lyn andrews

Far From Home

headline

First published in 2006
by HEADLINE PUBLISHING GROUP

First published in paperback in 2007
by HEADLINE PUBLISHING GROUP

2

Cataloguing in Publication Data is available from
the British Library

ISBN 978 0 7553 3195 6

Typeset in Janson by Avon DataSet Ltd,
Bidford-on-Avon, Warwickshire

Printed and bound in Great Britain by
Mackays of Chatham plc, Chatham, Kent

Headline's policy is to use papers that are natural, renewable and
recyclable products and made from wood grown in sustainable
forests. The logging and manufacturing processes are expected to
conform to the environmental regulations of the country of origin.

HEADLINE PUBLISHING GROUP
A division of Hachette Livre UK Ltd
338 Euston Road
London NW1 3B

www.headline.co.u
www.hodderheadline.com

FT
Pbk

My thanks go to Gail O'Connell (née Thomas) who gave me the inspiration for part of this novel in the form of the story of her step-aunts. To Carole McDermott who graciously afforded me the time from her very busy schedule to show me around her beautiful Georgian home, Rahan Lodge, on which I have based Harwood Hall. My thanks go also to my friend and neighbour Michael Guinan for patiently putting up with all my queries about aspects of life and locations in Rahan in the past. As this book is set in the 1920s it was necessary to include aspects of the turbulent days that led to the creation of the Irish Free State and eventually the Republic, although I have not gone into great detail.

Lyn Andrews
Tullamore 2006

Part I

Chapter One

Offaly 1919

'KITTY, DA WANTS TO speak to you. He's in the parlour.' Thirteen-year-old Annie Doyle's voice was full of curiosity as she relayed her father's instruction. Her dark brown eyes were fastened on her elder sister's back; Kitty was washing the dishes in the big earthenware sink and their younger sister Bridget was drying them and stacking them on the dresser.

Kitty paused, up to her elbows in greasy water. A frown creased her forehead. Da knew she had so many chores still to complete. Since Mam had died two years ago it had fallen to her to keep house and with no electricity or piped water it was far from easy.

'Did he say why he wants to see me and in the parlour no less?' she asked.

'He did not. Sure, isn't it Sunday evening and doesn't he always go into the parlour after supper and read his Bible?' Annie shot back. She'd just known that Kitty would be difficult about this summons. 'Am I to go back and tell him you're too busy?' she demanded, knowing full well that Kitty would never defy their father. He was strict with them all. He always had been, even when Mam had been alive, but at least he was fair.

Kitty wiped her hands on her coarse calico apron and shook her head. 'You will not! I'll just take off this apron then I'll go.'

'Ah, Kitty, 'tis probably only some small matter. Nothing to cause a fuss about and I'll finish the dishes,' Bridget, always the peacemaker, intervened.

Kitty smiled at her as she undid the apron strings and then tucked the few wisps of her long straight blond hair that had escaped from her chignon back into place. Bridget, at ten, was a rather plain child, she thought. Her grey eyes always seemed to be filled with apprehension and she had a habit of twisting her light brown curly hair around her finger when she was upset. She was also shy, and Kitty knew that Bridget missed her mother dreadfully. Even more than Kitty herself did.

'Aren't you a little treasure but this one here can help you, she doesn't seem to have anything else to do, unlike myself!'

4

Annie was stung. 'I have plenty to do. Isn't it my turn to bring in the turf this week?' But her protest fell into empty space; Kitty had already left the kitchen. 'Here give me that cloth and I'll finish up while you put all that clean delft back on the dresser.'

Bridget did as she was bid. 'Did Da look . . . angry?' she asked tentatively.

'He did not. He looked, well, serious though. As if there was something important on his mind.' Annie wrung out the dishcloth and began to wipe down the wooden draining board.

'He was worried about the work on Mr Harwood's carriage, I heard him say so to Reverend Joyce after the service this morning.'

'So did I. He said it was really the work of a coachbuilder but as there isn't one for miles around, he'd just have to do his best to sort out the damage. Aren't the gentry careless with their belongings? Sure, that carriage must have cost a fortune, wouldn't you think they'd be more careful with it and not go driving it into gateposts? Da's a blacksmith and farrier, not a carpenter or coachbuilder.'

Bridget carefully propped the large blue and white meat dish up on its edge at the back of the dresser shelf and nodded in agreement. The Honourable Mr Charles Harwood was the most important and influential man in the district, but a man whom she'd often heard described as 'a reckless, hard driver'.

Annie tipped the last few sods of turf into the range and looked around the kitchen. Everything was tidy. Kitty would have nothing to complain about when she came back. The big table in the centre of the room was covered in a green and white gingham-patterned oilcloth, which had been wiped down. In the middle of the table was a large bowl of russet apples that had been gathered from the small orchard at the back of the house. The chairs, all of which matched, had been neatly pushed into place. The range had been black-leaded yesterday and on the mantel above it was a plain, serviceable clock and a few china ornaments that Mam had bought over the years. Beside the range was Da's armchair, complete with a bright patchwork cushion, where he sat after supper every night – except Sunday. On the narrow bookshelf beside it were a few books and his pipe rack and tobacco jar. On Sundays, though, the pipes and tobacco remained on the shelf and the chair stayed empty. Sunday was a special day, he always said. It was the Lord's Day. Annie sighed and picked up the two large buckets that stood beside the door to the yard. Special day or not, the range and the fires had to be tended. She hated having to drag the buckets of turf from the open-fronted shed beside the forge back to the kitchen.

There was no help for it though. Coal was scarce and expensive and the electricity had not yet reached the rural areas of Ireland.

It was Bridget's job to fill the lamps and trim the wicks. Da had a fierce mistrust of candles, saying they were dangerous and pointing out the number of fires that had been caused by candles left unattended or carelessly handled. There was at least one oil lamp in every room of the house and the paraffin for them was stored in a large metal drum at the far end of the orchard, well away from the house and the forge that adjoined it.

When Annie returned to the kitchen with the turf Bridget was still alone, sitting close to the lamp on the side table, trying to thread a needle. Da insisted they spend Sunday evenings in some useful form of occupation and Bridget was reluctantly making a new quilt for her bed.

'Is she still in there with Da?' Annie demanded, stacking the turf box that stood next to the range.

Bridget nodded, her eyes wide with unease. 'It must be something very important, Annie. Have you no idea what he wanted?'

Annie shook her head slowly and sat down opposite her sister. Da had given her no inkling of what he wanted to speak to Kitty about but she was now beginning to feel as anxious as Bridget. What had

Kitty done or not done that merited such a lengthy lecture?

Crossing the hallway on her way to the parlour Kitty had stopped by the half-moon table on the top of which reposed a large aspidistra in a plain white china pot. Above it hung a mirror. As she gazed at her reflection, she wondered did she look older than her sixteen years? Had the extra work and responsibilities that she had had to shoulder these last two years caused the worry lines to appear on her forehead? She had never been classed as pretty but she didn't consider herself unattractive. Mam had always said that both she and Bridget were like 'ugly ducklings' that would one day turn into beautiful swans. Mam had always sounded so sure, so convincing when she'd said it that Kitty had come to believe it. It was just a matter of waiting. Annie was considered to be the beauty of the family. She took after Da with her dark brown eyes and thick dark curly hair. Kitty tried to smooth out the faint lines on her forehead with her fingertips and pinched her cheeks to give them some colour. Would she ever fall in love and get married and have children of her own? Would she ever be allowed to go anywhere to meet a nice lad or would she always have to stay here and keep house for her da?

'Ah, will you have some sense, Kitty Doyle! Sure, it won't be an easy matter for any of us to find a decent lad!' she admonished herself.

They were different to almost all their neighbours. They were Protestants in a country that was staunchly Catholic. They attended a different church: the old grey stone church a little further up the lane set in a field and surrounded by ancient, lichen-covered gravestones, the interior of which had none of the ornate trappings of the Catholic church at Killina. It was referred to as Rahan old church because it had been there for centuries, and the fact that it had been founded by a Catholic saint didn't seem to upset the present Protestant worshippers. The Doyles attended a different school to their neighbours' children too. It meant a long walk almost into Tullamore town itself and that was hard in winter when the snow was thick on the ground and the frost sparkled on the hedge-rows. Of course only Annie and Bridget went to school now; she'd left when her mam had taken ill. She sighed. No, it wouldn't be easy for any of them to find a husband in the parish of Rahan. Of course Da was a much-respected man, he being the only smith and farrier in the parish and everyone needed his services at some time. Da! She sucked in her breath. What was she thinking of standing here, gazing at her reflection and thinking about husbands and the like when her da was waiting? If he wasn't cross before he certainly would be now after she'd kept him waiting for what must be nearly ten minutes.

She knocked quietly on the parlour door before entering. ''Tis sorry I am, Da, to have been so long. I was just finishing the washing up.'

Thomas Doyle looked up from the passage he had been reading and laid the heavy Bible down on the top of the carved sideboard. 'Sure, I'm aware of the work you have to do, Kitty. Sit down, child.' His tone was not sharp.

Kitty sat on the edge of the overstuffed hide sofa. This room was only used once a week at the most but she dusted and polished the furniture regularly and the carpet was swept each week too. It was a fine room, she thought, one Mam had taken great pride in. The walls were covered in an embossed paper and were hung with pictures in fine mahogany frames. In addition to the sideboard and the sofa, there was a china cabinet, a plant stand, and under the window, which looked out over the small garden and the laneway, was a brocade-covered chaise. The window was covered with a white cotton lace curtain for privacy and heavy maroon chenille curtains for the practical purpose of keeping out the draughts.

Her eyes strayed to the top of the sideboard. A large, handsome brass and crystal lamp gave a good light. Beside it were photographs of herself and her sisters, and her da's parents stiff and formal in old-fashioned clothes. She frowned. There was something missing. For an instant she couldn't remember what it was and then a look of puzzlement filled her eyes. Where was the photograph of her parents on their wedding day that usually had pride of place in the centre?

'Kitty, I have something of great importance to tell you,' Thomas Doyle began, seeing the look of consternation that had crossed his daughter's face as she looked in vain for the photograph he had just an hour ago removed. He knew this wasn't going to be easy. He had practised all week in his mind the words he now had to speak. She was a good girl, a sensible girl, a dutiful girl but she was growing up; soon she would be a young woman and would need a husband of her own. He didn't want her to become an old maid like his sister Julia. Kathleen wouldn't have wanted that either. Poor Kathleen. She'd been a good wife and mother but, well . . . life must go on. He leaned forward, his large, calloused hands resting on his knees. He wasn't a tall man, standing only five feet ten in his stockinged feet, but he was broad-shouldered and strong. His once dark hair was now tinged with grey and his cheeks were veined and ruddy from long hours spent over the fierce heat of the forge. He was, he hoped, a devout man and not heartless. He had all their interests at heart.

Kitty was staring at him, biting her lip. She had a terrible feeling that what he was about to say would somehow upset them all. 'What is it, Da?' she asked quietly.

'I'm to be married again, Kitty. Hester Smythe has agreed to be my wife. I . . . I'm still in my prime. I'm not yet fifty and . . . and I have no son to follow in my footsteps.'

Kitty felt as though she had been slapped across the face. Instinctively she drew back, gripping the arm of the sofa tightly. 'Da!' It was a croak more than an exclamation of dismay and shock. 'But, Da! We . . . I . . . keep house just grand!' she stammered.

Thomas crossed his arms across his chest. He had expected this reaction and had steeled himself. 'You do indeed, child, but there's more at stake here than just "keeping house".' He paused; he couldn't bring himself to try to explain to her that a man had needs other than those of a meal on the table, clean sheets on his bed, clean clothes on his body. 'The good Lord saw fit to send your mam and me three daughters but no sons and a man *needs* sons. Hester is a good woman, a young, strong woman and it is as though I have been given a second chance to have the son I have always wanted. And there is something else, Kitty.'

Kitty was shaking her head, unable to take in the fact that soon Hester Smythe, a woman over ten years her da's junior, would be coming into this house to take her mam's place. She had seen her a couple of times lately, at church, which she had thought was odd. Hester lived in Tullamore and it would have been easier for her to attend church there instead of travelling the nine miles to Rahan. Now, it was abundantly clear just why she had made that journey. Kitty hadn't liked her either. She was tall and thin to the point of boniness, with a long face that reminded Kitty of Paddy Molin's old horse, a face framed with lank, mousy-brown hair. She had pale, insipid blue eyes that missed very little and she had no conversation to speak of.

'She . . . she's to be my . . . our stepmother?'

'She is so but, Kitty, I could not ask Hester to be my wife and to come and live here when I have three daughters at home. No woman would agree to that. So, I have arranged for Annie and Bridget to go and live with your Aunt Julia in Tullamore and you are to go to Harwood Hall. Mrs Harwood has very kindly agreed to take you and you will learn to be a lady's maid to Miss Elizabeth Harwood. There will be other duties as well but nothing you are not capable of.'

Kitty surged to her feet although the room seemed to be revolving sickeningly. 'No! No! Da, you can't do this to us! You can't send us away because . . . because *that one* doesn't want us here! This is *our* home! We're your daughters, you can't treat us like this!'

Thomas got to his feet. He hadn't expected her to take it so badly. 'Kitty, listen to me! It isn't just because Hester can't be expected to come in here with the three of you living here. I'm thinking of you. I don't want you to stay at home, become an old maid, nor your sisters either. With Julia they will be nearer to school, nearer to employment when they leave. You will have a grand position up at the Hall with the gentry, and the Harwoods *are* gentry. Where Miss Elizabeth goes, you will go too and in time you will meet a good man of your own faith. Don't forget the Harwoods are Protestant too.'

A wave of hurt and anger surged through Kitty. 'Don't try and fob me off with those excuses, Da. You don't care! You don't want us. *She* doesn't want us. And you're afraid you'll lose *her*! Lose your chance of a son! Oh, I hope Mam comes back to haunt you for driving us from our home.'

Thomas turned his back on her. She would come to accept the situation in time and to see that he really did have their welfare at heart. He picked up the Bible from the top of the sideboard. 'I want you to tell your sisters of this matter, Kitty.'

It was yet another blow and she clutched the

window sill for support. Her shoulders sagged and at last bitter tears welled up in her eyes. 'You . . . you coward! You . . . selfish, pathetic coward!' she gasped as she stumbled from the room. Never in her life had she spoken to him so disrespectfully, but now she didn't care. He deserved it.

Chapter Two

———◆———

THOMAS SAT DOWN HEAVILY, the Bible on his knee. It was closed, his reading forgotten. He truly hadn't meant to upset Kitty so much. He hadn't thought it cowardly to leave it to Kitty to tell his younger daughters of his plans. She was more capable of the task than he. She was closer to her sisters and would find the right words. She was being very unreasonable and it saddened him. Surely she must understand? He could point to at least three widowers they knew who had had to do the same thing. It was the custom. He'd made sure the girls would be well taken care of. Julia would be well paid for taking Annie and Bridget into her home; they would want for nothing. Kitty should be very grateful that he had obtained such a good position for her and she would be paid a wage too. It was all settled.

He stood up and reached into the sideboard cupboard and brought out a tumbler and a small bottle of whiskey. It had remained unopened since the day he'd bought it. He had never been a heavy drinker; indeed he had given up the drink altogether after Kathleen's death; but he now felt as though he needed a drop to steady himself.

Kitty stood with her back to the parlour door, tears falling down her cheeks. What was she to do? How was she going to tell her sisters this truly desperate news? She had to try to compose herself first. She couldn't go back to the kitchen until she had.

She groped her way down the hall, oblivious now of the mirror and the furniture, pictures and plants. Beside the kitchen door was another smaller door that led along a narrow passageway into the adjacent forge. Silently she made her way into her father's workplace. It was in darkness but she knew every inch of it from the hard-packed earth floor to the old smoke-blackened rafters. The furnace was kept damped down on Sundays and Bank Holidays: if it was left to die completely it took hours and hours to rekindle and reach the temperature needed to melt and shape metal. She sank down on a three-legged stool beside the embers whose reddish-orange glow threw deep shadows across the cavernous room. She was shivering as she glanced around. Everything was so familiar, bound up in her earliest memories of coming in as a small child, holding tightly to her mother's hand. She'd loved to watch as her da had hammered the white-hot horseshoes into shape on the big, blackened anvil, showers of sparks flying, to hear the loud hissing and see the clouds of steam as the finished shoe was plunged into a bucket of cold water. She'd never been afraid of the huge heavy horses that stood so patiently while the shoes were fitted. All around her hanging from hooks on the walls were scrolls and circle formers, rollers for making arches, winches, grinders, tongs and pokers of all shapes and sizes. Against one wall stood an old wooden press with small drawers that were filled with nails and screws and bolts for, besides the bread-and-butter work of shoeing the many horses that were essential to everyday rural life, her da made doorknockers, gates and railings, fireside tools, log baskets, braziers, toasting forks and even some farm implements. She'd come here with Mam every single day, usually to bring her da his dinner or big mugs of tea. When Mam had been sick she'd come on her own. It was thirsty work for 'Sure, isn't it as hot as the hobs of hell in there?' her mam had always remarked.

Kitty dropped her head in her hands and sobbed. 'Oh, Mam! Mam! Why did you have to leave us? I've tried my best but it's not good enough! I don't want to have to leave here, it's my home! It's *our* home! How am I going to tell Bridget she's to go and live with Aunt Julia? It will break her poor little heart.'

At last she wiped her streaming eyes with the hem of her skirt. She didn't care that it was her Sunday-best dress, which was now creased and stained. It was no use sitting here weeping, she had to go back to the kitchen and her sisters.

'Kitty! Kitty, are you in here?' Annie's voice, impatient and cross, came from the doorway.

Kitty got to her feet. 'I'm just coming.'

'I've been all over the house looking for you. I've even been outside into the laneway and Bridget's gone down to the orchard with a hurricane lamp and you know how she hates being there at night. Sure, what are you at sitting here in the dark, on your own?' Annie held the lamp she was carrying higher and gazed hard at her sister. 'What's wrong? You've been after weeping.'

Kitty knew there was no use denying it. She must look a desperate fright. Her face would be blotched and tear-stained, her eyes red and swollen and her hair had begun to come loose from its pins.

'Annie, come in and put down that lamp.' She indicated that Annie stand the lamp on the bench beside the anvil. She didn't want her sister to drop it in shock and set fire to the place.

'When you didn't come back I went and asked Da where you were. He said he didn't know but that you had something to say to us, no doubt in your own time. He . . . he was offhand, or annoyed. Upset. There was something wrong anyway. What have you to tell us?' Annie demanded, setting down the lamp.

Kitty reached out and took her sister's hand and a dart of fear came into Annie's dark eyes. 'Oh, God! What's wrong, Kitty? He's not sick?'

'He is not. He . . . he's getting married to Hester Smythe and we're to be gone from this house before he brings your one over the doorstep.'

Annie's eyes widened in shock and then her features contorted in fury. 'Mam's hardly cold in her grave and he's bringing *that one* in here in her place and putting us out! He can't do this, Kitty! He *can't*! I won't let him!'

Kitty caught her by the shoulders and drew her close. 'He can do what he likes, Annie, and there's nothing we can do about it. You and Bridget are to go to live with Aunt Julia in Tullamore and I . . .' Her voice broke. 'I'm to go to Harwood Hall to learn to be a lady's maid to Miss Elizabeth. 'Tis all arranged.'

Annie was shaking with rage. It was all so unfair, how could he treat them like this and just to marry Hester Smythe and she the ugliest woman Annie'd ever seen?

'He said he has to have a son to carry on after him;

that's the reason he's getting married again. But he can't bring her in here while we're here. It's not proper – and now I think on it, didn't Mary-Anne O'Hagan have to go to her aunt when her da married that woman from Kilbeggan?'

'I don't want to live with Aunt Julia, she's so old and miserable and she's a religious maniac, so she is! Always saying prayers and reading aloud from the Bible and church three times on a Sunday!'

Kitty was beginning to feel a little calmer. Still clasping Annie's hand, she eased her down on the stool she had recently vacated. 'It won't be so bad, Annie. You'll be nearer for school and you'll have all the entertainments of Tullamore on your doorstep.'

'Not that we'll ever be allowed over the doorstep to see them, she'll have us reading the New Testament morning, noon and night!' Annie retorted.

'You will when you're older and you'll find work there too.'

Annie was mollified a little until she remembered Bridget. 'What about poor Bridget? She'll hate it! She's afraid of her own shadow.'

Kitty nodded. 'I know, but there's nothing I can do, Annie.'

'She'll cry herself to sleep night after night and put herself into a decline and then God knows what will happen!' Annie prophesied darkly.

'You'll just have to make sure she doesn't. You'll have to be a comfort to her, help her settle in. You can't face Mam in the next life if you don't. I . . . I'll try to come and visit as often as I can, I promise.'

Annie was still openly mutinous. '*He'll* have to face Mam in the next life and explain everything and I wouldn't like to be in his shoes. She had a fierce temper on her when the mood took her, so she did. I hope she comes back and haunts him and Hester bloody Smythe!'

Kitty was scandalised. 'Annie Doyle! Don't you be after using such language! Now, we'd better go and find Bridget. Let's hope she's not still wandering around in the dark out there.'

Bridget *had* cried herself to sleep every night, despite everything both Kitty and Annie could do to reassure her. In her young life she had lost her mother and the love and security Kathleen's presence had given her. That had been hard enough to bear but she had had her da and her sisters when she felt lonely and vulnerable. Now she was to lose her da to another woman and Kitty to the Harwoods and she didn't want to live with her aunt, who seemed incredibly old and strict. Nor did she want to go to the town. She loved the countryside with its tranquillity, the birds in the trees and hedgerows, the many small, winding rivers that intersected the fields where the cattle grazed. She loved the brown-scarred bog land with its swathes of heather and furze, bright yellow in springtime. She often wandered along the banks of the Grand Canal in summer, watching the swans and moorhens, delighted when she caught a glimpse of the graceful flight of the heron or the vivid flash of a kingfisher. She picked daisies, yellow water buttercups, red campion and creamy white cow parsley from along the banks to put in the jug Kitty always kept on the kitchen window ledge throughout the summer months. But now her world had been turned upside down and she was so miserable that she didn't even want to get out of her small narrow bed each morning.

Kitty and Annie were despairing, worn out with their efforts to comfort, reassure and bolster her spirits. Bridget remained pale, wan and utterly miserable.

The following Wednesday Kitty was again sent for by her da. She stood in silence, her back rigid, her eyes downcast lest he see the hurt and anger in them, while he told her briefly that on Saturday morning he would take Annie and Bridget into Tullamore to their aunt and on the same afternoon he would accompany her up to Harwood Hall. She was to have all their things packed and ready by Friday evening.

When he had finished she nodded slowly.

''Tis for the best, Kitty,' Thomas said firmly. It

upset him that the girls were taking it so badly and yet it was the custom and had been for generations, so surely they must understand or at least try to.

Kitty's reserve broke. ''Tis best for you, Da, but I will never set foot in this house again, no matter how long I may live. I'll make my own way in the world and with no help or assistance from you.'

Thomas sighed deeply, but decided to ignore her defiance. 'Hester is coming to visit on Thursday evening. She wants to meet you. I expect you to be at least civil to her.'

Kitty stared at him in horror. ' We have to be polite to her? We have to serve her tea? Just a day before we are being forced to leave our *home* and because of *her*!'

Thomas frowned. 'Yes, I expect you to be civil and to serve her tea. She is a good woman, Kitty. She's not a monster as you seem to think she is. And you know full well it is the custom. Try to understand that, Kitty, please?'

Kitty just shook her head, bereft of speech. Angry and bitterly hurt, she turned away from him and left the room.

Annie looked up from the dish of apples she was peeling; Bridget was upstairs lying on her bed. 'What did he have to say?' Her tone was hopeful. Maybe, by some miracle, he had changed his mind.

'I'm to have all our things packed and ready by

Friday night. Come Saturday morning he'll take you both into Tullamore and then he'll return and take me up to the Hall.'

'So soon? Did he mention your one at all?'

'He did. She's . . . she's coming to visit on Thursday evening. She wants to meet us.'

Annie's eyes widened. 'Sure to God, hasn't she the brass neck. Isn't she responsible for us being sent away and we've to wait on her! Oh, I hate her, Kitty!'

'He said . . . he wants us to be polite to her and that we have to try to understand it's the way things have been done for years, it's the custom. I told him I would never set foot in this house ever again and I mean it, Annie! I want nothing from him – *nothing*! I'll manage on my own. I'll have wages, I'll save them. I'll have nothing to spend them on and maybe, one day, I'll have enough to get a place for us all to be together again.'

'Do you mean that, Kitty, truly?' There was admiration in Annie's voice.

'I do so. It might not be for years and years, but I do mean it.'

'Then I'll tell him the same thing myself.'

Kitty's features softened a little. 'Annie, you're only thirteen years old. You're just a child; you need him to pay for your keep. Even after you leave school you will need a roof over your head and, besides, it's his duty to mind you. Both you and Bridget are his responsibility

26

and even Hester Smythe can't change that. Wouldn't Reverend Joyce have something to say to him if he abandoned you entirely? You know how much he minds what the Reverend says and thinks.'

Slowly Annie nodded. Kitty was right but it was so frustrating that she too couldn't tell him that she wanted nothing from him. 'Will I go and tell Bridget?'

Kitty shook her head. 'No, I'll do it, but thank you for offering, Annie. We'll manage . . . somehow.'

On Thursday evening all three girls were silent and withdrawn. Kitty had laid the table with a clean linen cloth and her mam's best china. Annie had glanced defiantly at her as she'd carefully laid the dishes down, a look that said, 'I would sooner smash every piece than have your one drinking her tea from it.' Kitty had nodded and sighed.

'I know, Annie. I know,' she'd said softly.

Bridget sat by the range, her head bent, her hands clasped tightly together in her lap, and Kitty sighed again. Poor Bridget was taking it far worse than either herself or Annie and she hoped her sister would not break down during the visit of their prospective stepmother.

At five minutes to eight they heard the trap pull into the yard and Kitty and Annie exchanged glances.

'Sure, I hope the tea chokes her!' Annie hissed.

'Hush! We agreed to be polite,' Kitty hissed back.

Hester paused in the doorway, raising her eyebrows at Thomas. He quickly took her arm and gently guided her into the room. Kitty felt a little embarrassed, thinking her da looked like a moonstruck calf. Hester was dressed in a heather-coloured tweed two-piece, with a prim-looking white cotton blouse underneath the jacket; her mousy hair was tucked under a rather severe purple cloche hat. Kitty wondered just what her da saw in her; she was far from a raving beauty. In Kitty's opinion she wasn't even attractive.

'This is Kitty, my eldest daughter,' Thomas informed his bride-to-be.

Hester managed a tight little smile and extended her hand. ''Tis nice to meet you, Kitty.'

Kitty bit back the words that rose to her lips and took Hester's hand, briefly. 'Hester,' was all she could manage to say.

'And this is Annie,' Thomas continued.

Annie clasped her hands determinedly behind her back and was secretly delighted that Hester looked furious.

'Annie! Have you no manners on you at all?' Thomas's voice was sharp.

Reluctantly Annie took the proffered hand. 'Miss Smythe,' she said quietly. There, her da couldn't say she was being disrespectful or insolent.

Thomas decided to ignore the obvious rebuff. 'And this is Bridget, the youngest. Bridget, this is Hester.'

Kitty held her breath, knowing what a huge trial this was for her young sister but Bridget got up and shook Hester's hand and nodded, before sitting down again.

'She's very quiet,' Thomas confided, but Hester did not seem mollified. She looked critically at the tea table, but did not comment on Kitty's hard work. She was clearly not going to make an effort with these three uncommunicative girls who were obviously resentful of her presence here.

Thomas pulled out a chair for her. 'Sit down, Hester. There're biscuits and buns, Kitty is a good cook.'

'Good thing too, it will stand her in good stead up at Harwood Hall. Isn't it a grand job you're to have, Kitty? Didn't your da do well to get you a position there?'

'He did, although I suppose it would have helped if I had known about it sooner or it had been discussed with me at all.' Kitty's tone was quiet and without a trace of bitterness but she intended to let Hester know that she had had no say at all in the matter. She passed the teapot to Annie who filled it from the kettle that was boiling on the range.

Hester gave a little laugh, ignoring Kitty's reply. 'And, Annie and Bridget, aren't you lucky to be going to live with your aunt? Think of all the advantages you'll have. So near to school, so near to all the shops and entertainments. Sure, won't you be able to walk to things in a couple of minutes instead of having to wait to be driven the long miles into town.'

Annie glared at her. 'We both *like* living in the country.'

Kitty shot her a warning look and shook her head. They had promised to be polite but she could see that if Hester carried on like this there would be an outburst from Annie that would be far from courteous. She just wished the evening were over. There was nothing at all she liked about Hester Smythe but her da was obviously smitten with her.

It was a strained couple of hours with very little in the way of response from the girls. Thomas did his best to keep conversation on a light note but he knew the visit wasn't being a success and was relieved when Hester got to her feet and said she thought it time she went home.

As soon as her father and Hester had gone, Kitty dropped her head in her hands. She felt drained and tired.

'At least she got the message that she wasn't welcome, even though Da was trying to make her feel as though she was,' Annie said with a note of triumph in her voice.

'Can I go to bed now, Kitty?' Bridget asked tearfully.

'I think we'll all go. I don't want to be after getting a lecture from Da when he gets back. I've nothing more to say to him and I don't want to hear him going on about *her*! It's obvious he thinks the sun and moon revolve around her.'

'God alone knows why! Isn't she the most desperate plain-looking thing you ever saw?' Annie muttered sullenly.

Chapter Three

———

SATURDAY MORNING DAWNED CLEAR and crisp. The dew was heavy on the grass and the spiders' webs that festooned the hedgerows looked like delicate strings of pearls. Kitty had always loved autumn when the leaves on the trees began to turn to gold and russet and orange and the shorn fields lay quiet and peaceful in the morning mists. The smell of turf smoke was pungently sweet at this time of year and in the hedgerows blackberries and wild rosehips were abundant. The boughs of the old trees in the orchard were heavy with ripe fruit, apples, pears and shiny black sloes. This morning, however, she had no thought for the glorious October weather as she fastened the lids of their cases and zipped up the carpet-bags – it had been a mad rush to get everything washed and ironed and packed by the previous night but she had done it, and now her heart was heavier than it had ever been, heavier even than on the day her mam had been laid to rest in the churchyard up the laneway.

'Bridget's dressed and ready, but she's deathly pale, Kitty. Sure, I hope she doesn't go in a dead faint when Da brings the trap around.' Annie bit her lip. She had dreaded this morning but Bridget's unnatural calmness really worried her.

'At least she's not crying hysterically, as she has every night, poor lamb. Maybe she'll settle, Annie. Maybe she's come to accept it.'

Annie shook her head as Bridget, dressed in her good coat with a knitted beret over her light brown curls, came quietly into the room and sat down.

'You look nice and tidy and you'll be just . . . grand,' Kitty said, patting her sister's hand and trying to keep her voice steady. 'You've everything you need for school?'

Bridget managed to nod, but her eyes were haunted.

Annie took her dark blue tweed coat from the back of the chair and shrugged it on. Kitty handed her the narrow-brimmed blue velour hat with its pale blue grosgrain ribbon and Annie dutifully put it on. This morning she had no inclination to gaze in the mirror to see if it was on at the right angle.

The sound of the pony's hooves on the cobbles of the yard seemed very loud in the quiet kitchen.

Kitty hugged Annie tightly, tears stinging her eyes, but she was determined not to cry. She didn't want to upset her sisters and she wouldn't give her da the satisfaction of seeing her tears. 'Take care of yourself and Bridget. I'll come and visit you as soon as I can and don't forget what I promised you.'

'I won't and I'll not let him see I'm at all upset,' Annie answered with spirit but her dark eyes were bright with incipient tears.

Kitty turned to her youngest sister and hugged her too. 'Will I try and bring you something, Bridget?'

Bridget managed to nod just as Thomas Doyle strode into the room.

'You're ready, so? I'll take your things, come on out to the trap now,' he instructed, thankful that there appeared to be no hysterics in the offing, although Bridget looked very pale and there were huge dark circles under her eyes.

Kitty ushered her sisters out and helped them both up into the trap. The pony was sometimes inclined to be skittish but this morning it seemed to sense that this was no time for shying or impatiently pawing the cobbles. Kitty swallowed hard. Aunt Julia wasn't as bad as Annie made her out to be. The house was comfortable and she kept a good table. She was just a bit old-fashioned and set in her ways. At least they *knew* her; she was their da's sister. They weren't going amongst strangers as she was. Somehow she'd thought she would stay at home and look after her da, at least until she got married – and she'd thought that that day would be far in the future.

She bit her lip very hard as she watched her da manoeuvre the trap through the gateway and out into the lane. She intended to visit them as soon as possible, for surely she would get some time off, and even if she had to walk the whole way to Tullamore she would go and make sure they were settling in.

All the way into town Annie held Bridget's hand tightly in her own. Usually it seemed to take ages to cover the nine miles but this morning time flew by as though on wings. When they turned on to the Charleville Road both girls realised that within a few minutes they would be outside the neat terrace of Georgian houses where Aunt Julia lived and Annie's stomach began to feel as though it was full of butterflies. Bridget became even paler.

Their aunt was waiting for them and when the trap pulled up outside she descended the stone steps that led down from the front door.

'Ah, here you are then, girls! Come along inside; your da will see to your things.'

Annie managed a rather weak smile. Aunt Julia looked very old. She was tall and thin and her grey hair was pulled back severely into a small bun. Over the unfashionably long skirt and print blouse she wore a lavender-coloured knitted shawl. A pair of rimmed spectacles was balanced on the bridge of her nose and she peered short-sightedly at her nieces through them.

'You'll have had your breakfasts already, I'm sure, but I've the kettle on. You'll be in the want of a cup of tea after that drive and then we'll get you settled in. Won't it be grand not to have that desperate long walk to school and with winter coming on?' she prattled, clearly determined to be cheerful.

Still clutching Bridget's hand Annie followed her aunt into the house. They had been here on a number of occasions but now it was to be their home. She could see that Aunt Julia, like everyone who resided in town, considered that living in Rahan was like living in the back of beyond and that they should be very grateful to be moving to a civilised place like Tullamore where you didn't have to walk three miles to the nearest shop. She sighed to herself. All they could do was try to make the best of it until Kitty had enough money saved to find a place where they could all be together again.

Kitty was taking a last look around the kitchen when she heard her father return. She had gone on a last tour of the whole house, painful though it had been for every room held memories of Mam. Now all the things Mam had bought or made over the years and cared for so lovingly would belong to the second Mrs Doyle. Everything was clean and tidy. At least no one could say she had left the place in a mess.

With a deep sense of unhappiness and trepidation she buttoned up her brown wool coat with the black velvet collar and tucked her hair up tidily under the pink crocheted tam o'shanter. It was time to leave – for ever. She fingered the little silver cross on its chain that hung around her neck and which had belonged to her mam. 'Goodbye,' she whispered softly, picking up her carpet-bag. Her case stood beside the door and when her father appeared in the doorway she walked quickly past him and out of the house, her head held high and without a backward glance.

It wasn't far to Harwood Hall; they could have walked had it not been for the luggage, she thought as they crossed the humpbacked bridge over the canal. The outline of D. E. Williams' porter house and shop (known to everyone locally as 'the Thatch') came into view as they rounded the bend in the road. It was a place her da never frequented. Beyond there was a small farm and then a few cottages and above the trees to her left rose the square tower of the Catholic church at Killina. Around the next bend lay the gateway to the house that was now to be her home.

'It's a fine house and they are a fine family,' Thomas remarked solemnly, eyeing his silent daughter. Thank goodness this upheaval would soon be over and there had been no tears from either Annie or Bridget when he'd left them with Julia. But there had been no words of farewell from them either.

Kitty didn't reply; her gaze was fixed on the big white house at the end of the long sweeping driveway. The avenue was lined with trees and green pastures and paddocks stretched for as far as she could see. Cattle and horses grazed contentedly in their respective enclosures. She had often glimpsed the house from the lane and she had occasionally seen Mr Harwood at the forge, although it was usually his groom who brought the horses to be shod. She had seen Mrs Harwood and her daughter riding to town in the carriage and, like everyone else, had admired their fine clothes and fancy hats, but that was all. She had never spoken to any of them. They were strangers and they were the gentry.

'He is an important man, Kitty. He gives employment to many in this parish who would otherwise find no work. As well as the farm he has the factory from where squares of loose cut turf are taken by a narrow-gauge railway directly down to the barges on the canal to go up to the Curragh where the British cavalry are based and where the turf is used as bedding for the horses.'

Kitty knew this already and made no comment. She was in no mood to sit and chat amiably with her father. She also knew that the Hon. Charles Harwood was a Resident Magistrate and sat at the assizes in the courthouse in Tullamore but hoped that a lecture on this aspect of his work was not going to be forthcoming.

As they drew nearer the house seemed to grow in size and grandeur. It was a very imposing place indeed, she thought. A huge, gnarled old oak tree stood like a sentinel beside the second set of gates which led to an open area in front of the house and before they turned and drove down the left side of the place she saw clearly the flight of semi-circular stone steps that led up to the front door. There was a canopy over the door supported by pillars and the door itself was heavy and wide and painted crimson. The huge brass knocker gleamed in the pale sunlight. Black wrought-iron railings flanked the steps, railings she knew her da had made years ago.

She clenched her hands tightly in her lap, the sense of trepidation increasing by the minute. What would her life here be like? Would she be able to cope with everything? It would all be strange and unfamiliar to her. 'Don't be an eejit, Kitty Doyle! You will soon learn!' she said firmly to herself to bolster her spirits.

The back door, which was actually at the side of the

house, was opened by a girl of her own age dressed in the dark grey dress, white cap and apron of a maid of all work.

'This is my daughter Kitty. Mrs Harwood is expecting her,' Thomas said gravely.

'Sure, she is so and I'm to bring her and yourself straight to Madam. I'm Tess,' the girl said amiably, flashing Kitty a smile.

Kitty smiled back and they followed her down the narrow passageway that led out on to a wider passageway at the far end of which was a flight of stairs.

Kitty hardly dared to look around but the upper hallway seemed huge. The boards beneath her feet were highly polished and the sunlight that filtered through the fanlight above the front door picked out the ornate plaster coving and ceiling rose. The hall was painted in a shade of green Kitty had never seen before, a muted, sage-like tone. There was a huge crystal chandelier suspended from the ceiling and wide, highly polished doors led off from either side of the hall.

Tess knocked on a door to their right and entered. 'Ma'am, 'tis the blacksmith and his daughter that you were expecting,' she informed the occupant.

Kitty bit her lip. Now she was to be inspected like a prize heifer at a fair. She just hoped she would pass the scrutiny.

'You're to go on in,' Tess informed them, holding the door wide.

Clutching his hat in one hand, Thomas gave Kitty a gentle push and, swallowing hard, she stepped inside.

She was completely overawed by the size of the room and the furnishings but at least it was light and airy, for sunlight poured in through the four windows that seemed to stretch almost from the ceiling to the floor. Mrs Harwood was sitting in a brocade armchair near one of the two fireplaces, a piece of embroidery on her lap.

'So, you are Kitty. Come closer and let me have a good look at you. I won't bite.' There was a slight note of humour in the well-modulated voice, which had no hint of a local accent.

Kitty did as she was bid and found herself looking down into a pair of kindly blue eyes. She began to relax. Mrs Harwood looked very nice. She was small and fine-boned with pale skin and light brown hair that was cut in a short modern bob. Her knitted two-piece was of a soft amber colour trimmed with cream and she wore a long string of amber beads around her neck.

'Your father tells me you are sixteen and are used to keeping house.'

'I am so, ma'am. But not a house as big as this,' Kitty replied with a note of admiration in her voice.

'I don't expect you to, Kitty. I have a housekeeper, Mrs O'Shea, who manages admirably and to whom you will be responsible. Miss Elizabeth is the same age as yourself and will soon require a lady's maid of her own; Blanchard, my maid, is getting on in years and I don't want to tax her too much. But she will train you, once you have settled in and proved yourself to be diligent and reliable, as your father assures me you are.'

Kitty nodded enthusiastically.

'It's very kind of you, ma'am, to take her and give her this opportunity,' Thomas put in respectfully.

Amy Harwood nodded. The circumstances had been explained to her but she could not understand why he had to send his daughters away before bringing a new wife to the house. Mentally she shrugged; it was nothing to do with her. 'Well, then, Tess will take you to Mrs O'Shea who will show you your room and explain your duties and inform you of the wage you are to be paid. She will, of course, answer any questions you might have. I hope you will be happy here, Kitty.'

'Thank you, ma'am. I'm sure I will,' Kitty replied as Tess once again appeared and ushered them out.

'I'll be away home now, Kitty. Work hard, don't be insolent and don't forget to go to church on Sundays,' Thomas instructed as they once again reached the basement.

'Goodbye, Da,' Kitty answered coldly, turning towards Tess.

When Thomas had disappeared Tess looked at Kitty with raised eyebrows. 'Sure, isn't that the strangest way to part company with your own da?'

Kitty shrugged. 'I'll be after thinking that your da didn't send you here without asking you first did you want to come?'

'He did not but wasn't I glad to come all the same, there's ten of us at home and it's shocking crowded and they're always broke!' Tess answered with what to Kitty seemed like alarming frankness.

Kitty grinned at her. She liked her. 'And what is this Mrs O'Shea like, at all?'

Tess glanced quickly along the passageway. 'Sure, she's not the worst but she'll stand for no idling or shirking. Work hard and you'll get on just grand.'

'There must be plenty to do in a house this size?'

'There is so but aren't there enough of us to do it? Will we put your things in your room first? You're to share with me and Emer. You'll like her; sometimes she can be a bit of an eejit but there's no harm in her.' Tess took Kitty's small case and as they walked towards a door in the narrow passageway where Kitty had first entered Harwood Hall, Kitty felt that her arrival hadn't been as dreadful an ordeal as she'd anticipated.

Chapter Four

———————

KITTY WAS QUITE ASTONISHED to learn how much she would be paid a month. She had never had any money of her own, Da had given her a set amount each week for food and expenses and she had always had to ask him for money for their clothes. Now she was to receive what seemed like a small fortune just for doing all the chores she had done at home. She would also be fed and clothed. Two dark grey dresses and plain white aprons and caps for day wear and one black dress with a lace-trimmed apron and cap for 'best'. Stockings, of course, she would have to provide for herself, and underwear, but she already had plenty. Her black shoes were fairly new too. She was to have every second Tuesday afternoon off and one whole Sunday a month. It was more than she had expected.

She had liked Mrs O'Shea, a small, plump woman

in her fifties who had informed her that she was a woman who spoke her mind and stood no nonsense and as long as Kitty pulled her weight, was punctual, diligent and respectful, they would get along just fine.

'Didn't I say she wasn't the worst?' Tess said when she ushered Kitty back to the room she was to share with herself and Emer.

Kitty nodded and began to unpack her case.

'There's room in the presses for your stuff, then I'm to show you the kitchen and the scullery and the rest of the house and then we've to help prepare Madam's afternoon tea. She has it sharp at four-thirty. Dinner is always at eight, unless of course Himself is away on business and then Madam has it at seven, with Miss Elizabeth.'

'I thought there was a son? Was I wrong?' Kitty asked, laying her underclothes neatly in a drawer.

'You were not. He's above at the university in Dublin. Trinity College. I don't know what it is he's after studying up there but I do know that when he's finished he's to go off to England. His name is Henry and he'll be home for Christmas.'

Kitty thought he sounded very studious and intelligent. You had to be to go to university. 'I'll keep well out of his way.'

'Ah, he'll not bother you, Kitty. He hardly notices the likes of us. Come on now and we might get a bite to eat and a cup of tea before we start. That's if Cook is in a good humour,' Tess urged.

It was the biggest kitchen Kitty had ever seen and contained so many pans and dishes and utensils that she lost count. Mrs Connor, the cook, seemed pleasant enough and she was given a cup of tea and a slice of fruit cake and then told to go off with Tess and get her bearings, but not to take all afternoon about it as there was work to be done.

'This here is the scullery,' Tess informed her as Kitty peered into a medium-sized room next to the kitchen. 'All the washing and the laundry is done in here.'

'The water is piped in then?'

Tess laughed. 'Walked in, more like. Do you see the ass out there in the yard? All the creature does all day is walk round and round to draw the water up from the spring, and then it's piped in. We still don't have the electricity but I hear Himself has been thinking about having the place wired up and installing something called a generator to work it. I also heard that it would cost a fortune so I don't really expect we'll be after getting it soon. It would make life a lot easier, so it would.'

'Do all the servants live down here?' Kitty asked, following Tess back out into the passageway.

'Not all of us live in. There's meself, Emer, Mrs O'Shea and Cook live in. The rest come in daily.'

'My da does some work for Mr Harwood. Shoeing the horses mainly but now he's to mend the damage on the carriage.'

Tess rolled her eyes expressively. 'Sure to God there was a fierce row over that! It was all Miss Elizabeth's fault, she was doing the driving and didn't she take the turn into the drive too sharp and "Bang!" straight into the gatepost!'

'She can drive a carriage and pair?' Kitty was astounded.

'She cannot and wasn't that the top and bottom of it. She had coaxed and coaxed her ma to let her try and the Mistress was so fussed with it all that in the end she said she couldn't stand it any longer and allowed her to bring the carriage home from the school, with herself and James, the groom, supervising. There was hell to pay when Himself saw the mess she'd made of it.'

'Was she punished?'

Tess nodded. 'Had her allowance stopped for a month. No new dresses now until November. She had a puss on her for a week about that. She's spoiled rotten is that one but she can be as nice as pie when she feels like it.'

Kitty said nothing but hoped that Elizabeth Harwood would be 'as nice as pie' to her when she was finally deemed fit to be her maid.

'Those are all storerooms and pantries and both

Mrs O'Shea and Cook have their rooms over there,'
Tess said, pointing to the doors on the opposite side of
the corridor. 'Now, I'll take you up and show you the
dining room and the upstairs rooms. All very grand
and isn't there a fine bathroom up there too.'

Kitty had never seen a bathroom that was inside a
house. At home they had an outside privy and they
took their baths once a week in the kitchen in the zinc
tub that spent most of its life hanging on the yard wall.
Their daily ablutions were carried out in the tiny
scullery.

The dining room was on the opposite side of the
upper hallway to the drawing room, with two long
windows that overlooked the side of the house and one
that looked out over the front drive. The huge table
was highly polished and in the centre was a large,
ornate silver epergne which Tess informed her was
filled with fresh fruit each night before dinner. All the
windows had wooden shutters but were also flanked by
heavy royal-blue velvet curtains. Against one wall
stood the carved buffet, the top of which was covered
with a lace-edged fine linen cloth to protect the
surface from the array of silver salvers and dishes that
reposed there.

'It's my job to light the lamps and the candles
before dinner every night and do we get through some
candles!' Tess indicated the crystal oil lamps and the

many-branched candelabra that stood on a small sideboard.

By the time Tess had shown her upstairs to the long gallery-like landing Kitty's head was spinning. There were so many rooms, she was sure to get them all mixed up, she remarked to her companion and guide.

'You'll be fine in no time, Kitty. Wasn't I confused meself when I started in here for there's only four rooms in total at the home place.'

The opening of the door at the far end of the landing interrupted them and a slim girl with short wavy blond hair and startlingly blue eyes appeared.

'Oh, Tess, it's you. I thought it was Mama. Who is this?' Elizabeth Harwood looked at Kitty with mild curiosity.

'This is Kitty, Miss Elizabeth. Isn't she to be your lady's maid, when she's trained, that is,' Tess answered politely.

Elizabeth smiled. 'Mama said you were arriving today. How do you do, Kitty, are you settling in?'

Kitty smiled back, choosing her words carefully. 'I am so, miss. Everyone is very . . . kind and it's . . . it's lovely to meet you.' She thought Elizabeth Harwood was the prettiest girl she'd ever seen. Even though she'd seen her before it had never been as close as this. Elizabeth had beautiful skin, a little button of a nose and thick gold lashes fringed her wide blue eyes. Her dress was of a fine wool crêpe in a shade of blue that accentuated her eyes and was the height of fashion.

'I believe you are the same age as myself, Kitty?'

'I'm sixteen, miss. I'll be seventeen in January.'

'A month older than me. My birthday is in February, on St Valentine's Day actually. Papa always says it was the best St Valentine's Day ever and actually wanted to call me "Valentina", but, thankfully, Mama managed to dissuade him. Ghastly name, Valentina, don't you agree?'

Kitty didn't know what to say. Elizabeth was treating her as if she were an old friend instead of her future maid.

'If you'll excuse us, miss, Cook needs us to help in the kitchen. It's nearly teatime,' Tess interrupted.

'Of course. I'll take tea with Mama, is she in the drawing room?'

'She is so, miss.'

'Kitty, if there is anything you need, let Mrs O'Shea know. I'll no doubt see you tomorrow at Sunday service.'

'Yes, miss. And thank you, miss,' Kitty replied, a little confused.

'Didn't I tell you she could be as nice as pie when the mood took her? She likes you, that's a blessing, so it is,' Tess hissed as they went back downstairs.

As they reached the main hall the front door was

standing wide open and the tall, well-built figure of Charles Harwood could be seen on the top step, admonishing two boisterous golden retrievers to 'Stay!' The dogs obediently flopped down on the steps as he strode into the hall, clad in a tweed Norfolk jacket and plus fours, with a shotgun under one arm and a brace of pheasant in his right hand.

'Ah, Tess, just the girl. Take these down to Cook and tell her we'll have them for dinner after they've been sufficiently hung,' he instructed, handing the birds over to Tess.

'I will so, sir. This is Kitty Doyle. She's the blacksmith's daughter. She's come in here to work.'

'Ah, yes. My wife did inform me about you, Kitty. Your father is getting married again, I believe?'

'Yes, sir,' Kitty answered shyly, her cheeks reddening.

Charles Harwood did not miss the note of bitterness in her voice. Indeed it must be hard to be sent packing to make way for a stepmother, he thought. He vaguely remembered his wife telling him that the two younger daughters were to be sent off to a maiden aunt in town. 'Well, I hope you will be happy in our home, Kitty,' he said kindly.

Tess nudged her towards the stairs to the basement and Kitty was relieved to go. She didn't want to answer any further questions on her father's forthcoming marriage. In fact she didn't want to think of her da or Hester Smythe at all.

'I expect you'll go along with Mrs O'Shea to church tomorrow?' Tess said as they went back into the kitchen.

'She is a Protestant too?'

Tess nodded. 'The rest of us are Catholic and Madam lets us go to early Mass at Killina. Himself and Herself go into town to the church at Hop Hill and sometimes Miss Elizabeth goes with them and sometimes she goes with Mrs O'Shea down the lane to Rahan old church.'

Kitty nodded. Now she realised why the housekeeper had seemed familiar. She had occasionally seen her at Matins.

'Sure, I thought the pair of you had gone for good! Where did you get those birds?' Cook demanded, catching sight of both the pheasants and the two girls.

'Miss Elizabeth detained us and then didn't we meet the Master in the hall and he gave me these to give to you,' Tess replied, placing the birds on the table.

'Don't be after leaving them on my clean table, girl! Go and hang them up in the back pantry. I hope he isn't expecting them for dinner this night, they'll have to be left hanging for at least four days or they'll have no taste worth speaking of.'

'He said they'd have them when they'd been "sufficiently hung",' Tess called back over her shoulder.

'Kitty, child, you can start to set these trays. You'll find the cloths and napkins in the top drawer of the press next to the dresser. Use the second-best china – the ivy-leaf pattern – it's on the second shelf of the dresser by the window. Then fetch the milk from the marble slab in the pantry and fill the jugs and try not to slop it.'

'I'll be very careful, Mrs Connor.'

The woman smiled kindly at her. 'Sure, just "Cook" will do, Kitty. Everything must seem very strange and unfamiliar to you, child, but you'll soon learn. You only have to ask if you're unsure of anything. No one will bite your head off.'

Kitty smiled back. 'I think I'm going to like being here, Cook. I really do.'

'I hope so, Kitty. Now stir yourself.' She watched Kitty as she carefully laid the lace cloths over the trays. It was a shame, that's what it was. Throwing the poor child out of the only home she'd ever known just because he was bringing a new woman in there. Why couldn't they have all lived there together? But then, that was Protestants for you. They had some very peculiar notions.

By the time Kitty at last climbed into the single bed

under the window of the little room she shared with the other two maids she was very tired. It had been such a busy and emotionally exhausting day but she felt far happier than she had imagined she would. Everyone had made her welcome and there wasn't a single person that she hadn't liked. Before her eyes closed she prayed that her sisters were not too miserable after their first day with Aunt Julia, and she fervently hoped that she would not see her da tomorrow at church. Mrs O'Shea had told her she must be ready for the early service and she knew it was Da's habit to attend the later one, and for this she was thankful.

Chapter Five

———❦———

To Kitty's relief she had seen neither her father nor Hester at church and as the days passed she found that she was enjoying living and working at Harwood Hall. She particularly enjoyed the company of the other servants for in the two years she'd spent housekeeping for her father she had had little in the way of company. The work was no harder than her work had been at home and in fact the many appliances and the convenience of piped water made most things much easier.

On her first half-day off she had enquired about a lift into town but unfortunately none was forth-coming and it was too far to walk there and back in the time allotted to her. She was to be back in her uniform and in the kitchen by five o'clock.

'Wait until your first Sunday, Kitty, 'tis only two

weeks away. There's bound to be someone going into town. Even if you have to walk there, I'm sure you'd get a lift back,' Tess had advised, knowing Kitty was desperate to see how her sisters were faring.

So, it being a fine bright afternoon, she decided to take a walk around the house to familiarise herself with the gardens and outbuildings.

'Sure, I'd start with the kitchen garden and then the formal garden but I'd stay away from that turf factory. 'Tis dusty and noisy,' Emer warned.

'I'd like to see the little train,' Kitty replied, smiling.

Emer shrugged but smiled back. 'Suit yourself.'

Kitty walked down the path at the side of the house, which was flanked by large laurel bushes, and through the neatly laid-out kitchen garden with its vegetables and herbs. The formal garden was laid out mainly to lawns and rose beds and here and there the last roses gave splashes of bright colour. It must look beautiful in high summer, Kitty thought, and the family must sit out here as there was a wrought-iron table and chairs and a bench set in a little arbour. Beyond lay the yard and then the high wall that screened the turf factory from the house, and she crossed towards it. The doors to the big coach house were wide open; inside she glimpsed two well-cared-for traps but there was no sign of the damaged carriage. It must have been taken down to the forge.

On the walls hung various items of harness and a young lad was busy sweeping the floor.

''Tis a fine afternoon, Kitty!' he called.

She grinned at him. 'It is so and it's my first one off, Pat. I'm off to see the little engine.'

He threw down the brush. 'I'll come with you or you'll be falling over the tracks and all kinds of things.'

'I'm not an eejit, Pat Kearney, and you have work to do and I'll not have James blaming me for taking you away from it.' She laughed and continued on her way.

Beyond the wall was a scene so totally different from the tranquillity and elegance of the well-run house that she stopped and stood blinking in the sunlight. The ground was covered with black turf dust and gangs of men were loading piles of rough-cut square sods into the trucks of a small train. The little engine at its head emitted puffs of steam that mingled with the dust which seemed to cling to everything.

'I wouldn't stand there for long, miss, or you'll be black from head to toe.'

Kitty looked up. She didn't know the lad who had spoken to her. She judged him to be about eighteen and he was good-looking with dark curly hair and brown eyes. Nor was he wearing the dust-covered clothes of the workmen. His jacket was of a good Donegal tweed and his open-necked shirt was of a beige and green check.

'Do you work here?' she asked, feeling a little shy.

'I do. I mean I work beyond in the house.'

'You must be new then. I've not seen you before. I'm Niall Collins and I work for my da. He has a farm out at the Derries. I came down to see Frank Whelan, he runs this place – for Mr Harwood, that is. Da asked me to give him a message. I think I'd better escort you back beyond the wall, miss, or your clothes will be ruined entirely.'

'It's Kitty, Kitty Doyle, and that would be grand. I . . . I was just curious. I had no idea it would be so . . . dirty.'

'When you're moving turf on this scale it can't be anything else. Have you been at the Hall long?' he asked as, holding her arm lightly, he guided her across the tracks and towards the door in the wall through which she'd entered the yard.

'Only since a week Saturday. I'm to be lady's maid to Miss Elizabeth, eventually. I'm only just finding my way around the place.'

'Lady's maid! That's a piece of news. You've met Elizabeth?'

Kitty was quick to notice that he had not called her 'Miss Elizabeth'. 'I have so. I like her.'

'Indeed.' He raised one eyebrow quizzically. 'She has a temper, so I hear.'

'Doesn't everyone?' Kitty said, wanting to be fair to the girl. She *did* like her.

He laughed as he opened the door and they were once again in the yard. 'I suppose so. Well, enjoy the rest of your time off, Kitty. I have to go back and find Frank Whelan, but maybe I'll see you again.'

'Maybe,' she replied as she began to walk back towards the house and he turned away. She'd liked him. She hoped she would see him again.

Kitty was well into the routine of the house and had had a couple of hours' tuition from Blanchard, Mrs Harwood's attendant, in the duties of lady's maid by the time her Sunday off arrived. She had heard that James, the groom, was going into Tullamore on Sunday morning and would give her a lift. She had begged a jar of strawberry preserve from Cook, promising to scour all the pots until they gleamed as payment. Bridget loved strawberries and she had promised she would take her sister something.

It was a cold, blustery day. The wind was shaking the leaves from the trees to lie in a thick carpet on the drive. One of the gardeners would start to sweep them up next morning. She clutched her coat around her with one hand and her hat with the other as the trap rattled along the lanes towards town. James kept up a steady conversation for most of the way and she was quite thankful when they pulled up outside Aunt Julia's house.

'I'll be going back around two o'clock, if you'll be ready, Kitty.'

'Thanks. I will, it will save me the walk,' she called as he drove away.

'Kitty! You should have got word to me that you were coming,' Julia greeted her.

'Sorry, Aunt, but I had no way of doing so. There's been no time to go to the post office with a letter.' She felt a little irritated. Did she have to make a huge effort to make an appointment to see her own sisters?

'Well, come on in with you. Did you walk?'

'No. I managed to get a lift with the groom, he's calling back for me at two.' Kitty followed her down the narrow and rather gloomy hallway, contrasting it with the wide, spacious, airy one of Harwood Hall.

'Then I suppose you'll be wanting some lunch?' Julia was wondering if the small joint of lamb would stretch. She had hoped to mince the remains for a cottage pie for supper on Monday.

'If it's not a bother.'

'Kitty! Oh, it's been so long since we saw you!' Annie cried, launching herself bodily at her sister.

'Annie, can you be less boisterous? It's not at all ladylike to carry on like that,' Julia admonished.

Both girls ignored her and Kitty hugged Annie tightly.

'Now, Annie, sit down and let Kitty take off her coat and hat. Where's Bridget?'

Annie sat down. 'She was tidying her sewing basket, as you told her to. You said it looked like a rubbish heap,' she answered a little sullenly.

'I'll go and fetch her,' Julia said with a sharp note in her voice.

'Oh, Kitty, it's shocking here! She goes on and on about being neat and tidy all the time. You can't leave a thing out of your hand without being told to, "Tidy it away now, like a good girl". I could scream sometimes, so I could, and we have to read from St Paul's Epistles *every* night!'

'How is Bridget?' Kitty settled herself on the sofa under the window. The room was warm and comfortably furnished and indeed it was very, very tidy.

'She's very quiet, Kitty. Miss Schofield, her teacher, asked to see Aunt.'

Kitty was alarmed. 'Is *she* worried about her? Is she eating, Annie?'

'She doesn't eat much but she *does* eat.'

Kitty was thankful for that. 'What did Aunt say after she saw Miss Schofield?'

'Nothing much. She said she told her to give Bridget time to settle down.'

'Is she falling behind in her lessons?'

Annie bit her lip and nodded. 'She has to do extra work at home in the evenings now.'

Kitty sighed. Poor Bridget, she thought, but before she had time to deliberate further her sister appeared, accompanied by her aunt.

Kitty hugged her, noticing at once how thin Bridget was. 'I told you I'd come and see you as soon as I could and today is my first whole day off. I only get a few hours on a Tuesday afternoon. I brought you this. I know how you love strawberries and Cook makes the best preserve you ever tasted.' Kitty pressed the small jar into her sister's hand and was rewarded with a smile. 'I knew you'd like it.'

'How nice, we'll have some with the scones for tea. Now, Kitty, you must tell us all about that grand house and how you are getting on.' Julia was not going to miss an opportunity to hear all about how the gentry lived for she knew she would never get to set foot in the place herself. The ladies in her sewing circle would be all agog to hear about it too.

Kitty spent the next few hours telling them all about her new life. Annie and their aunt listened avidly, but Kitty saw that Bridget's attention often wavered and she seemed to be lost in a world of her own.

After lunch, which was a quiet affair for Aunt Julia believed it was the height of bad manners to hold a conversation at the table, Kitty helped her sisters to clear away and wash up.

'I can't believe how quickly the time has gone,' Annie remarked sadly as they returned to the parlour where their aunt was neatly laying out the silks she was using for her embroidery. Annie surreptitiously pulled a face at Kitty. Both she and Bridget had to make a cross-stitch sampler and they both hated sewing.

Kitty nodded. 'I'll come again next month and if by any chance someone is making a quick trip into town on my Tuesday afternoon off, I'll try and come then too.'

'It will be rather a waste of your time, Kitty. They'll both be in school,' her aunt reminded her.

'Oh, of course,' she answered dejectedly.

'Before you go, Kitty, I have some news for you, for all of you. I was going to tell the girls this evening and then write to you but—'

'What news?' Kitty interrupted.

'Your father married Hester yesterday. It was all very quiet and there is to be no honeymoon. Her things were moved in on Friday evening. He wanted me to let you know.'

Annie shot a hurt look at Kitty. He hadn't even

come to tell them himself, let alone have them at the ceremony.

Kitty shrugged. 'I suppose the entire parish knew before us,' she said flatly.

'Kitty, that is not the attitude to take at all! You go to church, I assumed you'd have heard,' Julia reprimanded her.

'I go to early service and no doubt Reverend Joyce didn't want to upset me further by informing me.'

'I hate Hester! I will never call her anything other than Hester Smythe! *Our* mam was Mrs Thomas Doyle!' Annie cried.

'Annie, don't be insolent! If ever you meet her you will address her properly as either Mrs Doyle or Stepmother,' Julia snapped.

Kitty rose. 'Then I hope none of us *ever* meets her, and if I ever have the misfortune to I will cut her dead! Thank you for lunch, Aunt. It's two o'clock, James will be here any minute.'

Julia said nothing as Kitty hugged her sisters and promised to visit again, but her lips were pursed in a thin line of disapproval. Kitty's attitude would only encourage further defiance from Annie and in her opinion the child was far too bold already. Oh, her brother might be paying her handsomely for the girls' keep, but they were a worry to her!

*

To Kitty's surprise, when she arrived back at the Hall it was to find Niall Collins sitting in the kitchen chatting amiably with Cook. He stood up as she came into the room and it was obvious that he was pleased to see her.

'I was passing this way so I thought I'd call in. Cook told me you'd gone into town to see your sisters but she very kindly offered me some tea.'

'Sure, wasn't it the least I could do, it being a fair way you've to travel home,' Cook remarked.

Kitty felt a little shy but quite flattered that he had obviously broken his journey home to see her. 'It was the first opportunity I'd had to see how they're getting on. They've gone to live with our aunt and neither of them wanted to go.'

He raised one eyebrow quizzically but before he could speak Cook intervened.

'And how did Bridget like the strawberry preserve?' she queried, trying to catch Kitty's gaze. As far as she knew the girl hardly knew him and it didn't do to go telling virtual strangers private family business.

'Wasn't she just delighted with it and Aunt Julia said they'd have some on the scones for their tea.'

Cook nodded. 'Don't forget you've promised to do extra work in payment.'

'But surely not right away? I was hoping Kitty might like to walk down to the gates with me?' Niall said.

Kitty looked questioningly at the older woman who shrugged.

''Tis still her afternoon off so I suppose it's up to her.'

'I'd like that,' Kitty replied, smiling at him.

They walked in silence to the stable yard and Kitty was surprised to see that he had brought the trap. He was obviously determined to speak to her alone.

'You've brought the trap. Sure, you needn't walk down the drive to the gates.'

'It is a fair way from the home place, that's why I drove here, but I wanted to see you again, Kitty.'

She felt herself blushing. He hadn't just been passing by. 'I'm glad you did.'

'How are you settling in? Has Elizabeth thrown any tantrums yet?'

'I'm doing just grand, so everyone says, and Miss Elizabeth has been very nice, as has her mother.'

He smiled down at her. 'Mrs Harwood is a real lady. She's greatly respected and admired. Why did your sisters go to live with your aunt?'

Kitty decided she would tell him. 'For the same reason that I was sent to work here. My da got married again and he couldn't bring Hester Smythe into the house with three unmarried daughters living in it.'

'Ah, I see. So your da is Thomas Doyle. I heard he

was married yesterday. You're the blacksmith's daughter.'

Kitty nodded. 'I'm the eldest, so I had to be found work. Annie and Bridget are still at school.'

'And what about you? Did you not want to come here?'

Kitty shook her head. 'It was such a shock. I suppose I thought I'd stay at home looking after Da and keeping house until . . . until I was older.' She had been about to say 'until I got married' but she thought that might sound too bold.

He smiled at her. 'Or until some lad swept you off your feet and married you?' Seeing the colour rise in her cheeks he became serious. 'It's a harsh custom, Kitty, as are many old-fashioned country ideas, but aren't you happy enough here?'

'I am so but I'm finding it hard to forgive him. It was the manner and the speed of it all. If only he'd done it gradually. Explained to us first, then let us get used to the idea, then let us meet her and perhaps get to know her. It was just *announced*! He never even told us he'd got married, let alone invited us – not that we'd have gone – he left that to Aunt Julia.'

Niall felt sorry for her. She was a very pretty girl and he liked her; he could see how the situation upset her. 'I suppose you'll come to accept it in time, Kitty.'

'I doubt it.'

'My mam is always saying "Time heals" and sometimes it's the truth.'

She smiled at him. She didn't want to pursue the subject but fortunately they had reached the gates that led out on to the road. 'Here we are then. I'll go back now, it's almost time for the Mistress's tea.'

He climbed up into the trap. 'Next time I have to come up here to see Mr Whelan, will I call in to see you too?'

'I'd like that, Niall,' she replied and she meant it.

Chapter Six

———

WHEN THE FIRST HEAVY frosts of mid-November covered the fields and hedgerows and fires blazed from early morning to late at night in every fireplace in the house, Blanchard informed Mrs Harwood that in her opinion Kitty was fit to be promoted to the position of Miss Elizabeth's maid.

'If she has any problems, ma'am, I will be there to supervise.'

Amy Harwood had nodded. 'With the Christmas season approaching Elizabeth will need someone of her own. I don't want to tax you too much, Blanchard.'

The woman had smiled gratefully. Her arthritis was far worse through the cold, damp winter months. 'Thank you, ma'am, for your consideration.'

Elizabeth was delighted for she considered her

mother's maid to be old-fashioned and rather censorious.

'It will be so nice to have someone of my own age to help with my clothes and hair and things,' she informed Kitty with an airy wave of her small white hand.

'I hope you'll find me satisfactory, miss.' Kitty was deferential.

'Oh, I know I will. Blanchard is rather . . . stuffy. Christmas is just around the corner and we always go up to Dublin in the first week of December to do the shopping and buy clothes. You can come with me, Kitty. Have you ever been to Dublin?'

Kitty blushed, feeling a little thrill of excitement. 'No, miss, never.'

'Oh, it's a grand place. Not as grand as London, of course, or so Mama says, but there are lovely shops. So very fashionable. We stay with cousins of Papa's, Eugene and Lavinia Harwood, in Fitzwilliam Street Upper. Their house is not as big as this but they do have electricity and hot running water. There will be no need for you to be running up and down stairs with jugs.'

'Oh, I'd love to see the place, miss, so I would. And perhaps I could buy some gifts for my sisters?'

'Yes, of course. They live with your aunt, so I hear? Did they not wish to stay at home with your stepmother?' Elizabeth had heard rumours and was curious.

'We had no choice, miss. Da wanted us all out of the place before he brought *her* into it.'

'How odd, but Papa is very pleased with the work he did on the carriage. It's as good as new. I suppose you heard all about that escapade? I know how the servants gossip.' Elizabeth was smiling.

Kitty couldn't help smiling back. 'I did, miss. Was he really very cross?'

Elizabeth laughed. 'Furious! He stopped my allowance for a whole month and it didn't matter how much Mama pleaded, he just refused to budge. Never mind, I'll have double this month and I can always persuade Mama to buy me whatever really takes my fancy when I've spent that. Henry always says I can twist her around my little finger. He'll be home for the holidays.'

'So I heard, miss.'

'He can be serious but he's fun sometimes too. I do miss him.'

'Shall I hang these up, miss?' Kitty asked, picking up three discarded dresses and a blouse from where Elizabeth had left them – on the floor.

'Yes, Kitty, and could you take my laundry down? It's in the basket in the corner there.'

Kitty did as she was bid and then went down with

the laundry to the scullery where Mary, the woman who did most of the washing, was rinsing towels.

'Miss Elizabeth's laundry, Mary.'

Mary raised her eyes to the ceiling. 'Sure, and most of it worn only for a few hours I'll be bound,' she grumbled.

'They're off to Dublin in a couple of weeks,' Kitty informed her, bursting to tell someone the news.

'And they'll bring back a fine heap of washing then!'

'I'm to go with them, won't that be grand?'

'Isn't it well for you,' Mary replied caustically.

'The house they stay in has running hot water and the electricity,' Kitty enthused undeterred.

''Tis to be hoped they have someone from the Royal Irish Constabulary minding the door too for there's shocking goings-on up there, I do hear tell.'

'What?' Kitty asked, wide-eyed.

Mary shook her head. 'This country is in a desperate state altogether after that palaver up there in nineteen sixteen at the General Post Office and then those lads blowing up the explosives and shooting dead the two policemen at Soloheadbeg on the very day the dail sat for the first time. 'Twill get worse before it gets better, you mind me.'

Kitty sighed. Ireland was always in a 'desperate state' or so everyone said. It was all to do with most

Irishmen not wanting to belong to the British Empire but that had been the case for centuries and she didn't think much was about to change, even though her da had often said it would have to one day. Even though he was a Protestant he was as fiercely nationalistic as his Catholic neighbours. Apart from their religion, they were all *Irishmen*, he had emphasised, and the British had never treated them decently. She pushed the thoughts away; she didn't want to think about her da at all.

There was great excitement as the family, with Blanchard and Kitty, prepared to go to Dublin: they were going to stay for ten days.

'Aren't you the lucky one!' Tess said enviously to Kitty. 'Sure, I've never been further than Athlone in my entire life.'

'I am so but won't I feel very dull and dowdy in my brown coat and knitted hat when everyone else is so fashionable.'

'You'll be better dressed than many. There's shocking poverty above, so I heard tell. Will you go to all those fancy shops with them?'

'I don't know. I'll have to ask Blanchard. Maybe they'll need me to carry the parcels.'

'They'll have them delivered,' Cook interrupted, having overheard. She could not see the point of Kitty going too. An extra pair of hands would have been more than welcome with all the extra work that the festive season demanded.

'Ah, never mind. Sure, you'll have some time off to do your own shopping,' Tess consoled Kitty as she saw her face drop.

'And wouldn't she be better doing that here in Tullamore and not be paying the fancy prices they charge for things above in Dublin? We work too hard for our wages to be lining the pockets of big fancy shopkeepers,' Cook said cuttingly.

Tess went off to collect the tea trays and Cook looked closely at Kitty. She knew Miss Elizabeth of old. The girl was very fickle with her loyalty.

'Kitty, don't you go taking too much notice of what Miss Elizabeth says. It doesn't do for servants to become too familiar with those who employ them; it doesn't do at all and only leads to upset and disappointment. You model yourself on Blanchard. You won't hear her gossiping and giggling with Mrs Harwood. And you mind yourself when you're above in Dublin; to my mind it's not a fit place for a young girl from the country to be wandering around at all. If you go shopping, go with Blanchard and take good care of your purse. If I were you I wouldn't take much money with you at all, then you won't be tempted to waste it or have some blackguard steal it from you.'

Kitty nodded. It was sound advice. After all, she only intended to get something for Annie and Bridget. She had to save.

Niall Collins had kept his promise and each time he came up to the turf factory he had called over to see her. Indeed sometimes she felt sure he had made a special journey. Each time she saw him her liking and her interest in him increased and she was certain he felt the same way. Tess had started to tease her about it, saying it was only a matter of time before they would be walking out. Kitty had laughed off the suggestion but she had begun to realise that it would be quite nice to be asked.

The following morning as she came downstairs with a large bundle of washing for Mary she was pleased to hear from Emer that he was in the kitchen.

'Will I tell him to come out to you?' Emer asked.

Realising there would be no privacy at all in the kitchen at this time of day, Kitty nodded and waited in the passageway.

'Here, let me take that for you. Sure, you can hardly see over the top of it,' Niall offered, smiling.

'I'll just pass it in to Mary then I can talk to you for a few minutes.' She hastily dumped her load in the scullery, not waiting to hear Mary's comments.

'I'm glad you've called today, I've something to tell you.'

It was one of the things he liked about her. She was direct in her manner. There was no shilly-shallying, no simpering, no fishing for compliments and yet she certainly wasn't what people would call 'bold'.

'You've had a fight with Elizabeth? They've increased your wages? You've got another job?'

She laughed, shaking her head. ''Tis none of those things. I'm to go up to Dublin with the Mistress and Miss Elizabeth and Blanchard, of course. They're going shopping for Christmas.'

He looked concerned. 'Kitty, you will take care? There's rumours of trouble above in the city. How long will you be gone?'

'Not long and I'm sure we'll all be safe. We're to stay with a cousin of the Harwoods in Fitzwilliam Street Upper. It's a very grand house I do hear, with every convenience, and I'm to go with them to the fine shops and maybe even do some shopping myself.'

He decided not to dampen her enthusiasm; she was obviously looking forward to the trip. 'You'll have a grand time, Kitty. It's a fine city. I'll call over when you come back to hear all about it. Just take care, I'd hate anything to happen to you.'

She was touched by his concern. 'Would you really, Niall?'

'Of course I would, Kitty.'

She ducked her head. 'I'd best get back to work now; there's so much to do. I'll see you when I get back.'

'You will indeed,' he replied. He'd make certain to call and see she'd returned safely.

Kitty was in a high state of excitement when they finally arrived at the tall Georgian town house in Fitzwilliam Street Upper. The city amazed her with its crowded streets, fine buildings and its traffic. Every street seemed to be crowded with carts, carriages, motor cars and trams. There was just so much to see and marvel at but she also noticed that there were many poor people on the streets too and gangs of ragged, barefoot children.

After dinner that night she sat with Blanchard and the other servants in the big kitchen below stairs. She had unpacked for both herself and Miss Elizabeth and had helped her young mistress dress for dinner. Now she would not be needed for a few hours. The butler was a dour man in his fifties who spoke only to the older servants but James, who had accompanied them with the luggage, was determined to find out as much as he could about what was going on in the capital.

'And is it true what we hear, Mr Kavanagh, that Mr de Valera is gone from dail eireann to America to get support for independence and that the military are becoming fierce hard on people?' he probed.

The butler nodded solemnly. 'It's getting desperate. There's shootings all over the place and whole streets have been burned to the ground as reprisals. The Lord alone knows where it will all end. Now there's talk of a new military force to be brought over. The "Black and Tans", I heard them called. Sure, they haven't even a proper uniform for them. Kitted out half in police and half in military gear. It's not safe to be on the streets at all these days.'

Blanchard looked fearfully at him. 'And did Himself not inform Mr Harwood of the dangers? Had the Master known I'm certain he would never have let Madam and Miss Elizabeth come to stay.'

'Ah, now, don't fret yourself. Sure, the gentry are safe enough.' The butler realised his mistake in painting such a black picture to a woman up from the depths of the country where they obviously heard little of what was going on.

'Well, I'll be certain to mention it to Madam. We must be on our guard and, Kitty, you are not to go out alone. It sounds far too dangerous,' Blanchard instructed firmly.

Kitty didn't know whether to be glad or sorry. She had been thoroughly alarmed by the butler's words and some of her excitement faded.

'I'm sure the ladies will be quite safe in the likes of Grafton Street and Stephen's Green. 'Tis the less wealthy areas of the city where the trouble is.'

'That may be so, Mr Kavanagh, but we must still be on our guard,' Blanchard replied firmly.

Miss Elizabeth, however, dismissed all notions of danger out of hand, making Kitty feel much better about the situation.

'Cousin Eugene says there's nothing to worry about. The military and the police have everything under control. Kavanagh is always full of doom and gloom. No one would dare to shoot at us! Anyway, I'm here to enjoy myself and I have no intention of letting a bunch of hooligans stop me. Now, Kitty, after breakfast tomorrow we're going to Brown Thomas and Switzer's in Grafton Street. Blanchard isn't coming with us, Mama says it's better she rests a bit, but you can accompany us. Oh, they have such stylish clothes!'

'Thank you, miss. I'll enjoy that.' Kitty felt her excitement returning.

Elizabeth looked her up and down. 'Do you have a decent coat, Kitty?'

Kitty was taken aback. 'I . . . I have my brown one, miss,' she stammered.

Elizabeth frowned. 'That won't do at all, Kitty. Of course you'll wear your best uniform but . . .' She crossed to the wardrobe and rummaged inside. 'Here,

I never really liked this coat. The colour doesn't suit me at all, black is so dull. I can't for the life of me think why I bought it.' She held out a black merino wool coat that had a deep shawl collar and cuffs edged in black velvet.

'Oh, I couldn't, miss! It's hardly been worn at all and it's very grand!' Kitty protested, certain that Mrs Harwood would not approve.

'I insist, Kitty. You must at least look smart and it's not too ostentatious. We can't have the commissionaire on the shop door turning you away. That would be *so* humiliating for Mama and for me.'

Kitty thought it would be very humiliating for herself too but she wasn't familiar with shops that vetted their customers. In fact she'd never heard of such a thing before. So she took the coat and thanked Elizabeth.

'And I think while we're here, Kitty, you can have your hair cut. That's if you would like to, of course,' Elizabeth added. She was enjoying this 'lady bountiful' role but it had suddenly occurred to her that Kitty might have views on something as personal as the length of her hair.

Kitty was delighted. 'Really? I'd love to have a more modern style, miss, so I would, but I . . . I didn't know if it was considered proper.'

Elizabeth laughed. 'I suppose Blanchard will pull a

face but we can say I insisted you have a modern style. I'm young and so are you and I won't have a lady's maid who is old-fashioned!'

'You're very good to me, miss,' Kitty said shyly.

'I like you, Kitty, and we get along famously, don't we?'

'Indeed we do,' Kitty replied, completely forgetting Cook's warnings.

Chapter Seven

———

THE DAYS SHE HAD spent in Dublin now seemed a far distant memory, Kitty thought as she pulled back the curtains in Elizabeth's bedroom that spring morning. She had been with the Harwoods now for eighteen months and no one had gone up to Dublin last Christmas. It had been far too dangerous. There was now open warfare throughout the country between the Army, the Black and Tans and the boys from the Flying Columns. The war for independence was being hard fought and the whole country was under martial law.

'Is it eight o'clock already?' Elizabeth asked sleepily from the depths of the bed.

'It is so, miss, and it's a gorgeous April day. There are daffodils everywhere.' Kitty smiled, looking out over the fields and meadows where spring flowers grew in profusion beneath the trees and hedgerows. 'I've brought up your tea tray. What will I be after putting out for you this morning, miss?'

Elizabeth was now sitting up, her blond hair dishevelled. 'Pour my tea would you, Kitty, while I try to think just what I am doing today. Oh, yes. I'm going to town with Mama.' She sounded dispirited.

Kitty poured the tea and handed it to her. 'Shopping?'

Elizabeth nodded, her expression sour. 'I do wish we could go further afield than Tullamore, the shops are so *dull*! But Papa has forbidden it. He says it's too dangerous to be wandering about the country with all the ambushes and fighting between the Black and Tans and the Irish Republican Flying Columns. *I* don't think it's that bad, there's no trouble around here, but he is adamant. If things go on like this I'm going to ask Mama to send me to England with Henry when he finishes in the summer. At least I'll be able to get some fashionable clothes there. I suppose you'd better put out my pale green dress and jacket, if you think it's warm enough to go without a coat,' she finished, throwing back the eiderdown and swinging her legs over the edge of the bed.

'Sure, it was a little chilly earlier on but that pale green is wool crêpe and the jacket is lined, so you should be warm enough,' Kitty informed her, going to the wardrobe. 'I'll lay it out and then I'll go and fetch your hot water while you have your second cup.' The memory of just turning on a tap, as she had done in the house in Fitzwilliam Street Upper, and of hot water gushing forth had long since faded.

'Would you like to come into town with us, Kitty? You could call and see your sisters?'

Kitty smiled at her mistress. Sometimes Elizabeth could be thoughtful, just as sometimes she could be utterly thoughtless. 'They'll be at school, miss, but thank you. I would like to go into town. It's Bridget's birthday next week and I'd like to get her something.'

'Then you can come in the carriage with Mama and myself. James will be driving,' Elizabeth added. She was still not allowed to drive and her mother hated having to drive herself. 'How old will she be?' she asked as an afterthought.

'She'll be twelve, miss. Annie is to leave school soon. She's to go and work in the hotel.'

'Really? Will she like that?'

Kitty shook her head. 'No, but she's no choice, Da knows the manager in there and told her she's lucky to get the job at all.' Annie had been outraged and had complained bitterly that she was to be a 'glorified skivvy'.

'Haven't you been "skivvying" for Aunt Julia all this

time? At least you'll get paid for it now,' she'd reminded her sister.

Kitty was ready and waiting in the hall when James brought the carriage round to the front door. She glanced surreptitiously at herself in the large gilt-framed mirror on the wall. Her blond hair was cut in a short bob and covered by the brown and cream cloche hat Elizabeth had given her. It was one she had discarded, as was the short brown jacket Kitty was wearing. Still, she looked fairly smart and a bit stylish, she thought. She was eighteen now and quite grown up and not bad-looking. She'd never be as pretty as Elizabeth, even if she had all the clothes and money her mistress had, but she wasn't unattractive. Niall Collins had even told her she was a 'truly lovely girl' the last time she'd seen him. Her features softened. True to his word, he'd come to see her when she'd got back from Dublin and they'd seen quite a bit of each other over the months. He hadn't asked her to 'walk out' with him but she had hopes that he would. He was fond of her, she could tell from things he said and the way he treated her. And she was fond of him too, but lately she had wondered was she falling in love with him? At least she knew he wasn't walking out with anyone else. She'd made enquiries. More to the point, he was the same religion as her and that mattered a lot. Had he been a Catholic she knew he would *never* have even bothered with her. She shrugged. That's just the way things were and probably always would be.

'Ah, good, you're ready and waiting, Kitty,' Amy Harwood said as she came downstairs, followed by her daughter.

'James is here with the carriage, ma'am,' Kitty replied, thinking how elegant Mrs Harwood looked in her deep plum-coloured costume, which was trimmed with lilac braid. A smart lilac cloche with a purple ribbon rosette at one side finished off the outfit. You would think she was going up to Dublin or to the Galway Races instead of just into Tullamore.

'I hear you will soon be able to visit your sister at the hotel? She's to leave school and start work, so Elizabeth tells me.'

'She is so, ma'am,' Kitty agreed, following them out and down the steps. She doubted she would ever get to see Annie at the hotel. She had heard they were quite strict about such things as social visits during working hours.

She was dropped off at the top of the High Street while James drove on to leave the carriage and the ladies in O'Connor Square, which was more central. She had a couple of hours to spend looking for a birthday present for Bridget and the few things she needed for herself.

She walked down and paused before the Bridge House Hotel, which was actually situated beside the bridge over the Tullamore River. It looked rather old-fashioned and, from what she could see through the windows, a bit dark and gloomy. She didn't think Annie would like it much at all. It catered mainly for commercial travellers.

'Good day to you, Kitty. You are looking well.'

She turned slowly to see her father and Hester standing on the pavement beside her. Hester was pregnant – again, she noticed. She looked tired and rather untidy. Her little stepbrother, young Thomas, was hanging on to the skirt of his mother's coat and was gleefully kicking the toes out of his boots on the kerbstone.

'Stop that, you little devil!' Hester hissed at him.

Kitty had of course heard of his birth but she had never seen him, nor had she wished to. He was very like her da, she thought. She made to turn away. She wanted nothing to do with her da or his new family.

'I have business in town and Hester finds shopping on her own tiring. Do you have long? Would you be able to go and see how your aunt is? I'd go myself but I'm late for an appointment,' Thomas asked, ignoring Kitty's hostility.

'Is she sick?' Kitty asked curtly.

'She sent word that she was having dizzy spells.'

Kitty looked alarmed. She'd not heard of this. 'I'll go up and see her. I have plenty of time.'

'Thank you, Kitty. Now, we'll be on our way before this lad has the toes of those boots kicked out entirely. He's too bold for his age by half.' Thomas took Hester's arm and Kitty turned away, but not before she'd seen the look of acute embarrassment on her stepmother's face at this criticism.

On her way up the town she bought a lovely little bracelet made of shells for Bridget and a pair of stockings for herself. It would be quite a walk to her aunt's house and then back again but she didn't mind as it was a lovely day.

When she reached the house it was to find the door open and two of the neighbours standing in the hallway.

'Mrs Maher, is there something wrong?' Kitty asked, noting the looks of distress.

'Ah, Kitty, thanks be to God you've arrived! I heard her banging on the wall and I came in with Mrs Kinsella here. We sent down for the doctor and he's here with her now.'

'What's wrong with her? I saw Da and he said she was having dizzy spells,' Kitty asked.

'Sure, Himself thinks she's been having little strokes,' Mrs Kinsella informed her.

'Should I go in to her?' Kitty was worried now.

'I would, child. You're family,' Mrs Maher advised.

Kitty went upstairs and along the landing to her aunt's bedroom. The door was closed so she knocked quietly on it.

Dr Hennessey opened it and looked enquiringly at her.

'I'm Kitty Doyle. Aunt Julia is my da's sister and my two sisters live here with her. They're at school.'

'You'd better come in, Kitty. She's had a severe stroke. She's very sick.'

'Oh, Lord!' Kitty cried, stricken.

Julia looked very old and somehow withered. Her long grey hair, done in two braids, framed a face suddenly wizened and sallow. Kitty looked up at the doctor. 'Will she . . . die?' she whispered.

He nodded slowly. 'I'm afraid so, child. She isn't conscious. You'd best go for your father.'

Kitty looked at him with concern. 'I don't know where he is. I mean I know he's somewhere in town, I saw him, but . . . we don't really get on. I don't know where he was going.' She was beginning to worry about her sisters. If Aunt Julia died, what would happen to them?

'I suggest you go and look for him. I take it he's her next of kin?'

Kitty nodded. 'I . . . I'll try and find him, sir.'

'Good girl. I'll stay with her until you locate him.'

She went back out on to the road, biting her lip in indecision. Just where should she start to look? He had said he had an appointment but that could be with *anyone*! And she would have to let Mrs Harwood know what had happened.

She hurried as fast as she could back into town and was so relieved when she almost collided with Mrs Harwood and Elizabeth as they came out of Danaher's Drapery.

'You must carry on and find him, Kitty. I'm so sorry to hear your news,' Mrs Harwood said kindly after Kitty had relayed the events to her. 'We're ready to go now but I'll send James back with the trap to bring you home. Will you be at your aunt's house?'

'I will, ma'am, and thank you.'

'I'd ask at the police barracks, Kitty. One of the officers might have seen him or they can look out for him,' Amy Harwood advised.

Kitty nodded and turned in the direction of Patrick Street where the Royal Irish Constabulary Barracks was situated.

She had almost reached there when she caught sight of her father and Hester. She crossed the road, waving to attract their attention.

'Kitty, what's wrong?' Thomas asked, taking in her expression.

'Aunt Julia is dying! You've got to come. Dr

Hennessey sent me to find you. You're her next of kin.'

'Merciful Lord! I had no idea she was that ill.'

'Thomas, I *have* to get home! I'm exhausted,' Hester complained.

Kitty glared at her. 'Haven't you yourself to blame for that?' she snapped. Hester was *tired*! Aunt Julia was *dying*.

'Hester, you'll have to take the child and drive yourself home. I'll be back as soon as I possibly can,' Thomas said sharply.

Kitty was out of breath by the time they reached Julia's house and the news that greeted them was the worst. Julia was dead. Kitty collapsed on the sofa in the parlour while her father went upstairs. It was such a shock. So totally unexpected. On her last visit, a month ago, Julia had seemed fine. Now what was going to happen to Annie and Bridget? Her da would of course see to all the funeral arrangements but what about her sisters? Where would they go? Hester wouldn't want them and she couldn't take them to Harwood Hall with her – and she hadn't nearly enough saved up to leave. Oh, this was dreadful. Bridget was still only a child and once again her world was to be turned upside down.

At last her father came down and saw Dr Hennessey out.

'Such a shock. A terrible, terrible shock,' he said, sitting down opposite her.

'Da, what's going to happen to Annie and Bridget now?' she demanded, biting her lip.

He looked serious. 'They will of course have to come home with me, for the present. They can't stay here.'

'For the present? ' she repeated.

Thomas looked worried. 'Hester has too much to cope with, what with young Thomas and the pregnancy. She is very . . . emotional at times.'

'You mean she won't have them?'

'I mean it's not . . . *feasible* as a permanent option.'

Kitty stared at him. What did he mean by that?

'When we get the funeral over, I'll write to Enid. She'll take them. It will be a great opportunity for them.'

Kitty's eyes widened and she gasped aloud. Enid was her da's only other sister but she had married years ago and gone to live in America. 'Da! Da! You can't send them to *America*!'

'What else am I to do with them, Kitty? Annie is too old now for boarding school, although Bridget is not.'

She was on her feet now. 'Let them stay! Never mind bloody Hester! Are you not master in your own home? It will kill Bridget! '

'Kitty, I'll not have you using language like that! You'll not talk about Hester like that or me either!

They are both still children and will do as I say.'

She was shaking with rage. 'Yes they are! They're *your* children and you want to send them halfway across the world on their *own*! What if anything happens to them? Will you even care?'

'Nothing will happen to them, Kitty. Stop being so dramatic. Once they're aboard an ocean liner they will be well looked after and Enid will meet them.' The solution was very clear in his mind. Didn't they call America the 'land of opportunity'? What better 'opportunity' would they have to get on in life? As usual Kitty was being hysterical. 'My mind is made up. It will be the best solution for everyone.'

'Don't you ask me to tell them, Da! This time you can do your own dirty work! If they refuse to go I . . . I'll go and plead with the Reverend Joyce to make you change your mind. You're a cruel, heartless, selfish man and I hate you!'

Chapter Eight

———◆———

KITTY HAD STOOD OUTSIDE on the steps until at last James had arrived to take her home. She was very thankful that her sisters had not arrived home for she couldn't have faced them. This time her da was going to have to break the shocking news to them himself.

'Ah, don't upset yourself too much, Kitty. 'Tis very sad about your aunt but the Mistress will give you time off for the funeral and once those girls are settled beyond with your Da and herself, sure, he won't be after sending them away. You mark my words, when your one sees how useful they are to her she'll come down off her high horse and say she couldn't manage without them,' James consoled her and Kitty tried to take some comfort and hope from his words.

Mrs Harwood was indeed very sympathetic when

Kitty informed her of what had happened. As soon as she'd arrived home, Mrs O'Shea had insisted she have a cup of strong, sweet tea and then personally escorted her to the drawing room.

'As soon as the arrangements are made for Miss Doyle's funeral, you must let me know, Kitty. It must have been such a terrible shock for you, arriving quite out of the blue and finding her so ill.'

'It was indeed, ma'am. And then for her to . . . die so . . . so quickly. I can hardly take it in but I'm so worried about my poor sisters.' Kitty was very near to breaking point.

Mrs O'Shea shot a warning look at Amy Harwood. She had already heard of Annie and Bridget's fate from Kitty but she didn't want the poor girl to have to repeat it and very probably end up in floods of tears. 'I'll be after informing you about all *that* later, ma'am.'

Amy Harwood nodded. 'Well, then, Kitty, you must go and have something to eat and then rest. Elizabeth can manage with Blanchard this evening. She isn't going out.'

Kitty nodded thankfully.

'Go down and see what Cook has for you,' Mrs O'Shea instructed.

'Might I have a word, Mrs O'Shea?' Amy Harwood asked as Kitty left, closing the door behind her. 'What is all this business with the child's sisters? Poor Kitty seems very upset.' She was fond of the girl, Kitty worked hard and was always pleasant and cheerful, and she did not like to see her in such a terrible state.

The housekeeper pursed her lips. 'Now that the aunt is dead, ma'am, it seems as though they are to be packed off to yet another of the father's sisters. This time he's after sending them halfway across the world alone – to America – and the youngest not even twelve!'

'Good God! Why is he doing that? They are far too young to be sent all that way unaccompanied. I wouldn't dream of letting Elizabeth go that far on her own and she's eighteen!'

Mrs O'Shea nodded her agreement. 'It's scandalous, ma'am. The new wife is in the family way again and is always complaining that she can't cope, that she's unwell and under such a strain, so I do hear.'

Amy Harwood frowned. So far as she knew Hester Doyle only had one child to care for and of course her husband. The family were not paupers, and she was certain that if the woman was indeed suffering the early effects of pregnancy, some domestic help could be found temporarily. The solution seemed very obvious to her. 'I would have thought that that being the case, she would have welcomed her stepdaughters for the help they can, and no doubt will, afford her.'

'My thoughts exactly, ma'am, but she's a fierce

contrary creature, so I do hear.' Mrs O'Shea sniffed. Just what Thomas Doyle had seen in such a plain, miserable and contrary woman as Hester Smythe she had never been able to understand. She was exactly the opposite to poor Kathleen Doyle who had been a fine-looking woman and as capable and cheerful as a soul could be, God rest her.

Amy Harwood sighed. There was no understanding some men. 'It seems such a heartless thing to do and so unnecessary.'

'Ma'am, the Reverend Joyce is coming to dinner tomorrow, is he not? Could you . . . possibly mention it to him?'

Amy Harwood was thoughtful. 'I could but he might not want to interfere and I myself am loath to say anything that might be construed as coming between a man and his wife.'

The housekeeper nodded. She understood that but surely it was worth a try? 'Could you not just mention it in passing, just drop it into the conversation, ma'am? It might help Kitty and save those girls a lot of heartache.'

'I'll mention it, Mrs O'Shea, but that's all. If the Reverend Joyce wants to take it further that's up to him.'

'Thank you, ma'am. If that is all, I'll be away now to my duties.'

Amy Harwood nodded and picked up the book she had been reading but she stared out of the window thoughtfully for quite a while before she opened the volume.

Amy Harwood did mention it to the clergyman after dinner the following evening.

'I hadn't heard that, Mrs Harwood. Julia Doyle's funeral is to be on Friday in Tullamore. I will not be officiating but I will of course attend, out of respect.' He frowned. 'It seems rather harsh to send those girls so far away.'

'They are very young, Mr Joyce,' Charles Harwood added, glancing at Elizabeth. He would be worried sick should his daughter have to travel so far alone.

'I'll have a word with Thomas about it but Hester can be . . . difficult and especially now she's . . . er—'

'I understand that but surely she must see that her stepdaughters can be of great assistance to her,' Amy interrupted.

He nodded. 'I'll speak to him about it.'

Amy smiled and changed the subject.

Elizabeth couldn't see why Annie and Bridget would be so upset. 'I'd just *love* to go to America! I've heard it's a wonderful place and I would be quite happy travelling on an ocean liner. There would be so much to do and such interesting people to meet and without

Mama giving me all kinds of instructions as to what I can and can't do.'

Kitty looked at her in amazement. 'They won't be just going for a visit, miss! They have to stay there, they can't come back, and they'll be terrified. They've never been further than Tullamore in their lives.'

Elizabeth was thinking of all the evening gowns and the cocktail dresses she would have and the balls and parties and the handsome young men who would accompany her to such entertainments. 'Oh, of course. I was forgetting that they won't be travelling first class and it won't be for a visit. But they might not have to go at all, Kitty. Mama was talking to the Reverend Joyce about it and he said he would talk to your father.'

Kitty's eyes lit up with hope. 'He did, miss? Oh, sure, I hope he can persuade Da to let them stay at home.'

Elizabeth was losing patience.

'Goodness, Kitty, can we drop the subject please? I really can't see why you are so upset. I could never really understand why you wanted to stay at home looking after the entire family, never getting paid a penny for it and probably no thanks either when you have a good job here, money in your pocket to spend how you choose and the opportunity to travel. And speaking of travel, after Easter I'm going to beg Mama to let me go to England at the end of May. I'm so sick of being stuck here. It's so boring. There's absolutely nothing to do and no one of any consequence to entertain me and even if there were I have *nothing* decent to wear. She'll understand and take me for a visit. We have cousins there, Harriet and Edmund. Would you like to come too, Kitty?'

Kitty nodded, but she was too taken aback by Elizabeth's insensitivity and still too distracted by her sisters' plight to be very interested in Elizabeth's plans for the future.

She was given the morning off to attend her aunt's funeral; it was an occasion that she was far from looking forward to. She had heard nothing from her father or her sisters and Mrs O'Shea had replied, when questioned, that there was no news from the Reverend either.

It was a dull, overcast day and that only added to her unhappiness. Young Pat Kearney who was driving her into town thought she looked very pale and sad in the black mourning outfit, but kept his thoughts to himself.

She was quite surprised at the number of people who filled the small church. Her father and Hester and her sisters were sitting in the front pew and she knelt beside Bridget, giving the child's hand a squeeze.

Bridget didn't look up and Kitty's heart plummeted. Had Hester insisted they go to America? She tried to look around, her eyes searching for the Reverend Joyce but she couldn't see him. She was surprised to notice Niall Collins sitting on the opposite side of the church. He nodded solemnly to her and she managed to smile a little tearfully.

It wasn't until the service was over and Aunt Julia had been buried in the small churchyard that she at last managed to speak to Annie.

'Are you to stay?' she whispered, drawing Annie away from the people who were shaking the hands of both her da and Hester, who had thankfully managed to find a neighbour who would look after young Thomas for the morning.

'For the time being. Reverend Joyce spent two hours talking to Da and herself. Oh, Kitty, when he told us that poor Aunt Julia had passed away it was bad enough but then when we got home and he said we were to go to Aunt Enid I just screamed and screamed at him and he . . . he slapped me! He said I was hysterical – maybe I was – and then poor Bridget collapsed. It was awful, Kitty! We . . . we were going to run away, we *were*, and then the Reverend came. I don't know how he knew.'

'I told Mrs O'Shea and she mentioned it to Mrs Harwood and Madam spoke to him.' Kitty was horrified at what Annie had just told her. Da had never raised a hand to any of them before.

'So, we're to stay and we've to help *her* as much as we possibly can. You know she's expecting again? I think it's disgusting, so I do, at Da's age! It's just *horrible* to think of them . . . doing that! ' Annie shuddered. She'd heard all about what was expected of you when you got married, her friend Violet Hickey had told her, and she didn't think she could possibly submit to such a thing – ever. At fifteen she thought it was the most revolting thing she had ever heard.

Kitty squeezed her hand. Annie would change her mind when she got older and met a boy she truly loved, but she was so thankful that the Reverend Joyce had managed to change her father's mind. She had to find him and thank him and when she got back she must also thank Mrs O'Shea and her mistress.

'Will you come and visit us, Kitty?' Annie asked. She still wasn't very happy about living at home but it was infinitely better than being sent to America.

Kitty bit her lip and then slowly shook her head. 'I swore I'd never cross the doorstep again. But you and Bridget can come and visit me or I can meet you somewhere and I'll see you at church on Sundays, if you come to early service.'

Annie smiled. 'Can we really come up to the Hall?'

'Just the kitchen. I don't think anyone will mind, as long as you're not going to be in and out of the place all day.'

'How can we be? Bridget will be at school and I'll be at work and you can bet *she*'ll keep us busy. She's downright lazy, Kitty, so she is. I had to get little Thomas up this morning and get him washed and dressed and fed. She was too tired or sick or something. I had to get Da's breakfast too; she said the smell of food turns her stomach. Bridget ironed his shirt and gave his suit a good brushing. I swear she doesn't do a hand's turn at all and you can be sure she won't be after getting out of her bed for early service on a Sunday.'

'At least I'll be seeing a bit more of you both now and I'm so relieved that you're not being sent away again.'

'We'll have to be going, Kitty. Da's looking around for us, no doubt Herself is tired – again!' Annie remarked cuttingly, seeing her father beckoning to them.

'I'm going to thank Reverend Joyce and then I'll have to get back myself,' Kitty said, hugging first Annie and then Bridget, who hadn't said a single word. 'Are you sure you're all right, Bridget? You're so quiet.'

'I'm grand, Kitty, really. It . . . it's just all so . . . upsetting.' Bridget was still very pale and thin.

'You'll be fine now, Bridget. Now you're back at home with . . . Da,' Kitty said before turning and going to find the clergyman.

She was making her way towards where young Pat was waiting with the trap when Niall Collins caught up with her.

'Kitty. I was so sorry to hear about your aunt.'

'It was good of you to come, Niall. You must be busy now that spring is here.'

'Not so busy that I couldn't come to pay my respects and Da agreed. We're too busy for both of us to attend.'

'You heard that Annie and Bridget are to stay at home?'

He nodded. 'You must have been worried?'

'I was but I feel much better now. I'll be able to see them more often; they'll be closer. Just down the lane.'

Niall looked at her closely. It wasn't really the right time for what he wanted to ask her, in fact some would say it was highly 'improper' and he cursed himself for not asking her this before, but he had to seize the opportunity.

'We've been friends for a while now, Kitty, and I'm . . . well . . . I'm very fond of you. More than fond really, and I was wondering if on your next Sunday off you might like to go into Tullamore with me, if Mrs Harwood doesn't object. A real outing where people would see us together, as a couple. But if you prefer to spend the day with your sisters, I'll understand.'

Kitty looked up at him, her heart skipping a beat. He had said he was more than fond of her and he wanted people to see them as a couple! Now she knew it was what she wanted too. She was more than 'fond' of him, she was falling in love with him. But this put her in a dilemma. 'I would love to, Niall, I want people to know that we're walking out together, but could we make it next month? I really do need to make sure Annie and Bridget are all right, especially Bridget. I don't think she's at all well.'

He took her hand and smiled at her, relieved. 'Next month will be grand, Kitty. The weather will be better too, more settled.'

'Then next month it is. I probably shouldn't say this, Niall, at least not here and at this very minute, but I'm so happy you've asked me,' Kitty replied, thinking the day had turned out far better than she had expected. She had completely forgotten that Elizabeth was determined to go to England at the end of May and that she was to go with her.

Chapter Nine

WHEN KITTY SAW HER sisters next she was very relieved to find that Bridget looked far better. She was much livelier and there was more colour in her cheeks. Things at home were not too bad, Bridget said, although Annie complained bitterly about her stepmother and her little stepbrother, Thomas. She declared that he was the most spoiled and wilful brat she had ever set eyes on but that Hester wouldn't hear a word against him.

'Ah, Annie, isn't he little more than a baby himself?' Bridget had defended him and Kitty had smiled. At least Bridget seemed to have taken to the child.

Annie had said she should have got word to them that Niall Collins had asked her out. She could have spent a few hours with them and still gone into town with him. She didn't get much pleasure out of life.

'I do so! Don't I have a grand life with every comfort and money in the Post Office too,' Kitty had retorted.

'Well, get word to him that you have Tuesday afternoon off,' Annie had persisted.

'And won't he be too busy to be dropping his work and jaunting off to town with me? Have some sense, Annie.'

'He might if he really likes you, Kitty.'

Kitty had looked at her thoughtfully. She really did want to see him and even though Annie was not aware of it, she now knew not just that Niall really did like her, but that she was certain that she was falling in love with him. More to the point, Elizabeth had already started to nag her mother to take her to visit their cousins near Liverpool. If she got her way who knew how long it would be before she got back and she didn't want to risk losing him.

She did get word to him and was delighted when a note arrived informing her that he was going into town to collect some things that had been ordered for the farm and if it wouldn't be too boring for her, she could accompany him. If she would like to go she should meet him by the Jesuit House in Rahan at one o'clock.

Knowing it to be her duty she asked Mrs O'Shea to

ask the Mistress if she had any objections and was relieved to hear that Mrs Harwood did not, as long as she conducted herself in a fitting manner.

'And, Kitty, I want to hear of no trick-acting or boldness out of you!' Mrs O'Shea had added. 'He's a decent-enough lad but you never know.'

Kitty had assured her there would be neither.

Elizabeth, however, was a little peeved. 'So, Kitty, you have a young man? You didn't say a word to me about him.'

'He's not my "young man", miss. I'm only going with him while he collects some things. It's not a proper outing.'

'It's certainly more than I'm allowed to do!' Elizabeth replied pettishly, knowing full well that if a young man she liked, and whom her parents considered acceptable, asked her out there would be no question of her not being allowed to go. Then she smiled. 'I do hope I'll meet someone at Cousin Harriet's. They have such a wide circle of friends.'

'I'm certain you will, miss,' Kitty replied, wishing Elizabeth would dismiss her and let her go and get changed.

It was quite warm for late April and so she decided to carry the hip-length cream wool cardigan that looked so nice over her blue dress with its short pleated skirt and boat neckline. She'd sewn a length of blue ribbon around the brim of her hat so it looked as though it matched the dress. She would have liked a string of long beads but hadn't been able to find anything at all. Still, she felt she looked well.

He was already waiting, perched on the farm cart, when she finally arrived outside the gates of the drive that led up to the large college run by the Jesuit priests.

'Am I late? I did hurry,' she apologised as he helped her up.

'No, I'm a bit early and don't you look very nice in your spring finery?'

She smiled at him shyly. 'I thought I'd bring the cardigan in case it turned chilly.'

'Ah, you never can tell at this time of the year. Get along with you now, Harvey.' He flicked the reins and the horse moved off.

They chatted amiably as they drove into town to the Agricultural Co-op and Kitty sat patiently while he went in and then reappeared and with the help of a young lad lifted the various boxes and sacks on to the back of the cart.

'Right, that's that done, now will we go and have a glass of lemonade or tea or something? Sure, it hasn't been much of an outing for you so far, has it?'

'That would be grand. It's very warm,' Kitty replied, swatting away the annoying flies that the horse had attracted, and feeling that her efforts at getting dressed up had not been totally in vain.

Over two glasses of cool lemonade in the more select of the town's two small cafés Kitty began fervently to wish that Elizabeth would give up her plans to travel. She did like Niall so and she felt that he had *really* wanted to see her today. He could have said he was too busy and that he would see her on her Sunday off, as previously agreed.

'This is lovely. It's certainly an improvement on catching up on my mending or just taking a walk or washing my hair,' she said, smiling at him.

'It's an improvement on me just driving into town and rushing back.'

'You won't get into trouble for not going straight back?' She was a little concerned.

'Not a bit of it. Sure, doesn't Da always stop off for a glass of porter on his way home?'

'Would you rather have had a glass of porter?'

'And leave you sitting outside the door of a pub? I hope I've more manners on me than that.'

She smiled. He was being very considerate, she was sure he would have preferred something stronger than lemonade, but no decent woman went into a public house.

On the way back, before they reached the stone wall that bounded the Jesuit College, he turned the horse into the entrance to a bohreen and let it graze on the lush grass at the edge of the ditch.

'Sure, you're going to get into trouble dawdling home like this,' Kitty chided but she was smiling.

'I wanted to talk to you, Kitty. Away from prying eyes.'

She looked down at her hands, her cheeks flushing.

He reached over and took her hands in his. 'Kitty, we've known each other for a good while now and I'm hoping that you're . . . well, that maybe you could learn to love me? I don't have to learn, I already know that I love you.'

Kitty felt her heart begin to beat faster. 'I don't have to learn either, Niall. I've fallen in love with you. I mean it,' she replied, her voice almost a whisper. Her emotions were all over the place. She felt elated, nervous, even a little light-headed. 'I must do, Niall. At least I know I've never felt like this before and I'm always so happy when I'm with you.'

He lifted her chin and looked into her eyes before kissing her tenderly.

She slid her arms around his neck. She *did* love him! She must do for she was beginning to tremble and the ecstatic dizziness had increased.

He at last pulled away from her and she rested her head against his shoulder.

'Oh, Kitty! You are so sweet and so lovely! These

next three weeks are going to seem like an eternity but we'll have a proper outing then, I promise. We can spend a whole day together and maybe even make some plans.'

She nodded. Now it *did* seem an eternity until her Sunday off but she couldn't bring herself to ask if he would have some time to himself on her next Tuesday afternoon. She couldn't expect him to neglect his work just to come to see her. She couldn't bear even to think that in three weeks she might well be on the other side of the Irish Sea. She would just have to pray that either Elizabeth changed her mind or something happened that would delay their departure until she'd had chance to spend a whole day with him and explain that she didn't want to leave him and that she would miss him dreadfully.

That evening while dinner was being served and Kitty was tidying away Elizabeth's discarded clothes and preparing to turn down the bed, she was surprised to hear that Annie had arrived and was asking to speak to her.

'What's wrong? Did she say?' she asked of Tess who had been sent to find her.

'She did not but she's a fierce puss on her,' Tess replied.

'Oh, now what?' Kitty exclaimed, hurrying downstairs.

Annie was sitting at the kitchen table, a glass of buttermilk in her hand, and Kitty could see by her sister's expression that she was angry.

'I told her to drink that and calm herself, she's upset,' Emer informed Kitty before disappearing with two covered vegetable dishes on a tray.

Cook raised her eyes to the ceiling. She wished the girl had not arrived at such a busy time, but there had obviously been some kind of a row down there at the forge.

'Annie, what's wrong?' Kitty demanded.

'I hate her! I *hate* her, Kitty! She's so selfish and spiteful and she's always going to Da behind my back, telling him lies about me. She told him I was as bold as a tinker's brat to her and I wasn't! Truly I wasn't. All I said was that when I start work I won't have time to be cooking every meal or standing for hours ironing. Now Da says I'm to mind myself and not upset her. He even said it might be best for me to stay at home; all the work might be too much for her when she has the new baby. I don't want to have to stay at home and wait on her hand and foot. It might not be much of a job but it's got to be better than *that*! At least I'll have my own bit of a wage.'

Kitty sighed. She hadn't expected there to be a fight already. 'Oh, Annie, try and hold your tongue. I know it's hard but just don't give her any excuse to complain to Da about you. If you don't want to have to stay at home you'll have to at least try to be civil to her.'

'Isn't it well for you to say that, Kitty? You don't have to live under the same roof as her!' Annie cried heatedly.

Kitty put her arm around her. 'I know that, but surely, Annie, it's better that than . . . being sent away. You'll feel better when you do actually start work. You won't be at home all day and you'll have company. There will be other girls of your own age working there too. Then when you're a bit older I'm sure Da will let you go out and you'll meet someone and get married and have a home of your own.'

Annie looked at her sister with horror, blushing furiously. 'I couldn't get married, Kitty! You know what . . . that means! I told you I couldn't even think about doing anything like . . . *that*.'

Kitty sighed and attempted to pour oil on troubled waters. 'Don't go getting yourself into more of a state. You won't always think like that, Annie, trust me. Besides, once she's had the baby she might be different. It might just be because of the way she is that she's being so difficult.'

'And pigs might fly!' Annie replied bitterly.

'I'd listen to Kitty if I were you, Annie. "Needs must when the devil drives", and you have to have a roof over your head, not forgetting that you have to think of Bridget,' Mrs O'Shea advised. It certainly wasn't the easiest of situations but the girl would just have to make the best of it until such time as she did get married or was old enough and had a decent enough job to support herself. Although she didn't hold out much hope of that, unless she was lucky enough to find herself a job in service, like Kitty.

Kitty glanced thankfully at the housekeeper, grateful for her words of support. 'Don't give her any cause for complaint and I'm sure Da will let you take up the job. The money will be welcome now there are more mouths to feed, I know that,' Kitty urged.

Annie nodded slowly, still reluctant, but she realised if she wanted to escape – even for a few hours a day – from her stepmother's hostile presence, then she would just have to do as they were advising her. 'I'll try, but it won't be easy.'

Kitty was greatly relieved. 'Good girl. Don't forget Bridget will help you. She always intervened when there were arguments between you and me. She's always been a little peacemaker.'

Annie managed a smile. 'That's true enough and she actually likes that desperate brat of a child so that puts her in Herself's good books, most of the time.'

'Sure, he can't be that bad,' Emer intervened, having returned from the dining room and catching the end of the conversation.

Annie rolled her eyes and grimaced. 'Maybe I just don't like children.'

'I've three brats of brothers meself, so I know they can be torments,' Tess agreed.

'Isn't it a good job you didn't want to be a teacher then?' Kitty smiled. 'You'd better be getting back, Annie, or Da will be cross. Maybe she's calmed down too by now.'

'Some hope, she's always as cross as a bag of cats,' Annie said glumly, getting to her feet. She envied Kitty. Everyone here seemed so pleasant and friendly.

Kitty gave her a quick hug. 'Don't be going in the door with that attitude. Just remember what I've said.'

When Annie had gone Mrs O'Shea looked at her kindly. 'She'll just have to learn that in life you have to rub along with people as best you can. She'll find there will be people she won't like when she starts work but she'll have to make the best of it.'

'She will. She's a lot of growing up to do,' Kitty replied.

Chapter Ten

WHEN KITTY SAW ANNIE again, after church, Annie informed her that things had improved a little at home, mainly owing to Bridget's efforts and her own at keeping her mouth shut. Kitty had nodded but her mind wasn't entirely on the situation at the forge. Elizabeth had informed her that her mother had finally agreed that they would go and stay with their cousins for the summer, in fact she had insisted they go and soon. Her father had concurred, saying it really was the best thing they could do. They were to leave in a little under two weeks' time: a week before she was due to see Niall again. She had been thrown into a panic and had finally decided that the only thing she could do was go over to his home on her Tuesday afternoon off and inform him that she would be away for three months. It seemed like a lifetime. She wanted so much to tell him that he was special and beg him not to forget her, but how could she? They had only just started to walk out.

'It certainly doesn't give us much time to get everything organised,' Blanchard had said, disgruntled, when she'd informed Mrs O'Shea of the decision.

'Tess and Emer can help and of course there's Kitty,' the housekeeper offered placatingly. There wasn't really that much extra to do, she thought, but the woman was nearing the age when she would retire and obviously didn't want to be doing all that travelling. It was an ordeal of a journey, she'd done it once herself. It took over two hours to get to Dublin, eight more on the ferry and then another hour to get out to the big house in Aintree where the Harwood cousins lived. Still, at this time of year the ferry crossing should be calm and they wouldn't be travelling steerage.

'And I'll need the three extra pair of hands. James is to come too and he's not at all delighted either,' Blanchard had informed her avidly interested audience of Cook, Tess, Emer and Kitty.

'Won't the Master need him here?' Tess had asked.

'Sure, he's perfectly capable of driving himself and young Pat will be here to see to the horses and the stable duties,' Mrs O'Shea had reminded her.

Blanchard had eased her stiff and aching bones

down into a chair beside the range. 'He's to attend to Master Henry.'

Mrs O'Shea's eyebrows had risen. This was the first she'd heard of it. Henry Harwood must be finishing at Trinity early.

'There's been a couple of ugly incidents above at the university. I suppose it's only to be expected when there's so much trouble and unrest in the entire country, so the Master has decided it's best for Master Henry to go to England, out of harm's way. I expect he doesn't want him to get mixed up with any undesirable political types,' Mrs Harwood's elderly maid announced peevishly.

The housekeeper shook her head warningly and frowned. It didn't do to be discussing such things in front of these young girls. 'That's entirely up to the Master and Mistress.'

Tess and Emer had exchanged glances. What kind of ugly incidents? Who were these undesirable political types?

'See what Miss Elizabeth has to say about it all. You know what she's like, speaks first, thinks afterwards,' Tess had whispered to Kitty a bit later on.

'I don't want to know. I've other things on my mind,' Kitty had whispered back, thinking of Niall.

The time seemed to drag interminably but at last Tuesday afternoon arrived. She had practised every night what she would say to him. She wanted to make him understand that it was with great reluctance that she was going, that indeed she had no choice and that she was very afraid that he would forget her. But choosing the right words was so very hard. She didn't want him to think she was bold – or worse, cheap.

She had a good wash and dabbed on a little of the lavender water she used for really special occasions. She had no fancy, expensive perfume like Mrs Harwood and Miss Elizabeth. She had washed her hair the night before and had brushed it until it shone. It was unseasonably warm for May so she decided to wear the white, fine lawn dress sprigged with tiny pink rosebuds that Elizabeth had given her. Elizabeth had said it was so babyish; it made her look as though she was only fourteen and not at all like the sophisticated young woman she really was these days.

Slipping it over her head Kitty peered into the mirror, wondering if it made her look childish too. She didn't think so. It had a square neckline piped with pink ribbon, short cape sleeves, a skirt gathered at the hipline with a pink belt and quite a short hemline. It looked cool and fresh and pretty. She had decided against a hat for she had nothing that was quite suitable, although it wasn't considered proper to go out without one. She'd confided in Tess who had said she could tie a length of ribbon around her forehead, like one of those new-fangled headbands she'd seen in one of Miss Elizabeth's magazines.

'Sure, aren't they the height of fashion? Wasn't the girl in the picture wearing one and she sitting in a motor car outside a grand house? So it must be all right. At least you've *something* on your head, but if you're not sure, Emer has that straw hat she wears for Mass. She'd give you a lend of it and you could put the ribbon around that.'

Kitty had decided against the hat: it hadn't looked at all right when she'd tried it on and both Tess and Emer had agreed with her.

She carefully tied the ribbon and tucked a tiny artificial rosebud into the bow to finish it off. The flower had been part of the fancy packing on a set of lace handkerchiefs Elizabeth had just opened and she'd rescued it from the wastepaper basket in her mistress's room. It did look much better than Emer's hat, she thought. She was quite delighted with the results of her efforts but decided to go out quickly and quietly in case either Cook or Mrs O'Shea saw her and reprimanded her for her lack of proper headwear.

It was quite a long walk out to the Derries and she wasn't sure exactly where the Collins farm was but when she finally reached her destination she was given directions by an old man who was painting his garden gate.

When she rounded the bend in the narrow laneway she was quite surprised to see that the farmhouse was much bigger than she had imagined it would be. It was a very substantial house of grey weathered stone with a slate roof built in an L shape. The windows were quite large and all those facing to the front had the blinds pulled down to keep out the strong sunlight. It gave the house a rather shuttered and unwelcoming air. The front door was firmly closed and she was too nervous to knock so she decided to go around the back and ask someone if she could see him.

She felt apprehensive and the headband was sticking to her forehead with perspiration from the combined efforts of her long walk and the heat of the sun. She hoped she didn't look all hot and bothered. There was a very tidy yard at the back of the house, flanked by an array of outbuildings, and beyond were the barns and sheds, byres and milking parlour. It was a much bigger place than many she had seen. They must be quite well off.

The back door was of the stable-door type, the top half of which was open, and she stood for a few seconds staring at it. She hoped he would be in but she doubted it. It must be well after two o'clock by now. The midday meal would be over. Well, standing here like an eejit wasn't going to help, she told herself. Resolutely she knocked on the lower part of the door.

The head and shoulders of a young girl appeared. 'Who are ye and what do ye want?'

'I'm Kitty Doyle and I'd like to see Niall Collins, please,' she replied, rather taken aback at this abrupt reception.

'He's not here.' The girl disappeared.

Kitty bit her lip. She wasn't going to be dismissed like that, not after she'd had such a long walk and taken such care with her appearance and so desperately wanted to see him. She knocked again, more determinedly this time.

'Didn't I just say he wasn't here?' came the annoyed voice from within.

'Who are you?' Kitty called.

'Rosie, who is at the door?' an older woman's voice called from the regions beyond the kitchen.

'A young one looking for Niall. I've told her he's not here, ma'am!' was the reply, delivered in loud, quarrelsome tones.

'Have the manners to ask her her name and bring her inside,' came the equally terse command.

The head and shoulders reappeared and the door was opened. 'She says ye are to come inside.'

Kitty stepped into the kitchen, which, apart from the kitchen at Harwood Hall, was the biggest she'd ever been in. It was well furnished, with a large range, many presses, two dressers and a large array of saucepans and utensils. It also looked comfortable and spotlessly clean.

Rosie, who was about fifteen years of age and was obviously a kitchen maid, had returned to her task of scrubbing the griddle pan and totally ignored Kitty.

A tall, middle-aged woman with light brown hair and grey eyes came into the room and Kitty noticed that the clothes she wore, while not entirely stylish, were practical and of good quality and cut. At the neck of her brown and beige checked blouse was pinned a fine cameo brooch. The grey eyes were regarding her with mild polite curiosity.

'Good afternoon, ma'am. I'm Kitty Doyle and I was hoping to have a few words with Niall,' Kitty informed her.

'My son is out in the fields with his father and the other men. Have you come far? Is it very important?'

'I've walked over from Harwood Hall and it is quite . . . important.' This was his mother, Kitty thought, feeling slightly perturbed as Rosie was now regarding her with avid interest.

'Rosie, leave that for now and go and help Carmel to bring in those sheets from the washing line. They'll be dry enough for ironing and I don't want them trailed in the dust of the yard,' Mrs Collins instructed firmly. She could see the girl was uneasy. She was well dressed, if a little too modishly turned out for her taste, and the skirt of her dress was very short. She wore no hat, just that little bit of ribbon around her head, and she had no gloves either, but she was polite and deferential. 'Please sit down, Miss Doyle.'

Kitty sat down on a straight-backed wooden kitchen chair. Obviously there were two maids. They must be more well to do than she had realised.

Rosie wiped her hands on her apron and went out with a very bad grace.

'You work at Harwood Hall, I take it?' Mrs Collins enquired.

'I'm Miss Elizabeth Harwood's lady's maid. I've been there for nearly two years.'

The older woman nodded. That explained the way the girl was dressed, she thought. The personal servants of the gentry tended to model themselves on their employers and from what she'd seen and heard of Elizabeth Harwood she was what was now being referred to as a 'flapper' or a 'bright young thing'. 'And you know my son?'

'We . . . we've just begun walking out, ma'am.' It surprised Kitty that he hadn't informed his mother of this fact.

Mrs Collins's eyes hardened a little. 'Indeed? He never mentioned that to either his father or myself. How old are you?'

Kitty became flustered. 'I'm eighteen and we . . . it's

only really become "walking out" recently but I've known him since I first went to the Hall.'

Mrs Collins compressed her lips. He'd not spoken of this acquaintance with her in all that time and hadn't she said she'd been there nearly two years? 'Where were you employed before you went to the Harwoods'?' she asked.

'I wasn't employed, ma'am. After my mam died I stayed at home and kept house for my da – he has the forge at Rahan – but he remarried and my sisters and myself had to leave. I went to Harwood Hall and my sisters went to live with an aunt.' Kitty was feeling very apprehensive. Mrs Collins's attitude had changed and these questions were unnerving her.

The older woman nodded. So, she was the blacksmith's daughter; she'd heard that they had been parcelled out when he'd taken a new wife. At least the girl wasn't a Catholic, as she'd feared, thinking that was the reason why Niall had made no mention of this liaison.

Kitty took a deep breath, determined not to waste her precious time. Time that was quickly running out. She *had* to try to see him; she had to make his mother realise that she was truly fond of him. 'I . . . I'm very fond of Niall, ma'am, and I was to meet him again on my Sunday off, but I'm to go to England with Miss Elizabeth and her mother before then and I wanted to see him and explain . . . how I feel and . . .' She decided not to mince her words. 'I don't want him to forget about me and meet someone else,' she pleaded. 'I'll be away for three months.'

'I see,' Mrs Collins replied. She looked intently at Kitty and felt a little pang of regret. She was a pretty girl with nice manners and she did seem sincere about Niall. Thomas Doyle's family was a respectable one but there was no wealth to speak of and no land. She pushed these thoughts aside. It was far better that she put a stop to this now before it went any further. There was no future for her with Niall. He was their only son and would inherit everything and Kitty Doyle could bring him no dowry for her father had a son and heir. Besides, it had been decided between herself and her husband that Niall would marry Margaret Maud Delahunty who would make a good wife and mother and would also bring land and money with her to the marriage. It was the only way to keep and increase wealth in such troubled times.

She leaned forward a little. 'Kitty, I'm very sorry to have to tell you this but it will do no good to speak to Niall. I'm sure that you are fond of him but there is no future for you with him. You have no dowry and we have other plans for him. Long-standing plans. I'll tell him you called and that you are going to England with the Harwoods. It's probably for the best and you said yourself that you have only just started walking out – if you can even call it that.'

Kitty gasped, feeling as though she had been kicked in the ribs. 'You mean . . . there's someone else?' Shock and bitter hurt filled her eyes.

Niall's mother nodded and then rose. 'I think it best if you went back to the Hall now, Kitty.'

Kitty pressed her hand to her mouth to stop the cry that had risen to her lips. She had never felt so hurt, humiliated and betrayed! He had said he loved her but he was promised to someone else! Promised to someone who had a dowry while she . . . she had nothing to bring him. With tears stinging her eyes, she stumbled from the kitchen and out into the yard. Then she broke into a run. She wanted to get away from here as quickly as she could.

Mrs Collins made no attempt to follow her. There would be no need to inform Niall of the girl's visit and she'd make sure that Rosie and Carmel kept their mouths shut about it too. She had said she would be in England with the Harwoods for three months and during that time they would prevail upon Niall to see sense and ask Miss Delahunty to marry him. Then when Kitty Doyle returned he would be safely engaged, if not married.

Chapter Eleven

———◆———

KITTY DIDN'T KNOW HOW long it took her to get back to Harwood Hall. Tears blinded her for most of the way and her breath came in sharp painful gasps. Somewhere along the way she tore off the pink ribbon headband and threw it aside. Once she fell, grazing her knees, ruining her stockings and tearing the skirt of her dress on the brambles that had tripped her. She didn't care any more how she looked.

At last she turned into the drive but as she made her way towards the house it was with a numbing sense of shock that she realised Elizabeth was coming towards her. She made an attempt to tidy herself but it was impossible.

'Kitty! Whatever has happened? You look . . . terrible!' Elizabeth exclaimed, taking her arm.

Try as she might Kitty couldn't stop the tears and

Elizabeth led her over to a bench set under the trees at the edge of the pathway.

'Was there some kind of accident? Did someone do this to you? If so Papa will call in the police.' Elizabeth had never seen Kitty in such a state. She was normally so tidy and so cheerful, Elizabeth thought as she urged her to sit down.

Kitty shook her head, beginning to calm down a little. 'No, no accident, miss, and I wasn't . . . attacked.'

'Then what is it? Your dress is all torn and dirty and your stockings are quite ruined.'

'I . . . I fell. I was running.'

Elizabeth was still mystified. 'Why?'

The pain and shame rose in an engulfing wave. 'Oh, miss, I'd been over to see . . . him.' Kitty gulped, she couldn't bring herself to say his name.

'Your young man?' Elizabeth pressed.

Kitty nodded. 'I wanted to tell him I'm going with you to Liverpool and wouldn't be able to see him but—'

'Where does he live?' Elizabeth interrupted; she was very curious to know just what had gone on.

'They have a big farm over at the Derries.' Kitty pushed her dishevelled hair from her hot, tear-streaked cheeks.

'You walked all that way and then ran back?' It was

absolutely *miles*! Elizabeth had never walked further than the end of the driveway.

'I did so but I didn't see him, miss. I saw his mother and she . . . she told me . . .' Sobs choked Kitty again and she couldn't go on.

'Calm down, Kitty, please. Here, wipe your eyes.' Elizabeth passed over her own handkerchief.

Kitty dabbed at her eyes and made a huge effort. 'She told me he was promised to someone else and besides that, I have no dowry to bring. No money and no land. So there is no future there for me. Oh, miss, I feel so ashamed and . . . and deceived!'

Elizabeth was astounded. 'No *dowry*! I never heard of such a thing in this day and age! Good grief, we might be under martial law but we're not living in the Middle Ages. And he's "promised" as you say, to someone else and he never said a word about any of it to you?'

Kitty shook her head miserably.

'Well, I call that downright deceitful. You're better off without him, if that's the way he behaves, and if they set such a store on an antiquated thing like a dowry, then you certainly don't want to get involved with any of them,' Elizabeth said firmly, oblivious to the fact that for generations her class had kept their wealth and lands safely in the family by 'suitable' and often pre-arranged marriages. She patted Kitty's arm.

135

'Dry your eyes and put him out of your mind, Kitty. Isn't it a good thing we're going to Liverpool soon? It's just what you need to perk you up again. Now, go on up to the house and wash your face and change your dress and then get a cup of tea. I'm sure you'll feel much better after that.' It really all was a bit of a storm in a teacup, she thought. Kitty had only been out with this lad once, you couldn't really call it courting at all and in her opinion she'd had a lucky escape. It would do her the world of good to get away from here for a few months.

Kitty rose and walked slowly towards the house. She supposed Elizabeth had been trying to help but her words hadn't brought much comfort at all.

She went straight to her room and tore off the ruined dress and stockings, thankful that there was no sign of either Tess or Emer. She bathed her face and her grazed knees and changed into her uniform. She brushed her hair but she still looked dreadful, she thought, and she felt dreadful too. What was she going to tell everyone? Now she was glad that only Tess and Emer knew where she had been going that afternoon; she hoped Elizabeth wouldn't say anything to Mrs O'Shea. It would be too humiliating for words.

Tess and Emer both agreed wholeheartedly with Elizabeth's sentiments when Kitty told them what had happened, but after she had gone to turn down Elizabeth's bed Emer sighed and shook her head.

'She was aiming a bit high, Tess. I mean apart from him being promised – and I never heard that before – they *are* well off. Herself has two maids and a woman who does all the washing and heavy work. She doesn't get her own hands dirty very often, I can tell you. I've heard old man Collins described as a "gentleman farmer" and they employ fifteen men, that's without the seasonal lads. Rosie O'Hanlon is my second cousin, she works there.'

'And our poor Kitty is only the daughter of the blacksmith, and an unwanted one at that! Sure, she'd get no dowry money out of him!' Tess replied.

'And Miss Elizabeth might call it antiquated and say we're not living in the Middle Ages now, but all these farmers expect a girl to come with money or land or both and she has neither.'

'Sure, she *is* better off out of it but she's heart-broken, so she is.'

Emer shrugged. 'She'll meet someone else and she'll forget all about him. Doesn't she have more of an opportunity than either of us? She's off to Liverpool, and aren't we the ones stuck here in the bogs?'

That night as she lay awake, Kitty tried to stop thinking about him, just as she tried to stem the tears, but she couldn't. Now that she'd lost him she realised just how much she loved him. She did, she thought, or it wouldn't hurt so much now. Oh, she had been almost deliriously happy since he had held her and kissed her and told her he loved her. Why had he told her that? Why had he arranged to see her again? Why had he ever encouraged her? He had known who she was, that she would have no dowry. He had known her for almost two years.

There was no satisfactory answer to these questions, no answer that would give her some comfort. Indeed the only answer was that he had just been using her. What had he hoped to get from her? She really didn't want to go down that road. She would try to forget him, as everyone had urged. She had her pride. Didn't she have her savings even though they weren't much? At least that money was her own; she'd worked for it. She hadn't been dependent on her da to give it to her, and she'd continue to save and one day if she ever did get married that money would be her dowry. She'd go to the altar with her head held high. She'd be as good as the one Niall Collins was promised to. No, she would be better for she'd have managed it by her own efforts, not those of her family.

In the days that followed she bolstered her spirits with that thought and as she became increasingly busy with the preparations for their departure she found she only had time to think about him before she fell asleep.

Cook said the place was getting to be like a lunatic asylum what with all the to-ing and fro-ing and Miss Elizabeth's tantrums. 'Won't I be glad when they've all gone and we get a bit of peace and quiet and I bet the Master is after thinking that himself.' The Master had already shut himself away in his study to escape the rumpus.

'Now isn't she fretting about the weather? Says she's not sailing if there's any wind, she'll stay the night in Dublin, for she'll be sick – and after the way she had the Mistress demented wanting to go in the first place,' Blanchard muttered to Mrs O'Shea. The weather had changed dramatically over the last week. It had become cold and windy and there had been some very heavy showers. Elizabeth was becoming insufferable lately, the older woman thought.

Kitty sighed. She was the one who had to put up with Elizabeth's constant mood shifts and her frequent changes of mind as to just what clothes were to be packed. Secretly, though, she agreed with Elizabeth's reluctance to undertake the ferry journey if there were high winds. It would be the first time she had ever been on the sea and she would be terrified if it were rough. Elizabeth had told her that once they had sailed back in a storm and the ferry had been tossed about like a cork and she'd been tipped right out of her bunk.

The sound of the waves hitting the ship had been so frightening, and then she'd been sick, just to cap it all.

Soon, however, to everyone's great relief, the weather grew calmer, the skies cleared and sunshine returned. The heavier clothes were unpacked and as Kitty rehung Elizabeth's wool dresses and costumes in the wardrobe and placed the cardigans and jumpers back in the drawers she resolved to repack her own small case that evening. They were to leave on the mid-morning train from Tullamore next day. The Harwoods would go in the carriage and she and Blanchard would go with James in the trap. Elizabeth and her mother would be travelling in a first class carriage, they would be in third class, but at least cabins had been booked for them for the ferry crossing. They wouldn't have to sit up all night in the public saloon.

'You'll have a grand time, Kitty. I wish it were me. I'd love to travel,' Tess said enviously as they got ready for bed that night.

Kitty smiled at her. She was feeling a little excited, despite having lost Niall Collins, although pangs of misery still assailed her.

'And won't it be great to have a room of your own? Cook says it's quite a modern house compared to this. She was in it once. She said there are grand little rooms up in the attic, very light and airy, and there is a special staircase leading down to the kitchen so the servants never have to use the front stairs at all. She said she was well treated too and had plenty of time off.'

'I heard it's quite a way outside the city, but that there's trams that will take you in,' Kitty replied. Elizabeth had chattered on for days about her cousins' home in Aintree, quite near to the racecourse where the Grand National steeplechase was held each year. 'Of course they have a motor car and a man who drives it for them and Mrs Harwood and Miss Elizabeth will go everywhere in that.'

'Do you think you'll get to ride in it too?' Tess thought it must be very grand to be driven everywhere in a motor car.

'I shouldn't think so but I won't mind going on the tram.'

'I wouldn't mind going somewhere other than just Tullamore,' Emer complained.

'If I get a chance I'll write and tell you all about it,' Kitty promised. She'd have quite a lot of writing to do, she thought, for she'd promised Annie that she would write to her too.

Her sister had been dismayed to learn that she would be away for three whole months and had Kitty not been so upset over the Niall Collins affair, she would have noticed that Annie had had a mutinous look in her dark eyes which did not bode well for the uneasy atmosphere that prevailed down at the forge, despite all Bridget's efforts to keep the peace. Her preoccupation would cost them dearly.

Part II

Chapter Twelve

———◆———

KITTY STOOD ON THE deck of the ferry in the damp air of the September morning and watched the misty, bluish purple shape of the Dublin mountains drawing closer. It had been so stuffy in the tiny cabin she shared with Blanchard that she'd got up, dressed and come up on deck. In some ways she was glad to be coming home and in others she wasn't. At least the country she was coming home to was far more peaceful now even though it was divided, the six counties in the north with their own parliament. The fighting and the destruction and hardship that followed it was over. In July a truce had been declared and now Mr Lloyd George, the British Prime Minister, had invited Mr de Valera to talks and there might soon be the real possibility that the rest of Ireland would become a

Free State. As far as she could see it was independence at last.

She had managed to write one letter to Tess and Emer and two to Annie, although she'd had no reply from either her sister or her companions – not that she'd really expected one. She had liked living in the house in Aintree, which had had any number of modern conveniences that made life so much easier. She'd liked Mrs Harriet Harwood's servants, too. They'd been friendly and the parlourmaid had taken her into Liverpool on the tram at the first opportunity.

She had of course seen the waterfront from the deck of the ferry when they'd arrived, and she had marvelled at the size and number of ships both in the river and the docks, but as they'd sat on the tram Tina had given her a running commentary on all the districts they had passed through. There were many fine buildings and houses and shops but, like Dublin, there were also slums and a great deal of poverty. She had been completely overawed by the shops in the city centre; some of them – department stores Tina had called them – were four and five floors high. Of course they couldn't afford to shop in most of them but she'd loved Blackler's where the prices suited her pocket.

It had all helped her to forget about Niall Collins, she thought, but how would she feel if she were to bump into him when she finally got back to Tullamore? In some ways she would be glad to return to the peace and quiet of rural life. It had been exciting to travel to another country and live not far away from a big city but she hadn't really got used to the hustle and bustle of the traffic or to the streetlights that stayed on all night.

They would be docking soon, she realised; she must go down and help Elizabeth with her things.

The motor car that belonged to the Harwoods' Dublin cousins would be waiting for them when the ferry docked and a conveyance had been hired for herself, Blanchard and James, both of whom were highly relieved to be back. Henry Harwood had remained in England but he had already gone to London to commence work in the offices of a respected firm of solicitors, the senior partner of which was a friend of Mr Edmund Harwood.

It was dark and the chill of early autumn was in the air when they finally arrived at Tullamore Station.

'I'll be glad to get to my bed this night,' Blanchard grumbled as James helped her into the trap.

Kitty took the rug from young Pat Kearney who had come to meet them. 'Put this over your knees, it will keep out the chill. No doubt Cook will have a fresh pot of tea made, that will warm us up.'

'Pat, give James a hand to put the luggage up in the

carriage,' Blanchard instructed the lad, for James was struggling with one of the two large trunks.

Mr Harwood was getting his wife and daughter settled in the carriage. He would drive them home himself.

How quiet it was, Kitty thought, and how dark the country lanes were with only the carriage lamps to light the way. By the time they reached Harwood Hall the chill damp of the night air had both herself and Blanchard shivering. Everyone was thankful to go inside where the rest of the staff were waiting in the hall to greet Mrs Harwood and her daughter and welcome them back.

'I'll have the tea trays brought up to the drawing room, ma'am, or would you prefer to take the refreshments in your room?' Mrs O'Shea enquired.

'Thank you, the drawing room will be just fine for me, Mrs O'Shea. Elizabeth, do you wish to go upstairs? You are very tired.'

'Yes, please, Mama. I've a headache too.' Elizabeth felt as though she had a head cold coming on.

'I'll come up with you, miss,' Kitty said. She, too, was tired but there was still work to do.

'Well, I'm going to pour myself a large brandy. You can really feel the chill in the air these evenings,' Mr Harwood announced, removing his overcoat.

'There are good fires in both fireplaces in the

drawing room, sir,' Mrs O'Shea informed him as she headed for the basement stairs to instruct Emer and Tess to take up the tea trays.

Kitty helped Elizabeth to take off her coat and hat, then turned down the bed and stirred up the fire that burned in the small fireplace in the bedroom.

'You'll feel much better after a good night's sleep in your own bed, miss. Those bunks on the boat are very narrow and quite hard.'

'Indeed they are not at all comfortable,' Elizabeth agreed.

But far better than trying to get any sleep in the public saloon, Kitty thought to herself; she'd been very grateful for a bed and some privacy.

Tess entered with the tray. 'Here we are, miss, and Cook baked some fresh scones this afternoon and there's jam and cream.' Tess set the tray down on a side table.

'I'm not hungry, Tess, thank you. Kitty, you can leave the unpacking until tomorrow. I'll go to bed as soon as I've had a cup of tea.'

Kitty followed Tess gratefully downstairs.

'There's tea and scones for yourself, Kitty; I'm sure you'll need something after that desperately long journey. Emer and I really enjoyed all the chat in your letter about the house and everything but neither of us are very good at the writing,' Tess said apologetically. 'Are you glad to be back then?' she asked, desperately trying to keep the note of dread out of her voice. Her poor handwriting wasn't the only reason she hadn't replied to Kitty's letter.

'I am but I did enjoy myself over there.'

Tess smiled at her as they went into the kitchen. 'Sure, you can tell us all about it later.'

Kitty looked around the familiar room; it was warm and comfortable and it was *home*.

'Kitty, child, sit down and have this tea and then there is something I have to tell you.' Mrs O'Shea shot warning glances at the other occupants of the kitchen. Let the girl get a hot drink down her first.

'Something important?' Kitty asked, beginning to feel a little uneasy as she sipped her tea dutifully.

'Tess, will you take Kitty's things down to your room? Let her have a few minutes' peace and quiet to have her tea. And, Emer, go and help Miss Blanchard. She's worn out,' Mrs O'Shea instructed. James had gone home and Cook had taken her copy of Mrs Beeton's *Household Management* to her room. She'd noticed a recipe and she wanted to write it out.

When the two girls had left Mrs O'Shea sat down opposite Kitty at the table. Oh, this was not going to be easy. What a homecoming for poor Kitty.

Kitty looked at the housekeeper's grave expression and her stomach turned over. 'What is it, Mrs O'Shea? What's wrong?'

'There are two things I have to tell you, Kitty, and I know you will be upset.' Mrs O'Shea did something she very rarely did; she reached across the table and took Kitty's hand. 'Firstly, Niall Collins has got engaged. I know you were fond of him, Tess told me, but I told her not to write and tell you.'

Kitty felt the sense of betrayal return even though she had had three months to get over him. Before he had just been promised, now it seemed so much more official. She nodded slowly. 'I . . . I'm over him now, I know it's for the best.'

'I'm sure it is, Kitty, and aren't you very young? There's plenty of time yet for you to meet someone.' She was relieved the girl was taking it so well. She sighed heavily. 'The second thing, Kitty, is that there was a terrible row down at the forge between Annie and your stepmother and . . . well . . . Hester Doyle miscarried her child and she blamed it on all the upset and so your father . . .'

Kitty clenched the older woman's hand tightly and her eyes widened with fear. 'What . . . what did he . . . do?'

'Kitty, I'm so sorry but he's sent Annie and Bridget to your aunt in New York. He took them down to Cobh himself and saw them on board the *Carpathia*. They will have arrived by now.'

Kitty stared at her, her eyes wide with horror. 'No!

No! They can't have *gone*!' She shook her head in bewilderment. 'I . . . I never even had a chance to say goodbye! Oh, how could he do this? How *could* he?' She dropped her head on to her arm and began to sob. Her poor, poor sisters! Oh, no matter how bad a row there had been it was just so *cruel* to send them thousands of miles away. She didn't know much about pregnancy but she didn't see how just a row could be the cause of a miscarriage and now she would never see Annie and Bridget again.

Mrs O'Shea gathered her into her arms. The poor girl was heart-broken and who could blame her? 'I informed the Mistress and we agreed not to tell you until you got home. Reverend Joyce has your aunt's address, so you can write to them. Hush now, child. There is nothing anyone can do about it. There's no use making yourself ill over it, it won't bring them back.'

Kitty raised a tear-streaked, stricken face. 'Bridget will die of heartbreak! She . . . she was just settling down, she was looking much better and she was fond of the little boy. How will she cope? How will they both cope so far away and with everything so *strange*?' A fresh wave of sobbing shook her. They'd both be terrified. Oh, how could Da do this? She hated Hester, really *hated* her!

Tess came into the kitchen and when she saw the

state Kitty was in she rushed to her side. 'Oh, Mrs O'Shea, isn't she destroyed entirely! Sure, Himself and Hester Doyle should be horse-whipped!'

The housekeeper silently agreed with her. She passed the sobbing girl into Tess's care. 'See if you can do anything to comfort her, Tess. I'll go up and see Madam and let her know that Kitty is in such a state.'

'Ma'am, will you ask her to tell Miss Elizabeth so Herself won't go tormenting poor Kitty in the morning with her airs and graces and headaches?' Tess begged. Elizabeth could be difficult, tactless and insensitive at times.

The older woman nodded. She would, but she'd have to put it more delicately than that. 'If you can't quieten her, Tess, there's a bottle of laudanum in my bureau drawer. Give her a few drops of that,' she advised.

Tess nodded. 'Did you tell her about . . . *him*?' she whispered.

'I did so and it didn't upset her as much as you thought it would. Now I don't think she'll even remember I said anything about him at all, she's that upset.'

'Kitty, will I take you to lie down, acushla? I'll stay with you and when Emer comes down we'll give you something to make you sleep,' Tess soothed.

Kitty let herself be led from the room and down the

passageway. Tess helped her on to the bed and pulled the quilt over her. Kitty was still fully dressed but she didn't care. She felt as though she would never care about *anything* ever again.

Emer arrived and was dispatched for the laudanum and the two girls stayed with Kitty until at last Kitty fell into an exhausted sleep.

Charles and Amy Harwood both looked concerned after the housekeeper informed them that she had broken the news to Kitty.

'She is taking it very badly, ma'am. I've told Tess to give her something to calm her and make her sleep. If she goes on crying like that she'll make herself ill.'

'Do you think we should have Dr Molloy out to her, Mrs O'Shea?' Mrs Harwood enquired. She had feared this reaction; she had been most disturbed when Mrs O'Shea had given her the unpleasant news about Kitty's sisters.

'I don't think that will be necessary, ma'am, but it's kind of you to ask. I don't know what kind of a state she will be in in the morning though.'

'Don't worry about that, Blanchard will be able to cope and I will explain to Elizabeth how dreadfully upset Kitty is. Perhaps it would be best if she had the day off, so she can rest and try to come to terms with it. You did tell her that the Reverend Joyce has obtained her aunt's address in New York?'

'I did so, ma'am, but I don't think she took it in. It would help if she had tomorrow off, I'm sure.'

Amy Harwood nodded. It was very upsetting. Oh, it had been such a difficult year with one thing and another.

She said as much to her husband after the housekeeper had left. 'I do think it was a cruel and heartless thing to do to those girls, though,' she finished.

Her husband nodded slowly. 'But it is not for us to comment on, my dear. I'm certain they will be well cared for by the aunt and Kitty will get over it, given time.'

Chapter Thirteen

———❦———

WHEN SHE AWOKE NEXT morning Kitty felt groggy and disorientated. For a few seconds she couldn't remember where she was or what had happened to make her feel so confused. Then with blinding clarity it came back to her. Her da had sent Annie and Bridget to America. She lay there staring at the ceiling. What was she to do? What *could* she do? What would be the use of going down to the forge and castigating him? While Hester was there he would never bring her sisters home. She couldn't go after them and bring them back, her da could legally stop her. It would be another three years before she was twenty-one and free of his parental control. She didn't have enough money to follow them and set up a home there for them all and probably her aunt and uncle wouldn't allow that. The girls had been entrusted to their care; she was still officially a minor. She was sure she would never see her sisters again. People held what were called 'American wakes' when relations emigrated because there was so little likelihood of them ever seeing the departing loved ones again in this life. Tears trickled slowly down her cheeks. She would never, never forgive either her da or Hester for this.

Her head was beginning to ache and she remembered that Tess had given her laudanum. She raised herself on one elbow and grimaced. Where were Tess and Emer? She must get up; there was all that unpacking to do, she thought miserably.

She got herself dressed and made her way slowly to the kitchen. The last thing she felt like was having to deal with Elizabeth, who probably wouldn't be in a good mood after all that travelling.

Mrs O'Shea looked up from her household accounts. 'Kitty, you were to sleep on. I told those girls not to disturb you. Mrs Harwood says you are to have today off and rest.'

Kitty sat down. She was very grateful for this kindness. 'They didn't disturb me but what about all the unpacking?'

'Blanchard and Tess are doing it and Miss Elizabeth has a heavy cold so she's staying in bed. Madam had a word with her this morning so she knows how upset you are. How are you feeling now?'

'Still shocked and hurt and . . . miserable.'

'It will take time, child, for you to come to terms with it.'

Kitty nodded. She doubted she ever really would.

'Now, have a cup of tea and some breakfast and then, as it's a pleasant enough day, why don't you go for a little walk to clear your head?' Kitty still looked half-asleep and her eyes were red and puffy. The result of all that weeping and the laudanum, the housekeeper thought.

'I'll have the tea but I'm not hungry, thank you.'

'A nice walk will bring your appetite back,' Mrs O'Shea said firmly. She was not going to let Kitty make herself ill and if she didn't eat that's what would happen.

In the days and weeks that followed Kitty gradually lost her air of despondency. Everyone was very patient with her; even Elizabeth, after she had recovered from her cold, was tactful about Kitty's loss. Kitty felt completely cold when she thought about her da. It was as if any feelings she had had for him had been frozen.

She had written to her sisters and begged them to reply, even if it were only a few scribbled lines. After two weeks of anxiously waiting she had a letter from Annie, the bold and untidy script made worse by the tears that had obviously fallen as her sister had put pen to paper. Mrs O'Shea had kindly allowed her to take the letter to read in her own sitting room and Kitty sat down at the small bureau and spread out the sheets of paper.

Dear Kitty [Annie had written],
The journey was desperate, as was the weather and Bridget was terribly sick and we were both terrified the ship would sink but eventually we got here and Aunt Enid and Uncle Ted were waiting for us. Aunt Enid says I have to tell you that she will take good care of us and you are not to worry. We are settling in and they have a comfortable apartment, as they call it. It's really just a set of rooms all on the same floor, the second floor of the building. But we miss you terribly!

Here the page was heavily stained and Kitty dashed away her own tears with the back of her hand.

Hester was *horrible*! I hate her! It all started in such a stupid way, her moaning and picking on me as usual. I wasn't insolent, Kitty, truly I wasn't! Then she started to scream at me, really *scream* and I yelled back at her and then she threw the sugar basin at me and it missed and broke. She said I had to clean it up and I wouldn't and then Da came in and she went on and on at him! Bridget was crying and so was I.

Kitty's hands had begun to shake as she pictured the scene.

Two hours later she started roaring in agony and then Da called the midwife and then she lost the baby. She blamed me! She said it was all my fault and that she wasn't staying under the same roof as me for another day longer, I had to leave. Then poor Bridget plucked up the courage to say if I went she was going too. Da was furious, really raging and then he said we would have to come here. We both cried and cried but he wouldn't change his mind at all. He wrote to Aunt Enid and then booked the tickets. He said there would be no American wake for us, we were going in disgrace. I hate him and I hate her and I don't care if I never see either of them again!

Kitty dropped her head in her hands and began to sob as she pictured her two frightened, heart-broken sisters being taken down to Cobh to be put aboard the *Carpathia*. Oh, if only she'd been here, surely she could have tried to sort this whole mess out? After a few minutes she calmed herself and read the final page of Annie's letter.

Aunt Enid says we must try and put it all out of our minds and concentrate on the future and we are both trying to do that. It's really not too bad here at all, even Bridget is settling down. You will write to us, Kitty? You won't ever forget us, will you? We remember you in our prayers every night.

    Your loving sisters,
    Annie and Bridget

Kitty folded up the now even more tear-stained sheets and stood up. How could she ever forget them? She would write every week.

'Ah, Kitty, they're bound to miss you but they're settling in and she doesn't say they hate it or that the aunt is desperate, so that's something to be thankful about,' Tess had comforted Kitty after she had returned to the kitchen.

It was two days later when Thomas Doyle came to the back door and asked to see Kitty.

Emer came and told her: 'Kitty, it's your da, wanting to see you.'

'I don't want to see him! I never want to see him again!' Kitty snapped.

'Kitty, I think you should at least see him and hear what he has to say, child,' Mrs O'Shea advised.

For a moment Kitty looked mutinous, then she nodded slowly and left the room. She found him standing in the passageway but she said no word of greeting, nor did she invite him to come any further into the house.

'I heard you were back, Kitty, and I felt I had to come and try to explain.'

'We've been back over two weeks and what is there to explain, Da? I didn't even want to see you, I'm only here to please Mrs O'Shea.'

'I had no choice, Kitty. It was all Annie's fault. She was making everyone's life miserable with her insolence and her tantrums!'

Kitty glared at him. 'You had no choice? You chose *that one* over us the day you decided to marry her! I don't want to hear your pathetic excuses. What you did was cruel and heartless and I'll never forgive you or *her*!' She turned on her heel and walked quickly away.

'Kitty!' he called after her, but she didn't stop or turn around. When she reached the kitchen she opened the door and then let it slam shut behind her.

As Christmas approached with all the usual fevered preparations, Kitty wondered how she would feel this year with the girls gone. She had bought some little gifts in Tullamore at the end of November and had carefully parcelled them up and posted them, to make sure they would arrive in good time. Annie was now working in a small hotel near Central Park and seemed to like it. Bridget was at the nearest school and said it was much more modern than her old school had been and Uncle Ted walked her there each morning on his way to work. They started school much earlier than they did in Ireland.

It was Bridget who wrote these days, Kitty noted, Annie seemed to have little time. Her younger sister's handwriting was much neater than Annie's though, and her letters were more detailed. Kitty was so relieved to realise that Bridget seemed to be adapting to her new life. Her aunt and uncle had four sons who were grown up and working, they'd never had a daughter so they spoiled Bridget, as did the boys, according to Annie. Kitty thanked God in her prayers every night that her quiet, gentle sister was being shown more love and kindness now than she'd had since their mother had died.

'There now, I told you they would be just grand, once they settled in,' Elizabeth reminded her after Kitty had confided the news to her. 'There was no need for you to get so upset and worried about them.' As usual Elizabeth had not really given the situation a great deal of thought. 'Now, I'd like you to come into town with me this afternoon. I have to go to the dressmaker and I need new stockings, so while I'm there you can go to Danaher's Drapery for them. Mrs Danaher ordered me a dozen pairs that should see me over the Christmas festivities. You know, Kitty, I think it's actually going to be quite entertaining this year, even though Henry isn't coming home. There are so many parties to go to!'

Henry Harwood was staying with friends in London.

Kitty smiled at her young mistress. 'You mean because we're at last being offered our independence?'

Elizabeth nodded. Of course it had only been offered; the politicians in Dublin hadn't voted to accept it but everyone said they would. She'd heard her father and Mr Whelan talking about it when he'd come over from the factory for some reason or other. They'd have the same status as Canada, a dominion, but still within the British Empire, and Mr Whelan had said there would be those who wouldn't be at all happy with that. After seven hundred years they wanted to be free entirely. They wanted Ireland to be a republic. Her father had replied that they should take it one step at a time and wasn't this a huge first step forward after all the bitter fighting? It was better to govern themselves and have their own parliament, free from interference. Mr Whelan had shaken his head and said but would it indeed be free from interference from London? She hadn't heard any more, she'd been bored and a little confused. She didn't understand politics nor did she want to. But people were now looking forward to the future with hope, hence the increase in social activities.

Kitty had left Elizabeth at Miss White's in Harbour Street. Miss White was a talented seamstress who had served her apprenticeship in Dublin and Elizabeth was delighted to have found her, although Elizabeth had said she was looking forward to taking trips up to Dublin to shop now all the trouble seemed to be over. Kitty had collected the stockings from Danaher's and had chatted for a while to one of the assistants and she was turning the corner from William Street into Harbour Street when she almost collided with Niall Collins. Her eyes widened and she felt her heart turn over.

'Kitty! I heard you were back. You look very well.' He was smiling at her.

She pulled herself together, drawing back from him. How dare he? He was acting as though nothing at all had happened, as if he weren't even engaged. She had nothing at all to say to him. Her eyes cold, she deliberately stepped aside and walked on, her head held high. She was very relieved to see Elizabeth coming out of Miss White's front door and hurried towards her.

'Kitty, you look as if you've seen a ghost! You're as white as a sheet,' Elizabeth commented.

It was an apt description, Kitty thought. He was a ghost from her past, one she wanted to forget. 'I bumped into . . . someone I would rather not have seen at all, miss. I'm grand now, it was a bit of a shock, that's all.'

Elizabeth looked across the road and saw Niall Collins still standing on the pavement at the corner, staring at them, a look of puzzlement on his face. She took Kitty's arm in a rare gesture of solidarity. 'I hope you ignored him, Kitty?'

'I did so, miss. He . . . he had the brass neck to look delighted to see me and said, "Kitty! I heard you were back. You look very well."'

Elizabeth tutted disapprovingly. 'And he only recently engaged to Margaret Maud Delahunty, so Mama told me. The impudence of him after he treated you so badly! She's no raving beauty I can tell you, you're far prettier than she is! Come along, we'll walk the other way back to where we left the trap.' Elizabeth had at last been allowed to drive herself but only in the trap. She knew her father was considering buying a motor car and if he did she intended to beg him to teach her to drive it. It was so old-fashioned these days to be seen in either a carriage or a trap.

Kitty didn't have much to say on the way home but Elizabeth chatted on happily, describing the evening dresses Miss White was in the process of making her for Christmas. Normally Kitty would have been quite happy to listen to all the details of colours and materials and trimmings and of how innovative and modern-minded the dressmaker was about skirt lengths, but now she wasn't really listening. She had almost forgotten how handsome he was, particularly when he smiled. He had looked genuinely pleased to meet her and she'd heard it in his voice too. Her heart had turned over. Was she still in love with him? If she were then she knew nights of heartache would surely follow. She had to forget him, she *had* to. He didn't love her, he was going to marry someone else and that was the end of it.

Niall stared after them, puzzled and hurt. Elizabeth had looked to be consoling her but why? Kitty was the one who had gone off to England without so much as even a note to tell him she was going or for how long or if indeed she was ever coming back. He'd been devastated when he'd found out; she'd said she loved him and he'd believed her. He'd intended to tell her that he hoped they could become engaged before Christmas but before that Sunday had arrived she had gone. He had been over and over everything in his mind. He'd done nothing to offend or upset her, he was certain. She had said she was so very happy when he'd left her. Now she had cut him dead. Looked at him as though he was a stranger and an offensive one to boot. He turned away, thrusting his hands deep into his pockets.

After she'd gone he'd felt so depressed and hurt that he'd been gradually worn down by both his parents who were insisting he marry Margaret Maud Delahunty. He'd become sick of the sound of her name and of the amount of money and land she would bring as a dowry, but eventually at the end of August, when he had realised that he didn't know when Kitty would return or if she even thought of him at all now, he had capitulated. He wasn't in love with his new fiancée. He didn't dislike her, but he thought she was a rather plain girl with not much of a personality and no mind of her own, for she seemed to obey her overbearing father completely. He was just *indifferent* to her, and was that a good start to any marriage? But the ring was on her finger now, ten acres of land had been given as an engagement present and he'd never hear the end of it if a breach of promise suit were embarked upon. His da would probably disown him for disgracing them. He walked on feeling utterly miserable and totally trapped.

Chapter Fourteen

———◆———

ELIZABETH WAS BITTERLY DISAPPOINTED not to be able to go to a ball that was being held at Charleville Castle on St Stephen's Night but she had developed a sore throat and a slight temperature and as it was a bitterly cold night her mother had been very firm about her staying in bed.

'I was so looking forward to it and to wearing my new pale green beaded dress,' Elizabeth said croakily to Kitty.

'You must be disappointed, miss, but if you're not well you wouldn't enjoy yourself. 'Tis best that you stay where you are, it's nice and warm and cosy in here and I'll bring you up a hot toddy,' Kitty soothed, stirring up the fire and replacing the green silk dress in the wardrobe. She could understand Elizabeth wanting to wear it, it was beautiful. How all those

171

beads would have shimmered under the lights in the ballroom.

'Oh, 'tis bitter out there and James says the canal is completely frozen over,' Tess announced, holding her hands out to the warmth of the range. She had her heavy coat on and a hat and scarf and had been out to help Mrs Harwood into the carriage, holding up the long skirt of her mistress's evening dress. 'Sure, the Mistress has need of her fur coat and all the rugs and I gave her a hot-water bottle too for her feet – she has only those satin shoes – but that will be stone cold by the time they arrive.'

'Did James make sure that those animals have the frost nails on their shoes?' Mrs O'Shea asked, looking a little concerned.

'He did so, didn't he have them down to the forge on Christmas Eve?' Tess glanced at Kitty. James had told her it was like a morgue down there and that Himself looked as miserable as sin. 'And well he might, serves him right!' she had replied with some satisfaction.

Kitty thought that she had had a pleasant Christmas by comparison. There had been a very fancy card and little gifts from her sisters, and Kitty had been cheered up no end to hear from Bridget that both she and Annie were actually looking forward to their first Christmas in America. They had had a gorgeous meal on Christmas Day in the Hall with all the trimmings, a gift of money from their employers and Elizabeth had bought Kitty a pair of black leather gloves. Kitty had been delighted with them. In Tess's opinion all three girls were better off away from the forge.

Kitty picked up the kettle. 'I promised Miss Elizabeth I'd take her up a hot toddy, she might get some sleep then. She's upset that she couldn't go but she's got a party to go to at New Year so she can wear that dress then.'

'Sure, I wouldn't mind a toddy myself, it would warm me up,' Tess remarked hopefully.

'You'll be after having a cup of tea and like it! There'll be no drinking spirits in this house for the likes of you, my girl,' the housekeeper rebuked her sharply. 'And I'll have a cup myself for I've to wait up for the Mistress. I told Miss Blanchard to go to her bed. This weather is shockingly bad for the poor creature's rheumatism. She'll be thankful when spring comes and she takes her retirement.'

'What will she be after doing then?' Emer asked, taking the bottle of medicinal whiskey that Cook handed her, which was kept under lock and key in Cook's private press, for James was not above helping himself to a nip.

'She's going to live with her widowed sister down in

Wexford where the climate will suit her more. 'Tis always warmer and drier down there,' Mrs O'Shea informed her.

'I'll take the toddy up and then I think I'll go to my bed too, if that's all right?' Kitty looked enquiringly at Mrs O'Shea.

The older woman nodded. 'It is so, and after you two girls have laid the table for breakfast and made up the fire in Madam's bedroom and dressing room you can go too. There's no sense in the whole household being up until God knows what time. James is going to come back later on to see to the horses.'

Kitty had made sure that Elizabeth was settled for the night and had gone to bed but she was still awake when Tess and Emer came in. She had said her prayers and then wondered what Christmas in New York had been like; she was sure Bridget would write soon and tell her. She resolutely pushed all thoughts of Niall Collins from her mind. She didn't want to wonder how he had spent the holiday or with whom.

'Kitty, are you still awake?' Tess whispered.

'I am so.'

'I've brought you an extra blanket, Mrs O'Shea said we might have one each, 'tis so cold tonight.' Tess deposited the blanket on Kitty's bed.

Kitty tucked it over her and snuggled down,

thankful for the housekeeper's consideration. There were no fires in their bedrooms.

All three girls were woken much later by Cook, her grey hair hastily tucked under a flannel nightcap, a heavy dressing gown clasped around her.

'What is it? Sure, it can't be time to get up already?' Tess muttered, sitting up and rubbing her eyes.

Emer groaned but Kitty could see there was something wrong by the look on Cook's face.

'What's happened?' she asked, getting up and clutching the blankets around her. It was bitterly cold. 'Is it Miss Elizabeth? Is it . . .' She didn't dare to think it was news of her sisters.

'Get dressed as quickly as you can, Kitty, and then go up to Miss Elizabeth. Mrs O'Shea is with her but the police are here. There . . . there's been a terrible accident—' Cook's voice broke.

Kitty clutched the woman's arm while Tess and Emer looked at her fearfully. 'What happened?' Kitty urged.

'The carriage went off the road and turned over and both Mr and Mrs . . . They're both . . . dead! Oh, poor, poor Elizabeth!' In her distress Mrs Connor dropped all formality.

'Oh, the Blessed Virgin have mercy on them!' Emer cried, crossing herself, and Tess burst into tears, but Kitty was already running from the room.

She ran up the stairs and past the burly figures of the police sergeant and constable standing in the hallway. It all seemed like a nightmare. They had gone off looking so elegant and smart, Mr Harwood in his white tie and tails and Mrs Harwood in a pale blue chiffon evening gown with diamonds and sapphires sparkling at her throat and wrists and now . . .

She didn't pause and knock on Elizabeth's door, she went straight in.

'Kitty! Thanks be to God! Stay with her, I'm going to send for the doctor,' Mrs O'Shea cried. She had her arm around the girl's shoulders and looked very shaken herself.

Elizabeth was sitting up, just staring ahead of her, her face paper white; her blue eyes looked vacant and she was trembling.

'Oh, Lord help us! I can't believe it!' Kitty exclaimed.

'No one can, Kitty! It's just so . . . terrible!' Mrs O'Shea's head was spinning, there was so much to do.

Kitty put her arms around Elizabeth as the housekeeper left the room. She knew how the girl felt, she'd lost her mam, but at least she had known her mother was going to die. When poor Elizabeth had gone to bed it had been in the knowledge that her parents were just going out for the evening; she was not to know that they were never coming back. Tears slid silently down Kitty's cheeks: tears of pity for her young and now orphaned mistress and tears of grief and shock at the deaths of a master and mistress who had been so kind and considerate to all their staff. She would never see Mr Harwood coming back from town in the carriage or striding into the hall with his shotgun over his arm. She would never see Mrs Harwood so elegantly dressed for a social occasion, a shopping trip or just being at home all day. How could she ever forget how kind Elizabeth's mother had been to her?

After the doctor had been and pronounced Elizabeth to be in a severe state of shock and had administered an injection, Kitty had stayed with her until she was sure she was asleep. Then she went slowly down to the kitchen.

Everyone was sitting huddled beside the range, all looking grey and exhausted. Tess and Emer were still sobbing quietly; James had his head in his hands.

'She's asleep. I wouldn't leave her until I was quite certain.' Kitty sank down in the chair Cook indicated, her legs suddenly feeling very shaky.

'Sip this, Kitty. We've all had a drop,' Mrs O'Shea urged, handing Kitty a small glass of whiskey.

'What's going to happen to her now?' Kitty at last managed to ask. The drink had burned in her throat and made her choke.

'The police are going to get word to the cousins in Dublin. They'll have to come down to arrange ... everything and Mr Henry will have to come home and then ... I don't know, Kitty. I just don't *know*!' Mrs O'Shea felt totally drained. She had done what she had thought would be best: there was only so much she as a mere housekeeper could do. Elizabeth's future and their own were in the hands of the family. The poor girl was still only eighteen and was totally incapable of coping with the situation. She wondered sadly whether Elizabeth would ever be able to cope with life without her parents. She had been totally spoiled and cosseted and life was so cruel.

Mr Eugene Harwood had arrived with his wife Lavinia late that evening. The house was so dreadfully quiet, Kitty thought, as though a thick dark cloud had descended upon it. She had helped to take down all the Christmas decorations and pack them away. This was no place now for holly and tinsel and shiny baubles. All the windows had the wooden shutters firmly closed over them but the winter sunlight poured into the hall through the fanlight above the front door and outside the heavy frost that still covered the landscape glistened and glittered. Mrs O'Shea had kept them all going with her composure and by making them carry out their routine tasks, but there had been people in and out all day. Shocked and horrified friends of the

178

family, members of the clergy both Protestant and Catholic, the police, the funeral directors, the doctor and the neighbours.

Elizabeth had remained in bed, only half aware of what was going on around her.

'I'm worried about her. I wish I could have coaxed her to take just some of this soup. There's only water passed her lips all day,' Kitty confided to Tess, returning to the kitchen with the untouched dishes.

'I hardly feel like eating myself, Kitty. She'll start to come to herself a little in a few days. Isn't that what the doctor said?'

Kitty nodded. Maybe Elizabeth would be better when some member of her family arrived. Maybe then she wouldn't feel so lost and alone.

After spending half an hour upstairs Eugene Harwood came down to the kitchen. He was older than Charles Harwood had been and looked weary and slightly stooped.

'I contacted Henry and he is coming home with every possible speed, Harriet and Edmund are sailing on the night ferry from Liverpool tonight; they will be here by lunchtime tomorrow. I will go myself to the station to collect them. Then when Henry arrives proper arrangements will be made for the funeral. There will have to be an inquest, of course.'

'I'll have the rooms ready, sir. Miss Elizabeth must

be very relieved to see you and know that her brother is on his way,' Mrs O'Shea replied.

He shook his head sadly. 'She is in such a state that I really don't think she understands a great deal. Lavinia is going to sit with her tonight.'

'All night, sir?'

He nodded.

'Then I'll take her up a warm drink and something to eat and make sure the fire is kept banked up. This weather shows no sign of easing at all. We are all very grateful that you've come, sir, and so quickly. It's been a desperate time for us too.' The housekeeper was very relieved that there was now someone else to shoulder the heavy responsibilities that had lain on her shoulders for the past twenty-four hours. With all the relatives arriving there would be plenty of work to keep them busy and occupy their minds, which was a small blessing.

Chapter Fifteen

———◆———

HENRY HARWOOD HAD ARRIVED the day after his cousins Edmund and Harriet from Liverpool and Kitty had been shocked at the change in him. He seemed to have aged ten years. Elizabeth was more awake and Tess said it broke your heart to see how destroyed entirely she was. She had sat for a whole morning, her face buried in a cardigan that had belonged to her mother, sobbing. No amount of comforting on the part of either Harriet or Lavinia or Kitty had been able to console her.

With the exception of her mam's burial, Kitty thought the funeral was the worst she had ever attended in her life. A verdict of accidental death had been declared and as she'd sat with the rest of the servants at the back of the church in Hop Hill where the Harwoods had worshipped, she had studiously

averted her gaze from the sight of her father and
stepmother who were sitting on the opposite side of
the aisle amongst the many people who had come to
pay their respects. She'd had to wipe her eyes
frequently but she was glad to see that Elizabeth was
holding up well under the ordeal. She looked very
pale and tearful, the pallor enhanced by her black
mourning clothes.

After the service they had all returned to the Hall
where they served hot soup and a buffet lunch to the
mourners invited back by the family. The future was
on all their minds. Only for Blanchard was there
certainty. She had declared that Amy Harwood's death
had 'finished her entirely' and that she intended to go
to her sister in Wexford as soon as was decently
possible. The rest of the servants, however, did not
know what lay ahead for them.

That evening Kitty was disturbed to hear that her
father had again come to see her. Had things been
different she would have welcomed him for even
though she was still dreadfully hurt and angry there
were times when she did miss him. Times when she
looked back to the happy days they had shared before
her mam had died. Had he not sent her sisters to
America she would have looked to him for some
comfort after the shock of the Harwoods' tragic deaths
and the sorrowful atmosphere that now pervaded the

house. She looked at the housekeeper enquiringly.

Mrs O'Shea nodded. 'Bring him into the kitchen, Kitty. It's what poor Mrs Harwood would have expected. No doubt he's come to pay his respects,' she advised. At least that would avoid any arguments for she knew how Kitty felt about him.

'You're to come into the kitchen. Mrs O'Shea says so, 'tis what the poor Mistress would have wanted,' Kitty informed him, giving him no time to inform her of his reason for being here.

'Will you sit down, Mr Doyle?' the housekeeper asked politely.

Thomas looked uncomfortable and fiddled with his tie. 'Thank you, but no. I came to say how sorry I am about the tragedy and to see how Kitty is . . . er . . . coping.'

'I'm upset, we all are, but I'm managing well enough,' Kitty replied quietly, not looking at him.

'And do you know what will happen now? Has anything been said?' Thomas was still hesitant.

'Sure, we've heard nothing and it's not our place to be asking things like that and especially not today,' Kitty replied.

'I didn't mean to sound insensitive, it's just that Hester was asking —'

'And is Mrs Doyle well now?' Mrs O'Shea interrupted. She had a very good idea just what it was that Hester Doyle wanted to know. Would Kitty be going back to the forge?

'She is so, thank you, ma'am.'

Kitty glanced at him, her expression cold. She was certain Hester had sent him, no doubt to find out if she intended to go back home. She was far from ready to forgive him.

Thomas gave up. 'Well, I'll be away home now.'

'Thank you for coming, Mr Doyle. I will convey your condolences to the family and as you can see Kitty is coping very well.' Mrs O'Shea's tone indicated that there was nothing more to be said.

Kitty returned to her chores and it was Emer who showed him out.

The day after the funeral they were all summoned to the drawing room.

'Sure, I'm dreading this,' Tess whispered and Emer nodded. It wasn't going to be easy to find other employment.

Kitty too was very apprehensive. She looked on this place as home for in her mind she had no other. She would not go to her da's house, even if he ordered her to or begged on bended knees – which was very unlikely. Not after the way he had treated her and her sisters. She wondered if Aunt Enid would give her a home too? But she would still have to find work.

Henry Harwood was standing by the grand piano,

flanked by his much older cousins. He looked calm enough, Kitty thought, although it was impossible to read anything from his expression.

'I've called you all here to inform you of my . . . our plans,' he corrected himself, remembering his distraught sister. 'I have talked it over with Edmund and Eugene and I have decided to take Elizabeth to live in England. There are too many memories for her here and my work is in London. It is not practical to maintain a home here, so the house will be shut up . . .' He faltered for a second but gathered himself and continued: 'That does of course mean that you will all have to find other employment, except for Kitty. She will come with us and stay with Elizabeth in Aintree. Miss Blanchard has informed me of her impending retirement and will leave for Wexford at the end of the week. My . . . father would not have wished you to be thrown out of work like this, so we have agreed to pay you all a severance fee appropriate to your status and length of service. It may help you until you can find other work.' He paused again, his gaze passing over them all. 'I would just like to say, on behalf of Elizabeth and myself, how much we appreciate the long and loyal service you have given to us . . . all, and the kindness and consideration shown over the years and especially this last week. Thank you.'

'Sir, can I ask will you require us to stay on to pack and close up the house?' Mrs O'Shea asked. She had thought that this would happen, but had given no indication to anyone of her fears. He was treating them fairly, he was not obliged to give them anything, but she knew it would not be easy for her to find another position locally and she felt she was too old now to have to move to Dublin.

'Thank you, Mrs O'Shea. That will be much appreciated,' Eugene Harwood replied, for Henry had turned away, his gaze fixed on the frosty pastures beyond the window, and he knew the boy was struggling to maintain his composure.

As they filed out and went back downstairs, Kitty breathed a sigh of relief. She had liked the house in Aintree and the servants and she would get used to living there.

'Put the kettle on, Tess, I think we all need a cup of tea. It wasn't entirely unexpected – not by me – but it's another shock we have to contend with,' Mrs O'Shea announced.

'What will you do, Majella?' Blanchard asked of Cook, using Mrs Connor's Christian name. As she was retiring she felt it appropriate. The title 'Mrs' was a courtesy. Majella Connor had never married.

'Start a novena to St Jude right away. I'll not get a position like this in a hurry.'

'Well, I'm not going back home to live, sure the place is like a bear-pit!' Tess announced.

'And what will you be after doing?' Emer demanded. She had no wish to go and live at home herself but there was no alternative.

'I've cousins in Australia. I'll go out to them and make a fresh start, I'm only young. Why don't you come with me, Emer?'

'*Australia*! How much will the fare cost? It takes weeks and weeks to get there and what if we don't like it?' Emer cried.

'We'll just have to get on with it. Sure it can't be that bad, at least we'd never be half frozen by winters like this,' Tess replied.

Emer thought about it. So many people had to take the immigrant ship but it was so *far*! 'I don't know but I'll think on it.'

'Isn't it well for you young girls? Aren't you able to go off to any part of the world and find work?' James said disconsolately. He had a wife and family to think of. He took a gulp of his tea. 'And it's not good for all the lads who'll be thrown out of work when the turf factory is closed down.'

'Sure, can't Mr Whelan keep it running? He never said anything about closing it down,' Tess reminded him.

'But will they still need the turf up at the Curragh?

With the British Army looking set to leave this country, will there be an Army camp up there at all for much longer?' James was not to be swayed from his mood of pessimism.

'Well, that's Mr Henry's decision and we can do nothing about it. We have to look to ourselves. At least you'll keep your position, Kitty,' Mrs O'Shea said firmly.

'And I'm very thankful for it because wild horses wouldn't have dragged me back to the forge. It would have been New York for me. I think you're very brave, Tess, and I think it's right you are to go. Good luck to you.'

Tess smiled at her. 'I feel much better now I've made up my mind. All I have to do now is coax this one here to come with me.'

'Your da might have something to say about it, Tess. Don't they look for the bit of money you pass over to help put food on the table?' Emer reminded her.

'I'll deal with Da. Won't I be after sending money home when I've got settled? So he can't be complaining about that,' Tess replied determinedly.

Mrs O'Shea got to her feet. 'If we've all finished, you girls can wash up and then I'd better start making a list of all that needs to be done.'

The feeling that they were all living in a kind of limbo seemed to fade as the work of packing up and covering the furniture with dustsheets began. The Harwood relations departed to Dublin but Edmund and Harriet stayed on, as did Henry. They were to travel to Liverpool at the beginning of the following week taking Elizabeth and Kitty with them.

Elizabeth was very quiet and withdrawn and still had bouts of sobbing but Kitty felt that once they had left Ireland she would start to get over her grief. At least she had started to eat again, she thought as she packed her mistress's many clothes.

She had written to Annie and Bridget and told them the sad news and had given them the address in Aintree to send all future letters to. Her father had come up to the house but she had flatly refused to see him and the housekeeper had assured him that she would be very well cared for and that she was a good, sensible girl who would not get herself into any kind of trouble.

Tess and Emer had left at the end of the week. Tess was resigned to staying at home until her passage could be arranged, which she hoped wouldn't take too long. Emer had decided against going with her and was going to Dublin instead where she was sure she'd find work of some kind. Kitty's admiration for Tess had increased when she heard this; it was a long way to go alone.

'Didn't Annie and Bridget go all the way to America and they got there safe enough?' Tess had remarked, but she did feel a bit apprehensive about the journey. She would sail from Liverpool and hoped to see Kitty for an hour or two, if Kitty could get the time off.

'Be sure and write from time to time and let me know how you are getting on,' Kitty had instructed Emer, hugging her before she set off for her home, but realising Emer probably wouldn't bother.

On her last night at Harwood Hall Kitty stood in the yard and looked out over the cold, damp gardens. The heavy frost and ice that had caused the tragedy had gone, to be replaced by milder, wetter weather. She was leaving here for ever, she thought, and that saddened her. She loved the house and the gardens but would she ever set foot in Ireland again? Was there any reason for her to come back, she asked herself, drawing her coat closer to her and shivering a little. She'd lost her mam and Aunt Julia. Her sisters were so far away that she'd probably never see them again either. She didn't *want* to see her da or Hester or little Thomas, and Niall . . . he was lost to her too. He'd marry the Delahunty girl and have a family. Tears pricked her eyes. She felt very alone and suddenly fearful until she determinedly shook off the mood. She'd make a future for herself on the other side of the Irish Sea and in the meantime there was Elizabeth to think about. She would have to try and help her mistress recover her former spirits.

Chapter Sixteen

———◆———

EVEN THOUGH IT WAS the depths of winter the journey hadn't been as bad as Kitty had anticipated. It was still very cold but by the time they reached Dublin the wind had dropped a little. The sea had still been choppy but she had slept for most of the ferry crossing. It was still dark when the boat finally docked and they made their way up on deck to disembark. Even at this hour on a cold, wet and blustery January morning the Pier Head was busy. Under the streetlights she could see the lines of trams waiting at the terminus. The trains on the overhead railway that ran for eight miles from the Herculaneum Dock in the south to the Gladstone Dock in the north were packed with men on their way to work in the docks and factories and warehouses. Out in the river a departing Cunard liner blazed from bow to stern with lights and the Mersey ferries were resolutely ploughing their way across the dark choppy waters, bringing more people to work in the city.

She was very thankful that she was to travel for the last stage of the journey with Elizabeth in the second car; it was a closed vehicle and it would at least be warmer. She had never travelled in a motor car before and was a little nervous. She tucked the rugs around her mistress and then settled back against the leather upholstery and tried to get used to the rather bumpy sensation.

It was just beginning to get light when they turned into the drive of the house. It wasn't nearly as long as the drive at Harwood Hall, she thought as they rounded the bend and the house came into view. The walls looked pale grey in the diffused light, although they were startlingly white in broad daylight. Lights were burning in the downstairs windows and from the leaded glass of the hall door a myriad colours spilled on to the front steps.

'We're here, miss,' Kitty informed Elizabeth who had dozed off, for she hadn't slept well on the crossing.

Elizabeth opened her eyes and gave a little sob. 'Oh, Kitty, I was so happy when I visited here last summer. So excited knowing I could go shopping and be entertained in high style. I had my poor, dear mama with me then. Has it really only been a few weeks since . . . since the accident? It seems like an eternity and how am I going to cope, Kitty, with all the happy memories of Mama being here in this house with me? How am I going to think of it as my new home?'

'You'll be fine, miss,' Kitty consoled her.

Wearily, Elizabeth let Kitty help her from the car into the house.

The servants were waiting in the hall in respectful silence. The maids had black ribbon edgings to their caps and aprons, the butler and the boot boy wore black armbands.

They were all greeted deferentially and Edmund and Harriet and Henry were shown to their rooms. Tina accompanied Kitty and Elizabeth upstairs and helped Kitty to get Elizabeth settled in and then informed her that breakfast was to be served in a quarter of an hour, if she was hungry.

Elizabeth nodded and then dismissed both Kitty and Tina.

'She doesn't look the same at all. She was so excited and full of herself last time she was here,' Tina said as she took Kitty down to the kitchen for a cup of tea and some hot buttered toast.

'She took it very badly. We all did,' Kitty replied.

'I couldn't believe it! It must have been awful.' Tina was sympathetic. She was twenty and had been with the household since she had left school at fourteen, starting first as a kitchen maid.

Kitty nodded. 'Oh, it was really desperate and I'm the only one that was kept on.'

'I heard that the house was closed up. But I'm glad they kept you on, Kitty, and you'll both settle down here. You liked it when you were here last.' Tina smiled, the corners of her brown eyes crinkling. Tendrils of short, curly light brown hair had escaped from her cap.

'I did though I was glad to go back – then. But now my sisters are in New York and I'll never speak to my da again because it was he who made them go. I only found out that they'd gone when I returned. I never even got to say goodbye to them.'

'Oh, God! That was cruel of him.' Tina had never heard of the like before.

'It was but they seem to have settled there . . . Then I heard that the lad I was . . . well . . . fond of had got engaged to someone else and then . . . then there was the accident. So, you see, there's nothing left for me back there.' She had said nothing to Tina about Niall when she had been here before.

'You've had a dead hard time of it, Kitty, but as far as that feller goes, there's plenty more fish in the sea. I go dancing on my evening off, would you like to come? It's not far to the Aintree Institute where they have the dance. It might cheer you up a bit, take you out of yourself.'

'Would it be proper, with everyone in mourning?' Kitty wasn't sure about it and she didn't want to offend anyone.

'It's not for another two weeks and we're not exactly family, are we? I'll ask first though.'

Kitty felt relieved. 'I've never been to a dance before. How do we get there?' She thought it was very good of Tina to ask her.

'On the tram, it's not far and we can get the last one back at eleven.'

'Don't they mind you staying out so late?'

'Not as long as we behave ourselves and don't go bringing fellers back with us. Come on, let's get something warm inside you. Make sure you don't mention the dance until I've sorted out the lie of the land,' Tina advised her as they reached the kitchen.

Harriet Harwood agreed that Kitty could accompany Tina to the dance. It was very correctly run; the Committee were highly responsible. Kitty didn't mention it to Elizabeth as she felt her mistress might view the outing as less than sensitive.

'I've nothing suitable to wear,' Kitty confided to Tina after permission had been given. 'I've a few nice things that Miss Elizabeth has given me but they are all for spring or summer.'

'That grey tweed skirt you have is nice; can you afford a new blouse? You don't have to go into Liverpool, there are some good shops along Walton Vale and that's only a couple of stops on the tram. Pink or lemon look lovely with grey.'

'But wouldn't a skirt and blouse look a bit ordinary? Shouldn't I dress up more?' Kitty was still unsure.

'No, it's not a ballroom. Lots of girls wear skirts and blouses or ordinary day dresses.'

Kitty felt quite relieved and decided she could afford a new blouse; after all it would be her first dance.

She was delighted when she was asked if she would go along to the local shopping centre to pick up some things for Mrs Harriet Harwood. It meant she wouldn't have to ask for a few hours off. Tina had been right, it was only a few stops on the tram and she alighted at the Black Bull public house where the road forked. She was surprised at the number and variety of the shops that lined both sides of the main road.

She quickly completed the errand she had been sent on, then looked around her. On the opposite side of the street she spotted some premises sandwiched between Ziegler's pork butcher's and Timpson's shoe shop, above which was the name 'A. Page – Gowns'. She stood gazing into the window but realised the prices would be beyond her pocket. Instead she walked on and stopped outside 'Lucy Johnson – Ladies' Outfitter', which looked more promising.

The assistant was very helpful and she finally selected a pink crêpe-de-Chine blouse with pearl buttons up the back and a floppy bow at the neckline. It had short sleeves with a narrow cuff, which had caused her to hesitate for a moment, but she had been assured that it would be quite suitable for her purpose as the building in question was adequately heated.

She bought a cheap pair of pearlised earrings at Woolworth's Bazaar which she thought would match the buttons of the blouse and then she went into Ellinson's Grocery. Elizabeth had been very fond of a type of chocolate biscuit that had been served on their visit last summer but which had proved to be unobtainable in Tullamore. Ellinson's looked to be a very high-class grocers and Kitty wondered if they would stock them. It might tempt her mistress to eat, she thought, for Elizabeth's appetite was still very poor.

It was quite a large shop but rather old-fashioned in its layout, compared to the other shops she had visited. The shelves were well stocked though and her gaze wandered over Hartley's jams, jellies and bottled fruit, packets of Lyon's tea, Cooper's coffee, and Tate and Lyle's demerara and refined sugars. Finally she caught sight of the packets of Jacob's biscuits.

'May I help you, miss?'

Kitty turned and saw a middle-aged man approaching. He was not wearing an overall or a brown shop coat but a three-piece suit, which she noticed was rather shiny in places. He had a nice, friendly smile though and his eyes were kind, she thought.

'I'm looking for a packet of Jacob's Premium Orange Chocolate Fingers, please.'

He went behind the counter and immediately located a packet. 'A wise selection if a trifle expensive, but quality always costs more.' He smiled at her. She was an attractive girl but obviously not very well to do, judging by her clothes. She was very probably in service.

'How expensive?' Kitty asked cautiously.

'A shilling, I'm afraid,' he replied a little apologetically.

It was verging on extortionate, Kitty thought as she hesitated. 'Are you the manager?'

He shook his head. 'No, I'm the proprietor. Stanley Ellinson. I'm having staff problems at present – my two assistants have gone to a funeral. They should be back in an hour but I couldn't close up. Are the biscuits for yourself?'

Kitty shook her head. 'I wanted to buy them for my mistress. We've just come to live here, her parents were killed in an accident and she still has a very poor appetite. She really likes those biscuits and I thought . . .'

'You're Irish?'

'I am so, from Tullamore in Offaly, and so is Miss Elizabeth.'

He nodded, looking regretful. So, she was Elizabeth Harwood's maid. The tragedy had been reported in the *Walton Times* for Mr Edmund Harwood was an important man in the area. Indeed, the Harwoods were good customers. 'Well then, let's say the biscuits are sixpence.'

Kitty smiled at him. 'Sure, that's very good of you, Mr Ellinson.'

'And you are?' he enquired politely, thinking she might come in again on Elizabeth's behalf.

'Kitty Doyle,' she replied, handing over a thrup'penny bit and three pennies.

As she left he wondered whether he should have given her the biscuits, then he shook his head. Business was business, after all. His father had always said, 'Look after the pennies and the pounds will look after themselves,' and he'd found it to be a wise maxim.

As she made her way back to the tram stop Kitty felt quite satisfied with her purchases. Perhaps the biscuits would tempt Elizabeth and she had her blouse and earrings for the dance. She was really looking forward to it.

*

She had enjoyed herself very much, Kitty thought as, two weeks later, she and Tina joined the queue at the tram stop. She pulled her coat closer to her for it was very cold. Over the blouse she wore a heavy cardigan but there was already a dusting of frost on the pavements and as the tram trundled into sight, sparks shot into the night air as the trolley ran over the icy wires.

'Oh, thank God for that, my feet are freezing in these shoes,' Tina said thankfully as they both paid their fares and were urged to 'Move along inside there, girls! We all want ter get 'ome ternight!' by the conductor.

The tram moved off down Warbreck Moor and Kitty reflected on the evening. She'd been surprised to find that the dance was being held in what had looked like a village hall, except that it had two storeys. The dance floor was in the black and white mock Tudor upper storey and was already packed when they'd arrived. She had been relieved to notice that none of the girls and young women was really dressed up, many like herself wore a blouse and skirt. There was no alcohol allowed but soft drinks and biscuits could be purchased. She had been anxious that she wouldn't be able to copy the steps of the other dancers and that she wouldn't be asked to dance at all, but she needn't have worried on either count. There wasn't really room for intricate steps or grand dips and flourishes and she'd been asked up by half a dozen different lads, but none had asked her more than once.

'Yer haven't got much ter say, have yer? Bit of a quiet one, aren't yer?' one lad had remarked.

She had just nodded and smiled at him. I suppose I am a quiet person, she'd thought but she wasn't offended by his remarks. There had really been no one who had aroused more than a passing interest. Maybe she had unconsciously been comparing them to Niall, she thought now. She sighed. That was something she would have to put a stop to.

Chapter Seventeen

———◆———

AT LAST THE LONG winter was over, Kitty thought
thankfully as she went out into the garden that
April afternoon to inform Elizabeth that her brother
was on the telephone. It was a beautiful day with
bright sunshine and blue skies and a mild breeze was
shaking the pale pink petals of blossom from the
ornamental cherry trees. It lay in a thick carpet on
the edge of the lawn. Spring flowers bloomed in all the
neatly kept borders and the birds darted between
the trees and bushes, moss and straw in their beaks to
add to the nests they were building.

It was quiet out here for beyond the gardens lay the
stables and then the racecourse and the surrounding
fields. Elizabeth liked to sit in the shelter of the garden
wall and take her afternoon tea. Sometimes Harriet sat
with her but today she was alone.

'Miss, your brother is on the telephone from London!' Kitty called when she was within earshot.

Elizabeth smiled and got to her feet. 'I'll be there directly, Kitty. Run ahead and inform him.'

Kitty turned and began to run back to the house. She still marvelled that it was possible to speak to someone miles and miles away from the comfort and privacy of your own home. Of course there were public telephone boxes but she had never had cause to use one, nor would she know how to.

The telephone was in the hall and had been answered by Harriet who was still talking to Henry.

'She's coming right now, ma'am,' Kitty whispered before going upstairs. Elizabeth had looked so pleased; she missed her brother, Kitty knew. He had gone back to London two weeks after they'd arrived here. Elizabeth was much better these days, more like her old self, and had started to go out again. Of course there were days when she was miserable and tearful and sometimes snappy, but that was only to be expected. It would take her a lot longer than four months really to get over her loss. Kitty herself had settled in. Of course she missed Tess and Emer and Cook and Mrs O'Shea, but she was adapting to life here. She and Tina had become close friends and they went to dances and the cinema together.

She had had one letter from Tess who had finally

arrived at her cousins' home in Brisbane after a long but quite enjoyable voyage. She had promised faithfully to write the day Kitty had gone into Liverpool to meet her before she sailed. Tess seemed to like her new country and was not sorry she had made the decision to leave Ireland.

Elizabeth would come upstairs to find her as soon as the conversation was over, she thought, but she had a few minutes in which to read the letter from Bridget that had arrived in the afternoon post. She took it from her pocket and sat on the stool beside the half-open window. She smiled as she scanned the lines of neat writing. Her aunt and uncle were taking Bridget for what they called a 'little vacation' in July when it got unbearably hot in the city. They were going 'upstate' to a house beside a lake and already Bridget was excited about it. Annie of course was very disappointed not to be going, she had to work, but there were compensations: she had been seeing quite a lot of a lad called Davie Molloy who was a porter at the hotel where she still worked and whose parents had come from Cork. Everyone liked him, so Bridget wrote, but it was such a shame that he wasn't the same religion, although that didn't seem to be as important in America. Kitty frowned at this: there were always arguments and disagreements in mixed marriages, or so her mam had always said. Still, Annie was only sixteen, which was a very young and impressionable age. She would need the approval of both her father and her aunt and uncle before she could even think about getting married, and she knew her father would refuse to allow Annie to marry so young and to a Catholic to boot.

Bridget wrote at some length about her school friends and of how she too would be leaving school next year and was looking forward to earning money of her own and being thought of as grown up. Kitty folded the letter and tucked it back into her pocket as she heard Elizabeth's footsteps on the landing.

She was folding some clean underclothes to replace in the drawer of the dressing table when Elizabeth entered, her cheeks flushed.

'Kitty, great news! Henry is coming to visit me, just for a few days at Easter, but I'm so happy! It's months and months since I last saw him and it's not the same thing at all just to talk on the telephone. He says he's got something planned for me. It's a surprise but he's certain I'll be delighted. He's getting the train on Maundy Thursday and staying until the following Wednesday morning. Harriet says if it's fine we can all go to Chester on Easter Monday, to the races. Oh, I do hope it won't rain.'

Kitty smiled at her. She and Tina had planned to go to New Brighton for the day by train. She had never been to the seaside before and Tina, mimicking Kitty's accent, had said it was a 'grand place altogether'.

'I'm so pleased he's coming to see you, miss, really I am,' she said, wondering just what kind of a surprise he had in store for his sister.

Henry Harwood duly arrived on the Thursday evening and was greeted with cries of delight by Elizabeth. Kitty noticed that he, too, seemed to have recovered some of his old spirits but she was saddened to hear later that night from Elizabeth that he intended to sell Harwood Hall, if he could find a buyer. Surely this wasn't the surprise?

'Don't you mind, miss?' she asked.

'No, not really, Kitty. Of course it was my home, I was born there, but I can never think of it in the same way, not after what happened. I don't think I would ever want to go and live there again and besides, it's much too big for just Henry and myself. Henry intends to stay in London so it makes sense to get rid of it, but he says it might not be very easy to sell. Naturally he will want a large amount of money for it and he doesn't know of anyone who could afford it. Most people who could already have a big house – and then there's the situation . . .' Elizabeth, sitting at the dressing table, had begun to brush her hair and now she frowned at her reflection.

'What situation, miss?'

'Haven't you heard, Kitty? There's civil war now in the Free State. Mr de Valera has declared that the Irish Republican Army is illegal and there is terrible fighting between anti-treaty and pro-treaty forces. Henry says we are fortunate to be away from it all and I agree with him. Who knows where it will all end?'

Kitty hadn't heard and she too wondered where it would end. She thought briefly of her da but realised that he would do everything in his power to stay out of trouble, but what of Niall? She had no idea of his views. Had he joined one side or the other and if he had, what would happen to him? 'Did Mr Henry say there was fighting in Tullamore, miss?' she asked tentatively.

'He hadn't heard there was, but it won't make it easy for him to sell the house and he's worried that one side or the other will set fire to it.'

This horrified Kitty. 'But, sure, why should they do that? Your father didn't take sides and neither did Mr Henry and there was no trouble around Rahan during the fight for independence.'

Elizabeth shrugged. 'Who knows, Kitty? Don't worry about it; just be glad you are well away from it all. I am.'

Kitty nodded, but she hoped that neither side would senselessly burn down such a beautiful old house.

It hadn't rained on Easter Monday and the family had all gone off to Chester, which left the staff with little to do until they returned. Kitty and Tina had begged a few hours off in the afternoon and had gone for a sail on the ferry, just to New Brighton and back.

So they had joined the crowds on the Landing Stage, paid their tuppence and boarded the ferry. They had taken a walk along the promenade, got a pot of tea for two and a scone each for sixpence in a café, spent another tuppence on the amusements and had then boarded the ferry for home.

'We'll go for longer next time. Summer is coming, the evenings will be longer and the family always go off for a holiday, so we'll have more time off,' Tina consoled after Kitty had said a couple of hours wasn't enough to see and do everything and she'd wanted to paddle. She'd never felt sand under her feet or dipped her toes in salt water, although Tina assured her that the aforementioned salt water was freezing cold even in summer.

'But if they go away I'll have to go too, as Elizabeth's maid,' Kitty had reminded her.

'God, aren't you dead lucky! They always go to France, to Brittany.' Tina had been openly envious.

'Sure, I think I'd sooner go to New Brighton and Southport with you than have to travel all that way,' Kitty had replied conciliatorily.

Judging from the fact that a bottle of champagne had been opened after dinner that night, the family had had a profitable day at the races, so Tina remarked to Kitty as she brought a pile of dirty dishes back down to the kitchen.

'Ah, it's well for them. I hope Miss Elizabeth enjoyed herself,' Kitty answered, noting the glance of disapproval Cook shot at Tina.

'Kitty, Mr Henry wishes to see you. He's in Mr Harwood's study,' the Harwoods' butler informed her as he returned from upstairs.

Kitty looked puzzled. What did he want to see her about? she wondered.

Tina raised her eyebrows but made no comment as Kitty left the kitchen.

Henry Harwood was sitting at his cousin's desk, which was covered with what looked like lists of figures; there was a half-empty coffee cup at his elbow. 'Ah, Kitty, come in and sit down.'

She had never been asked to sit down before, she thought nervously as she sat on the edge of the brocade Victorian slipper chair he had indicated. She clasped her hands tightly together in her lap and waited.

Henry stood up. 'We decided today that Harriet is to take Elizabeth on a world cruise. We're hoping it will do her good, help her to get over her loss and of course broaden her education and outlook on life.' He paused. They were also hoping she would meet a suitable and wealthy young man. Elizabeth had been thrilled with the idea of travelling in such luxury. 'They will be away for approximately a year as Harriet feels they should experience certain places in more depth.' What Harriet had said was that should Elizabeth meet someone, they would of course want to spend time with his family and friends. There was no point in rushing things; they had plenty of time on their hands.

Kitty looked at him in amazement. 'Am I to go too, sir?' She hoped not, she certainly didn't want to have to traipse all over the world and be away for so long.

'No, Kitty. They will be well looked after by their stewardesses.' Henry had been adamant about this when Elizabeth had complained that Kitty always attended to her needs.

'I see, sir.' Kitty was very relieved.

'But, Kitty, I'm afraid that it will be impossible for me to keep you on here for all that time and when Elizabeth returns her situation may have changed and also her plans. Even if it hasn't, there are enough maids here to wait on her. I do realise that this must be a shock to you, but I'm afraid our financial situation has altered.'

It was exactly what he had told Elizabeth and it was

true. He needed to sell Harwood Hall and quickly. He had had to close the turf factory; there was no call now for turf for the Curragh. That had put a great many people out of work, which was regrettable. He had lodgings in London and a prominent lifestyle to maintain and he was only a junior member of the firm. Then there were Elizabeth's expenses and he couldn't expect Edmund to bear the cost of them; his cousin had very generously offered to help with the cost of the trip, concurring with Henry that Elizabeth was more likely to meet a suitable husband on a first-class world cruise than here in Liverpool. Of course the substantial amount of money he'd won today would help with the expense too. His father hadn't left as much as he'd expected and then there were death duties to be paid. He just couldn't afford to keep Kitty for a whole year doing virtually nothing.

Kitty just stared at him. He was telling her that she no longer had a job or a home. They had brought her all this way and now . . . now she was to be let go. What was she going to do? she thought in panic.

Henry noticed her sudden pallor, her dazed expression and the fear in her eyes. 'Of course they won't be going until the beginning of next month and we shall endeavour to find you other employment. There will be a little severance money. You're not being thrown out on the street, Kitty.'

'But, sir, I . . . I . . . look on this as my home and I'm not trained for any other kind of work,' Kitty managed to stammer, feeling the colour rush to her cheeks. She hadn't wanted to leave Harwood Hall and she didn't want to leave this house either; there was no other place she could call home. She didn't want to go back to a country that was being torn apart by civil war and she *wouldn't* go back to her da's house.

'Don't get upset, Kitty. You're a very capable girl. We'll find you something suitable, and lodgings as well,' Henry promised.

Slowly Kitty got to her feet. She was utterly devastated. What kind of a future lay ahead of her now?

She felt as though she couldn't face anyone. Not Tina and certainly not Elizabeth. She had bent over backwards to help Elizabeth over the last four months, especially in those terrible dark days after the accident. Surely, surely Elizabeth could have prevailed upon her brother to keep her on. Her wages weren't enormous by any means and she could have worked in the kitchen, done anything in the house, until they returned from their travels. What had he meant when he had said Elizabeth's situation might have changed when she returned? Oh, it was all too much to take in.

She turned and ran down the hall and out into the darkened garden, thinking of the night not so long ago when she had stood in the garden of Harwood Hall. Was she never to have a home of her own, a place that was secure and safe? She had once promised Annie that she would find somewhere where they could all be together. That dream had been shattered when they'd been sent so far away, she thought. Suddenly she wished she had the money to buy Harwood Hall and bring her sisters home to live there, but it was just another futile dream. She didn't even have a job now.

Chapter Eighteen

———❖———

KITTY WAS QUIET AND very dejected in the days that followed. Tina had been outraged when she'd heard what was to happen to Kitty.

'It's a living disgrace, that's what it is! They dragged you all the way over here from your own country and now they're giving you the push! He can't be *that* hard up if he's paying for her to go travelling for that long, those trips cost hundreds! He doesn't pay you a fortune and what's up with her that she didn't stand up for you? Well, there's gratitude for you, I must say! A law unto themselves, they are! It's pure bloody selfishness, that's what it is.'

'He said they'll find me another job and lodgings and there'll be a bit of severance money.' Kitty was trying to be fair but she felt bitterly hurt and let down.

Tina was scathing. 'A few shillings just to ease his

guilty conscience and you can bet she's going to spend pounds and pounds on new clothes that he'll have to pay for.'

Kitty knew this to be true. Elizabeth seemed to have forgotten about her loss and, enthralled with the impending trip, was totally engrossed in the cruise itinerary and literature and her planned shopping trips for all the outfits she would need.

'Oh, Kitty, it's such a shame that you'll have to find another position. I will miss you but Henry says it can't be avoided. You'll manage just fine, I'm sure. You always seem so . . . adaptable,' was all Elizabeth had said on the subject.

Kitty was certain that Amy Harwood would have been horrified by her son's behaviour but poor Mrs Harwood was lying in the churchyard at Hop Hill.

It soon became apparent to Kitty that the Harwoods seemed to be in no hurry to find her alternative employment; they seemed to be concerned only with their travelling arrangements.

'I'm after thinking that I'll have to find a job and somewhere to live myself,' she confided to Tina.

'Typical! I'll get the *Echo* and we'll have a look in the "Situations Vacant" section. If there's nothing in that we can ask the other servants if they know of any jobs in the offing,' Tina said, practically.

They scoured the Situations Vacant columns but

there was nothing that Kitty was either qualified for or had experience in.

'I suppose if everything else fails, I'll have to go round the factories and ask.'

Tina was horrified. 'You're not going to work in a factory – you'd hate it! They're shocking places, and some of those girls are dead rough! Mouths on them like sewers!'

Kitty was trying to be optimistic. 'That place down Long Lane, Hartley's is it? That doesn't look too bad. They make jams and marmalades and preserves and I've seen some of the girls they employ and they don't look or sound desperate.'

Tina hesitated. 'I suppose not but I think it's quite hard to get in there: they pay decent wages and provide overalls. Most places pay buttons and expect you to work until you drop! No, we'll ask around or you could put a notice in a couple of the shops. The newsagents and tobacconists usually charge a penny to display notices.'

'Sure, I've never heard the like before. What will I put on these notices?'

'Something like "Quiet, hard-working girl, willing and capable, requires any suitable employment. References available. Apply within."'

'It's worth a try, but I can't just rely on that. I'll have to try to find something.'

'There's always the Labour Exchange, I suppose,' Tina said, not sounding very optimistic about that option.

Kitty put postcards in the windows of three shops and duly went to the Labour Exchange. It was a wasted visit as the only work that seemed to be available was indeed in the factories and she really didn't like the sound of either rope or animal feed factories, nor the soap factory, and the wages they were offering were very small indeed. She'd never be able to keep herself and pay for lodgings on such amounts. Neither was there good news from any of the other servants. Decent work was very hard to come by.

After a few days she went back to the shops where her postcards were displayed to see if there had been any response. She desperately hoped there would be. To her acute disappointment there had been no enquiries. She decided to leave them there for a further week and handed over the money to the shopkeepers. Then she wandered disconsolately along Walton Vale. As she drew near Ellinson's a girl ran out, pulling on her jacket, and she saw Mr Ellinson appear in the doorway behind her, looking hot and flustered and anxious.

'Is there something the matter, Mr Ellinson?' she asked, remembering how he'd only charged her sixpence for the biscuits she'd bought for Elizabeth.

At first he was so preoccupied that he didn't recognise her. He ran a hand through his hair.

'It's Kitty. Kitty Doyle. I bought some biscuits for Miss Elizabeth Harwood.'

'Ah, yes, I remember now.'

'Is something wrong? You look . . . worried.'

'I'm in a bit of a fix. You see, one of my assistants didn't come in this morning and now the other one has had to dash off as she's needed at home urgently, which leaves me to cope with what will be a busy couple of hours on my own. I don't suppose you could help out at all?'

Kitty was taken aback. She felt sorry for him but she had no experience at all of shop work. 'Well, I . . . I suppose I could try but I've never worked in a shop before. I'm a lady's maid, don't you remember? I told you.'

Stanley Ellinson seized the opportunity. 'Oh, it's not at all hard, Kitty. I'm sure you could manage and you can ask me if you get into difficulties. It's just for a couple of hours and it would really help me out.'

Kitty nodded. She didn't care what Elizabeth would say about her absence.

She tried her best to be efficient but she had to ask him all the prices and where things were kept. The customers were for the main part patient and helpful but when the shop was finally quiet she was relieved.

'Kitty, thank you. I would never have managed on my own.'

'Sure, I wasn't much help at all. Didn't I have you harassed, asking the price of this and the price of that and where will I find tea and coffee and biscuits and all manner of things.'

'You were very willing, you worked hard and you were very polite and considerate to the customers.'

She smiled at him. 'They were very polite and considerate to me considering I was such a desperate eejit!'

He smiled back, thinking she was very attractive and he was truly grateful to her. 'I'd say you were far from an "eejit". You pick things up quickly. Once I'd told you a price you remembered it. I'm both impressed and grateful.'

'I'd better be getting back now, Mr Ellinson. I said I'd only be out for about half an hour.'

He nodded. 'Well, thank you once again, Kitty. Let me see you out and if you are ever passing by do call in.'

As she walked to the tram stop Kitty thought it hadn't been that bad working behind a counter. She supposed that once you were used to it it could be quite enjoyable. At least you got to meet lots of people.

Preparations for departure were reaching a frenetic pitch when Harriet Harwood asked Kitty to go to

Walton Vale to pick up an order of basic toiletries that had been placed at Boots Cash Chemists, and Kitty had been glad to escape from the house.

The thoroughfare was busy and after she had duly picked up the parcel she walked along to look in the window of Lucy Johnson's shop. There would be no more shopping here, she thought sadly. She'd bought a few nice things over the months. Nothing wildly expensive, just a lace collar she'd added to a plain jumper, her first pair of silk stockings and a petticoat trimmed with a bit of lace. Whatever job she managed to find she probably wouldn't earn as much as she did now and she would have to pay rent. She would need what savings she had and she'd have to be careful with them too. They wouldn't last for ever.

She'd better go and see if there had been any replies to her advertisements but she didn't hold out much hope, nor did she want to pay out more money for them. Again there had been no interest and this time she took back her postcards, tore them up and stuffed the pieces into her bag.

She turned and walked towards the tram stop. She didn't want to go back and have to listen to Elizabeth enthusing over her latest purchases or exclaiming in mock horror how she didn't know how she was ever going to be ready to leave by the appointed day. When she reached Ellinson's Grocery she stopped, remembering now with growing bitterness how she had sought out and bought the biscuits that Elizabeth so liked, just to cheer her up. Elizabeth *was* very shallow and selfish, as Tina had reminded her. It was getting harder and harder even to be civil to her mistress now.

Should she go in? Mr Ellinson had said if she was passing she should. She pushed open the door and looked around. The shop was quiet and a young girl was idly rearranging some jars on a shelf.

'Would Mr Ellinson be in at all?' Kitty asked hesitantly.

'Mr Ellinson! There's someone here asking for you!' the girl called out.

Stanley Ellinson emerged from the back of the shop. 'Kitty Doyle, how nice to see you.'

'You did say if I was passing . . .'

'I did. Come through.'

Kitty followed him into the tiny office at the back of the shop.

'I hope you didn't get into trouble for being back late the other day?'

'I'm past caring,' Kitty answered truthfully.

He looked concerned. 'Is everything all right at the Harwoods'?'

'They're going away. At least Mrs Harwood and Miss Elizabeth are.'

'Away?'

'On an extended cruise.'

'I see, and I suppose they are taking you along with them, lucky girl.' He smiled at her but was surprised to see that she didn't look very happy at all. In fact she looked decidedly dejected.

'They are not, Mr Ellinson. I'm to be let go. "Given the push" as my friend Tina puts it. They can't afford to keep me on, so Mr Henry says. I don't know what I'm going to do, sure I don't!'

He was very concerned to hear this. He hadn't heard that Henry Harwood was in financial difficulties, and besides, if he could afford to send his sister off on an extended cruise surely he could pay the girl's wages?

'They said they would find me a job and lodgings but I'm not trained for anything other than domestic service and they don't seem to be in much of a hurry to do anything. I think they've forgotten. I've been looking in the newspaper, I've been to the Labour Exchange, I've even had advertisements in the windows of three shops along the road here.'

'I'm so sorry to hear that.' She wouldn't find it easy to get another such position. Very few people now had houses big enough to warrant employing domestic staff and those who did lived in Liverpool or in Newsham Park and their servants had usually been with them for years.

Kitty sighed. 'I'd best be getting back now. They're waiting on these things from Boots.'

'Wait, Kitty.' An idea was taking shape in his mind.

'What for, Mr Ellinson?'

'I'd like to . . . discuss something with you.'

Kitty nodded. A few more minutes wouldn't matter. Harriet Harwood could complain all she liked; she'd be off to Southampton on the boat train on Sunday.

Stanley Ellinson gestured that she should sit down. His germ of an idea was growing and growing. She needed a job; she needed a place to live. He needed someone reliable to look after this shop for him. The girls he had were totally incapable of that, thinking of nothing but what they would spend their wages on and where they would go at the weekend. He'd had a succession of them over the past year and they all seemed to be tarred with the one brush. He had two other shops, where thankfully he'd managed to find decent staff, and he was thinking of buying another. If he did, that would need his attention until he'd made sure it was profitable. What if she came to work for him here? She must be a fairly bright girl if the Harwoods had brought her with them from Ireland.

'Now, Kitty, sit down there and listen to what I am about to say,' he instructed, taking off his jacket and hanging it on a coat-hanger on the back of the door.

Kitty wondered what exactly he had in mind. Was

he going to ask her about Henry Harwood's finances, whether any problems there could possibly affect his business? She looked around. It was a very small room but extremely tidy.

'I am prepared to offer you a job here, Kitty. Serving behind the counter, as you did the other day. I have two other shops as well as this one and I'm thinking of buying a fourth and I'll be very busy with that and the people you seem to be able to employ these days are not at all up to scratch.'

Kitty was completely taken aback. 'Sure, I . . . I don't know what to say. Will I be able for it, Mr Ellinson?'

'I'm sure you will, you coped very well. You'll soon learn all there is to know, Kitty, and you must be honest and diligent and reliable otherwise the Harwoods wouldn't have employed you.'

'I am so! And I'm loyal.' Kitty was beginning to think it wasn't a bad offer at all. It would make a change from being at the beck and call of Elizabeth.

'We can sort out your wages later.'

Kitty frowned. 'I'd love to accept, Mr Ellinson, but . . .'

'But what? Please speak plainly, Kitty.'

'I'd have nowhere to live, Mr Ellinson. They are leaving on Sunday.'

'We can sort this out too. There are a couple of

rooms above the shop here.' He leaned across the desk and nodded. 'They're not large but I think they'll be adequate. I can find you some furniture, I'm sure. My own house is quite large and I don't use all the rooms, so there will be pieces spare.' He was thinking of the house in Orrell Park that had belonged to his parents. The furniture was very old-fashioned but still serviceable and there was bedding and towels, crockery and pans. More than enough to spare. He lived alone and frugally.

'Oh, that would be grand!' Kitty was feeling much better already.

'Shall we go up and have a look at them? Have you time?'

She smiled at him. 'Sure, I've all the time in the world.' Now she didn't care how late back she was.

She followed him up a narrow and rather dark staircase on to a cramped landing. Both rooms were quite small but then she'd never had a really large room of her own. She'd had to share a bedroom most of her life, first with her sisters, then with Tess and Emer. Only at the house in Aintree had she had a room by herself; now she was to have two. The one at the front of the building that overlooked the busy road had a fireplace, the other, which overlooked the yard at the back, did not.

Stanley Ellinson was frowning. 'I'm afraid they

need a bit of a clean and a coat of paint wouldn't go amiss either.' He hadn't been up here for a while and hadn't realised how shabby they were.

'I could give them a good clean before you bring any furniture in,' Kitty offered, knowing Tina would give her a hand.

'And I could get young Georgie the delivery lad to give them a coat of whitewash.'

Kitty clasped her hands together in delight. Two rooms of her own. Was this the security she had been looking for, a place of her own? She'd make it a home, she *would*. 'You're being very good to me, Mr Ellinson, really you are.'

'You're helping me out, Kitty. And I think we'll get along very well as long as you work hard and are totally reliable.'

'Indeed I will be,' Kitty promised, knowing she would do her very best to fulfil all his expectations. 'When I get back I'll tell them they needn't bother themselves looking out for me. I have a job and lodgings.' That gave her a great deal of satisfaction. She didn't need the Harwoods any more, just as they obviously didn't need her.

'I'm sure Mrs Harwood will be relieved, she has my assurances that you will be my responsibility and I'll see that no harm comes to you, Kitty.'

'I'll tell her that but, sure, I don't think they really

care what happens to me, as long as they don't have to pay me,' Kitty replied bitterly.

'I'll have that bit of rubbish that's up there removed. Will you let me know when you will be coming to give the place a clean?' he asked as they went back downstairs.

'I will so. They're going on Sunday so I expect I'll be finishing up on Saturday.'

'Will they want you to move out immediately?' Saturday was always the busiest day of the week.

Kitty frowned. 'I don't think so. Sure, they can at least give me a few days, they haven't done anything yet to find me somewhere else to live and work.'

'Well then, I'll wait to hear from you, Kitty,' he said with some relief. He'd get her settled in, see how she was shaping up and then he'd put an offer in for the shop in Walton Village.

Kitty collected her parcel and then held out her hand to him. 'You'll not regret this, Mr Ellinson, I promise.'

He shook it warmly. 'I have the distinct feeling that we are going to get on very well together, Kitty Doyle.'

Chapter Nineteen

'WHERE'VE YOU BEEN? SHE'S having ten fits up there!' Tina cried when Kitty at last returned and dumped the parcel down on the kitchen table.

'Sure, she can have as many fits as she likes, I don't care! I've got myself another job and a place to live,' Kitty announced, her eyes sparkling and her cheeks flushed.

Tina stared at her in astonishment. 'What? How? When?' she at last managed to ask.

'I bumped into Mr Ellinson and he's offered me a job and there're two rooms above the shop I can have all to myself.'

Tina recovered herself. 'I didn't know you knew him that well. You're sure there are no strings attached?' She was a little suspicious; this was all a bit sudden.

'What kind of "strings" would there be at all? He

can't find good staff and he's after buying another shop and will want to mind that.' Kitty couldn't see what there was to be worried about. Surely her friend wasn't being a begrudger?

'He can't be short of a few bob then and he is *old*. How did he know you were looking for a job?'

'I told him about things here. Will you give me a hand to give the rooms a good clean, after they've taken themselves off to Southampton? I said I'd clean them up and he's going to have them whitewashed.'

Tina nodded. She was very curious to see where Kitty was going to live and hopefully learn more about Stanley Ellinson. It all seemed a bit too good to be true. Did he have some kind of ulterior motive? After all, he hardly knew Kitty. 'You'd better go up and tell them the good news,' she instructed.

Elizabeth was surrounded by clothes and shoes and hatboxes; cases and a large cabin trunk also added to the clutter in the bedroom. Kitty could see her mistress was definitely in a state of agitation but mentally she shrugged. She would only have to put up with Elizabeth for a few more days.

'Kitty! Where on earth have you been? I've been asking for you for hours, there's so much to do and hardly any time at all to fit it all in. Did you get the tissue paper? I do hope there's enough or everything will crease so.'

Kitty produced a large wad of tissue paper from the top of a cupboard. 'There's plenty here, miss, and I've been talking to my new employer, that's why I was so long.'

Elizabeth stopped sorting through the piles of new and very fancy underwear that covered the bed and stared at Kitty. 'Your new employer?'

Kitty felt a quiet sense of satisfaction. 'Yes, miss. I'm to go and work for Mr Ellinson, the grocer. He has three shops and I'm to work in the one in Walton Vale. I'll live above the shop. I'll have two very nice rooms all to myself.' There, that had wiped the peevish look off Elizabeth's face, she thought triumphantly.

'Good heavens! I didn't even know you knew him. Did you ask him for the job?'

'Sure, I did not! Wasn't it offered to me? I'll be moving out as soon after you've gone as is practical. He's having the rooms . . . decorated for me.' She had been going to say 'whitewashed' but decided 'decorated' sounded far better, as though he was going to endless trouble.

'Really?' Elizabeth wasn't actually that interested. Of course she was glad Kitty had found something, although she didn't think working behind a shop counter was any kind of a step up in life, rather the opposite, but it did settle the matter and if Kitty was happy with it then it was nothing to do with her.

'Good. I'll tell Harriet the news. Now, can we start and pack all this underwear in tissue and put it in that case, and all those stockings too?' Elizabeth had dismissed Kitty's situation from her mind. Did she have enough underwear, she wondered? Then she sighed. Harriet had said it could be laundered on the ship, her stewardess would see to it, so she supposed there would be enough.

Harriet Harwood sent for Kitty that evening and they discussed Kitty's new situation. Harriet showed some satisfaction, relieved the problem had been solved, and informed Kitty that she could stay until the end of the following week. Then she handed her an envelope, as Henry had instructed her to do. Kitty thanked her politely, put it in her pocket and returned to the kitchen.

'Did she thank you for all your hard work and loyalty over the years?' Tina enquired.

'She did not but then I didn't expect her to. Hasn't Elizabeth got her all worked up into a state of nerves?' Kitty replied.

'I'll be glad when the pair of them have gone and we can get some peace and quiet. They've got the whole place turned upside down and I'm sure Mr Edmund will be glad to see the back of them too.'

It was with sighs of pure relief on the part of the entire staff (and secretly of Edmund Harwood too) that Harriet and Elizabeth finally departed with their luggage to Lime Street Station on Sunday morning to catch the boat train to Southampton. As the car disappeared around the bend in the drive Tina turned to Kitty and grinned.

'Come on, let's tidy up and then we'll go down to see these new rooms of yours. You did let him know we are coming today?'

'I did so. I sent a note in the post and I managed to get the cleaning stuff from Appleton's. It's all in one of the sheds in the yard. It will be a bit awkward to take on the tram but . . .' She shrugged.

'We can put it on the parcel shelf by the door and the conductor can keep his eye on it,' Tina advised.

They struggled down to the tram stop with buckets and scrubbing brushes and soap and a broom and a mop, laughing and joking about what a sight they must look – and on a Sunday too.

'Like a pair of charladies on an outing!' Tina giggled, feeling carefree now she'd been released from weeks of chaos.

'I 'ope youse girls aren't goin' far with that lot!' the conductor remarked when the tram arrived.

'Just a couple of stops, honestly. Will you keep your eye on it all?' Tina asked him.

'Who's goin' ter be scarperin' with all that on a

Sunday? Everyone's havin' a day off, except the likes of me and youse two, by the look of it,' he replied rather glumly.

To their relief Stanley Ellinson was waiting for them. Tina thought he must be forty-five if he was a day but he seemed pleasant enough. He'd always been courteous and obliging whenever she'd gone to the shop, which hadn't been very often and usually on the instruction of Mrs Harwood. It was more than could be said for the two girls he employed.

'I see you've come prepared,' he said, noting the cleaning utensils.

'We have so. This is Tina, she's going to help me,' Kitty introduced her friend.

'The ladies have finally left so here we are,' Tina informed him.

'Follow me then. I had the rubbish removed before I locked up last night.'

Tina exclaimed how nice and cosy the rooms were and said they'd be even better after a clean and a lick of paint.

'And I've picked out some furniture, Kitty, I'll have it brought down here. When do you have to leave?' Stanley Ellinson asked.

'Not until the end of the week, so by then we should have everything done here, Mr Ellinson.'

'Good. Then I'll leave you girls to it. I'll call back

later on to see if you've finished and then we can lock up.'

Tina thought he was really quite nice, in a quiet sort of a way. He wasn't bad-looking either, although rather pale, probably because he spent so much time in his shops. He had light brown wavy hair and grey eyes. He was obviously a confirmed bachelor; he wasn't short of money; he was a good businessman and probably had quite a high standing in whatever circles he moved in. She had to admit that she couldn't see anything sinister in his offering Kitty a new start. Kitty would probably do very well at the new job as she was totally reliable.

'Right then, let's give this floor a good brushing before we attempt to scrub it. There's years of dust up here,' she remarked, running her finger over the grimy window ledge and grimacing. 'Once these windows have been cleaned you'll get a great view of everything that's going on up and down the road and it's so convenient for all the shops, the cinema and the trams,' she added, thinking that Kitty might well see more of life than she did.

By the time Stanley Ellinson returned they had the place looking clean and tidy. They were both tired and a little grubby from their efforts.

'You have worked hard. There's a big improvement already,' he remarked, looking around.

'Won't it look just grand when it's been freshened up and there's furniture in it,' Kitty enthused.

'You must both be tired and thirsty. Would you like to come with me for a cup of tea? I'm sure we can find somewhere open,' he offered, thinking it was the least he could do. They had indeed worked hard.

'That's very good of you, but, sure, look at the state of us! We're not fit to be seen,' Kitty cried, pushing her hair out of her eyes.

'We couldn't go showing you up. Is there a kettle downstairs?' Tina added. They were both dying for a cup of tea but he couldn't take them anywhere decent looking the way they did, especially not on a Sunday when everyone was wearing their best clothes.

'There is. We'll make a pot of tea in my office.'

'That'll be grand. Then we'll get off. There's still plenty to keep us occupied back there. We only did a quick tidy this morning.' Kitty smiled, untying the dirty apron and following him down the stairs.

They got a few curious looks on the tram going back but they ignored them.

'I have to admit that he's not a bad old stick. Set in his ways and a bit on the fussy side though,' Tina commented.

'He's not the worst and he didn't need to offer to take us for tea,' Kitty agreed.

'So, you think everything will be ready for you to move in on Friday?'

'I do so and I'm beginning to look forward to it.' Kitty was being truthful. The sooner she got settled in the better, she felt.

'You didn't need to say you'll go into the shop on Tuesday to start the job.'

Kitty glanced at her friend. Tina sounded a little put out but Kitty wanted to show willing. 'I've officially finished working for the Harwoods so I might as well go in there. I've a huge amount to learn and it's not going to be easy.'

Tina smiled at her. 'Just think, this time next week you'll have done almost a full week in the shop and you'll be settled into your new home. I'll miss you, Kitty.'

'I'll miss you too, Tina, but won't you be able to come and visit me whenever you get the chance?'

Tina brightened up. 'I will, and with those two off gadding around the world I'll have much more time off. We'll all have things a lot easier now.'

Kitty nodded but she hoped that Edmund Harwood wouldn't think he was wasting money paying servants for doing very little and follow Henry's example and get rid of a few.

As she lay in bed that night she wondered how she would feel living entirely on her own for the first time.

Would she be lonely? There had always been someone to chat to in the past. But there would be plenty of people in and out of the shop all day and probably Mr Ellinson would stay on for a bit after they closed, to see to the takings. In the evenings there would still be the traffic and a certain number of pedestrians on the road outside. She could sit by the window and watch what was going on. Then there would be evenings when Tina would come and visit, although she doubted there would be much money for things like dances and the cinema now; they would have to stay in. Of course she wouldn't be lonely. It would be a very different kind of a job but she would look on it as a challenge and she would make sure she did it well. She wasn't sure how the two girls Mr Ellinson already employed would treat her. If the worst came to the worst she was sure he would get rid of them and then maybe she could help him interview new girls, girls who she felt would be more suitable. Then her position would be quite clear to them from the start and there would be no resentment or jealousy.

She closed her eyes, thinking that tomorrow she must write to her sisters and give them yet another new address, but at least this time she hoped it would be permanent.

Chapter Twenty

———————

ON TUESDAY MORNING SHE arrived for work at eight o'clock sharp and for the first time in years she wasn't wearing the uniform of a domestic servant. As the weather was quite mild for the beginning of May she had worn a skirt and blouse and a long-line cardigan. Stanley Ellinson had given her a navy blue overall and had introduced her to Mavis and Beryl, the other assistants. As the day wore on she found both girls a little on the lazy side and very frivolous in their attitude.

'You're dead serious, Kitty! You've got to have a bit of a laugh or you'd go mad'! Mavis had chided her. 'This job is dead boring at times and some of the customers are a bit snooty and can be flaming awkward.'

'I'm just naturally quiet, I always have been, and I've so much to learn,' she'd replied.

'This must be a big change for you, Kitty, but you wouldn't catch me going into service. Waiting hand and foot on the likes of people too damned lazy to pick up their own stockings and having to say "Yes, ma'am" and "No, ma'am" all day! Not on your life!' Beryl had added, after she'd found out where Kitty had previously worked.

'It wasn't all that bad. I liked living at Harwood Hall,' Kitty had replied defensively.

'It's a turn-up for the book for that old miser to let you live upstairs. He can be a right misery guts at times, I can tell you.' Beryl had pulled a face and jerked her head in the direction of the back office.

Kitty had said nothing but had thought Stanley Ellinson was anything but an 'old miser' or a 'misery guts'. In her opinion he was a kind and generous man who didn't deserve to be spoken about so disrespectfully.

She had been polite and obliging to the customers, who seemed to like her, even though she frequently had to ask the other girls where things were and their prices. After Mavis and Beryl had left that evening she'd gone through to the office.

'Well, Kitty, how did your day go? I heard a couple of favourable comments about you,' her benefactor asked, looking up from his cashing up.

'I managed but there's so much I don't know. I've

come to ask you, Mr Ellinson, could I stay on for an hour each evening to learn where everything is and all the prices? Then I won't need to be asking Mavis or Beryl all the time. I feel such an eejit.'

He frowned. 'Have they not been co-operative? Did they say you were an "eejit"?'

'Oh, no. It's just that I could give the customers a better service if I *knew* those things.'

He nodded. She wasn't complaining and she was showing a willingness to learn. 'That will be fine, Kitty. It takes me an hour to cash up and make a note of what needs to be reordered and go over the deliveries with Percy one of the delivery boys.'

She turned to go. 'Then I'll go back and make a start.'

'You don't have to tonight, Kitty. It's your first day; you must be tired. Get off home now.'

She smiled at him. 'This is my home now, or it will be by Sunday night, and I don't feel at all tired.'

He smiled back at her. 'Well then, go and make a start.'

She was indeed tired by the time she got back to the Harwoods' house and her head was spinning trying to remember all the prices, but at least she did now know where all the dry goods were stacked.

'Do you intend to stay behind every night?' Tina enquired, thinking that Kitty was taking this conscientiousness a bit too far.

'Until I know where every item is kept and how much it costs. The two that are in there are lazy and offhand but at least they know the price of a jar of jam and where it is on the shelf. It makes me feel such an eejit.'

'Did you get on all right with them? They weren't nasty or anything with you?'

Kitty shook her head. 'Not at all.'

By the end of the week she had learned a great deal and Stanley Ellinson was pleased with her progress. On the Friday evening he had shown her the large order books and explained his method of weekly stocktaking. He'd also taken her upstairs to show her the newly painted rooms and the furniture that he'd had brought down.

'It's lovely, really it is,' Kitty exclaimed, although privately she thought the furniture was very dark and old-fashioned and too large for such small rooms; it seemed overpowering. It was of good quality and had been well cared for, she could see that, and she really shouldn't be so picky, she told herself, it was small-minded and ungrateful.

'So you'll be moving on Sunday?'

She nodded. 'There's not a lot to pack. I was going to ask you, Mr Ellinson, could I buy a few groceries from the shop? I'll need things to tide me over.'

'Of course, Kitty. Take what you need and we'll

settle up next week.' He had installed a small Baby Belling electric cooker for her and a gas ring, so she could boil a kettle.

On Saturday night when she returned to the house Tina had a pot of tea made and there was a cake with chocolate buttercream icing on the top set out on a china cake stand.

'It's for you, this is your last night, so I begged Cook to make it specially,' Tina explained.

'Oh, Tina, that's so kind.' Kitty felt quite overcome.

'It's to celebrate your new life – your independence, if you like.' Tina poured out the tea and handed Kitty a knife with which to cut the cake.

'I'm still accountable to Mr Ellinson. I can't do exactly as I please.' Kitty defly cut two slices and transferred them to the side plates Tina had laid out beside the cups and saucers.

'But at least at the end of the day your time is your own and you'll have every single Sunday off,' Tina reminded her.

Kitty was surprised at the note of disgruntlement in her friend's voice. Tina had never seemed discontented before. 'Are you getting tired of being in service?'

Tina took a bite of cake and shrugged.

An unpleasant thought occurred to Kitty. 'They're not going to give you the push as well, are they? Has anything been mentioned?'

'No, I've heard nothing like that but it's just that . . . well, sometimes I do get a bit fed up.'

Kitty bit her lip. She hoped her new situation hadn't made Tina restless and discontented. 'It's going to be hard work at the shop, much harder than working here, and I'm not going to earn a fortune. Just what I'm paid here.'

'I know that. Oh, I suppose it's just that I'm going to miss you.' Tina finished her tea and stood up, shaking off her mood. 'Come on, I'll give you a hand to pack your things. I'll parcel up the rest of the cake and you can take it with you, have it after your tea tomorrow night.'

Kitty nodded and looked around the kitchen. This was the last time she would sit here with Tina. Her days with the Harwoods were over. It seemed so long now since that day her da had taken her up the drive of Harwood Hall. She hadn't wanted to go, she'd been afraid of what faced her, but she'd been happy there, until Annie and Bridget had been sent away and she'd lost Niall. Sadly she wondered where he was now and what he was doing. Was he married? Was he involved in the bitter fighting that was tearing the newly independent country apart, dividing families and friends? Did he ever think of her? Probably not.

'Cheer up! You look as miserable as sin,' Tina urged, breaking into her reverie.

Kitty smiled. 'I was just thinking about the day I first started working for Mrs Harwood – Mrs Amy Harwood, God rest her. She was lovely, much nicer than Harriet or Elizabeth.'

'That wouldn't be hard!' Tina commented acidly. Their treatment of Kitty still rankled with her.

'No, she was kind and considerate.'

'And she was Irish, don't forget that,' Tina added.

'So is Elizabeth,' Kitty reminded her.

'You wouldn't think so. You'd think she was more English than I am. Do you miss Ireland, Kitty?'

Kitty looked thoughtful. 'I suppose I do but there's nothing there for me now. I once thought there was but . . .' She shrugged.

'You mean *him*? I told you, Kitty, you're better off without that feller, the way he treated you.'

'I know and besides he's probably married by now.'

'If he's not dead in a ditch! From what I've heard there're terrible things going on over there. Fathers and sons killing one another, brother fighting brother.'

Kitty shuddered. 'Oh, Tina, don't be after saying things like that! I wouldn't wish him any harm. He didn't seem the type to be interested in politics, I hope he's stayed out of it all.'

'So do I, for the new wife's sake. It's not easy being a widow, my poor mam can tell you all about that. Six of us at school when my da died and only the Burial

Club money. She had to go out scrubbing floors morning and evening just to keep food on the table until us older ones went to work. Oh, for heaven's sake, we're getting morbid! Let's get your things together so you can shake the dust of this place from your shoes in the morning. Isn't that what they say when someone moves on to better things? Life's *got* to be better for you now, Kitty.'

'It will be. I just know it will,' Kitty replied firmly, pushing all thoughts of Amy Harwood, her time at the Hall and Niall Collins from her mind. It was a great opportunity for her and she was determined to make the most of it.

Part III

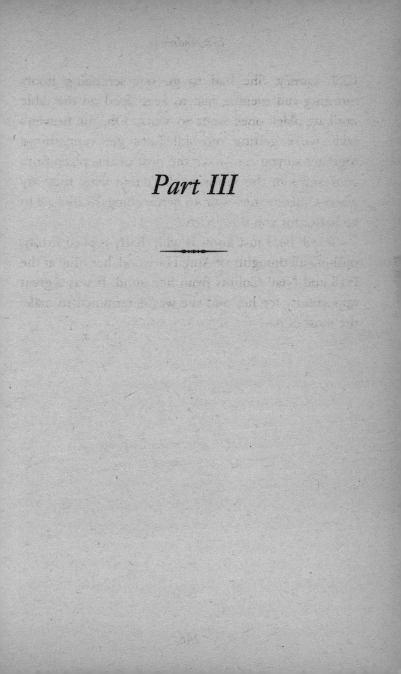

Chapter Twenty-One

—◆—

SHE REMEMBERED HER DETERMINATION now as she climbed the stairs on a cold, dark December evening. The wind was whistling around the building and a shower of hail rattled against the windows. She switched on the light and shivered. The little room looked gloomy and cold. The fire she'd lit at lunchtime was almost out. She drew the curtains, shutting out the miserable weather, and stirred up the embers, tipping more coal from the small brass scuttle on to them. Coal just didn't seem as welcoming or as aromatic as turf, she thought, remembering how her mam had always kept a great fire going, especially in the winter months.

She took off her navy overall and pulled on a thick cardigan and then put the kettle on the gas ring. Wearily she settled herself in the armchair beside the fire. They had been so busy this week. Christmas was approaching and that meant they stayed open later. It pleased Stanley Ellinson, of course, that business was so brisk but as he seemed to spend more and more time in his new shop, it meant that she had more to do. She had been delighted when in September he had decided that she was more than competent enough to take over the running of this shop for him. It hadn't of course delighted either Mavis or Beryl, who had both declared that it was sly and underhanded of him to promote her over their heads when she had only been there five minutes. They had both given in their notice and left. She hadn't been sorry to see them go for in her opinion neither of them did a decent day's work. She had helped Mr Ellinson select their replacements and both had proved to be good, reliable workers. It was a good thing too with things getting so busy, she thought. It was a challenge but was life really so much better for her now than it had been?

She treated herself once a month either to the cinema or to the dance at the Aintree Institute, both of which were in easy walking distance. The first time she had gone to the dance she had been very self-conscious and shy. It was the first time she had been to such an event alone. She had sat at the back of the room, clutching a glass of orange juice and praying she wouldn't have to sit there alone all night. If no one spoke to her or asked her to dance she would be so mortified, she'd thought. However, she needn't have worried. She soon got chatting to two other girls who lived down Longmoor Lane, by the fire station – so they had informed her.

'We come here most weekends, don't we, Flo? You tend to get a better class of feller. Of course some of them do go for a pint before they come here but I've never seen anyone drunk and there's never any trouble,' the girl called Ivy had informed her.

'I've never been here on my own before. I came with a friend, she works for the Harwoods. I work in Ellinson's Grocery just down the road.'

'Well, you can sit with us whenever you come. What's your name?' Flo had asked.

'Kitty, Kitty Doyle, but I can't afford to come here very often. Haven't I to keep myself?'

Ivy had nodded. 'I thought you were Irish. It's not easy having to pay for everything yourself. Flo and me live at home so we have more to spare for nights out and such, but whenever you do come sit with us. Mind you, we usually don't sit for long, do we, Flo?'

Flo had giggled. 'And I don't think you will either, Kitty. Look, there're three fellers heading this way already. Which do you fancy, Kitty?'

She had looked a little embarrassed. 'Sure, I don't

mind which one asks me to dance. 'Tis better than being a wallflower,' she'd answered.

They hadn't sat out much; all three of them had been asked to dance and she had enjoyed herself. At the end of the night she thanked Flo and Ivy for their company and promised that next time she came she would certainly make sure she sat with them.

The kettle began to whistle and she got up and made herself a cup of tea. She'd have to liven herself up a bit, she thought, as Tina was coming tonight for a quick visit. She hadn't seen her friend for a while. There had been so much to do. In June Tina had informed her that now the house was virtually empty Mr Edmund had decided that the place should be given a thorough turning out and that some rooms were to be redecorated. So, throughout the summer months a succession of workmen had been in and out and Tina and the rest of the staff had had plenty to keep them occupied.

The room was getting warmer now and looked much cosier as the firelight picked out the reds and oranges in the patchwork cushions on the two easy chairs. On the floor in front of the fire was a rag rug Kitty had bought at a jumble sale and had washed and hung over the line in the back yard to dry in the hot July sun. She'd been delighted to see how bright the colours were after all the grime had been washed away.

She sat gazing into the fire as she finished her tea. She supposed she was happy enough. She was kept fully occupied during the day and had the company of her two assistants and the customers. She received regular letters from Bridget. Stanley Ellinson called at least once a week to take the money to the bank and Tina came as often as she could. But lately, especially as the evenings were long and dark, she sat here on her own for hours feeling increasingly lonely and dispirited until she went to bed. She had tried reading but the light was bad and often she couldn't concentrate. There was nothing to see from the window either now: people stayed at home on winter evenings. She had too much time on her hands, that was the trouble. Time to think about the future and the past. Even her visits to the cinema and the company of her new acquaintances, Flo and Ivy, at her monthly trip to the dance, didn't seem to help.

There were nights when she couldn't keep the memories of the brief time she had shared with Niall at bay or stop herself from going over and over in her mind why he had acted that way. Then there were nights when she remembered the happy days in the forge at Rahan before her mam had died, when they'd been a family, and that always made her feel very alone. And, despite everything, she missed her da.

There was peace at last in Ireland but there was still

a great deal of bitterness on the part of the defeated anti-treaty men. To her relief Harwood Hall had survived although it was looking neglected and overgrown, so Bridget had informed her. Her sister occasionally received a letter from their father, which Kitty supposed he wrote out of a belated sense of duty. It also gave her some satisfaction to know that Henry Harwood had been unable to find a buyer for it.

She got up, glancing at the little clock on the mantelpiece. Tina would be here soon and she'd been daydreaming when the fire needed mending, the table had to be set and she had to tidy herself up.

She had rushed around and just completed the chores when the doorbell that had been installed rang. She ran down the stairs to the back entrance and opened the door. 'Come on inside out of the weather.'

'I hope you've got a good fire going, Kitty! I'm half soaked, the flaming umbrella blew inside out when I got off the tram,' Tina complained, leaving the now useless brolly at the bottom of the stairs.

'I have so, it's nice and warm up here and the kettle's boiled so I'll whet the tea.'

Tina took off her wet coat and hat and settled herself in a chair by the fireside. As Kitty handed her a mug of tea she could see her friend had some news. She laughed. 'I can see by your face that there's something you're bursting to tell me. Are they cutting short their trip? Has Elizabeth found herself a husband?'

Tina laughed. 'Neither, as far as I know.'

'He hasn't found a buyer for Harwood Hall, has he?' Kitty hoped that wasn't it.

'No. Will you just give me time to get a word in edgewise, Kitty? I'm leaving. I've got another job,' Tina announced.

'Where? I didn't think there were any other big houses near here. The only other one I know of in the area is Knowsley Hall and doesn't the Earl of Derby live there and it's *huge*, so I hear. Are you going there?' Kitty was incredulous.

'Don't be daft, Kitty! He's the Lord Lieutenant of the county and a peer of the realm. They wouldn't have the likes of me in that place, nor would I want to work there. No, it's not in service at all.'

Kitty felt relieved. If Tina had been going to work there she would hardly ever see her, it was a good distance away. 'So what are you going to do?'

Some of the excitement went out of Tina's eyes. How would Kitty take this? she wondered.

'I'm going away to sea, as a stewardess. I'm dead lucky to get it. My brother, our Gerry, sort of spoke for me. He's been a steward with the Booth Line for years. The money is much better and I'll get to see places I never dreamed I would. They don't carry huge numbers of passengers so I won't be rushed off my feet and I'm so sick of working for that lot! When you left I realised that I was wasting myself, that I could do better.' It all came out in a rush.

Kitty tried to look pleased and excited for her friend but it was so hard. Now she was going to lose Tina's company and she was the only friend she had. 'I'm delighted for you, Tina,' she managed to get out at last.

'They are quite long trips though. They go to Portugal and then to Brazil, and halfway up some big river there, the Amazon I think it's called.' Tina was a bit dubious herself about being so far from home but Gerry had said he'd be there to keep his eye on her.

'How long will you be gone for?' Kitty asked.

Tina bit her lip. 'Nine months.'

Nearly a whole year, Kitty thought, feeling very miserable.

'Oh, I know it's a long time but it will fly, you wait and see, and I'll write and tell you all about it. We haven't seen much of each other lately, I know, but you're very busy and you have to agree that you do like your new job and this place. I'll have plenty of time off when I do get back, we can spend lots of time together then.'

Kitty nodded as enthusiastically as she could and

tried hard to be interested as Tina chatted on about her new job and change of lifestyle.

When Tina had gone, promising to call again before she left aboard the *Hildebrand* in two weeks' time, Kitty started to clear away the tea things, but a wave of loneliness flooded over her and she collapsed at the table. The long winter months stretched ahead endlessly. She would come up here every night to sit alone, miserable and neglected, without any kind of company or friendship. She was nearly twenty years old and there was no one in her life to give her companionship, let alone love or affection. She dropped her head into her hands and began to cry.

It was almost half an hour later when she realised that there was someone outside on the landing. She raised her head and wiped her eyes. The knock came again on the door and she realised that it must be Stanley Ellinson. He had keys but he never invaded her privacy. He always knocked on the door to her small living room, and usually he told her in advance of when he intended to call. Getting to her feet she prayed he wasn't coming with bad news; she felt utterly dejected as it was. She called out to him, bidding him enter, then turned away from the door and busied herself with putting more coal on the fire.

'It's a wild night out there and cold with it. I hope I'm not disturbing you, Kitty. I've brought the catalogue from Terry's so we can discuss just which boxes of chocolates to order for Christmas. They're very high-class confectioners and I've found certain boxes have been very popular in the past. This year they have three entirely new ones and I'd like your opinion on them.'

Kitty turned around reluctantly. She didn't want to discuss which boxes of chocolates to stock.

He was taken aback to see her tear-stained cheeks and puffy eyes.

'Kitty, you've been crying! Whatever is wrong? Has something upset you?' He was genuinely concerned; he'd never seen her so upset.

Kitty felt so utterly wretched that she didn't attempt to deny it. She nodded.

He put the catalogue down on the table and gently helped her to a chair. 'Is it the work? Are you finding it too much? I know I've been up at the new shop for long periods but—'

'No, it's nothing to do with work. It's . . . Tina came to see me tonight and she's . . . she's going away to sea for nine months,' she stammered, the tears again threatening to overwhelm her.

He patted her hand and looked mystified.

'Oh, Mr Ellinson, I'll miss her! I'm so lonely! I have no one . . . close. I sit here every night all on my own!' She broke down again.

He nodded as understanding dawned. She had not been used to living alone, she must indeed find the evenings very long and forlorn. He handed her his handkerchief. 'Hush now, Kitty. I do hate to see you so distressed.' He tried to comfort her. There were times when he felt lonely himself, although he was accustomed to living on his own. He had done so since his parents had died ten years ago. He found it was best to keep yourself occupied but she was very young and hadn't been very kindly treated by life so far. He had learned a little about her over the months and he felt sorry for her.

Kitty wiped her eyes and tried to pull herself together. She didn't want him to think she was ungrateful. He'd given her a job and a home after all. 'I'm sorry. I didn't mean to break down like this. I'm not ungrateful, truly I'm not!'

'I don't think you are, Kitty. I find it helps to keep busy in the evenings. Take up an interest, a hobby. I collect stamps. I find it very interesting and it passes the time. And of course I have all the accounts to do.'

Kitty nodded. Neither sounded very interesting to her. 'I'll find something to do, Mr Ellinson.' She was feeling a little bit better; maybe he was right.

He smiled. She was such an obliging girl and quite pretty too, when she wasn't overcome by tears. 'When there are just the two of us together, do you think you could call me Stanley? I really do hate to see you so miserable, Kitty.'

She managed a weak smile. 'I'll be just grand now, Stanley. I was just feeling a bit sorry for myself.' She hesitated over his name. It seemed very strange not to call him Mr Ellinson. She got to her feet. 'Shall we have a cup of tea and look at the boxes of chocolates? I don't want you to feel as though you've wasted your evening.'

He nodded, relieved that she had recovered her good humour. 'That would be "grand", as you say, Kitty, and I certainly haven't wasted my evening. I'm just glad I could cheer you up.'

Chapter Twenty-Two

STANLEY ELLINSON THOUGHT A great deal about Kitty over the next few days and it seemed to increase his own sense of isolation. He tried to concentrate on his accounts and his stamp albums but he was restless and edgy. He had never been very good with girls even when he'd been younger and his mother had urged him to go out more. He was a shy man, a little introverted and he had put all his energies, and in fact he'd put everything into building up his business. But now he realised he was fast approaching middle age and it would be pleasant to have someone to talk to after supper or take for walks on summer Sunday afternoons, someone who shared his interests. And of course he had no one to leave his shops to when the time came for him to meet his Maker. That thought weighed heavily on his mind. What was the point of it all if there was no one to leave it to? his father had always said.

Kitty was easy to talk to and she knew the business. She also had a good eye for detail; she had picked out just the right chocolates that would appeal to his customers. She was attractive, she had a pleasant nature and he was definitely happier in her company. But did he love her? he asked himself. Did he even know what love was? Was it really necessary for a successful marriage? His mother had always said it was better to have mutual respect and interests, affection certainly; love would follow and children always brought you closer together. Kitty was much younger than himself but she wasn't flighty or irresponsible, and he certainly thought of her with affection. She was a quiet, well-mannered girl with many good qualities; indeed those very qualities had been instrumental in making him offer her the job in the first place. He was certain they would make her a good wife too. She was lonely, her family was far away and now her only friend was going away too. By the end of the week he had decided that he would ask her to tea on Sunday afternoon.

Kitty had tried to recover her good humour and during the day she succeeded, but each night the feelings of sadness and increasing despair returned. She had received a letter from Bridget full of all the plans for the forthcoming Christmas holidays. It had already snowed heavily in New York, which gave the whole city the look of a Christmas card. The shops were full of lovely things and were decorated beautifully too. They were going to start their shopping soon and Uncle Ted was going to bring home the tree next week. Annie was terribly excited as Davie was going to take her to her first real dance and she was to have her first dance dress and black patent-leather pumps. Bridget herself was going to buy something new to wear as she was now working in Petty's department store and would get what she called 'staff discount'. Family and friends would surround everyone, Kitty thought. There would be parties, dances and outings for everyone – everyone except herself.

She thought of all the Christmases when they'd been children and those she'd spent at Harwood Hall. Even the year of the accident, the holiday itself had been happy, until St Stephen's Night. She wondered what Tess and Emer would be doing this year; Elizabeth would no doubt be having a whale of a time, wherever she was. Even Tina would be enjoying herself for they must celebrate aboard ship. She didn't dare to think about Niall: that would have been too much to bear.

She was very surprised when on Friday afternoon young Violet told her that Mr Ellinson had just arrived and wanted to see her in his office. He hadn't told her he was coming here this week; there was so much to do in the new shop, this being the first Christmas season under his new management.

She closed the door behind her and shivered. The little office was rather chilly. 'You wanted to see me, Stanley?'

He smiled at her although he felt rather apprehensive. Even in her plain navy overall and the white cap she wore over her hair, she was indeed a pretty girl and so young. She wouldn't even be twenty until next month.

'Yes, Kitty. It's just a flying visit, I have to get back to Walton Village as I'm expecting a large delivery and I want to make sure everything I ordered actually arrives. I . . . I was wondering if you had any plans for this Sunday afternoon?'

She was surprised. 'Plans? No, I'm not doing anything special.' She was not looking forward to her day off but she had intended to write to her sisters.

'I . . . was thinking, perhaps you would like to come to tea . . . with me?' He felt awkward and a little embarrassed.

Kitty's eyes widened in amazement. 'At your house . . . your home?'

'Yes, indeed. I live at number ten Osterley Gardens. It's just off Orrell Lane.'

Kitty knew where it was. It was a quiet cul-de-sac, just a ten-minute walk away, and they were big houses. She realised he was patiently waiting for her answer. 'Yes. Yes, I'd like that, Stanley, thank you.'

He smiled, feeling very relieved. 'Good. Shall we say half past three?'

Kitty smiled back. It was very kind of him to invite her. 'Half past three on Sunday. I . . . I'll look forward to it.'

He nodded and picked up his hat and gloves from the desk. 'Right. I'd better be off now.'

She followed him out into the shop, which was busy, and as it remained so for the rest of the day she had little time to dwell on the matter.

That evening, however, after she had closed up and gone upstairs, she did think of his invitation again. It *was* kind and thoughtful of him; he must realise how lonely and quiet Sundays were for her. Half past three would give her ample time to write to Bridget, give her rooms their usual clean and do her bit of washing. Even though she was weary after the long busy day, she felt her spirits rise. She'd wash her hair on Saturday night and press her good dress. She might even try to get along to Lucy Johnson's and buy a bit of velvet ribbon and retrim her one good winter hat. She wondered if she should take something. Perhaps a cake or some scones?

She was ready by three o'clock on Sunday afternoon and she scrutinised her reflection in the mirror in the bedroom. Her hair was clean and shiny; her dusky pink wool dress with the white broderie anglaise collar suited her fair complexion and had been neatly pressed. She wore the pearlised earrings and she carefully positioned her brown felt cloche hat with its new band of pink velvet ribbon to show them to the best advantage. She'd given her brown winter coat a good brush and she had brown and pink Fair Isle patterned gloves and a small brown handbag. Quite smart and stylish, she thought.

She picked up the cardboard box that contained the Victoria sponge cake she'd bought and went down the stairs, locking the door behind her.

When she reached Osterley Gardens she took out the small mirror from her handbag and tucked a few wisps of hair that had been blown across her forehead by the wind back under her hat. She certainly didn't want to arrive looking untidy. Stanley Ellinson's home was in the left-hand corner of the squared cul-de-sac. It was a three-storey, detached Edwardian house fronted by a small and neatly kept garden. The paintwork was dark brown and there were cream cotton lace curtains at the windows.

She took a deep breath and opened the small wrought-iron gate and knocked on the front door.

'Right on time, Kitty, but then you are always punctual,' Stanley greeted her, smiling.

'I wasn't sure exactly how long it would take so I left a bit early, and I brought this, for our tea.' She handed him the cake box.

He took the box from her and opened the door wide. 'That was very thoughtful of you, come inside and let me take your coat and hat.'

It was a rather dark hall, she thought, glancing around yet trying not to appear avidly curious. All the woodwork had been varnished and the wallpaper was of a very old-fashioned and busy design of flowers and leaves in deep plum and dark green. The pictures on the walls were old-fashioned too, set in heavy ornate frames, and the carpet, although of good quality, had seen many years of wear.

He took her coat and hat and hung them with care on the mahogany hallstand.

'Come through into the sitting room. I've a good fire, so it's warm,' he urged, ushering her into the room.

It was warm, Kitty thought, and quite comfortable. After the hallway it was brighter than she had expected with the weak winter sunlight coming in through a large bay window. As she had expected the furniture was big and dark and of good quality, like the pieces that dominated her small rooms. They had come from this house. Bright cushions and a fireside rug livened the place up as did pale green curtains and a tall standard lamp with a pink-fringed shade that stood in one corner. On a small side table covered with a lace cloth, china cups and saucers and plates were set out. There was a three-tier matching cake stand too, with small sandwiches on one tier, scones on another and iced fairy cakes on the third.

'This is lovely, Stanley. You've gone to such trouble.'

He looked pleased. 'Sit down by the fire and warm yourself, Kitty. I'll just go and make the tea.'

When he'd left the room she scrutinised the furnishings more closely. There were old sepia photographs on the sideboard, obviously his parents and grandparents, judging from the Edwardian and Victorian clothes and hairstyles. The bookcase was crammed full of leather-bound volumes. The antimacassars on the backs and arms of the chairs and the sofa had been embroidered by hand. On a table in an alcove stood a large wireless set and on the shelf beneath it were neatly stacked what looked like photograph albums. It was a homely room and not short on creature comforts. The china was delicate and patterned with blue flowers and the cutlery was silver. She leaned back in her chair, feeling more relaxed.

He returned with the teapot, milk jug and sugar basin on a tray, also covered with an embroidered cloth. 'Now, will I pour or would you prefer to?' It was the first time he had ever entertained anyone and he wanted to get things right.

'I'll pour if you like?' Kitty answered a little shyly. She was wondering what they would talk about and at what time he expected her to leave. It was rather daunting to sit and chat informally with your employer, she thought. She knew very little about him.

He watched her as she poured the tea carefully. She looked very attractive in that pink dress. She had good taste too: nothing loud or flashy and the little earrings suited her. He'd never seen her wear them before. She seemed perfectly at home here, he thought with affection as he took the cup and saucer from her and added milk and sugar.

'I see you have a wireless, Stanley. Do you listen to it a great deal?'

'I like the News and sometimes there are good plays in the evenings. I try to listen to the *Book at Bedtime* programme too, but I have to admit that quite often I fall asleep and so lose the thread of the story.'

She smiled at him over the rim of her cup. 'You must get very tired running between four shops, doing all the accounts and the ordering. Especially at this time of year.'

'I do, Kitty, but I enjoy my work. It's my life, you see, I've invested more than just money into the shops.'

'That must be very . . .' She searched for the right word. 'Satisfying.'

'It is but lately I've been thinking is it worth it? I have no one to leave it to.'

'Have you no brothers or sisters then?' she asked.

'No. Just a cousin and he lives on the south coast, in Dorset. We exchange Christmas cards, but that's all. I haven't seen him since we were children.'

Kitty nodded but thought it was rather sad. It wasn't that far away, not like New York.

'You have two sisters, I understand. In America?'

'I have so, in New York. They have both settled very well with my aunt and uncle. Better than I would have imagined. I was very upset when my da sent them away, as I knew I would never see them again. I don't get on with my da and stepmother. I have a step-brother too but he's only a small child. My stepmother was the reason we were all sent away from our home.'

He leaned forward in his chair. 'Why was that?' he asked. She looked upset and annoyed.

During the next few hours she told him all about herself and her family and her jobs first at Harwood Hall and then at the house in Aintree. But the one person she didn't mention was Niall Collins.

He thought she had coped very well with everything and said so. She smiled at him and apologised, saying she hoped she hadn't bored him to death.

'Not at all, Kitty. It's a very interesting if rather sad few years you've had to endure.'

She stood up, not wanting to wear out her welcome. 'I think I had better be going now, Stanley. I've taken up enough of your time and you've been very kind. I've enjoyed my visit and the tea.'

'Would you like to come again next Sunday? We could listen to the wireless.'

'Would you want to be bothered with me at all? It's getting near to Christmas and you'll need a day's rest.'

'I'd love you to come and I was thinking, Kitty, would you like to come and have some lunch with me on Christmas Day? There's no sense in us both sitting on our own, then of all times.'

Kitty's smile was one of pure pleasure. She had begun to dread having to sit alone in her little room on Christmas Day. 'I'd only be delighted, Stanley. I wasn't looking forward to it, if the truth be told.'

'Then that's settled and we'll have a most enjoyable time. Now let me get your coat and hat and I'll walk with you to the bottom of Orrell Lane. Sometimes there are some unsavoury types hanging around the Windsor Castle public house.'

'Sure, there's no need for you to be dragging out in

the cold, Stanley. I can catch a tram for just one stop if you're worried about me.'

'Then let me walk you to the tram stop, Kitty. It's the least a gentleman can do.'

Kitty nodded. No man had ever been as concerned for her welfare before. He was indeed a gentleman and she was looking forward to visiting again next Sunday.

Chapter Twenty-Three

Kitty had gone again the following Sunday and once more she had enjoyed her visit. As Christmas approached she found time to pay a very quick visit to Brierley's Gentlemen's Outfitters further along the road and bought three white handkerchiefs embroidered with the letter 'S', which they had wrapped nicely for her. She had to take him a little gift, she thought, in return for his hospitality. She wished she had both the time and a proper kitchen, then she could have baked some mince pies to take with her as a little contribution to the festive meal. Unfortunately she had neither, she thought ruefully.

She had asked him about the preparation and cooking of the festive meal. She couldn't expect him to do it all and wait on her, he was her employer, after all. He'd said he was used to cooking for himself, nothing fancy, of course, but she had insisted that she at least help with the cooking and serving, if not the preparation.

She was delighted when she arrived at his house on Christmas Day to find that he had put up a small tree.

'Isn't that a grand sight! When did you find the time? We have been rushed off our feet all week.'

'I brought it home last night.' He was pleased. He'd bought it and the decorations on his way home and even though he'd been exhausted he'd stayed up to make the effort and it had been worth it. Usually he didn't bother with a tree; he made do with a few sprigs of holly stuck over the mirror above the fireplace.

'I brought you a little gift.' Kitty held out the packet.

He blushed with pleasure. How kind of her to spend her money on him. 'Thank you, Kitty. You're very thoughtful.' He opened it carefully, smoothing and folding the wrapping paper and placing it on the table. 'They're very good quality and they have my initial on them too.' She had gone to so much trouble. He bit his lip and looked embarrassed. He hadn't thought to get her anything. 'I'm afraid I haven't got you anything. It's very remiss of me to be so mean-spirited.'

She smiled at him. 'Sure, didn't you get the lovely little tree and aren't you giving me my dinner too?

That's more than enough, Stanley. I bought those as a thank you.'

She really meant it; she wasn't upset. He smiled at her. 'And talking of dinner, I'd better go into the kitchen and see how it's doing. Help yourself to a glass of sherry, Kitty, and I think I'll have one too.'

'I'll do that, Stanley, and I'll bring them into the kitchen so I can help you. I did promise I'd help.'

She poured two glasses from the decanter that stood on a tray on the sideboard and sipped the sweet liquid. There had always been decanters of sherry, whiskey and port in the drawing rooms of both Harwood Hall and the house in Aintree but she'd never touched them. She'd not tried sherry before and she wrinkled her nose. It was rather sickly, she thought. Still, she was being treated as an honoured guest so she would drink it and not pull faces.

She had to admit that it was a very good dinner and there was a plum pudding and mince pies to follow. Shop-bought, he'd admitted with regret, he wasn't much good at baking. They'd listened to the wireless, which she had found fascinating, and they'd played cards and he'd shown her all the stamps he had collected. She had feigned great interest but she couldn't for the life of her see what was so enthralling about postage stamps, although he was engrossed. He'd pointed out a few that were rare and therefore worth quite a lot of money, but as they'd already been used once and couldn't be stuck on a letter again, she couldn't quite understand why.

At six o'clock she said she had thoroughly enjoyed the day that was in it but she had better be getting home. He felt disappointed as he'd hoped she would stay until at least eight. He too had enjoyed the day; it was such a change to have pleasant company and he was loath to see her go. How much more like a home the house had seemed: it made him realise just how much he missed having a family.

'Can I prevail upon you to come to tea tomorrow, Kitty? Of course I don't want to put pressure on you if you'd rather not or if you have something you need to do, but it's been such a pleasure having your company.' He meant it. She seemed to bring warmth and happiness into his life.

She didn't know what to say. There was nothing else she had to do on Boxing Day, as they called St Stephen's Day over here, but would it seem a bit bold?

'And there is all that food left. Such a shame to let it go to waste,' he added.

She nodded. 'Waste not, want not. My mam always used to say it was wicked to throw food away when there are people starving. Will half past three suit?'

'Make it three o'clock and perhaps if it's a fine day we could go for a walk first? Now I'll walk with you tonight and no arguments,' he said firmly, holding out her coat.

He'd seen her safely home and when he returned he thought how silent the house was. Her presence had seemed to bring the place to life. He looked around. That was what the house needed: a woman's touch; the sound of cheerful voices and laughter. The more he saw of her the more he realised that she would be the perfect companion. He went upstairs to his bedroom and took out a small box of polished wood inlaid with ivory and mother-of-pearl. It contained his mother's few pieces of jewellery. He took out a ring and held it up to the light. The three diamonds sparkled. It had been his mother's engagement ring and he had made up his mind to ask Kitty to marry him tomorrow.

Kitty thought the neighbours must be thinking of her as a more than regular visitor as she went up the path the following afternoon, but she shrugged the thought away. Everyone had visitors at Christmas and it was better than sitting on her own, but she did hope the stamp albums would remain unopened today. She had carefully peeled the stamp from Bridget's last letter though, thinking that maybe he would like to have it.

They had gone for a short walk and then had tea and listened to the wireless and she was relieved that although he thanked her for the stamp and placed it carefully in an envelope, the albums hadn't been brought out. It did seem as though there was something bothering him, however, although she couldn't think what it was. Maybe it was a problem with the new shop? She insisted on clearing away the dishes and decided to ask.

'You seem a bit preoccupied, Stanley. Is it something to do with the shop in Walton Village?'

He'd been trying to find a way to broach the subject all through tea but hadn't found the right opportunity. 'No, everything is fine there. I'm very pleased. Business was very good. But I do have something I'd like to ask . . . say to you, Kitty.' He felt a knot of apprehension in his stomach and his mouth was suddenly dry.

'What is it?' she asked.

'Kitty, I . . . I've got to know you much better over the last weeks and in fact I've become quite . . . er . . . fond of you. I know I am much older than you but . . . but would you consider marrying me?' There, it was out. He'd done it.

She was utterly dumbfounded.

He rushed on. 'We get on well together, I'm a temperate man, I'm not short of money and this is a large house. You wouldn't want for anything, Kitty, I promise. Could you possibly . . . consider it?'

'Stanley, I . . . I don't know what to say, sure I don't!

You've been kindness itself to me but . . . marriage?'
She gripped the back of a chair to steady herself.

'I'm not expecting you to say you . . . love me,
Kitty. But . . . but perhaps you could come to in time,
and even if that's not possible affection would do.' He
fingered the ring in his pocket. Was he being too
forceful? Was he rushing things?

'Stanley, I . . . I don't love you. I have to be
truthful,' she stammered. She remembered what it felt
like to be in love; the way she had felt when Niall had
held her and kissed her.

'I wouldn't expect anything else from you, Kitty.
You are a very honest person.'

She was trying to gather her scattered wits. Should
she refuse him this minute, dismiss it out of hand?
Would she be throwing everything away if she did?
Oh, what a dilemma! What a terrible position he had
put her in! she thought. He had been good to her but
she'd never expected *this*! 'Could I . . . could I have
some time to *think* about it, Stanley, please? It's
very . . . sudden,' she at last managed to ask.

'Of course, Kitty. Take as much time as you need,
I won't press you. I know it's a big decision.' At least
she hadn't said an emphatic 'no'. There was at least
hope, and now he realised that his affection for her
was growing and he prayed she wouldn't turn him
down.

She felt a little calmer although still shocked. 'I'll let you know before New Year's Eve, I promise.'

He managed a smile. 'Thank you, Kitty, and I do sincerely hope that the new year will bring us both . . . happiness.'

She lay awake for the next three nights, tossing and turning. She didn't love him, and he was so much older than her. She had loved Niall but he was lost to her for ever – and had he even loved her at all? Niall's betrayal still hurt and she still felt bereft at the way she had been forced from her home and separated from her sisters. She had looked on Harwood Hall as a home too and she'd been brought from there to this country and then abandoned by the Harwoods. She longed for some security, loyalty and certainty in her life and Stanley would give her all three. He was a good, kind friend and she was comfortable with him but marriage was for a lifetime – until death us do part: could she commit herself for all that time? But what kind of future did she have at all? Would she always be alone, ending her days as an old maid? Never having anyone to care for her, always having to work to support herself and never having a child of her own? It was a bleak and depressing vision. Stanley was kind and considerate, he had said she would never want for anything and she would have a comfortable life. Maybe she *would* grow fond of him in time, it wasn't unheard of. She was torn by indecision and doubt and fear but she had promised him an answer so she would have to make up her mind. She had no one she could turn to for advice. Tina had sailed, Tess was thousands of miles away as were Annie and Bridget. She had lost contact with Mrs O'Shea and her father couldn't care less about her. She had heard nothing at all from him for a year. Her Aunt Julia was dead and Aunt Enid didn't really know anything about her. She tried to think what her mam would have advised but any thought of her mother only made her more confused. She just didn't know what to do.

Stanley had stayed away from the shop when they reopened after the holiday and she was thankful but she knew she was fast running out of time. Her head ached constantly and she felt exhausted and irritable but at last she reached a decision. She would accept him. She couldn't face a lifetime of loneliness and despair. Marriage couldn't possibly be worse than that.

Once she'd made up her mind she felt better, much calmer and strangely grown up. Looking back she realised she'd never been a giddy or frivolous girl. In fact, she thought sadly, her youth had been over the day her mam had died. She wasn't yet twenty but she felt thirty. Because she hadn't yet reached her majority she would need her father's permission although she couldn't see that he would object. She would write to him immediately she had given Stanley her answer; perhaps he would enclose a brief note too. Stanley. Stanley Ellinson would be her husband. She would be Mrs Ellinson. Once she had hoped to be Mrs Collins but that flimsy, fanciful hope had been dashed. Better to be Mrs Ellinson than Miss Doyle. At least she would be cared for and well respected.

Stanley was so overcome with delight and relief when she told him she would marry him that tears brimmed in his eyes and he was unable to speak. Instead he clasped her hand tightly and nodded.

'I'll have to have my da's permission, Stanley. I won't be twenty-one for another year. Would you like to write, too?'

He recovered his composure. 'Yes, of course, Kitty. It's only right that I do to assure him that I will look after you and that I can afford to support you and give you a good life.' He delved into his pocket and drew out the ring. 'Will you wear this, Kitty? It belonged to my mother.'

'It's beautiful and I'll be proud to wear it but not for work, of course, it's much too good.'

He slipped it on to her finger and she smiled. 'I'm after thinking it will have to be made smaller or I'll lose it.'

'That's easily arranged and shall we set a date? Will

your father and stepmother wish to come over?'

'No! I don't want them here, Stanley.' She was adamant.

He nodded, he could understand.

'I don't think we should have a long engagement, do you?' She didn't want to wait months; she might change her mind.

'No, there's no need to wait. As soon as the banns are called we can go ahead.'

'Then shall we say the beginning of February? I'll ask Violet to be my bridesmaid, I can't think of anyone else. Tina won't be back until October but I'll write and tell her. She left me the shipping agent's address in Manaus.'

He nodded. 'I'll have to find someone to replace you, Kitty, but it won't be easy. There'll be no need for you to work after we are married.'

She felt a little disappointed but people would talk if she carried on working: they would say he could more than afford to keep a wife. But she would miss chatting to the customers. 'Of course, but perhaps I should try to train Violet. She's a sensible girl and could manage until you found someone with more experience.'

'You let me worry about things like that, Kitty. I'll make all the necessary arrangements.'

*

Kitty was surprised how quickly the time went. There seemed so many things to do. Besides working in the shop all day, she had to pack up her belongings in the rooms above it. She had written to Annie and Bridget and to Tina and to her father, and Violet had been delighted to be asked not only to stand for her but also to go with her to buy her wedding outfit.

She had chosen a cream dress and because it was winter she had decided to buy a tan wool coat, edged with cream braid, to go over it. A clutch bag in tan leather, matching shoes and gloves and a cream cloche hat completed the ensemble. Violet had asked had she not wanted the traditional long white wedding dress and veil but she had replied that they wanted a quiet affair, so the coat and dress were more suitable and she would get good wear out of them.

It was a dull, blustery day when she and Violet arrived at St Peter's Church. There was only the Reverend Platt, Mr Spinks the verger, Stanley and his best man awaiting their arrival. Both she and Violet carried small posies of early spring flowers.

'You look lovely, Kitty. Very smart and elegant,' Stanley greeted her, smiling.

She smiled back, feeling a little nervous and apprehensive. Annie and Bridget had sent a lovely card which had arrived in the early post that morning and to Bridget's neatly written message wishing her every joy and happiness, Annie had added that it did seem a pity it was to be such a quiet affair with no long white dress. It had caused her a moment's reflection on how different things might have been had she been marrying Niall at home in Ireland. She had resolutely pushed the thought away. She was doing the right thing, she *knew* she was. She wanted security and peace of mind and someone loyal and reliable to look after her, always, and Stanley was that person. She passed her posy to Violet and took his hand. In just a few minutes she would be Mrs Stanley Ellinson.

Chapter Twenty-Four

KITTY PULLED BACK THE curtains in the bedroom and frowned. Heavy flakes of snow were falling from grey clouds that were laden with yet more snow. She shivered, pulling her warm dressing gown more closely around her. Beyond the window the garden and the other houses in Osterley Gardens were cloaked in a blanket of snow. It looked quite pretty but it made life more complicated. Transport would be disrupted, walking was difficult and people did not want to venture out. Only the children took great pleasure and enjoyment from the snow-covered streets. Today was her birthday. She was twenty-one years old and she had been married for almost twelve months.

Stanley had been up for over an hour, she thought, turning away from the window. He rose early summer or winter but had urged her not to get up to see to his breakfast, as she usually did, not when it was so bitterly cold and her birthday to boot. She looked longingly at the comfortable warm bed then sighed. It wasn't fair on him for her to be lying in bed while he lit the fires downstairs, boiled the kettle and made breakfast.

She got dressed, pulling her clothes on quickly for the room was icy cold. There had been a fire in the small fireplace last night but it had long since gone out. She sat at the walnut dressing table to brush her hair and saw how pale she was; there were dark circles under her eyes too. She also thought she looked far older than her years. She certainly felt older.

She hadn't found marriage easy. Oh, he was a kind and generous man but he was so dull, so set in his ways, so serious. And he was so utterly predictable. He was quite happy as long as his life ran like clockwork. He had a rigid routine, which he insisted on sticking to, and became quite cross when it was disrupted, as she had found out on a few occasions. When she looked ahead, the future didn't seem even mildly exciting. They never went anywhere, except for a walk on a Sunday afternoon if the weather was fine. She would have liked to have gone occasionally to the cinema or even a dance but his life revolved around the shops. Sometimes she wondered was he interested in anything else at all other than work? He always asked when he returned home each evening, 'How was your day, Kitty?' but she knew he wasn't really interested. She would answer with the obligatory, 'Just grand, Stanley. And how was yours?' which gave him the opportunity to describe it in great detail. Detail which was becoming extremely tedious and hard to bear. She was convinced that he simply did not know how to enjoy himself, that it wasn't a priority in his life at all. He made few demands on her sexually, which didn't really upset her. She had found his fumblings embarrassing.

She sighed. She really shouldn't complain. She was lucky to have such an easy life. She stood up but felt giddy and sick and caught the edge of the dressing table to steady herself. She was pregnant and she knew she was going to have to tell him soon. She wondered how he would take the news. Babies totally disrupted your life; she knew that from having younger sisters. He was an only child. The nausea was passing and so she decided to go downstairs.

'You should have stayed in bed until this room warmed up, Kitty.' Stanley was sitting at the table with his breakfast, a copy of the *Grocer's Gazette* open on the table beside him.

'I was wide awake so I thought I'd get up. I feel dreadfully lazy lying in bed.'

He smiled at her. 'It's your birthday and it's a special birthday, too. Many happy returns and congratulations on coming of age, Kitty.' He pushed a small package across the table towards her.

She sat down and opened it. Inside was a leather box and inside that was a gold cross on a fine gold chain. 'Thank you, Stanley, it's really beautiful. Will you put it on for me?' It was very pretty and it was the first piece of jewellery he had bought her. Everything else she had, including her wedding ring, had belonged to his mother.

'Don't you think it would be better to save it for a special occasion?' he asked cautiously.

She frowned, looking a little puzzled. What did he mean? Did he intend to take her somewhere this evening, as a celebration?

'I mean like church on Easter Sunday or Christmas.'

The hope died. She nodded. 'I have a surprise for you too, Stanley. You know I haven't been feeling very well these last few weeks, well, I'm going to the doctor's today—'

He looked alarmed. 'It's nothing serious, is it, Kitty?' he interrupted.

'Not at all. I'm going to have a baby.'

The look of incredulity that had come over his face gave way to delight. 'Oh, Kitty! That's wonderful news!' He had been hoping that she would conceive, that he would have a son and heir, but he had begun to have some doubts. They had been married for nearly a year and although she was young and healthy, up to now . . . He reached across the table and took her hand.

'When?'

'I think about the beginning of May.' She was so relieved by his obvious delight. 'But the doctor will give me a more accurate date.'

'You will have to take care of yourself now, Kitty. You must get plenty of rest and eat sensibly. Let me know what we need and I'll have it all delivered. I don't want you going out in weather like this, you may slip and fall.'

'Stanley, the exercise will do me good. I'm not an invalid.' She was loath to give up doing her own shopping. Even though he had often suggested the groceries be delivered, she enjoyed going out. It was the only time she ever had chance to chat with people. 'And we'll have to think of a cot and a pram and baby clothes. I thought I might take a trip to Frost's on County Road, they stock things like that. Or maybe the shops in town.'

'Not yet, Kitty. Wait until the weather gets better,' he urged.

'Would you like to come with me?' she asked. He might enjoy helping to choose a pram and a cot.

'I'll leave things like that to you, my dear, besides I

don't have time.' He glanced at the clock on the mantelshelf. 'And speaking of time, I really must go now. Take things easy today and be very careful walking to the doctor's.' He was shrugging on his overcoat.

Kitty got up and fetched his scarf and hat and gloves. 'I will. I'll see you this evening, Stanley.'

He kissed her on the cheek as he always did and left.

She sat down again and poured herself a cup of tea. In five months' time, all being well, she would have a child of her own. The thought brought a great surge of joy rushing through her. Her baby. Someone who would love her, really love her, for she doubted Stanley knew the meaning of the word. A child who would depend on her for so much. It would have the best of everything, she vowed, and then at last there would be laughter and joy in this house. Things that it sadly lacked. There would be birthday parties and such excitement at Christmas. For the first time since her marriage she felt really happy, young and more *alive*.

Dr Lipman confirmed that she was indeed pregnant and congratulated her sincerely. 'I'll get in touch with Mrs Caldwell, the midwife, she'll come and visit you and advise you of everything you will need. You'll be having your confinement at home, I presume.'

Kitty nodded although she hadn't really thought about it.

'And I will want to see you regularly for check-ups. Now, I recommend gentle exercise, healthy eating with plenty of liver, a good source of iron, and green vegetables and fruit. The morning sickness should pass soon. A little rest of an afternoon might help too. Mr Ellinson is delighted, I take it?'

'Yes, of course.'

'Then I'd like to see you in four weeks' time but if you have any pain or bleeding you must go straight to bed and call me.'

Kitty nodded and rose. 'Thank you, doctor.'

'Take care on your way home, Mrs Ellinson. The pavements are treacherous.'

Kitty paid him and left.

The snow had almost stopped, just a few flakes now fell, but she walked slowly and carefully back to Osterley Gardens, her head full of dreams and plans. There were plenty of bedrooms in the house, they could make one into a nursery with pretty wallpaper and curtains and a nursing chair. When she was due summer would be on its way and she would go for long walks with the baby in the pram. She'd have a canopy for the pram to keep off the sun and a lace-edged pram set. She'd take the tram to County Road on Saturday, the roads should be better by then. She felt fine, perfectly healthy and very happy.

When she arrived home she found her neighbour

Nancy Williams clearing the snow from her path.

'It's treacherous underfoot, Kitty. I know it all looks very pretty but it does make the pavements dangerous,' she called, leaning on the handle of the broom.

'Ah, sure, it's not too bad, Nancy.'

'Have you been shopping?' Nancy asked amiably.

Kitty shook her head. She was so delighted with herself that she was bursting to tell someone her news. 'The doctor's surgery. I'm . . . expecting.'

Nancy's face lit up with a smile. 'Congratulations! Come on in and we'll have a cup of tea to celebrate, unless you'd prefer a little drop of sweet sherry?'

Kitty laughed. 'Tea will do just fine, thanks.'

'Wait until I tell our Gloria, she loves children. If ever you're stuck for someone to mind the baby our Gloria will be delighted,' Nancy offered on behalf of her young daughter.

Kitty thanked her although she couldn't envisage a situation where she would need the girl's help. Gloria was at work all day and she and Stanley never went out at night. Still, it would be comforting to have someone like Nancy Williams to confide in during the coming months, she thought as she followed her neighbour into the kitchen.

*

She had tidied up and made a steak and kidney pie for supper and had changed out of the clothes she wore for her domestic chores. She had a wash and put on her dark green wool skirt and the cream twin-set edged with green that matched it so well. She didn't have a vast wardrobe of clothes but those she did have were good and stylish, although she realised that soon most of them wouldn't fit her. She'd have to add maternity smocks to her shopping list.

As usual the supper was ready, the table was set, the fire made up and the curtains tightly closed against the weather when she heard his key in the front door.

'I left a little early as the trams are not running to time at all and business was very slow all day,' he informed her, holding his hands out to the blaze of the fire. 'How was your day, Kitty?'

'I went to see Dr Lipman this afternoon and he confirmed it. Mrs Caldwell, the midwife, will call to see me to advise me on everything.'

He nodded. 'Did he say he would organise the hospital?'

She was startled. 'Hospital? I'm going to have the baby here, at home, Stanley. I'm perfectly fit and well, the doctor said so, there's no need for hospital. Sure, it's only if there's any danger of complications that you have to go to hospital.' She had never in fact heard of anyone having a baby in hospital. Her mam had had them all at home and so had everyone else, even Hester. Even after she'd miscarried Hester hadn't gone to hospital.

He looked anxious. 'I just thought it would be less . . . disruptive and more comfortable for you.'

Less disruptive for you, she thought with a dart of annoyance. 'I'll get the supper,' she said and left the room.

After the meal they sat by the fire and she hoped he wouldn't go into more detail about how slow business had been today. 'I thought I would go along to Frost's on Saturday. The roads should be better by then – the snow might even have gone. I thought we could have a room done up as a nursery?'

He frowned. 'Do you think that is really necessary?'

'Of course the baby will be in with us for a good while but people do put them in their own rooms, if they have the space. Not that we did, I always had to share with Annie and Bridget. Elizabeth Harwood was the only person I knew of who had always had her own room.'

'I was thinking today, Kitty. Do you think you should write to your father and tell him the good news? I mean, it's only polite to let him know he is going to be a grandfather.'

Kitty didn't reply. She had no wish to contact her da at all. She had received just one letter from him, giving his permission for her marriage and wishing her well. Bridget had written that he had been very impressed with the letter Stanley had included. He was pleased that Kitty was marrying so well, she had done far better for herself than he could have imagined and he had urged both Bridget and Annie to follow her example when the time came, and not marry a 'waster or a blackguard'. Annie had been highly indignant, Bridget wrote, thinking he was referring to Davie. Both her sisters had congratulated her but had expressed the opinion that they hoped this Stanley Ellinson wouldn't be too *old* for Kitty. She had smiled at that at the time.

'I'll write to Annie and Bridget and no doubt they'll let him know but, sure, I doubt he'll be delighted, nor Hester either. They'll have no wish to see our child,' she said firmly, thinking how different things would have been if her mam had been told she was going to be a granny. But then if Mam had lived she probably wouldn't have even been in Liverpool, let alone have married Stanley Ellinson.

'Whatever you think best, Kitty,' he answered, twiddling the knobs on the wireless set.

Chapter Twenty-Five

HER PREGNANCY HAD BEEN uneventful and people said she had blossomed. Stanley had been most attentive and considerate, even moving into one of the spare bedrooms when she became uncomfortable and restless in the latter weeks. She had found Mrs Caldwell, the midwife, a great comfort. She was a down-to-earth, practical woman with years of experience who answered all her questions truthfully and bolstered her spirits when she became very apprehensive as her confinement drew closer. In the end she had had a relatively easy birth after seven hours of labour. She had been very grateful though that Dr Lipman had attended too, it had been very reassuring.

'There we are, Kitty. A fine, healthy boy and with a strong pair of lungs, too,' Mrs Caldwell had announced, placing the baby in her arms.

Kitty had been exhausted but happier than she had ever been in her life as she stroked the tiny, red and wrinkled cheek with something akin to sheer wonder. This tiny scrap of humanity was hers! A surge of protective love had washed over her.

Stanley had been called in and had looked as proud as Punch when the doctor had shaken his hand and congratulated him heartily.

'I have two boys of my own, Mr Ellinson, and they can be a bit of a handful at times but I wouldn't be without them,' Dr Lipman had confided, beaming at both Kitty and Stanley. 'What are you going to call him?' he'd asked.

'Edward Stanley Joseph,' Kitty had replied, smiling tiredly at her husband. He had suggested the child be called Thomas Stanley Joseph after Kitty's father, himself and his father but Kitty had refused point blank to have him called after her da and stepbrother and he had reluctantly acquiesced.

In the weeks that had followed Edward Ellinson had proved to have a very healthy pair of lungs indeed. He was a colicky baby and Kitty was worn out and irritable. Stanley had had no idea at all just how much of a difference a baby would make to the household and to his ordered life. His sleep was broken, his meals were often late, and the tidiness of his home was a thing of the past. The house seemed to have been completely filled with all the requisites for a baby, which he viewed with great consternation. Surely such a tiny thing didn't need such a vast array of bottles, nappies, clothes, bedding, a pram, a crib and a cot, he had remarked rather testily to Kitty upon returning home to find only cold cuts and cheese and bread for his supper. Clean nappies had been draped over the fireguard, steaming gently and blocking the heat from the room. A pile of clean baby clothes had been folded and lay on the sofa, waiting to be put away, and worst of all there had been no clean shirts that morning. Kitty had always run the house so efficiently that he had taken it for granted that there were always clean shirts hanging in his wardrobe. It was all very annoying, he'd thought.

Kitty had lost her temper, worn out with trying to keep up with the housework, the washing and the cooking with a fractious and constantly wailing baby in her arms. She was the one who got up with him in the night to feed and change him and then try to get him back to sleep. 'I thought you were delighted with him? You wanted a son and heir to leave the shops to, isn't that what you told me?' she snapped. 'Sure, I sometimes wonder if it's the only reason you married me, that and being your unpaid housekeeper!'

Stanley realised he had been tactless and apologised. She was just as tired as he was and she had to put up with the child crying all day too. These days he was glad to spend his days in his well-ordered shops.

Some really beautiful clothes had arrived from Annie and Bridget, who urged her to have Edward's photograph taken and send it to them, although she wondered when she would ever get the time to do that. There was hardly any time to scribble a few lines to them.

June was hot and sultry which didn't help, she thought as she climbed out of bed after yet another sleepless night and drew the curtains. Bright sunlight streamed into the room and she blinked. The heat affected Edward, bringing him out in a rash even though she only dressed him in a vest and a nappy, which was covered by a pair of plastic pants. They didn't help much either, making him sweat, but there was no help for it.

She picked him up from the crib and gave him a cuddle. 'Sure, when are you going to sleep all night for your mammy?' she asked, smiling tiredly down at him. He had her eyes but apart from that he was a miniature version of Stanley. 'Come downstairs and Mammy will give you a nice wash, your milk and then a clean nappy.'

Stanley raised himself up on one elbow. 'What time is it?' he muttered.

'Just after half past six. You don't have to get up just yet. I'm taking Edward downstairs.'

He grunted and lay down, thankful for another half an hour's sleep.

By mid-morning Kitty was bathed in perspiration. The kitchen was stifling and her arms were aching from all the washing and rinsing. The baby was asleep in his pram in a shady corner of the garden and she was trying to catch up with her housework while he slept. Wiping her hands on her apron she muttered a curse under her breath as she heard the knock on the front door.

Mrs Caldwell was standing on the step. 'How are things, Kitty? I thought I'd just drop in and see how you are coping. Has he settled down since my last visit?'

'Come on in. He's asleep in his pram in the garden and I'm trying to catch up.' She ushered the midwife through into the kitchen.

The older woman glanced around. 'Put the kettle on, Kitty, and have a bit of a break, you look as though you need it.'

Kitty nodded and filled the kettle.

'You look worn out, girl. Is he still giving you a hard time of it?'

'Do you mean Edward or Stanley?' Kitty asked with sarcasm.

'Oh, dear. I take it Mr Ellinson is finding it hard to accept the changes?'

Kitty nodded, busying herself with the teapot and cups.

'Why don't you take Edward to see Dr Lipman? I'm sure there is something he can give him for the colic, although he will grow out of it, believe me. You could ask him for a tonic for yourself too. It might help.'

Kitty poured the tea and sat down opposite her. 'Even I didn't think it would be this hard. My mam had three of us and she seemed to cope perfectly well.'

'Kitty, this is your first baby and you are naturally anxious and a bit over-protective. Once he's over this patch and more settled things will gradually get back to something approaching normal.'

'Stanley hates things not running to plan, his plan.'

The midwife sipped her tea. 'It's his child too, Kitty, but it's often hard for older men when they become fathers for the first time.'

'I know and I'm not criticising him, really. He works very hard all day and I suppose he's entitled to a decent meal on the table, a clean shirt each morning and a good night's sleep.'

'And he'll get all three, it will just take a little time. Tell him that, Kitty. Tell him I said so and I've plenty of experience in these things. And while you are so exhausted it would do you good to have a little rest when Edward is asleep, instead of running around like a headless chicken trying to do everything and wearing yourself out still further. I'm sure in this hot weather Mr Ellinson wouldn't mind cold meat and salad. He'll not waste away and if you go on like this you *will* and then where would both he and the baby be? Perhaps he could get you a bit of help, temporarily? Someone to do a bit of cleaning and the washing and ironing?'

Kitty looked doubtful. She wasn't sure Stanley would understand.

'It's worth a try, Kitty. You're going to make yourself ill if you go on like this.'

'I'll mention it tonight and I will go and see the doctor.'

The midwife finished her tea and stood up. 'Good. I'll call next week to see how you are. Now, I'll just go and have a peep at Edward, I won't wake him.'

Kitty saw her to the door, vowing to take her advice. At least she could suggest it and if he agreed she would be very grateful.

Dr Lipman was most sympathetic and gave her a bottle of medicine for Edward and a tonic for herself but she felt very weary as she pushed the baby home in his pram.

The post was lying on the floor in the hall. She

picked it up and frowned. There was a letter from Ireland and no one wrote to her from home. She knew Bridget had informed her father that he had become a grandfather. Was this a letter of congratulation? She hoped not. She looked closely at the envelope: it wasn't da's handwriting. Was it from Emer or Mrs O'Shea, she wondered? But how could it be, they didn't know her address. She took it through with her to the kitchen, after lifting Edward from his pram. It was nearly four o'clock and he would need feeding soon, so she'd see to him first and she'd give him a spoonful of medicine as the doctor had directed.

To her relief he seemed far more settled as she put him in his crib. Usually he screwed up his little face and began to wail, drawing his legs up in pain. Now he lay quietly on his back, waving his tiny fists in the air and watching her as she attached the little blue and white pompoms suspended on a piece of blue ribbon to the top of the crib.

She quickly cleared and then reset the table. She washed the lettuce, tomatoes, radishes and watercress and sliced the cucumber. She put them all in a large bowl and covered it with a clean tea cloth and placed it in the larder on the marble slab. Later she'd cut the ham and tongue and the bread and butter. With any luck, when Stanley arrived home it would be to a sleeping son and an attractive-looking meal and she would be able to mention that Mrs Caldwell had suggested they get someone to help. There was still a mound of washing and ironing but she was just too hot and tired to tackle either and the room was far from tidy.

She picked up the letter and opened it slowly. It was from Hester. Her father was very ill, she wrote, he wasn't expected to recover. He had been delighted to learn that he was a grandfather but now it was upsetting him that he would never see his grandson, or Kitty. Kitty set her lips in a tight line. It wasn't upsetting him that he would never see Annie or Bridget. What did he expect her to do? Drag herself and a young baby all the way back to Rahan? Did he expect Stanley to take them?

She returned to the letter. Hester wrote that she was at her wits' end, trying to cope with young Thomas and her second son William and the fact that she would be left a widow. The forge would have to close; there was nothing else she could do. It would be years and years before either of her sons could run it and they might not even want to. There was no one else she felt trustworthy and efficient enough to run it in the meantime.

So, what does she expect me to do about it? Kitty thought angrily. Is she expecting me to go back and help her out? She was quick enough to get rid of us, so she can just get on with it, Kitty determined. She wasn't even sure she would reply.

Stanley was quite surprised when he arrived home. He was hot and weary and had expected a cross baby and a cross wife and no meal. Instead there was an appetising-looking salad and cold meat, with bread and butter and even some scones. Edward was asleep in his crib and even Kitty looked less pale and tired.

'This is very nice, Kitty. How was your day?'

'Not as bad as usual, although I did receive a letter from my stepmother.' She poured him a cup of tea as he sat down.

He looked at her with mild curiosity. 'Not your father?'

'No. He's very ill. Hester says he isn't expected to recover.'

'Oh, Kitty, I'm so sorry. You'll be going over to see him?'

She shook her head. 'I don't think so. It's such a long journey and I can't leave Edward. Besides, Hester seems to think she has the right to ask me to go and help her out. She seems to forget all the heartbreak she caused myself and Annie and Bridget.'

'But, Kitty, he is still your father! You must go and make your peace with him before it's too late. You'll be sorry if you don't. He had his reasons for sending you all away, even if I don't agree with them. You *must* go.

I insist. Take Edward with you. I'm sure your father would like to see him.'

'You think it's going to be an easy matter for me to take a baby that young all the way to Offaly?' Kitty was surprised by the firmness in his tone.

'I'd come with you if I could but you know it's impossible. I'll book the ferry. Is it possible to book your seats on the train and arrange for transport to meet you? You will travel first class, that will make things easier.'

'I suppose you could book the ferry but I can't see how you could organise the train and transport.' Kitty was realising that she would have to go and she was becoming resigned to it. He *was* her father and he was dying. No matter what he'd done in the past, she would have to go and see him now.

'Send a telegram to your stepmother and ask her to arrange the travel over there.' Stanley was very good at organisation. To him it was a simple matter.

'From her letter Hester seems to be in such a state that she couldn't organise a tea party.'

'There must be someone who could help her?'

Kitty thought hard. 'I suppose the Reverend Joyce would do it.'

'Then suggest it. You word it and I'll send it off first thing in the morning and I'll book the ferry. When can you be ready?'

Kitty stared at him. He was very eager for her to go and she was certain it wasn't entirely to do with her da's condition. She sighed. He was probably thinking he'd get a bit of peace and quiet with herself and the baby gone. There was no point in her mentioning the midwife's visit now. 'By Saturday and how long should I stay?'

'Stay for as long as you are needed, Kitty. Who knows how long the poor man has left.'

'I'm not going to stay for months, Stanley! I'm not going to be a skivvy for *her*! I have enough with Edward to take care of. I'll stay for two weeks, three at most, and that's my final word on the matter.'

Chapter Twenty-Six

THE JOURNEY HADN'T BEEN as bad as she'd expected it to be. The weather continued fine and warm and people were very kind and helpful, but most of all the medicine seemed to be working wonders for Edward was a far quieter and more contented baby. It had helped that she had travelled first class in a cabin and as she'd lain, drifting into sleep, she had thought of the last time she had made this journey. She had been coming with Elizabeth to start a new life, thinking she would never see Ireland again. Now she was going back as a wife and mother to a house she had sworn she would never enter again.

It was the Reverend Joyce himself who was waiting at Tullamore Station when she alighted from the train. Hester had sent a telegram saying she would contact him but there had been no mention that he would meet her in person.

'Kitty, I'm so glad you have come.' He took her bags and ushered her to where his pony and trap were tied up. She looked tired, he thought, but wasn't that only to be expected? She looked so much older too, but of course she hadn't had an easy life and now she had the responsibilities of a husband and baby. 'Your father will be so delighted to see you both. He's very ill, I'm afraid. A tumour on the spine. It appeared suddenly after Christmas although he said nothing until he became too ill to work and Hester called in the doctor.' He shook his head sadly.

Holding Edward firmly Kitty let the Reverend help her up. 'And now she says she can't cope.'

He didn't miss the note of bitterness in her tone. 'Ah, Kitty, I know you dislike her but can't you put all that aside for the moment?'

Kitty said nothing but fussed over Edward, making sure the strong sun wasn't in his face.

'How long will you be staying? Your husband must be a very considerate man,' Reverend Joyce ventured, not wishing to pursue the subject of the relationship between Kitty and Hester Doyle.

'He is but I can't expect him to fend for himself for ever. Three weeks is the longest I can manage.'

He nodded. He doubted Thomas Doyle would last

longer than a week. 'Mrs Joyce has been down at the forge with young Mary Wrafter, helping Hester to get things ready for your arrival.'

'Sure, that was very good of her.' Kitty wondered just what kind of a state the place must have been in if Hester needed the help of the Reverend's wife and maid.

He asked about Stanley and his business and about Bridget and Annie as they drove down the country lanes towards Rahan. Despite her reluctance to stay with her stepmother in what was her old home and the trepidation she felt on having to see her father on what she now knew was his deathbed, she couldn't help her spirits rising as she gazed across the green fields and the hedgerows, all so quiet and peaceful under the blue sky and summer sun. Overhead the leaves of the trees rustled in a gentle breeze. As they crossed the narrow stone bridge over the Grand Canal she looked along the bank: the reeds were tall and green and splashes of yellow and pink and cream indicated where the wild flowers grew. She glimpsed a flash of bright turquoise feathers and smiled. You would never see a kingfisher in Liverpool.

As they passed the gates of Harwood Hall Kitty peered intently up the drive. 'Is it still shut up and empty?'

'It is indeed and beginning to look rather forlorn

and neglected. Mr Henry Harwood is desperate to find a buyer but so far no one wants to take it on.'

Kitty was curious. 'Is it still furnished?'

'No. A few things were shipped across to England but the rest went for auction. Such a shame to see it all sold for half of nothing but then there isn't much money around, Kitty. Times are very hard, but at least the country is peaceful now, thank God. So many have died, some have been executed by the Free State government and others are in prison, including Mr de Valera, although there are hopes they will all soon be released.'

Kitty nodded and they travelled the rest of the way in silence.

They drew up in the yard behind the forge and Kitty thought how much smaller it now seemed than when she had been a child. The Reverend helped her down as his wife appeared in the doorway.

'Kitty, welcome back. You must be exhausted. Come inside out of the heat. Is this your son?' She smiled, peering closely at Edward.

Kitty had always liked her. She was a very homely woman and not at all prim as some clergymen's wives were. 'Yes, this is Edward and he has been so good. I was worried he would be as cross as a bag of cats all the way.'

'He's a fine child, Kitty. He has your eyes.'

Kitty smiled. 'But he's his da's son all right. He's very like Stanley.'

The kitchen looked neat and tidy and there was no sign of her two young stepbrothers. Hester was making the tea and as her gaze rested on her stepmother Kitty felt the bitterness rise up in her. This had been *her* home and this woman had been responsible for driving her from it and her poor sisters too.

'It was good of you to come, Kitty. He's been asking all morning what time you would arrive.'

Kitty stared at her in silence, shocked by the change in the woman. She was thin and haggard and she looked worn out. Her clothes looked grubby and creased and her hair needed washing.

'Sure, how could I not come, Hester? He's my da when all is said and done,' she said quietly.

'I'll put Kitty's things in her room,' Reverend Joyce said, thinking you could cut the atmosphere with a knife.

Mrs Joyce took charge. 'And we'll all have a cup of tea before Kitty goes in to see her father. Sit down, dear, Mary will see to baby Edward. She's very capable.'

'Sure, why wouldn't I be, ma'am, there's seven little ones in our house,' Mary informed them, expertly taking Edward from Kitty and bouncing him up and down in her arms, to his delight.

'He's taken to you, Mary.' Kitty smiled, very grateful for the refreshing tea and the fact that Edward hadn't started to cry.

'You're to have your old room. I've moved young Thomas in with myself and William,' Hester ventured.

'Thank you.' Kitty at least managed to be civil, although she wondered how she would feel sleeping once again under her father's roof.

'Well, Kitty, if you've finished your tea? He knows you've arrived and is very anxious,' Reverend Joyce gently reminded her.

With a heavy sigh she got to her feet. 'I'd better take Edward in too.'

'Leave him with Mary for a little while,' Mrs Joyce urged. She thought it wise to let Kitty make her peace first. She hadn't seen her father in years and she was going to get a shock.

Kitty gasped in both shock and horror when her gaze fell on the man lying in the bed. This couldn't be her da! Her da was a big, strong man who wielded the heavy hammers without effort. This man was little more than a skeleton, a small, shrunken, wizened shadow of the man she had last seen in the kitchen of Harwood Hall after the Harwoods' funeral. His eyes seemed huge above his shrunken, paper-thin cheeks.

Mrs Joyce gave her a gentle push forward. 'He's very sick, Kitty, and in a lot of pain.'

She moved to the bedside and took a thin, wasted hand in her own. Her throat was constricting and tears were pricking her eyes. 'Da! I . . . I came as quickly as I could. Stanley is sorry he couldn't come too, but he has . . . commitments.'

'Kitty. I . . . wanted to . . . see you and . . . the baby.' It was little more than a whisper and she had to bend over to catch his words.

'Don't try to speak, Da. You must rest and save your strength.' She realised now that Stanley had been right to insist she come. He didn't look as though he would last another day.

'Plenty of time for that, Kitty. I wanted to tell you . . . I'm so . . . sorry, for everything.'

'Hush, Da. It's all right now. Don't let's talk about it all, it's in the past. Annie and Bridget are quite happy in New York and I have Stanley and Edward and a lovely home. It . . . it's all turned out well.' It hadn't, she thought. If he hadn't sent her away she would never have ended up marrying Stanley. She would still have had her youth and her freedom and might have married someone her own age. But she wouldn't have had Edward, she thought, and she didn't regret that.

'And you . . . brought him to see me?' It was a painful effort to speak.

'I did so. Will I go and fetch him?' She was struggling to keep her voice calm.

He managed to nod and then closed his eyes.

She clutched Mrs Joyce's arm as they left the room. 'Oh, I didn't realise! I . . . I hardly recognised him!' she whispered.

'I know, Kitty. Cancer is a terrible disease.'

She took Edward from Mary without a word and went back into the bedroom.

'Here he is, Da. This is Edward Ellinson, your grandson.' She laid the baby gently down on the bed beside him and the tears again threatened to spill over as he reached out for his grandson.

'Your mam . . . would have been so . . . proud of you, Kitty. 'Tis such a pity that I won't see him grow up.'

Kitty swallowed hard. 'With me living in Liverpool you wouldn't have seen much of him anyway, Da.'

He reached for her hand. 'Stanley is a good man, I felt that when I read his letter. I've no need to worry about you and that eases my mind, but Annie and Bridget . . . I should never have done . . . that to them, Kitty. They were too young. Your mam would never have forgiven me and now . . . now I have to face her.'

Once she would have taken great satisfaction from hearing him say that but now it seemed irrelevant. 'Ah, Da, don't think like that! Sure, Mam will understand, she'll not blame you. And aren't they both happy over there? I doubt they'd ever want to come back. Isn't that bold Annie courting a lad named Davie Molloy?' She smiled at him, trying to lighten the atmosphere.

He nodded and feebly squeezed her hand. 'She's too young for all . . . that.'

'Annie's no fool and Aunt Enid will make sure she doesn't go astray. I'll make sure I keep in touch,' she promised.

He nodded again and she could see he was very tired.

'Hester . . . she's not good at . . . coping.'

Kitty didn't want to go down this road. She wasn't going to promise anything. 'She'll manage, Da. I'm sure we can sort someone out who will keep the forge going until Thomas and William are old enough.' She picked up Edward. 'Now, you really must rest and I must feed this little one or he'll start roaring and we don't want that.'

He closed his eyes, completely exhausted but feeling far more relieved in his mind. It was good that she was here. She was such a sensible girl, just as his Kathleen had been.

The Reverend and Mrs Joyce departed, taking young Mary with them and Kitty fed and changed Edward and then went to unpack. She had greeted her two small stepbrothers cheerily and had even managed a short conversation with Hester, feeling a little sorry now for a stepmother who was about to become a widow. It would be difficult staying here, she thought as she unpacked, but what else could she do? She would just have to try and make the best of it. In her opinion her da hadn't got much of a bargain in Hester. She was lazy and spoiled and seemed utterly unable to manage things on her own. Maybe she would marry again; it might well be the best thing all round for she was certain Hester wouldn't be interested in bringing up her two small sons alone or in keeping the forge going. She would have to write to her sisters too and that wasn't going to be easy, but perhaps they had realised when they'd been sent to America that they would never see their father again. She sighed. It was going to be a very fraught and difficult time.

Chapter Twenty-Seven

<hr />

THOMAS DOYLE DIED TWO days later and he had been in such agony that Kitty would not have wished him to linger further. Hester had become almost hysterical and Kitty had been hard put to calm the older woman.

'Hester, do try to pull yourself together! Aren't you upsetting the boys even more with all that wailing and aren't they confused and miserable enough as it is, poor little souls? Sure, their world has become a dark and frightening place and you're terrifying them!' she had said, her own grief evident in every line of her body.

Mrs Joyce had intervened. 'Kitty is right, Hester, but I'll go and ask the doctor to give you something to calm you. You are going to have to be strong these next few days for the boys' sake,' she'd admonished firmly yet kindly.

To Kitty's relief Hester had managed to pull herself together for the funeral. The neighbours had all been very supportive, as they always were in times of trouble, and she had been so grateful for all the help that had been given. She was relieved that her visit would not be prolonged; she intended to return to Liverpool the following week. The Reverend and Mrs Joyce had been a tremendous help and, as she'd stood in the small graveyard beside the old Rahan church and watched her father's remains being committed to the earth, to lie in the same grave as her mother, Kitty felt that at last her da was at peace.

She wondered if it would have suited him better to have remained a widower. But maybe he had enjoyed having Hester as his wife, at least in the early days. Had he not remarried he might well have ended up a lonely man, for she supposed that both herself and her sisters would have left to get married eventually. But then perhaps she or indeed Annie might have married someone who would have been willing to take over the forge, which had been in the family for generations. She knew Hester had no interest in it, apart from the income it provided, and she doubted either Thomas or William would either without Da to encourage or teach them. And the reason he had married again had been solely to produce a son and heir who would keep the business in the family – just as Stanley had done, she thought ruefully.

In the days that followed she felt stifled in the house and not solely by the weather. Hester seemed incapable of making the effort to keep the home going; it was left to Kitty to cook and clean and look after both Edward and her young stepbrothers. She decided to push Edward in his pram to the rectory.

'Kitty, isn't it a grand day for a walk. Come in and we'll have tea in the garden,' Mrs Joyce greeted her warmly.

When they were settled and young Mary had brought out the tea Kitty decided to confide in the minister's wife. Edward was fast sleep under the shade of the big ash tree close by.

'I've come to tell you that I'm returning to Liverpool at the beginning of next week. I can't in all conscience leave Stanley to fend for himself much longer, now that Da . . . is gone.'

Mrs Joyce nodded her agreement but looked worried. 'What about Hester? You've seen the way she is.'

'In truth, Mrs Joyce, Hester is not my concern. She is much older than I am and I have had to cope with far worse things. I lost my mam, my home and my sisters. I lost two kind and considerate employers when the Harwoods were killed and then Henry Harwood decided he could not keep me on, even though they had taken me to Liverpool. And now I've lost my da too. Sure, it may sound heartless of me but she will just *have* to get on with life. She has those two boys to think of, not just herself. My responsibilities are to Stanley and Edward now.'

Mrs Joyce nodded. She could see Kitty's point of view entirely. 'Of course they are, Kitty. You must go home. I'm sure we can get someone to help Hester until she feels she can manage. Maybe I could spare Mary for a short while.'

Kitty thought that Mary might have something to say about that, the girl wasn't an eejit and would be well aware that it would be she who would be running the household, but she said nothing.

Mrs Joyce refilled their cups and Kitty thought how quiet and serene it was here in the rectory garden. 'Can I ask you something?' she ventured.

'Of course, Kitty.'

'Have you heard anything about . . . Niall Collins?'

Mrs Joyce glanced at her, wondering what interest she could have in him. 'Only that he married Margaret Maud Delahunty and that they are expecting their first child. That latter piece of information I only heard a few weeks ago so I presume it has only just been confirmed. Was there something specific?'

Kitty shook her head. It had been stupid to ask, she

thought. He was married and so was she. She had Edward and now Niall was to be a parent too. She smiled at the Minister's wife. 'I met his mother once, that's all.'

'I believe she is delighted at the news and why wouldn't she be? She doted on Niall, spoiled him I often thought. I also thought she was rather ... domineering and manipulative. I don't think he had a great deal of choice in the matter of a wife, but that's just my opinion. In all other ways she's a good woman.'

Kitty pushed all thoughts of him out of her mind. 'I was thinking of going up to Harwood Hall, just to take a look at it, before I go back.'

'Sure, it can't do any harm. It's very sad to see it so neglected. He can't sell it, you know.'

'I heard. Times are bad. I wonder what will happen to it – eventually?'

'Who knows? If it's not sold I suppose it will go the way of so many other big houses and estates in Ireland now they no longer have the tenants' rents to sustain them and the British landlords have gone, although most of them were absentees anyway. Let go to rack and ruin until there is nothing to be done but pull it down.'

Kitty sighed and rose. 'I'd better be on my way. Thank you for the tea.'

She hadn't intended to go up to Harwood Hall this

afternoon but she was loath to go back to the forge so she pushed the pram over the bridge and along the lane.

She stopped when she reached the gates and looked up the long drive. There were potholes in it now and the verges were overgrown, the paint on the gates was peeling and patches of rust were showing through. She shook her head. The drive had always been so well maintained. The nearer to the house she got the sadder she felt. The shutters were closed over all the windows but the panes were grimy, the paintwork of their frames blistered by the summer sun and the cold winds of winter. The steps up to the front door were chipped and the railings Da had made were missing a few stanchions here and there. The big brass door-knocker was tarnished and pitted and lichens stained the canopy above the door. Weeds were growing in the guttering and clumps of moss were visible on the roof.

She wheeled the pram around to the side door, noticing how ragged and overgrown the big laurel bushes were. The door was locked and bolted so she continued on to the gardens at the back. The roses were still blooming, struggling amidst the tangle of weeds and wild flowers that had sprung up around them. The once well-tended lawn now resembled a meadow and the boundary fence was broken down in places. Brambles had taken over the shrubbery. There was no sign of the wrought-iron table and chairs where Amy Harwood had taken tea on summer afternoons such as this.

She made her way to the kitchen garden and then the yard. The doors to the coach house were sagging on their hinges and needed painting. Grass was growing between the cobbles and beyond the high wall the turf factory was silent and deserted. Who knew what had happened to the little engine and its trucks? She turned away. She had so many memories of this place and it depressed her to see it in this sorry condition. She could only try to imagine what the interior was like. Had the winter storms caused the rain to seep through the roof, ruining the beautiful plasterwork of the ceilings? The floors, once so highly polished, would now be dull and covered in dust. The beautiful curtains would be musty and damp and eventually rot. The chandeliers would be dull and festooned with cobwebs. Mrs Joyce had been right. If it wasn't purchased soon and brought back to life it would go to rack and ruin. Once before she had wished she had the money to buy it and now she felt that desire again – but it was just an idle dream. She had no money of her own. Oh, Stanley saw that she wanted for very little but it was his money. She looked around again and sighed. Maybe someone would come along who wanted it. Maybe Henry Harwood would change his mind and come home, but she doubted it. She manoeuvred the pram over the uneven terrace; she would have to go back. The sun was slipping lower in the sky.

The following day she went into Tullamore, taking her two small stepbrothers with her but leaving Edward with Hester and young Mary who had been sent to help out. She wanted to send a telegram to Stanley informing him of her impending return; she needed to book her train and ferry ticket and there was grocery shopping to be done.

She had completed all her tasks and as the boys had been good she had bought them a pennyworth of sweets each.

'Now, that should keep you quiet on the way home. So I want no trick-acting out of you!' she instructed as they came out of Mrs Flannery's shop.

'Kitty Doyle! I never thought to see you again!' Mrs O'Shea cried with delight.

Kitty was equally surprised and pleased. 'Mrs O'Shea! I thought you had moved away. How are you in yourself? Don't you look grand?' The house-keeper was very well dressed and wore a really beautiful hat.

Mrs O'Shea smiled at her. 'I did move but then I met someone I hadn't seen in years and, well . . . I'm Mrs Clooney now and I moved back here. Himself has a fine business here in town. Don't tell me these two belong to you?'

Kitty laughed. 'Not at all! They're my step-brothers. I . . . my poor da died recently so I came over from Liverpool.'

'I heard about it. I'm so sorry, Kitty, but you seem to have made your peace with him. Are you still with Elizabeth?'

Kitty took her arm and as they walked she told the former housekeeper of her dismissal, her good fortune in meeting Stanley Ellinson and the job he'd given her, and then her marriage and Edward.

'You were indeed fortunate, Kitty, and now haven't you a grand life.'

Kitty had to agree. 'Yesterday I went up to look at the Hall and it's so neglected. Sure, it would break your heart to see it all shuttered up and looking so . . . forlorn.'

The older woman shook her head. 'A desperate shame! When I remember how Mrs Harwood loved the place and how well we all kept it. I hope he does manage to find someone to buy it. And how are your sisters getting on? Do you hear from them?'

'They settled very well. They love it now and Annie is courting and even Bridget is working.'

'They'll not come back now, Kitty, any more than you will.'

'I know. Isn't it strange how things work out.'

'It is so, I never thought I'd end my days as the wife of a man like Paddy Clooney and with no end of comforts showered on me. Me that has spent my life making other people's homes run like clockwork. Have you the time to come home with me for a cup of tea, Kitty?'

'That would be grand and we can really have a good chat.' Kitty was delighted to see the woman again and it prolonged her time away from Hester. She might not have another opportunity before she returned to her real life in Liverpool.

Chapter Twenty-Eight

———◆———

IT WAS HARD TO believe that it was a year since Da died, Kitty thought as she watched Edward attempting to push his little wooden truck across the grass. She smiled; he was such a beautiful child with his curly blond hair and mischievous smile – and he *was* a mischievous lad. Into everything when she took her eyes off him for a few seconds. It was pleasant in the back garden with the trees overhanging the wall and the riot of colour in the small triangular flower beds that Stanley tended with such care. Flower beds into which Edward made all too frequent invasions with his truck, to the detriment of the salvias, petunias and marigolds.

'He's determined to mow down every last flower!' Tina laughed.

'And Stanley will have ten fits if he does. Sure, it

will be all my fault for not minding him properly,' Kitty predicted. Tina was home on leave and had come to spend the afternoon.

Tina got to her feet and ran across the grass and lifted the child and the truck, turning them in the opposite direction. 'Now, off you go in that direction and leave Daddy's lovely flowers alone, you little villain!'

'Thanks. He has me worn out with his antics,' Kitty said as Tina returned to her seat in the deckchair in the shade.

'Does Stanley really blame you?' She could never really understand why Kitty had married such a staid man.

'He does so but I'd have to have eyes in the back of my head to watch that child and do my housework and cooking. Stanley does like his meal on the table when he gets home and the place tidy and a clean shirt every day and I don't suppose it's too much to ask, he does work very hard.' Kitty thought back to the days after she had returned from Ireland. Things had improved as Edward had grown and the tonic had helped too. Life had gradually returned to something resembling normal.

'Wouldn't you think he'd want to do the house up a bit, make it more . . . modern?' Tina mused. The place was like a mausoleum with all that heavy dark furniture and awful old-fashioned wallpaper and paint.

Kitty rolled her eyes expressively. 'He says it's fine as it is. You'd have thought I was desecrating his mother's memory when I mentioned having the sitting room redecorated in pale green and cream, buying a new carpet and curtains and getting rid of the old sofa and chairs. He is very set in his ways. He doesn't like change one bit.'

'He'll have to move with the times in his shops or people will go elsewhere,' Tina warned.

'I daren't mention that.'

'Oh, my new ship – the *Hilary* – is just lovely! You should see the cabins, lovely pastel colours and lots of white paint and the public rooms are as grand as those on any Cunarder,' Tina enthused.

Kitty smiled at her. 'You really enjoy it, don't you? How can you get used to being away for so long?'

'I hardly notice it. I get on so well with all the crew and my ladies are just that. Ladies. Not the flashy flapper type like Elizabeth Harwood. They're usually older and really interested in travelling and seeing different people and their cultures and ancient civilisations. And of course we only carry a dozen passengers.'

'They'd have to be a bit different to the likes of Elizabeth Harwood to want to go sailing into the jungle!' Kitty replied. She had been amazed when Tina had told her that the ship actually sailed for one thousand miles up the river Amazon, through dense jungle where there were all kinds of exotic birds and animals and also enormous insects and snakes. She had listened incredulously when Tina had described the city of Manaus, a proper city with houses, offices, shops, churches and even an opera house right in the middle of the jungle. Tina loved her work, her passengers were all refined, cultured ladies and the two stewardesses were treated as ladies too by the rest of the crew. The work wasn't hard or demanding (stewards did the heavy tasks), the food was very good as was their own accommodation – things that on other bigger ships were far inferior. The only thing Tina complained of was the overpowering, steamy heat but she said it was a small price to pay.

'Did I show you the lovely bag Mrs Fanshaw gave me at the end of the last trip?' Tina delved under her chair and passed a small clutch bag made of crocodile skin over to Kitty. 'She actually bought it for me in Manaus.'

'It's lovely, Tina. She must have thought a lot of you.'

'And she gave me a good tip as well. My sister Joan's got her eye on it but I told her if she touches it I'll kill her!'

'Oh, Lord! There he goes again!' Kitty darted up

and scooped Edward up, just in time to save a row of French marigolds from certain destruction. 'I think I'd better take him indoors for his nap while we have our tea or we'll get no peace.'

Tina followed Kitty into the kitchen and glanced around without much pleasure. Obviously Stanley Ellinson's refusal to modernise extended to the kitchen as well. She was very glad she had her own money and was accountable to no man for it. She boiled the kettle and filled the teapot. Kitty had everything laid out on a tray and Tina carried it all out into the garden.

When Kitty returned she poured the tea and handed her friend a cup.

'Have you heard how your stepmother is getting on?' Kitty had written with all the details of her father's funeral and Hester's apparent inability to cope with anything.

'I get the occasional letter from the Minister's wife. They managed to find her someone to do the house-work when young Mary flatly refused to set foot in Hester's house again, saying she'd sooner give notice and go on the Parish.'

'Can Hester afford it?'

Kitty shrugged. 'I don't think Da left her penniless and work is so hard to find in Ireland, especially in the country districts, that she won't be paying much.'

Kitty still sounded bitter, Tina thought, and she didn't blame her. Any money that had been left would have gone to Kitty and her sisters if he hadn't married Hester in the first place.

'She also said those two boys are let run wild and are the boldest brats in the parish. Mrs Joyce thinks it will do them the world of good when they are old enough to go to boarding school and she's probably right.'

'Won't that cost a fortune?' Tina was wondering where Hester was going to find the money for fees.

Kitty shook her head. 'No. There're so few Protestants that the Church will pay.'

'Isn't she the fortunate one! Strikes me that when she's packed the lads off she'll be living the life of luxury, getting waited on. Has she done anything with your da's business?'

'There have been rumours, according to Mrs Joyce, that if she gets a decent offer she'll sell it. I don't know where people are taking their animals to be shod these days, but if she hangs on to it for much longer she won't find it easy to sell. Once people go somewhere else they seldom come back.' Kitty thought sadly of how hard her father, her grandfather and great-grandfather had worked to build that business. Some of her fondest memories were of watching her da work, shaping the white hot metal not only into horseshoes but pokers and fire-irons, fancy railings, log baskets and so much more.

The same would be true of Stanley Ellinson's customers if he didn't keep them up to date, Tina thought.

Kitty decided to change the subject. 'Has anything been heard of Elizabeth Harwood? I look in the local paper but I've never seen her mentioned. A couple of months ago I read that Mr Edmund is going to retire.'

'I did hear that she had met some titled bloke dim-witted enough to want to marry her but whether he did, I don't know. I've not a scrap of interest in any of them, Kitty. We're both well out of it.'

'Harwood Hall is still up for sale and getting more and more dilapidated, according to Mrs Joyce.' Kitty often thought of the house and wondered how it had fared through the winter months.

'Who has that kind of money these days, Kitty? And wouldn't you want something with a bit of comfort in it instead of a cold, draughty old place like that with no electricity or gas or even running water? Lord above, it's nineteen twenty-five not eighteen twenty-five!' Tina thought the place sounded dreadful and couldn't understand why Kitty held it in such affection.

'There's no gas or electricity in most of rural Ireland and not much piped water either,' Kitty said simply.

Tina rolled her eyes. 'Then hasn't the Free State got a lot of catching up to do?'

'They would if they had the money. Sure, it's a new country, everything takes time,' Kitty said, thinking of the dreadful slums that existed in areas of Liverpool. She was certain that the City Fathers weren't short of the money to pull them down and replace them.

Reluctantly Tina rose. 'I'd better be going, Kitty. I've got new uniforms to wash and iron and I'll have to start my packing.'

'Will you be sorry to be leaving your mam?' Kitty gathered the tea things on to the tray.

'I miss her but I don't miss the rest of them! They do nothing but fight, it would drive you mad! I've got permission to have Mam aboard for afternoon tea tomorrow and she's so excited about it she's given herself one of her headaches.' Tina grimaced. 'I'll write to you and don't forget to write back. You've got the agent's address?'

Kitty nodded and ushered her indoors.

The following morning she had her shopping to do but decided to walk to Stanley's shop in Walton Village. It was a lovely summer morning, the often oppressive heat of July and August was still weeks away, a breeze was wafting the small white clouds across a blue sky and although it was quite a long walk, she didn't mind. She had never been to Stanley's most recent acquisition. She usually went to the shop where she had worked. She could have had her order delivered and sometimes in the winter months she did, but she liked to walk. People stopped and chatted to her, admired Edward, and she liked to see what all the other shops along Walton Vale had in stock.

It took her the best part of an hour to get there, even taking a few short cuts, and the sun had grown stronger. Edward had fallen asleep beneath the fringed canopy of the pram and looked like a sleeping cherub, she thought. He was still asleep when she reached the shop so she put the brake on and left him outside. He would come to no harm and she could keep her eye on him through the window.

Stanley was very surprised to hear from his senior assistant that his wife had arrived and that his son was asleep in his pram outside the door.

'Kitty, you never mentioned you intended to visit this morning,' he greeted her, coming through from the office at the back.

'I'm not visiting, Stanley. I've come to do my shopping and just to see the place.' She had been glancing around and Tina's words had come forcefully back to her. The place was very dark and dismal-looking even on such a sunny day. The shelves were crammed to capacity but nothing was attractively displayed, as quite often things were in other shops she'd been in.

And there wasn't the convenience of things being clearly marked with their prices.

'Well, if you give Ada your shopping list I'm sure she'll get everything together for you. Would you like to come through to the office and have a cup of tea? It really is a long walk. I think you'd better bring Edward in too. We can put the pram in the yard at the back, it will be safer,' he fussed. He didn't think it at all safe for babies to be left in their prams unattended and had said so but Kitty always replied that that was nonsense, who would want to harm a baby and besides, how was she to shop and watch him at the same time? Everyone left their children in their prams.

Kitty went through, leaving him to wheel his son around to the back entrance and Ada to assemble the groceries. It was very similar to the office in the other shop and, as she lit the gas ring and placed the kettle on it, she supposed they were all the same.

When they were sipping their tea she decided to tentatively suggest he make some improvements. 'Do you not think it would be well to mark things with their prices, Stanley?'

He looked a little taken aback. 'But the girls know the price of everything, Kitty. What need is there of all the extra work in writing out tickets?'

'So that customers can see for themselves without having to ask.' It seemed perfectly logical to her.

He leaned forward across his desk. 'Kitty, you know that my customers have no need to *ask*. That is what I have built my reputation on. Ellinson's are high-class grocer's. We are not the Co-op.'

Kitty didn't think there was anything wrong with the Co-operative stores. There was always a good selection and prices were very competitive and you got a dividend. She sometimes shopped there.

'I understand that, Stanley, but don't you think things would look far more *attractive* if they were displayed more prominently, rather than everything being crammed on the shelves?'

He frowned. 'I employ people who know exactly where to lay their hands on *everything*. There is no need for gimmicky displays, cluttering up the counters and the floor space. Customers like to have plenty of room to move around.'

She tried again. 'The place would be so much lighter and brighter if you got rid of those heavy window blinds and installed a nice bright awning outside,' she suggested, keeping her tone light and breezy.

'Kitty, for heaven's sake! The blinds are there to keep the sunlight from ruining the window display and I have no intention of wasting money on gaudy awnings that will be of no use at all for most of the year. And I would be grateful if you left the running of the business to me. I have years and years of experience. It has nothing to do with you at all, my dear.'

She knew it was no use. He wouldn't change. He wouldn't even *consider* changing anything. He did things exactly as his father had done, over thirty years ago. He certainly wasn't going to move with the times and that concerned her.

'I'm sorry, Stanley. I didn't mean to upset or offend you. Well, I'd better be going home now.'

He nodded and rose, placated by her apology. She ran the house efficiently and that's all he wanted. 'A woman's place is in the home' his mother had always said and he was in total agreement with her sentiments. Kitty should leave the business in his capable hands and not come inspecting his premises and making fatuous and impractical suggestions.

Chapter Twenty-Nine

———◆———

As Christmas approached Kitty knew from Stanley's behaviour that something was worrying him and she suspected that it was the state of business. Times were hard; there was a great deal of unemployment and hardship; even those who had never had to count the pennies before were now being more frugal. When she did her own shopping she noticed more and more expensively dressed women shopping in the likes of the Co-operative Stores. Women who especially at this time of year had their groceries delivered were trudging home carrying their own shopping bags. The area they lived in was affluent but on the odd occasion when Kitty travelled into Liverpool the signs of poverty on the streets appalled her. Groups of men and boys standing on street corners looking gaunt and desperate. Hordes of children barefoot, their clothes little better than rags, begging for pennies. All of them thin and undernourished, many suffering from rickets. The women with their shawls drawn closely around them in the freezing weather as they stood patiently in the long queues outside the pawnshops.

She had done her Christmas shopping but as she was on her way home the tram had been held up on Scotland Road. A cart had overturned when the shire horse that had been pulling it had slipped on the icy cobbles and gone down. The traffic was in chaos as the police on duty waited for the vet to arrive to put the poor creature out of its misery. She glanced out of the window of the stationary tram and down the narrow street of soot-blackened, crumbling houses. Even in this weather many of the front doors stood open and small children, some not much older than Edward, were sitting on the worn and broken steps. Her heart went out to their mothers who must be desperate to keep food on the table and some sort of fire in the hearth. Obviously there was nothing left over for boots or shoes or a warm coat for the little ones. One little lad was wearing what was quite clearly a cut-down man's jacket, which swamped him, and from which two bare and filthy feet protruded. She hugged Edward tightly as he sat on her knee, thanking God that he had warm clothes and boots and that he had always had plenty to eat.

She mentioned the poverty she had seen to Stanley that night after supper. 'Sure, it would tear your heart out to see them. Their little feet bare and in this weather.'

He shook his head in sympathy. 'It's always the children who suffer most. There's no work and I hear the conditions laid down for Parish Relief are so stringent that many men refuse to face the humiliation. Mind you, they can always seem to find the money for beer. The pubs are never empty, but I suppose it's the only bit of respite they have.'

Kitty wondered what bit of respite their poor wives had; none at all, she suspected. 'Stanley, is there something worrying you? You've been quiet and preoccupied lately,' she ventured.

He sighed heavily. 'There isn't much you don't notice, is there, Kitty? Business is very slow for the time of the year. Very slow indeed. Usually everyone is rushed off their feet.'

She had thought as much. 'I see.'

'There's been no demand at all for the fancy boxes of chocolates I ordered, in fact I'm beginning to think I shouldn't have ordered quite as many luxury lines this year and most of them are perishable. I've noticed that at least a dozen of my best customers whose orders are always substantial and include just such luxury items have ordered very little.' He shook his head gloomily.

'Could you not sell them off at a reduced price? People might be tempted to buy them if you display them with a ticket saying something like "Special Purchase" or "Perfect Christmas Gift".' Personally she thought that he should instigate a special weekly offer. Choose one slow-selling line, display it prominently with a marked-down price: she was sure it would work. People had to be tempted to buy these days and they might increase their purchases; word would soon get round that there was always a weekly bargain to be had at Ellinson's. She looked at him anxiously, thinking of the last time she had made suggestions and been told it was none of her business.

Stanley looked thoughtful. She might have a point. It irked him that she was interfering and it went against his way of conducting business, but he was seriously worried that things were so slow and he didn't want to make a loss. It would be no use selling the chocolates off after Christmas, it would be too late then. 'I'll consider doing that, Kitty. I'll see how things go.'

She smiled at him. 'If it works, Stanley, you could consider doing it on a weekly basis, with slow sellers.'

He frowned. 'Now, Kitty, let's not get carried away. Ellinson's do not want the reputation for being "cheap" shops.'

She nodded, but privately thought that surely it would be better than seeing the profits drain away and maybe even being forced to sell one of them? She sometimes wondered if Stanley, for all his experience, really did understand business?

Stanley was quite pleased when Kitty's suggestion seemed to work, although he had convinced himself that it was his idea. Business, however, was still slow and so he decided to close early on Christmas Eve. Normally they stayed open until half past ten, as did most of the shops.

'That will make a nice change, Stanley. We can have an early supper, listen to the carols on the wireless and then fill Edward's stocking,' Kitty had replied when he'd told her of his decision. 'What time should I expect you home?'

'I'd say around half past six to a quarter to seven. I'll cash up at Walton Village first then do the other shops. The girls can lock up. They're all delighted to be able to get home a few hours earlier than usual.'

She nodded as she put the final touches to the decorations on the Christmas tree.

She'd made a special effort with the table, laying out the best china, polishing the silver cutlery and placing a vase filled with holly and mistletoe in the centre. She'd had a busy afternoon, preparing all the vegetables for next day, making the stuffing for the goose and finishing wrapping the Christmas presents while Edward had his nap. There was home-made soup, to be followed by a steak and kidney pie, Stanley's favourite, and a blackberry pie for supper.

Edward had had his bath and was sound asleep in his room and she changed into her dark blue pleated skirt and pale blue jumper with the navy edging that toned nicely with the skirt. She fastened the gold cross and chain around her neck and clipped on the small gold stud earrings that had been his gift to her last Christmas. She didn't expect jewellery this year, not with the decline in profits, but she didn't mind.

By seven-fifteen she was getting a little anxious but not seriously worried. Something might have cropped up. There might even have been a mad, last-minute rush and he'd decided to stay open for a while longer. She turned the oven down to its lowest setting and removed the soup pan from the stove. It would only take a few minutes to reheat that. She poured herself a small glass of port, which she infinitely preferred to sherry, and sat down in a fireside chair.

At eight o'clock she switched off the oven. She was beginning to get a little angry. If he was staying open he should have let her know. Hadn't she told him supper would be ready? Hadn't she gone to the trouble of asking him what time he would be home? He could have sent one of the delivery lads up to tell her he'd be late. The supper would be ruined at this rate. She decided against having another glass of port and started to assemble the toys she'd bought for Edward. They wouldn't fit into a stocking; she'd just put the sweets and fruit and shiny new penny in that. The rest she would put into a pillowcase. She would lay out the little sailor suit she'd bought him for she intended to have his photograph taken after the holiday. He would now sit still for longer than a few minutes and Bridget was complaining bitterly that she didn't even know what her only nephew looked like.

Thinking of her sisters, Kitty smiled to herself. Annie's romance with Davie Molloy had taken a serious turn, Bridget had informed her in her last letter. Annie had confided that he was saving hard for an engagement ring and was trying to pluck up the courage to ask Aunt Enid and Uncle Ted for Annie's hand. Now that Da was dead, they were her guardians and as Annie was still under twenty-one she needed their permission. It was hard to think of Annie getting married, Kitty thought, remembering that Davie was a Catholic and also that she had determined that she wasn't going to worry about the fact. As long as he was good to Annie, and her sister was happy, that was the main thing. She still pictured her the way she'd been the last time she had seen her: the angry, bitter, discontented young girl who'd sat in the kitchen at Harwood Hall clutching a glass of buttermilk. Of course she'd been sent photographs of both her sisters and now Annie was a very pretty young woman with big dark eyes and short, wavy dark hair. Bridget too had blossomed into a lovely girl with a serene expression in her grey eyes and light brown hair cut in a bob. Both photographs were now in frames and displayed prominently on the mantelpiece.

By half past ten she was alternating between fits of anger and gnawing anxiety. Where was he? Why hadn't he come home? Surely, surely he must realise that she'd be worried sick? The supper was ruined and he hated waste. Why hadn't he let her know? She paced the floor restlessly, going from the sitting room, to the kitchen, to the hall and back again. She checked on Edward from time to time but he was fast asleep, clutching his little woolly rabbit, which was looking a bit worse for wear these days. Occasionally she peered from behind the curtains into the dark street but there was no sign of him. There was no sign of anyone.

She went to the front door and opened it, standing on the step shivering as she peered intently out. The cul-de-sac was quiet and deserted although lights burned in all the houses.

At twenty past eleven she was seriously considering going to ask Gloria or Nancy Williams if they could sit with Edward while she went to look for him. Christmas Eve was not exactly the right time to be asking such a favour but she was getting desperate. She only chatted to a couple of the neighbours as people tended to keep themselves to themselves but Nancy Williams next door was a nice enough woman. Ten minutes later she was wondering if she had left it too late – perhaps they would be going to bed – when she heard the knock on the front door. Stanley never knocked, he always used his key and her heart dropped like a stone as she went to answer it. He *must* have had an accident, she told herself. Someone was coming to inform her of that; probably he would be in hospital. She steeled herself as she opened the door.

'Mrs Ellinson?' the sergeant from the Liverpool City Police enquired. Another officer in plain clothes accompanied him.

'I am so. Will you come in, please? I presume you've come to tell me that Stanley has been in an accident?' She managed to keep her voice calm and indicated that they should follow her into the sitting room.

They glanced briefly at each other and then looked around the room. Obviously she'd been waiting for him to come home for supper, the table was nicely set, and equally obviously there was a child in the house for a bulging stocking was tacked up at one side of the fireplace. That surprised them, as did she. They'd expected the wife to be middle-aged and any family well beyond the Santa stage.

'I think you'd best sit down, Mrs Ellinson,' the CID man suggested kindly.

Kitty sat down on the edge of the sofa. Oh, God! What were they going to tell her? An image flashed through her mind: two burly members of the Royal Irish Constabulary standing in Harwood Hall on St Stephen's Night – the night the Harwoods had been killed. 'Oh, God! You've come to tell me he's . . . he's dead!' she cried.

'I'm afraid so. It's a shocking case. A constable on his beat along Walton Vale noticed a light in the back of the shop and went to investigate. He found the back door open and Mr Ellinson lying on the floor. The office was a shambles; he had obviously put up a fight.'

'You mean he . . . he . . .' Kitty couldn't finish, she was utterly dazed.

'Obviously a robbery that went very wrong. There were two empty cash boxes on the floor. He was dead when the officer found him. I'm so, so sorry, Mrs Ellinson, and on Christmas Eve, too.'

Understanding was dawning on Kitty. Her eyes

widened and her hand went to her throat. 'He was . . . *murdered*!'

The CID man nodded gravely. 'When we catch whoever did it, he'll hang.'

'Is there anyone who will stay with you, luv? Family, friends?' the uniformed sergeant asked. Glancing around, his gaze fell on the empty glass and the almost full bottle of port wine. He got up and poured a glass and then handed it to her.

Kitty gripped it with shaking hands. *Murder!* She couldn't believe it. Things like that didn't happen in this neighbourhood.

'Drink that up, luv, it may help. Is there anyone we should contact?'

Kitty shook her head. 'No. No one. My sisters are in America. My only friend is away at sea.'

She was Irish; obviously any other relatives she might have were still over there, the sergeant thought. 'What about neighbours?'

'Mrs Williams next door,' Kitty managed to croak. She was feeling a little light-headed. Poor Stanley!

'I'll go and fetch her.' The CID officer stood up. It was always difficult but there were certain questions he had to ask her and they couldn't be put off. The longer they left it the less likelihood there was of catching the bastard.

'Is there just the one child, luv? Would you like to

go and see if it's all right?' The sergeant felt so sorry for her. Any death was a shock but a murder was even more dreadful and she was so young and seemingly all alone.

Kitty nodded. 'Edward, he's upstairs.'

He helped her to her feet and guided her up the stairs. The little boy was fast asleep. Poor little mite, he thought. A fine bloody Christmas this would be for them both.

'He's . . . fine. 'Tis best we don't disturb him. He . . . he won't understand,' Kitty whispered.

He nodded as he closed the bedroom door quietly. 'That's a blessing in disguise, luv.'

Nancy Williams and her eldest daughter were ushered in, both looking pale and shocked.

Nancy hugged Kitty. 'Oh, Kitty, what a terrible, terrible thing to happen! I'm so sorry. Poor Stanley! Such a quiet, mild-mannered man. He'd not hurt a fly.'

At her words Kitty broke down and tears poured down her cheeks. The two women eased her down on to the sofa and Nancy put her arm around her. 'It's all right, Kitty, luv. Gloria and I will stay with you. Gloria, go and put the kettle on. What she needs is a cup of strong sweet tea. In fact I think we all do.'

Gloria Williams nodded and went into the kitchen while her mother attempted to calm Kitty down. The two men looked uncomfortable and reluctantly the officer in plain clothes got out his notebook.

'You don't have to take a statement *now*, do you?' Nancy asked, looking even more shocked.

'I'm so sorry but the more information we have, the quicker we will catch whoever committed this crime,' he replied regretfully.

'Let her have her tea first, please,' Nancy Williams begged.

Kitty did feel a little better after the tea and said so.

'Just take your time, Mrs Ellinson. Now, did your husband usually cash up last thing?'

'He did, but tonight he said he was closing the shops up early. He said he'd be home at about half past six. Business hasn't been great this year.'

The man nodded as he wrote it down. Half the city was out of work. Then he frowned. 'You said "shops". Did he own more than one?'

Kitty nodded. 'He has . . . had four.'

'And had he been to the other shops first?'

Kitty was trying hard to think clearly. 'Probably. The one on Walton Vale was the nearest to home so he would have left it until last and locked up himself.'

'So there would have been quite a large amount of money?'

'Not as much as in other years but a good bit.'

'Perfect motive. It's hard to come by large amounts of money legally these days. And that was his routine? He did that every day?'

'Yes. He always took it to the bank on Fridays so there wasn't a large amount here in the house over the weekend, and if there was a decent enough amount by Tuesdays he went then too. But with it being Christmas and the fact that takings were down I . . . I suppose he intended to bring it home with him.' Her head was beginning to ache.

'So he could have been watched. There's a manhunt on now, all leave in this division has been cancelled, so we'll be asking the question: Did anyone notice a man or men hanging around in the vicinity in the previous weeks? Mr Ellinson didn't mention to you that he'd noticed anyone suspicious hanging around near the shop?'

Kitty shook her head. 'He didn't say anything but then he had been so worried that he probably wouldn't have noticed.'

'Please, isn't that enough? The poor girl just isn't up to all this,' Nancy Williams interrupted.

The notebook was shut. 'That's all for now, Mrs Ellinson. If you remember anything, anything at all that you think might help, you will get in touch?'

Kitty nodded, relieved to see them both get to their feet.

'Gloria will show you out,' Nancy Williams informed them.

'We're so very sorry, Mrs Ellinson. If there is anything we can do?' the sergeant said as he turned to leave.

'You can give her some peace and quiet, she hasn't taken it all in yet,' Nancy Williams said sadly, shaking her head.

Chapter Thirty

⸻

The DAYS THAT FOLLOWED seemed like a nightmare to Kitty. Somehow she had managed to get through Christmas Day with the help of Nancy and Gloria Williams. She thanked God that Edward was too young to understand but he had frequently looked enquiringly towards the door and said, 'Dada,' one of the few words he had so far mastered. He would never know the full horror of the circumstances in which his father had died and she hoped he would never learn. She was filled with revulsion and pity when she thought of poor Stanley fighting for his life, trying to protect his hard-earned money, while some thug beat him. He had been such an inoffensive, honest and kindly man; he hadn't deserved to die like that. Oh, he'd had his faults but he'd been good to her and she supposed he had loved her in his own way.

If she were honest with herself, she knew she had never really loved him, but she had been fond of him, and he had given her Edward. And now Edward would never know his father, and it was such a tragedy, for Stanley had had so many good qualities and he had truly loved his son. If she hadn't had her child, life would have been very empty, she realised that, but she did miss Stanley. It was only Edward that kept her sane, she confided to Nancy.

Stanley Ellinson's brutal death was reported in all the newspapers, even the national press carried the story and a huge police search ensued. Four days after Christmas the police arrested a man in the south end of the city. A publican had become suspicious of one of his customers and the seemingly endless amount of money he was spending. He wasn't a regular, in fact he was a stranger to the district. When the room he was renting was searched, the police found a stash of notes under a loose floorboard and a bloodstained cap. The police sergeant, whose name was Draper, came the following day to inform Kitty.

'I'm glad you caught him. It makes me feel that Stanley will have the justice he deserves.'

'And you too, Mrs Ellinson, you're a widow with a little boy to bring up. And, believe me, justice *will* be done. Oh, he'll get a fair trial but I'm sure he'll be found guilty and he'll hang. A life for a life.'

'Sure, it's not revenge I want, sergeant, just justice,' Kitty said a little sadly.

'It *is* justice, Mrs Ellinson. Death is the penalty the law demands for murder. And of course the money he stole will be returned to you in due course.'

She'd nodded but she had little interest in the money.

As the weeks of January slipped by Kitty wished Tina had been home for she missed having someone she could really confide in: Nancy Williams had been wonderful but she was so much older. But Tina wouldn't be home until March.

After the funeral she had written to her sisters and to Mrs Joyce and the minister's wife had written back immediately saying they were praying for her and for Edward and if she felt the need to return for a visit then she was welcome to stay with them.

As she lay awake at night or wandered restlessly and aimlessly around the house she thought about it. She even contemplated going back permanently but what was there for her in Ireland? Now she needed something to occupy her mind and keep her busy through the short winter days. Oh, she could find things to do in the house and Edward was only twenty months old and so demanded a good deal of attention, but she was beginning to feel that there was no purpose or structure to her life.

The shops had been closed until the week after New Year as the staff had been very shocked and distressed but she had realised that she would have to open them again as the girls all needed their wages and she felt it would be letting Stanley down if she just let things slide.

She hadn't fully realised that Stanley had left everything to her until the following month when his will had been explained to her. The shops, the house and quite a large sum of money that Stanley had both saved and inherited himself meant that now she was quite a wealthy woman. The solicitor had asked if she would sell the shops. She could live quite comfortably on what she had and what they would realise. She had shaken her head and he had surmised that she intended to put a manager in each one.

She had thought about doing so but then changed her mind. She would promote the senior assistant in three shops, she would run the fourth herself and she would supervise them all, as Stanley had done. It would be hard work but it was just what she needed, she told herself. She had to pull herself together, concentrate her mind and her energies on something so why not the business? She would find someone to look after Edward for, say, the mornings and all day Saturday – the busiest day of the week. He was at an age where he wouldn't fret or mope without her for a few hours. He even mentioned his 'dada' less frequently now.

She mentioned it to Nancy Williams in the hope that she could recommend someone.

'Are you quite sure you feel up to it, Kitty?' the woman asked with some concern.

'I need something to occupy me. Apart from Edward, life seems so empty and pointless. I always worked before I was married.'

'But you don't need to, do you?'

Kitty smiled at her. 'No, Stanley left me comfortably off but I don't want the shops to start failing. I was wondering if you knew of anyone who would come and look after Edward for me each morning and all day Saturday? I'll need someone reliable and trustworthy. I would pay them well.'

Nancy looked thoughtful. 'Gloria is fed up with her job. They pay her buttons in that place. Would you like me to ask her? Edward does at least know her.'

'Do you think she'd be at all interested?' Oh, that would be wonderful. Kitty so hoped she would want to do it.

'I'll ask her tonight. She'd have to give a week's notice. When do you intend to start?'

'I hadn't really given it that much thought but after she's worked her notice, I suppose.'

'You don't feel a break would do you good? Didn't you say someone had asked you to visit them in Ireland?'

'I did so but I think it's better if I stay and do something constructive, and besides, I've no real wish to be making that journey in the depths of winter.'

'Well, if you're sure I'll have a word with Gloria,' Nancy promised.

To Kitty's delight Gloria said she would love to escape from her dead-end job and look after Edward and have some more free time, so they agreed a wage and Gloria said she would give a week's notice the following morning.

Now that she had made the decision Kitty began to concentrate on what she must do next. She would visit the shops in turn and explain to the girls what she was about to do; they had been coping remarkably well all this time but it wasn't fair to leave them to do it any longer. She would also make notes of what needed to be done in the matter of modernising the shops and of ideas to increase business. Suddenly, for the first time since Stanley's death, she felt animated. The apathy into which she'd sunk most of the time disappeared.

Next day she wrapped Edward up warmly and pushed him to the shop in Walton Vale. A little shudder ran through her as she went into the office where Stanley had died but she told herself he wouldn't have wanted her to feel any fear. Her mam had always said there was nothing to fear from the dead, only the living. The room had been tidied and scrubbed.

Violet put her head around the door. 'Are you all right in here, Mrs Ellinson?'

Kitty smiled at the girl. 'I'm just grand, Violet. Come on in, I wanted to talk to you anyway.'

Violet came in and stood in front of the desk. It seemed strange to see Mrs Ellinson sitting there instead of him.

'I'm going to take over here in about a week's time. I'm going to promote the senior assistants in the other shops and I'll be visiting them all a couple of times in the week. From now on the takings will be banked every day. I'm sure I can trust you to go along to Martin's Bank on the corner of Orrell Lane each lunchtime with the previous day's money.'

'Oh, indeed you can, Mrs Ellinson.' The girl was enthusiastic.

'And I think we'll make some changes to all the shops. They're very gloomy and a bit off-putting, don't you think?'

Violet wasn't used to being asked her opinion on such things and she looked doubtful.

'Those window blinds can go for a start and we'll

do a bit of reorganisation with the stock and I'll write out price tickets for everything. I'll have time in the evenings. I have lots of fresh ideas and if either you or Maggie think of anything I'd only be delighted to listen.'

Violet smiled. Kitty Ellinson wasn't going to let the grass grow under her feet, she could see that. 'Well, there was something, but . . .' she started hesitantly.

'What? Sure, you can tell me, didn't I just say so?' Kitty urged.

'It's these overalls. Don't you think they look a bit . . . drab and old-fashioned?'

Kitty looked critically at the plain navy-blue shop coat and the plain white cap and nodded. 'Aren't you just right? What if we can get something in cream, edged in dark green? I know they would get grubbier much more quickly and it would mean you having to wash and iron them more often but you could have two each instead of just one of those old blue things, couldn't you? And if we do away with the cap completely and have just a plain dark green Alice band to keep your hair tidy, how does that sound?'

'Much better. We'd look so much smarter.'

Kitty looked thoughtful. 'I could have the letter E embroidered on the top pocket of the overalls in green and on the front of the Alice band in cream. Then it would be more like a proper uniform and less like an overall. And I'll have this room painted, get rid of this desk, which is far too big, and find one smaller. We could get a card table and a couple of chairs in here too, then you could have your lunch in here instead of in a corner of that dingy stockroom. There's already a gas ring and a kettle and I'll bring some decent cups from the house.'

Violet thought it sounded wonderful and, leaving Kitty poking around in the desk drawers, she went and told Maggie, the other assistant, about Kitty turning out to be 'a new broom'.

'Thank God for that! It's about time something was done to liven things up, no disrespect to poor Mr Ellinson, but it's terribly old-fashioned in here. Have you been in Costigan's lately? They've got new tills and paper bags printed with the shop name on them and they have everything displayed better too.'

'You tell her about the tills and the paper bags: she said if we thought of any good ideas we were to tell her, that's why I suggested we get rid of these awful-looking things.' Violet grimaced, pulling at the sleeve of her overall.

'I'm dead chuffed she's dumping these caps. Mine gives me a shocking headache by the end of most days.'

Violet rolled her eyes expressively. 'All we'll need then is more customers.'

Kitty thought the paper bags were a great idea and she wondered about the cost of having full-sized bags printed too: bags with handles that could be used again and which would be a good advertisement for the shops, especially if they could incorporate some kind of slogan. 'Ellinson's for Quality Groceries', she mused. Or 'Ellinson's for Quality and Value', or 'Value and Variety at Ellinson's'. She liked the sound of that. She'd make enquiries. And she would visit all the grocery stores in the vicinity of all her shops to see if there were any other improvements she could make.

The prices Stanley had paid his suppliers would have to be looked at too, as would the prices they charged. She wanted to keep the high quality but these days money was so tight that the prices had to be competitive to get customers in. The first thing she was going to do was instigate the 'Ellinson's Bargain of the Week'. There must be things that could be attractively displayed and sold at a markdown price? She might even put an advertisement in the local paper announcing it. It would all cost money to start with but it was about time some money was invested and she was certain it would be worth it in the long term. You had to speculate to accumulate, she told herself firmly. It wasn't what Stanley would have done, in fact he would have had ten fits, but he had left the shops to her and she was going to run them *her* way. And she was determined she would make a success of it, never mind her deceased mother-in-law's strictures about a woman's place being in the home. You had to move with the times these days.

Chapter Thirty-One

—◆◆◆◆—

TINA ARRIVED HOME ON leave and at once came to visit her friend. She could hardly believe her eyes when Kitty took her down to the shop.

'You've worked miracles! This place used to be so dismal that it's a wonder anyone shopped here at all!' She was full of praise as she glanced around in amazement. The place had been painted; new lights and shelving had been fitted. There were still plenty of goods on the shelves but now there were displays of fancy biscuits and packets of different types of tea on the counter ends. To one side was a small circular table covered with a yellow and white gingham cloth; jars of jam and marmalade and honey were arranged on it in tiers and a printed notice declared them to be the 'Special Purchase of the Week'. You could pick any two for sixpence.

'This month's theme is "Teatime" – hence the displays of tea and biscuits and preserves,' Kitty informed her. 'We have a different theme each month. We had "Home Baking", which included Shrove Tuesday – pancakes – last month. Next month it will be Easter.'

'I've got to hand it you, Kitty, you've got a good business head on you.'

'Which is more than could be said about poor Stanley, God rest him.'

Tina nodded. She'd been so shocked and full of pity for Kitty when she'd received her letter. Hadn't the poor girl had enough to put up with in life already, she'd thought, but Kitty was coping with everything remarkably well and Tina thought she actually looked better since she'd become a widow. That's a dreadful thing to say, she chided herself mentally, but it was true. Kitty looked very smart and attractive in a black and white checked coat with a black velvet collar and a black velvet cloche hat that sported the black tail feathers of a Bird of Paradise curled around the brim. Her face was far more animated, her eyes had a new sparkle and Tina noticed that she smiled more frequently.

'And are all the shops the same? Do you have these theme things in all of them?'

'They are and we do. The "theme things" as you call them were Ada's idea. She's my manageress at

Walton Village but all the girls put their ideas forward.' Kitty beamed at Violet and Maggie, both of whom were serving customers.

'And don't they look much smarter without those awful old navy things. I wish I could swap the starched cap I have to wear when I'm on duty for a nice Alice band. It would be much cooler when we're in the tropics. It really is a smart and modern uniform, Kitty,' Tina enthused, thinking it made the white sharkskin dress and small pleated cap which constituted her working clothes look rather dull and boring.

'Come through to the back and we'll have a cup of tea, or would you rather wait until we got home?' Kitty enquired.

'Here will be fine, I'm eaten up with curiosity to see what you've done with Stanley's old office.' Tina laughed. She never would have thought that her friend would make such changes.

'We got rid of the desk and all the old furniture, had it painted, put a nice blind up and it's now an office cum "rest room".'

Tina nodded approvingly. It hadn't been a very big room to start with but now it looked so different. She liked the beige and white tiled linoleum on the floor, the cream walls and the window blind that had a bright yellow edging. In one corner was a neat cabinet where Kitty kept all the paperwork and on top of this reposed a vase of yellow catkins. There was a small desk under the window and on the opposite wall a card table and three chairs. The table could be folded up when not in use but now three cups and saucers patterned with yellow flowers and green leaves and a matching sugar bowl and milk jug were set out on it.

'It's much nicer to have somewhere clean and bright for the girls to have their tea and their bit of lunch and in that corner I've put up a mirror and a shelf so they can tidy their hair and keep their bits and pieces together.'

'I just hope they appreciate everything you've done, Kitty.'

'Indeed they do. Maggie says it's a pleasure to come to work now and her mam was "gobsmacked" – whatever that means – when she heard they have their tea in china cups and with a cloth on the table too. It's the little touches I find they appreciate most and, sure, what's a bit of paint, a few cups, a tablecloth and a vase of flowers at the end of the day? I throw the cloths in with my own washing and if Stanley's mam had one china tea set she had a dozen and the flowers or whatever come from the garden. We have pink roses on the china at Walton Village, blue forget-me-nots at Walton Road and lilac sprays at Rice Lane. And there's still plenty of stuff at the house. I've had all the delivery boys rigged out with a sort of uniform and the bikes have been repainted. My next project is to have a proper inside toilet and washbasin put in for them. Sure, isn't it desperate to have to go out to the old privy in the yard in the winter months in all the rain and sleet and wind?'

'You'll have people queuing up to work for you, Kitty, it's like a home from home for them.'

Kitty nodded slowly. 'I only want them to have the kind of working conditions I had when I was in service. Apart from Henry deciding he couldn't keep me on, the Harwoods were good to their staff. Even when the Hall was closed up all the rest of them were paid a bit of severance money. They weren't flung out on the road without a penny. He said it was what his parents would have wanted and 'twas the truth.'

'And is business picking up?' Tina enquired, thinking Kitty must have spent quite a bit of money on doing the shops up.

'It is so. You can hardly get in the door at the end of the week and we've cleared a lot of lines that Stanley had trouble selling. I've also managed to come to an arrangement with most of my suppliers. Isn't it only common sense for me to be getting a discount if I order more frequently, which is what a lot of shops can't do these days as money is so tight? My customers don't have a struggle to make ends meet but they still like to think they're getting good value for their money and they like a bargain too. I have two ladies who have asked to be informed of what next week's special purchase will be and they both live in those huge houses in Walton Park near the station. *And* they have servants because it's the maids who come in to find out.'

Tina nodded in approval, her esteem for Kitty's business sense rising still higher.

'I heard the other day that some shops are being built on that brand-new housing estate out at Fazakerley and that they are going to extend the tram lines and build a terminus there. It's called a "model estate" and people can only get a house there if they can prove they have a decent, steady job. All the houses have front and back gardens and inside bathrooms too, and there's to be shops, a cinema, churches, a library, a community hall and even a welfare clinic.'

'I heard about that. It's all very go-ahead, Mam said, and I know that Mr Hayes, our Chief Steward, has applied for a house and he'll probably get one too. Even though he's away so much he has a wife and two daughters. Are you thinking of taking one of the new shops?'

Kitty nodded. 'It sounds just the kind of place for an Ellinson's Grocery shop.'

Tina was concerned. 'You'll wear yourself into the

ground at this rate, Kitty! Running between five shops and keeping a home going too and don't forget there's Edward.'

'Edward is fine. He's the most important thing in my life, and always will be, but he's adjusted to me being out and he loves Gloria. She's so good with him. Sure, that girl should have been a nanny or a teacher but Nancy said she wouldn't apply herself to her books and they weren't going to waste all that money on her training. I don't know what she'll do when Edward is old enough to go to school but I'll worry about that nearer the time.'

'I still think you're doing too much, Kitty, and you can't afford to make yourself ill. You're Edward's mother, don't forget. You're all the family he has.'

Kitty bit her lip. Tina was right and she knew what it was like to be alone. Perhaps she should give more thought to taking on another shop, but she was young and healthy and she would get someone to do the housework if need be. She hated to miss such an opportunity for she was sure there would be fierce competition for those shops, just as there was for the houses on that estate. The people who were going there *needed* shops and they would all have decent incomes.

Tina smiled and got to her feet. 'Don't overreach yourself, Kitty, that's all I'm saying. I'm not what you call a begrudger. Now, shall we wash these cups and go along to Tyler's? I need a new pair of black shoes. Mam remarked that these are starting to look shabby even after a good polishing and they spoil the look of the outfit altogether.' Tina glanced down at her feet and frowned. These days she hated to think she looked anything less than smart and stylish and Kitty looked as though she'd just stepped off the cover of a woman's magazine.

After Tina had gone and when Edward was in bed Kitty tidied up the sitting room. Then she poured herself the single glass of port she allowed herself each night to help her unwind and sat on the window seat gazing out at the darkening evening sky. A brisk wind was rattling the branches of the trees and the first daffodils were appearing in the flower beds. It was hard work running a business but she enjoyed it, she thought. She had come a long way from being a maid at Harwood Hall and she was certain she could go much further. Granted, she had been fortunate that Stanley had left her four shops but they'd not been increasing business and he'd had no interest in adding to them. Now they were once again showing a healthy profit and why shouldn't she add to them? Poor Stanley had been firmly stuck in the past, he wasn't ambitious or far-sighted enough to look to the future, but she was.

She glanced around the room; it wasn't just the shops that had been redecorated. Gone was the brown varnish and gloomy wallpaper. She had new curtains and a nice carpet; she had got rid of a lot of the furniture which made the room look much bigger. She had packed away most of the ornaments and all the old photographs. The ones of Annie and Davie and Bridget had replaced them. She had found a good one of Stanley and had bought a lovely frame for it and it now stood on the sideboard with the one she had finally had taken of Edward in his velvet sailor suit, clutching a toy ship that Tina had bought for him. She hadn't had the heart to get rid of Stanley's treasured stamp albums; they were still stacked neatly under the wireless.

She had modern appliances in the kitchen and she had moved the old-fashioned double bed out of the bedroom and replaced it with a new single one. There were times when she did miss Stanley and occasionally she caught herself listening for his key in the front door. She owed him so much and now she felt glad that he had seemed to be happy enough in their short marriage. It hadn't been a love match and it had never been exciting but it hadn't been without affection and companionship and respect.

Her thoughts turned to Niall Collins and she wondered just how his marriage was working out.

How many children did he now have? Were his parents still alive? Was he grateful for the dowry his wife had brought him? She would never forget that day she had met his mother or the humiliation she'd felt. Well, now she was a woman of both property and wealth but it was far too late. She still wrote to Mrs Joyce but she never mentioned him and neither had the minister's wife. In her last letter Mrs Joyce had told her that Hester had smartened herself up and the reason for that was a certain Walter Sullivan, a bachelor farmer who had shown an interest in her stepmother. As Kitty had little interest in Hester or what she did, she had shrugged and dismissed it from her mind. Irish bachelors were renowned for staying just that – bachelors – and she was certain that this Walter Sullivan would think very carefully about taking on the likes of Hester Doyle and two unruly boys – boys that were none of his blood, even if they would one day inherit the forge. Providing Hester didn't sell it before then, as it was still being rumoured she would.

She finished her drink and got up to switch on the standard lamp and draw the curtains. There were still a few things she had to attend to before she went to bed, and sitting here musing wouldn't get them done.

Chapter Thirty-Two

—◆—

THE YEAR WAS CERTAINLY one of vastly contrasting weather, Kitty thought as she sat in the office of the shop on Walton Vale. July so far had been scorching hot with the sun beating down from a cloudless blue sky day after day with not even the slightest of breezes to give some relief. The room was stifling even though the window was wide open, as were both the front and back doors of the building. It was such a change to the way the New Year of 1927 had started. There had been fierce winds in January, in Glasgow eight people had been killed in what the newspapers had called a hurricane and in February there had been dense freezing fogs. It had been so bad that all the ships on the river Mersey had been fogbound for days and nights on end and in the English Channel ten had collided and three had sunk. Spring had come as a welcome relief but the weather had become very warm in May and as the months advanced the temperatures had continued to rise.

Kitty fanned her cheeks with a sheet of paper and tried to concentrate but her head had begun to ache. In front of her was the letter she had received concerning yet another shop she was contemplating taking on. A further new model estate was being built at Norris Green and her venture in Fazakerley was doing so well that she had jumped at this opportunity as soon as she'd heard about it. She had a week to put in her application.

Maggie put her head around the door, looking hot and flustered. 'Mrs Ellinson, what are we going to do about the butter and lard and margarine? It's so hot that they're in real danger of just melting into puddles.'

Kitty sighed and pushed the letter aside. 'What state is that ice in that came this morning?' she enquired, thinking of the large zinc tubs filled with ice that stood in the storeroom. It was the only way they had of trying to keep things cool and fresh but it didn't last long and it wasn't cheap.

'It melts so quickly. The tubs were half full of water last time I checked.'

'We'd better bring all that kind of stuff into the storeroom, put it in the tubs and pack as much ice as we can around it. If customers ask for it we'll have to go up and get it. It will mean running up and down in this heat but it will be ruined entirely if we leave it in the shop. I'll give you a hand. The Lord alone knows how the dairies are managing. There must be gallons of milk turning sour.'

'Anyone selling ice cream will be making a fortune, I'll bet,' Maggie said glumly. The thought of running up and down stairs all afternoon didn't appeal to her at all and she wouldn't have minded an ice cream herself.

After she'd helped the two girls move the stock of rapidly melting fats, Kitty went back to her desk and began to write out her application for the shop on what was going to be called 'Broadway'. It was in an excellent position as far as she could judge from the small copy of the plans that she had been sent. There would be a large catchment area and it would be well served by the tramway system. She considered that to be important as very few people had cars and it was far from easy having to carry shopping home on foot for any distance, whatever the weather. It would mean more work for her. There were endless things to think about and organise to get new premises up and running; she knew that from her experiences with Ellinson's in Fazakerley, but she was sure it would prove to be just as successful. She had her competitors of course, Costigan's, Peegram's and the Home and

Colonial Stores to name but a few, but she kept up to date with everything and read the *Grocer's Gazette* and the *Retail Grocer* avidly.

She leaned back in her chair and rubbed the back of her neck, which felt damp with perspiration. Six shops, what would Stanley have thought of that? As Tina had said admiringly, she was building up a chain, which might one day rival that of the Co-operative. She smiled to herself; she doubted that. They were a much bigger outfit than Ellinson's would ever be, even if she finished up with over a dozen shops. Still, it was a chain if only a small one. 'Not bad for a bit of an eejit from the bogs of Ireland,' she said aloud.

She was called out into the shop as there was a sudden rush of customers and she hated people to be kept waiting for too long. She worked efficiently alongside Maggie and Violet. Today was Tuesday and Eileen, the latest addition to her staff, only worked on Thursdays, Fridays and Saturdays as she helped her sister to care for their invalid mother.

'There we are, Mrs Watson. Two pounds of sugar, two of plain flour, half a pound of lean boiled ham and a packet of Rich Tea biscuits.' She assembled the items on the counter.

'Thank you, Mrs Ellinson. I'll leave you the weekly order, if I could have it delivered on Friday as usual I'd be grateful.' The woman passed Kitty the list and delved into her purse to pay for the things on the counter, thinking that it was nice to see Kitty Ellinson, who certainly had no need at all to set foot behind a shop counter, paying such attention to her business. It showed she hadn't got above herself and taken on all kinds of airs and graces.

Kitty was counting out the woman's change when she was startled to see Gloria Williams come rushing in.

'Gloria! Where's Edward? Sure, you haven't left him on his own, have you?'

'No! Mam's with him but she said she thinks you'd best come home, he's not at all well.'

'There's an awful lot of sickness going around, Mrs Ellinson. It's the heat,' Mrs Watson said gravely, preparing to leave.

Gloria was upset. 'He was off colour all morning and wouldn't eat his lunch but he got worse and so I asked Mam to come and have a look at him. She thinks you should call the doctor.'

Kitty was seriously worried. Oh, he had suffered with a few childish ailments and colds up to now but nothing serious. 'Has he been sick? Does he have a temperature or a rash?' she asked as she lifted the counter flap and took off her overall.

'He's very hot and is complaining that his head hurts. I can't see any signs of a rash, but he was playing with the little Townsend child from Edgeley Gardens last week,' the girl answered.

'And is she sick?' Kitty demanded as she snatched up her hat and bag from the office.

'Mam said she'd seen the doctor's car outside on Friday afternoon but she hadn't heard what was wrong.'

Kitty had a few quick words with Violet and then followed Gloria out.

When she got home she could see by her neighbour's face that she was worried. 'Where is he, Nancy? What's wrong?'

'He's in bed, Kitty, but I don't like the look of the poor little mite at all. I've sent for Dr Lipman I was that worried.'

Kitty ran upstairs, her fear increasing. The little boy was lying on top of his bed and she could see he was burning up. She fell to her knees beside him and took his hand. It felt clammy and limp.

'Edward! Edward, Mammy's here! Do you feel sick? Tell Mammy where it hurts.'

'All over but my head hurts very bad, Mammy.'

She put a hand on his forehead. 'The doctor is coming right away and he'll make you all better again soon,' she soothed. She hoped she sounded more confident than she felt. He'd never been like this before and she was very frightened. She felt guilty now that the business had become almost all-absorbing. It was nothing compared to the place Edward held in her heart and without him everything was pointless.

To her relief the doctor arrived within a few minutes and Nancy ushered him upstairs where Gloria informed him of Edward's symptoms and the fact he had been playing with little Hannah Townsend the previous week.

'Let me look at him but if he's been in contact with Hannah then I suspect it's scarlet fever,' he said gravely.

'Oh, no!' Kitty cried, her eyes widening in fear. He was only three years old, little more than a baby.

'There's a lot of it around and it can be quite serious. We should be very thankful that we live in a decent area for I hear diphtheria is rife in the poorer areas of the city and that there has been one case of cholera confirmed on the dock estate. A man has been taken to the fever hospital, although it's believed he is of foreign origin. The ship in question has been quarantined. This weather is not at all healthy.' He shook his head as he examined the little boy. It was as he'd expected.

'It's scarlet fever, Kitty, but don't worry, it's seldom fatal. Keep him sponged down with cool water and try to get him to drink plenty of fluids. You'll have to stay with him. You won't be able to go near those shops of yours, it's contagious, and when he recovers all the bedding, toys, books and clothes that he's had contact with will have to be burned. I'll keep my eye on you too and, Mrs Williams, will you watch young Gloria?'

Nancy nodded. Kitty was so relieved that he had said it was seldom fatal that she didn't give a second thought to the disruption this would cause her business. All that mattered was that Edward should get well again.

'Kitty, don't be alarmed if his skin starts to peel. It's a sign that he is recovering and it's quite normal with this disease.'

Kitty thought it was quite the most horrible thing that had happened to her precious son in his short life, apart from losing his father she reminded herself, but she doubted that Edward even remembered Stanley.

She nursed him devotedly day and night for the next four days, even though she felt utterly exhausted. It broke her heart to see him suffer but all that mattered was that her precious son should get well again. Dr Lipman was as good as his word and called in to see him, giving her advice and much-needed encouragement. She had been dozing in the chair at the foot of the child's bed when he at last crawled out of the bed and tugged at her skirt.

'Mammy, I'm hungry!'

Kitty scooped him up in her arms, tears of relief

and exhaustion in her eyes. 'You're better! Now, what would you like? An egg and some soldiers?'

He nodded and she carried him downstairs, relief that he had come to no harm giving her strength.

He got stronger but was puzzled when, starting with small patches, his skin began to peel.

'Mammy, look, I'm coming to bits!' he'd cried.

Kitty had laughed and reassured him but it hadn't been as easy to placate him when she'd told him some of his favourite toys, including his battered little rabbit – now minus one ear – would have to be burned.

'But Mammy will buy you some nice new things and look, poor rabbit is all broken. Wouldn't you like a brand-new one with two ears?' she'd consoled him, but it had been useless and he'd become so upset that she'd given in over the woolly toy. Sure, I can't see that fretting over it will do him any good at all, she'd said to herself. She'd give it a good wash in Dettol.

She had been so preoccupied while he'd been ill that she hadn't even seen a newspaper or listened to the wireless and the application for her new premises was still lying on her desk in the shop. But now she read with concern that there were epidemics of all kinds of diseases raging in the slum areas and she immediately began to worry that Edward would catch something else.

As she sat in the chair in his room watching him

sleep her fears grew. What if he caught the dreaded diphtheria? His throat would close over and he would choke to death and there would be nothing either she or Dr Lipman could do that would save him. It was too terrible to think about. And the weather showed no sign of changing, it was hot and sultry and even though the window was wide open there was little movement of air in the room. And there was August to get through yet before the cooler days of September arrived. She couldn't put him at risk; if she lost him she would lose all reason for living herself. He needed to be away from the city. Away from the hot, crowded and dirty streets. She had fought a constant battle with the flies all summer and had spent a small fortune on flypapers and DDT. The rubbish in the gutters and the manure left on the roads by the horses that pulled the many carts attracted them. She'd heard customers say that parts of the city stank to high heaven. No, he was so precious to her that she would have to take him away somewhere where there was fresh air, no streets full of traffic, no crowds of people to pass on disease. She could pick something up from any one of her customers or deliverymen and bring it home to him. It would be hard to leave everything she had worked so hard for but her son's life was far more important. She would sell up and she would go home to Ireland. Home to Rahan where there were green fields for him to run and play in and little risk of terrifying epidemics each summer. Where the wind blowing across the midlands from the west coast was pure and clean. She was sure Mrs Joyce would be delighted for them to stay with her until she found somewhere to live. She would not stay with Hester.

She propped her chin up with her hands and looked out of the window and in her mind she saw the white walls of Harwood House rise up at the end of the long curving drive. She had always loved that house. If Henry Harwood hadn't found a buyer then she would buy it, no matter what kind of a state it was in now. She had a good head for business and she would point out that in its present condition she would expect him to reduce his price and be grateful that someone was willing to take it off his hands. Even if it was his sister's former lady's maid.

Chapter Thirty-Three

———•◦⋈◦•———

As soon as Edward was fully recovered Kitty determined to go and see Mr Blackwell, the solicitor. It had been Tina who had suggested it when she called to see her, bringing a toy for Edward and a strange polished gourd inside which there were large nuts.

'Sure, I've never seen the like of it before, what is it?' Kitty had asked, a look of puzzlement on her face.

'It's what the Brazil nuts grow in. That's them inside. It's a sort of curio, I suppose you could use it as an ornament.'

'I've seen Brazil nuts in the shops but I never knew they grew like this.'

Tina had settled herself down on the sofa. The oppressive heat didn't seem to be affecting her, Kitty thought, but then she supposed her friend was used to it.

'And the poor little mite was ill, you must have been worried sick.'

'Half out of my mind! Thank God he's over it now. But I've come to a decision, Tina. He is more precious to me than anything I have in this world and I can't risk him catching something from which he won't recover, so I'm selling up and I'm taking him home, back to Ireland.'

Tina had stared at her open-mouthed. 'Are you mad?' she'd at last managed to cry. 'Sell everything you've worked so hard for? The shops, this house? What will you do there?'

'I don't know but I'll find something. I won't be short of money so it's not a pressing matter.'

'Kitty, you have thought this through properly? I don't want you to regret it and I'll miss you terribly.'

Kitty had smiled. 'I've thought of nothing else and I won't regret it. I hardly see you anyway, you're away for nine months of the year. We write regularly but it's not the same, is it? I'll miss you too, but you can come and visit me. You have a month's leave each time you get home.'

Tina had nodded. She visited Kitty as often as she could when she was home on leave; well, she would just have to go to Ireland. She'd never been there and it was a good deal nearer than South America.

'What will you do, stay with your stepmother to start with?'

'No! I'll stay with Mrs Joyce and I intend to buy Harwood Hall, if it's still for sale.'

Tina had stared at her as though she was a raving lunatic. 'Now I know you've gone completely mad! Didn't you tell me it was virtually derelict a couple of years ago? For God's sake, Kitty, there's no electricity or gas, no proper water supply and it will cost a fortune in repairs, furnishings, heating – that's if it hasn't collapsed! What in the name of God do you want a huge house like that for when there's just you and Edward?'

Kitty had laughed. 'I knew you'd say all those things, I just knew it! Well, won't I have a fortune to spend on it and labour is cheap. There'll be plenty who will be glad of the work and I've always loved that house. Perhaps one day Annie and Bridget might come and visit us. I can afford to pay their fares. They'll never come back to live, I know that, they're happy over there, they've made good lives for themselves. I once promised Annie that one day I'd find a place where we could all be together and now I have, even though it will never be their home. And there will be plenty of room for you, you might even like to bring your mam on a bit of a holiday. Aren't you always saying she deserves one?'

Tina had realised there was no changing her mind, so she had grinned. 'And there's something really satisfying in the fact that you first went there as a servant and now you'll be the mistress. I'd love to see Elizabeth Harwood's face when she learns her maid will now be sleeping in what used to be her room! What will you do, get in touch with Henry Harwood?'

'I have no idea of how to get in touch with him.'

'Go and see that solicitor feller. He'll know how to go about it and, Kitty, tell him you don't want Henry Harwood to know who you are.'

'Why not?'

'Because he might refuse to sell it to you or put the price up.'

'Well, last time I heard he was desperate to sell it. I'm expecting him to lower the price, seeing as it's in such a shocking state of repair.'

'Then tell the solicitor just to inform him that Mrs Kathleen Ellinson wishes to buy it. He won't know who you are. He probably doesn't even remember you at all.'

'No, I'll say all I want him to know is that a Mrs Ellinson wants to buy it. He probably didn't even know my surname; if he remembers me at all it will be as Kitty, not even Kathleen, but I want to be on the safe side. And I'll ask Mr Blackwell to handle the sale of the shops and this house too,' Kitty had said determinedly.

'What about all your staff? They're going to be a bit upset.'

Kitty had already thought of that. 'I want it to be made a condition of the sale that they be kept on and on their present wage.'

Tina had smiled. 'You've thought of everything, haven't you?'

'I've had plenty of time to think, Tina,' Kitty had replied.

A week later on a day that threatened a storm, Kitty went to see Mr Blackwell, who had been Stanley's solicitor. She told him all her plans and he listened carefully, making occasional notes.

'I know who the Harwoods' solicitor is; I'll contact him straight away, Mrs Ellinson. You can leave everything in my hands. You do realise that the sale of all five shops, their stock in trade and the goodwill and reputation, plus the house in Osterley Gardens, will amount to a very large sum of money?'

Kitty nodded. 'I'll need it, Mr Blackwell, even if Henry Harwood reduces his price. The house was in a sorry state the last time I saw it and that was a few years ago.'

He leaned forward, his hands clasped together as he studied her. He was quite surprised that she had turned out to be such an astute businesswoman but she still didn't seem to grasp that she would be a very wealthy woman indeed. The reputation of her shops alone would ensure that they were snapped up and at a price well above what she had in mind.

He smiled at her. 'I think you will find that you will still have a great deal of money left, Mrs Ellinson. I would invest it carefully for your son's future. Have you any ideas about that that I could assist or advise you on?'

Kitty smiled back. 'Not really, although after I've got myself settled I might open an Ellinson's Grocery shop in Tullamore, which will be my nearest town.'

'You intend to start another chain of shops?'

'Perhaps.'

'I'd think very carefully about that, Mrs Ellinson. The Free State is a poor country whose economy isn't as stable as ours and there is still tension between the two governments. There are economic restrictions in place which I suppose some people would say are tantamount to an economic war. I would say there are very few people in the rural towns and villages who could afford to shop at an Ellinson's type of grocery and I assume you would also find it difficult to source many of the items you now have on your shelves. There is the difference in value too between the Irish pound and the British pound, although that will be greatly to your advantage. However, I wouldn't advise you to take your entire fortune with you. I would leave the bulk of it in the security of a bank here, just in case. Much better to be safe than sorry.'

Kitty nodded. These were things she hadn't considered. 'I'll take your advice, Mr Blackwell. I'm not at all well versed in such things.'

'Right, I'll get the process started and I'll contact you as soon as there is any progress. I don't think you will have long to wait in the matter of the sale of your businesses; the purchase of Harwood Hall may take longer. Have you decided when you wish to return to Ireland?'

'As soon as it is possible. I'm terrified for my son's health.'

'I'm sure he will come to no harm, Mrs Ellinson. I'll move things along as quickly as is possible but it won't be a matter of weeks, I'm afraid.'

'I don't intend to wait months, Mr Blackwell! I'll stay no longer than the end of this month. If Mr Harwood can't or won't sell, then I'll find another house.' She meant it although she would be terribly disappointed.

'Then you had better leave me an address in Ireland where I can contact you.'

'Care of Mrs Joyce, the Rectory, Rahan, Tullamore, County Offaly. That will find me.'

He wrote it down as she rose and held out her hand. 'Thank you, Mr Blackwell, you have been most helpful. I look forward to hearing from you.'

When she returned home she began to make lists of things she had to do. The storm that been threatening broke and the room was illuminated by flashes of lightning and rain sheeted down the window panes. At least it should cool things down a bit, she thought.

She must decide what furnishings she would keep from this house and what she would sell. There were things to be disposed of too. She would have to call a meeting of all her staff; she must tell them her plans personally and reassure them that their jobs were safe. She would have that meeting here on Sunday afternoon. She would also have to tell Gloria and Nancy Williams of her impending departure: she knew Gloria would be upset. She wondered if she should ask the girl whether she would like to go with her? Edward would miss Gloria and as everything would be new and perhaps strange for him at first it might help him to settle. She would make that a priority.

Gloria had been upset to hear the news but Kitty had suggested that she go with her and Gloria had agreed to think about it and discuss it with her parents. Kitty had told her that she could return at any time if she wasn't happy, and Gloria had said it was a great relief to know that. She had never been away from home before.

The staff meeting had gone far better than Kitty had expected. Everyone had been very apprehensive when they'd arrived, not knowing what to expect. It was unheard of for an employer to invite employees to their home for tea on a Sunday. Kitty had explained the reason for her decision to sell but had reassured them that little would change.

'Whoever buys the shops won't be after making huge changes, not if they've any sense at all. The way Ellinson's shops have been run is part of their success so you probably won't even notice the difference and it will be written into the conditions of sale that you are all to be kept on with no reduction in your wage either,' she had told them, noting the glances of relief that passed between them all.

'We'll notice that we won't be seeing you popping in and out and I for one will miss you, Mrs Ellinson,' Ada had said, knowing she spoke for them all.

When they had all gone she cleared everything away and tidied up, then she sat down to write to Mrs Joyce. She explained that she was returning home for good at the end of this month as she refused to expose her son to the diseases that raged in this city throughout the summer months. She asked if it would be too much of an imposition for herself and Edward and possibly Gloria, who was in effect Edward's nanny, to stay until she bought a place of her own. For obvious reasons she did not want to stay with Hester Doyle. She confided that she wanted to buy Harwood Hall but asked the minister's wife not to disclose this to anyone other than her husband, for she was not sure if Henry Harwood would sell it to her. He might think it demeaning to sell his former home to someone who had once been a servant there. She sealed the letter and put it on the sideboard; she'd post it in the morning.

She was delighted to receive a reply the following Friday and equally delighted to learn that Harwood Hall was still for sale. It would, however, need an army of workmen and cleaners to make it habitable. Mrs Joyce wrote that she would love to have them all to stay, there was plenty of room, and for as long as was needed. Not a single soul would she tell of Kitty's plans and she had hidden Kitty's letter in a safe place for young Mary was not above poking and prying. Kitty was to let her know the exact date of her departure and the time of her arrival and they would meet her at Tullamore Station. Was she to inform Hester they were coming? she enquired.

Kitty thought about that. She supposed her stepmother would hear of it so it would do no harm, although she had no intention at all of visiting Hester. The post had also brought a letter from Bridget who declared that she thought it truly wonderful that Kitty was going home and that both she and Annie couldn't believe that she was going to *buy* Harwood Hall and live there with just Edward and maybe Gloria. Bridget wrote that Annie had said Kitty must be a millionairess now and did she think her sister could contribute something to the cost of Annie's forthcoming wedding? Everything was terribly expensive and Annie really wanted it to be a special day. Kitty smiled at that. Well, Annie would have everything she wanted. At least she was marrying the lad she loved. She would have liked to invite her sister and her new husband to spend their honeymoon in Ireland, all expenses paid by herself, but it wasn't possible. Harwood Hall, if she got it, would not be ready and when Annie did come she wanted Bridget to come too and you couldn't ask a bride to bring her sister with her on her honeymoon. No, that visit would have to be sometime in the future.

She had thought at length about how she would feel if she met Niall Collins and his wife. She knew she would, it was inevitable in such a small place. It wasn't a big city like Liverpool, full of strangers. She supposed he would have changed, she knew she had, but did she really still care for him the way she had once? It was something she wasn't at all sure of, something she wouldn't know until she actually saw him again; and even if she did she would just have to put it out of her mind and get on with her life. She had done it before; she could do it again.

Chapter Thirty-Four

THE WEEKS THAT FOLLOWED seemed totally chaotic and Kitty found herself living in a house where she was surrounded by packing cases. She had thrown out all kinds of things; some of the items of furniture she wanted to keep had already gone into storage where they would remain until she sent for them. She had booked their tickets and had sent Mrs Joyce a telegram giving dates and times. To her delight Gloria had decided to accompany them. She'd 'give it a try', was how she'd put it, and she too was busy packing.

To her surprise and relief she had had a letter from Mr Blackwell informing her that Henry Harwood had more or less jumped at the chance to get rid of what he now saw as a millstone around his neck and at a much reduced price, although those weren't the words the solicitor had used. Everything had been set out in formal legal terms. She hadn't expected to hear so soon but she wrote instructing him to proceed with the purchase. There had been a great deal of interest in the shops but so far there had been no firm offer. She had thought the price the solicitor had asked was outrageously high but had deferred to his judgement. She supposed she could always take less if they looked as if they were going to stick. Her own house had been quickly snapped up, and at the price she had asked: it was in such a very desirable and popular area.

There hadn't been much time to visit the shops but the week before she was due to leave she went and said goodbye to all her staff. As she left the shop on Walton Vale she stood on the pavement and looked up at the cream sign above the door with the name 'Ellinson's Grocery' painted in dark green lettering. The colours were a sort of trademark, chosen the day Violet had suggested they change the overalls. She felt a pang of sadness. She was selling something that was a part of her. Then she shook herself mentally. Wasn't Edward a part of her too? They were not worth risking his health for.

Tina had been a great help and when the day of their departure finally arrived she came to the ferry with them to see them off.

'Now, you've got everything and you'll have someone to help you with the luggage and meet you?'

'It's all arranged, stop worrying.'

'You should have bought a car, Kitty. I'm sure it would be quicker and more comfortable to drive from Dublin and they'd have taken it over on the ferry with you.'

Kitty laughed. 'Ah, sure, I couldn't drive one of those things. I'd be terrified I'd run off the road and into a ditch!'

'You could have learned. You can do anything when you put your mind to it.'

Kitty studied her friend's expression speculatively. 'You just want me to arrive looking like the gentry!'

'Well, you're going home with more money than a lot of the gentry have these days, Kitty Ellinson, and don't you forget it!'

Kitty hugged her. 'I'll miss you, Tina. You promise to come and see me and to write?'

'I will, and when I'm sitting on deck of an evening I'll think of you rattling around in that big, falling-down old house.' Tina was smiling but there were tears in her eyes.

'It won't be a "falling-down old house" when I've finished with it, you wait and see. Now, Gloria, you'd better kiss your mam and then take Edward while I make sure all the luggage goes on board. The cabin numbers are on the tickets,' Kitty instructed, handing Gloria an envelope.

Tina hugged her again. 'You've a lovely evening for it. There's not a breath of wind.'

Kitty nodded and glanced back at the waterfront of the city that had been her home for these past five years. In some ways she was sorry to be leaving, it was a fine city and its people were friendly, witty and generous. It had been good to her; she had made a success of herself here. There was a firm offer in for her shops and at almost the price that had been asked for. Tina was right. She was going home a very wealthy woman.

'You'd better go on board yourself, Kitty, now,' Nancy Williams urged, 'and don't worry about our Gloria. She's a sensible girl.'

Kitty thanked her. 'You will come and visit us when we have the house fit to live in?'

'You'll be having such a succession of visitors at this rate that the place will be like a hotel!' Tina laughed, giving her friend a gentle push in the direction of the gangway. She stood with Gloria's parents and sisters and watched as Kitty went aboard.

'She'll be fine, Tina. She's going home,' Nancy Williams said kindly as Tina wiped away her tears.

It was quite amazing what having money did, Kitty thought as the following afternoon they all alighted from the train. Mrs Joyce had arranged for two porters to see to the luggage and the station master himself came out to greet her. There was no sign of a pony and trap, instead a shiny black car was waiting, hired especially for the occasion.

'Sure, aren't we arriving in the height of style?' Kitty smiled delightedly as she greeted the minister and his wife, while Gloria looked around with avid curiosity as she held tightly to Edward's hand.

'We took the liberty of arranging everything; you have to admit that you have come up in the world now. Welcome home, Kitty!' the Reverend Joyce greeted her.

'No, it wouldn't do at all for you to be seen driving in a trap and besides there wouldn't be room for all of you and the luggage,' Mrs Joyce added.

'But one of the first things I must do is get myself a pony and trap. I'll have to have transport and Gloria certainly isn't used to walking miles,' Kitty laughed as they ushered her towards the car.

'We'll get all that sorted out in the next few days but for now let's get you all to the rectory. Mary is to have the tea ready and she's so excited that you're coming home.'

'She doesn't know about the house?' Kitty asked anxiously.

Mrs Joyce shook her head. 'Not at all! Didn't I say my lips were sealed? Is it all going well?'

'It is. Mr Blackwell will be sending me the deeds very shortly. I still can't believe it. If you don't mind, I'd like to go up and look at it after supper. It will still be light.'

Mrs Joyce nodded. Kitty had a big job on her hands to restore that place to its former glory. It was a sorry sight.

They unpacked with the help of Mrs Joyce and a delighted Mary Wrafter who had said wasn't it great that she had sold all those grand shops and come home with pots of money. It just showed you that it wasn't only the lads that could go off and make their fortunes. Kitty had laughed but Mrs Joyce had admonished the girl for being so bold.

After supper she and Gloria got Edward to bed and as she gently stroked his cheek, Kitty felt she had done the right thing. He would be safe here. He would grow up in the country with room to run and play and learn to fish and to ride. And he'd make many friends. Gloria was getting on famously with young Mary who was promising to take her to the next dance to be held in the parish, and extolling the virtues (or lack of them) in all the lads who would be there. Mrs Joyce was listening intently to all this and intended to keep a watchful eye on Gloria who had obviously never been to a country dance before.

It was a beautiful evening, Kitty thought as she

drove the Joyces' trap along the lane and up over the canal bridge. The sun was a huge fiery ball of orange, low in a sky now shot with streaks of vermilion and purple, and its dying rays had turned the still, calm waters of the canal into a wide ribbon of molten gold. The air was heavy with the scents of a summer evening and it was so quiet. Only the sound of the pony's hooves broke the stillness. For the first time in months she felt a sense of peace and contentment. It really was good to be home.

At last she turned the trap into the wide gateway and looked up towards the house, as she had done so many times before. She drove slowly up the potholed drive, the long shadows of evening masking the unkempt verges and straggling lines of trees that marked the boundary of the paddocks. She pulled up beneath the massive old oak tree and got down, tying the reins to a low branch. The white walls of the Hall looked welcoming, half covered by the Boston ivy, the leaves of which would turn bright red and orange next month before they started to fall. There were weeds, waist-high now, growing around the front steps and some of the window panes were cracked and broken, resembling sightless eyes staring unseeingly into the gathering twilight. It was so neglected, she thought, as she walked nearer. So forlorn and *unloved*. She went up the steps and reached out and touched the tarnished doorknocker. It was *hers*! It was really *hers*! A feeling of pride and joy surged through her, of such magnitude it made her shiver. She would love it and tend it, making it into the gracious, happy home it had once been. She wouldn't feel lonely or isolated here. She would fill it with people. Tina and her mother, Nancy and her daughters. Her own sisters Bridget and Annie and Annie's Davie. Maybe even Aunt Enid and Uncle Ted who had been so good to the girls. It would be filled with Edward's laughter and that of his friends. It would never again be referred to as the home of the gentry. All her neighbours would be welcome.

She stepped back a little and looked up at the creeper-clad walls. She had no keys yet so she was unable to go inside, but she dreaded to think what faced her when she did. Still, she had such great plans. Once all the building-repair work was done she would go up to Dublin for furnishings. She would buy the best of everything; she could certainly afford it. It had come as a shock when she had fully realised just how much money she had. Annie's estimation hadn't been far wrong and she had determined to take Mr Blackwell's advice on investing a good deal of it for Edward's future.

She should go around to the back of the house before it grew dark, she thought, because the gardens would be a wilderness now.

'It's finally been sold, although I hear he had to drop his price. An Englishwoman has bought it.'

She was startled at the voice that interrupted her deliberations; she had thought she was alone and she'd heard no one approaching. She stood rooted to the spot, not even attempting to turn around. She would recognise his voice anywhere. Her heart began to beat in an odd jerky fashion but she realised she would have to answer him.

'I know. I bought it. It's mine.' She was thankful she had managed to keep her voice steady.

'So, you are Mrs Ellinson then?'

Kitty reached out and caught hold of the wrought-iron railings her da had made so many years ago and held on tightly to steady herself. She still didn't turn around. 'How do you know my name?'

'My da had to go into town to see his solicitor today. Henry Harwood had written to your man with some instructions. It's not a secret, not that I heard anyway. I came up here to have a look at the place for the last time. I sometimes come here for a bit of peace and quiet. I . . . I used to come quite often at one time. I didn't expect you to be here, I didn't think you would be coming until it was made habitable. It puzzled me too that an Englishwoman would want to come and live in the back of beyond. We're miles and miles away from Dublin.'

So, he had often come back here for 'a bit of peace and quiet'. Were things *that* bad at the Collinses' farm? Kitty wondered. She took a deep breath. 'I only arrived today and the reason I bought the place is that I . . . I came here often too in the past. In fact I used to work here, when Amy Harwood was alive. I was Elizabeth's maid.'

Slowly Kitty turned around but she was still unable to look at him. She kept her eyes fixed on the steps at her feet. Her heart was racing.

'God Almighty! Kitty Doyle, is it you?' He hadn't recognised her voice; he barely recognised her. She was beautiful. In the rays of the dying sun her hair shone like a gold halo. She wore a dress of some flimsy, floaty lilac-coloured fabric that showed off a trim, slender figure and he couldn't be certain but he thought there were tears sparkling on her downcast lashes.

Kitty was desperately trying to stay calm and in control of her emotions as at last she came down the steps towards him. He was older but she thought he had never looked so handsome.

'I'm Kitty Ellinson now, Niall, and I've brought my son home. He was very ill with scarlet fever. A city is no place for a child to grow up.'

His emotions were playing havoc with his composure. 'And your husband?'

'Is dead. Stanley left me four shops and a house. I built up the business until it was a huge success but . . . but it wasn't worth Edward's health. So I decided to come home. I always loved this house so I bought it.'

He thrust his hands deeper into the pockets of his trousers. She must be a wealthy woman. It still hurt the way she had left without a word and even more so the way she had treated him the last time he'd seen her in Tullamore with Elizabeth Harwood. 'I see. So now you've come back to lord it over us all?'

A retort rose to Kitty's lips but his smile took the sting out of his words. 'I have not. As I've just said, I've come home for Edward's sake.'

'Where are you staying? Surely not here? Didn't Henry Harwood mention the state it was in?'

'I knew it had fallen into almost a ruin so I got it at a good price and I'm staying with the Reverend and Mrs Joyce until it's fit to live in.' She stepped closer to him. There was so much she wanted to ask him. She wanted to cry out that he had broken her heart, he had betrayed her, but she fought down the impulse.

'Then you kept in touch with everything that was going on?'

'I did so.'

'Well, I wish you well of the place, Kitty. I'd best be getting back now, 'tis late.'

She didn't want him to go, not yet, but what excuse

could she give to keep him here? She sighed. 'I'd best be getting back myself. Sure, I said I wouldn't be long and I am tired after the journey.'

'I take it the trap belongs to the Joyces?'

She nodded. 'Have you transport? Surely you didn't walk?'

'I left the bicycle outside the gates, as I always do.'

For a second she had hoped he had walked, then she could have offered to drive him home but what was the point in that? She would have been driving him home to his wife. She unhitched the pony and led it down the driveway; he walked beside her. The trees threw long shadows and she was unable to see his face clearly but there was one question she had to ask.

'I heard you married: how is your wife?'

He stopped and stared down at her. 'Did they not inform you?'

'Of what?' she asked.

'She died giving birth to Aoife.'

She laid a hand on his arm. 'Niall, I'm so sorry. I really didn't know, it was never mentioned in Mrs Joyce's letters. You have a daughter?'

He nodded. 'Ma takes care of her.'

''Tis a pity she never knew her mother. Edward hardly remembers Stanley. Stanley was much older than me. He was forty-seven when he was murdered.'

He was horrified. '*Murdered!* My God, Kitty!'

'A robbery that went wrong. They hanged the man who killed him.'

'And you coped with all that alone?' His voice was full of admiration. She obviously hadn't had it easy.

'I had to, there was no one else. Annie and Bridget are in New York and Tina, my friend, was away at sea.' They had reached the end of the drive and it was nearly dark.

'Let me help you up into the trap,' he offered, reluctant to let her go. There was so much he wanted to ask her. When she was settled he handed her the reins. 'I was wondering, Kitty, if . . . if I could perhaps see you again? We've a lot to catch up on but if you're too busy or you feel—'

'No! No, I'd like that, Niall,' she interrupted.

He smiled at her. 'When?'

'I'll be up here again tomorrow evening, is that too soon?'

'That'll be grand. I'll see you then.' He slapped the pony on the rump and it started into a trot.

She turned to wave but the bend in the road hid him from her sight.

When she reached the rectory it was to find that Mary had gone home, Gloria was in bed and Edward too was fast asleep.

'You look tired Kitty, you must be worn out. Gloria was,' Mrs Joyce said kindly.

'I am so and if you don't mind I think I'll go up too. Sure, it's been a long day.' She didn't tell the minister's wife that she had met Niall Collins or that she was meeting him again tomorrow evening; she wanted time to think about it first.

'You'll feel better in the morning. Goodnight, Kitty.'

A nightlight was burning in the room she was to share with Gloria and Edward and she smiled. Edward looked like a sleeping cherub. Her thoughts turned to a little girl who would no doubt also be asleep, a little girl who had never known her mother; and tears came to her eyes. She had never expressed an interest in Niall to Mrs Joyce so there had been no reason for her to inform Kitty of that tragedy. She sat down on the edge of the bed and eased off her shoes. What did she feel for him? she asked herself, but she already knew the answer. She still loved him, after all these years. She had never loved anyone else and he wanted to see her again. Could she trust him this time? He'd broken her heart once. Was he now attracted to her wealth? Was he looking for a mother for Aoife? She would just have to see how things went tomorrow evening. But she would be careful. She couldn't stand to have her heart broken again.

Chapter Thirty-Five

——◆——

THE FOLLOWING EVENING SHE took a pen and a jotter pad with her, telling Mrs Joyce that she wanted to make some notes. She had been up to the house that afternoon with Gloria and Edward but she explained that she really hadn't been able to concentrate on structural things with Edward running around and Gloria exclaiming that she'd never seen such a big house, even if it did look to be in a terrible state.

Niall was waiting for her, leaning against the trunk of the old oak, and her heart turned over. She would have to keep a tight rein on her emotions but maybe this evening she would find out why he had lied to her all those years ago.

He held the pony's bridle as she prepared to alight. 'I wondered if you would come. I heard that you were here this afternoon. Will I tie him to a branch?'

She nodded. 'There's not much goes on in this parish that doesn't get gossiped about, is there?'

He laughed, relieved that she had indeed come to meet him. 'Very little, but you are causing quite a stir. No one seems to know much about you at all and I'm not after being the one to enlighten them, unless of course you want me to?'

'No, not yet anyway.'

He helped her down and they walked towards the house.

'When will you be making a start on it, do you think?' he asked, thinking how fresh and lovely she looked in the cool blue and white dress, a thin white cardigan around her shoulders.

'As soon as I have the keys, which should be any day now. I'll go into town and find an architect and surveyor. Then I'll know what needs to be done first. I dread to think of the state it's in inside. 'Tis such a shame, poor Mrs Harwood would turn in her grave.'

He nodded. She was so confident and self-assured. The girl he'd known would never have dreamed of consulting architects and the like.

They went up the steps together and Kitty reached out and touched the peeling paint of the front door. 'I remember the day I first came here. Tess showed me around and I met Elizabeth and then as we came downstairs this door was wide open and Mr Harwood was standing just here where we are now, telling the dogs to "stay". He gave us a brace of pheasants to take to Cook.'

'It was a long time ago, Kitty. You've changed.'

'So have you, Niall.'

'What happened to Elizabeth? Why did you not stay with her?'

'The last I heard she was going to marry someone with a title. Someone she met when she was off on her extended cruise. I didn't go with her, I was let go. Told I was no longer needed, that they couldn't afford to keep me on while she was away. That's when I went to work for Stanley.'

He thrust his hands deep into the pockets of his trousers. He *had* to ask her.

'Why did you not tell me you were going to England with Elizabeth, Kitty? Even if you couldn't have got away you could have sent a note.'

She stared at him and then took a few steps closer. What did he mean? She had tried so hard to see him. 'I told your mother. I walked all the way over to your place to see you but by the time I arrived you were back out in the fields working. She knew, Niall! I told her we'd just started walking out. I told her where I worked, who I was, how old I was, how long I'd known you – everything!'

Being this close to her made him realise that she

was the loveliest girl he'd ever seen, but really a girl no
longer: she was a young woman. 'You saw Mam?' He
was puzzled. His mother had never mentioned it.

'I had no choice but to go with Elizabeth. I told
your mam that and it was then that she told me I had
no chance with you. I had no dowry and anyway you
were more or less promised to someone else. I was so
humiliated and so . . . so bitterly hurt and upset. I ran
all the way back here. I was utterly devastated.'

He reached out and laid his hand on her arm.
'Kitty, I never knew! She never told me! I swear it! I
thought you hadn't really meant what you'd said, that
you were just flirting, playing with me. I had no idea
how long you would be away or if you'd even come
back at all.'

She wanted desperately to believe him. 'But you got
engaged, you married her!' she cried. His hand on her
arm was making her tremble.

'They were at me day and night and I was so
miserable because I thought you didn't care! And then
I saw you in town with Elizabeth and I wanted to ask
you to explain, hoped we could start again, but you cut
me dead. Kitty, I would have taken you without a
penny! I loved you and you broke my heart!'

Still she held back. It was a huge effort not to throw
her arms around him and cry out that she had loved
him too, she hadn't just been flirting with him, and sh

still loved him. 'That day in town I was angry and hurt, Niall. I thought you had just used me. Then I went to Liverpool with Elizabeth after the accident. I married Stanley because I had no security. He gave me a job and a home. He was a good man but I never really loved him. There was just . . . affection between us.'

He took her hand. 'I never loved Margaret even though I tried and she knew it. When I think of all the pain Mam caused! The way she's made us suffer. Margaret's life wasn't easy either; they didn't really get on. I'll never forgive her, Kitty!'

She couldn't hold out any longer. 'And now, Niall? Is there anything left at all for . . . us?'

'Kitty, I never stopped loving you and when I saw you yesterday I desperately wanted to tell you that but I didn't know if you still cared. I was afraid even to ask.'

Tears filled her eyes but they were tears of joy. 'Oh, Niall! I never stopped loving you either!'

He took her in his arms and held her tightly. 'Kitty, this time I'm not letting you slip away from me.'

It was a long time before either of them could both speak but when they drew apart he stroked her cheek. 'Kitty, I'm afraid to ask you and maybe it's just too soon, you've only just arrived back, but . . .'

She reached up and kissed him again. 'But what?'

'Would you consider picking up where we left off? We've both changed, there are so many things I don't know about you and things you don't know about me, but in time . . .'

'Do you mean should we start "walking out"?'

'I mean, should we consider an engagement? I'll understand if you feel I'm rushing you, but I love you.'

'You're not rushing me, Niall. There's so much I want to learn about you but would it be a long engagement, do you think?'

'Not if you don't want it to be.'

'I don't but I don't want to be gossiped about either. Can we keep it a secret between ourselves?'

He nodded and they sat down on the steps. The heavy summer dusk was falling. 'When I think of all the wasted years, Kitty . . . It's going to be hard facing Mam and not having an almighty fight.'

She leaned her head on his shoulder. 'I know but try not to; sure, what good will that do now? And there are some good things that have happened, we should think of them. I have Edward and you have Aoife and now I have this house. And we . . . we have each other.'

'When will I see you again?'

'Tomorrow evening. Haven't I enough good reasons to be coming up here? I brought a pad and a pen but I haven't written down a single thing, but I can list at least a dozen things that need urgent attention. When I get the keys I want you to come inside with me.'

'I'd like that, Kitty. I really would.'

Reluctantly she got to her feet. 'We'd both better be going.'

He drew her close and kissed her. 'Goodnight, Kitty. I love you.'

Chapter Thirty-Six

NIALL FOUND IT HARD to keep his temper under control when he walked into the kitchen of his parents' house. He had always considered it to be home but now he felt like a stranger. A stranger who had been duped and bullied and denied the love he had always craved – and for what? So they could amass more land, money and a half-baked social position. His mother had treated Kitty disgracefully that day and had caused immeasurable heartache and misery for them both.

'Where have you been until this hour? The child was asking for you before she went to bed,' his mother demanded, putting down the book she had been reading. Her forehead was heavily lined from constant frowning and her tone was sharp.

Things had not turned out as she had planned at all.

The marriage between Margaret Maud Delahunty and Niall had been far from successful and she often felt guilty that she had pushed him into it. He had grown surly, taciturn and resentful. The only child of the marriage had been a girl, not the grandson she had hoped for who would in time inherit the farm, and girls often made unsuitable marriages to men who cared little for the land. Margaret had compounded that failure by dying, leaving her to bring up the child, an unwelcome added responsibility for a woman of her advancing years. She should be taking things more slowly, not running around after a two-year-old. And she felt guilty that at times she hadn't made life easy for her deceased daughter-in-law. The farm was not doing as well as she'd anticipated either; there was an economic war going on with Britain, which badly affected the prices they expected for their beef and dairy products. In fact the country was in a depressed state and there was growing poverty and mass emigration.

'I went up to Harwood Hall. I met the woman who has bought it,' Niall answered, noting with grim satisfaction the look of astonishment that came over his mother's face.

'You met the Ellinson woman? Did she tell you why she's bought the place?'

'To live in when it's been repaired and refurnished.' He was watching her carefully.

'Then she must have more money than sense. Sure, it will cost a fortune.' She glanced across at his father who had put down the *Farmers' Journal* and was listening intently, and then back at him. 'Do you know her, Niall?'

'Didn't I just say I met her there?'

'Sure, she must be worth a good bit. Didn't Himself tell me this morning that she paid Henry Harwood a tidy sum for that old wreck of a place and all the land, but then land isn't worth what it used to fetch,' Myles Collins said grimly. The British were refusing to import Irish beef cattle and dairy products and they were Ireland's only export market. Now this English woman was coming to live at Harwood Hall and no doubt lord it over them all.

'She was pleasant enough and she's a very attractive woman. She's a widow with a little lad.'

His mother looked at him quizzically. 'Is that so? She can't be very old then?'

'No, not very old. I expect you'll see her soon enough in town,' he replied and left the room before he could be interrogated further.

Kitty saw Niall the following evening and to her delight she received the keys to Harwood Hall the day after that. At once Gloria begged that they should go up there and see what it was like inside, as it was all so exciting, but Kitty explained that she wanted to go alone. She didn't want the shock to be too great if it was really in a desperate state and also she had waited so eagerly for this moment that, selfishly, she wanted time and some peace to enjoy it.

Niall was again waiting for her that evening and she handed him the bunch of keys, her eyes shining. 'I've no idea which ones are which and the door could be hard to open. It might have warped.'

He put his arm around her and took the keys. 'I can see you're delighted with yourself but are you prepared? I don't want you to be desperately disappointed.'

'I won't be. Don't I know full well it will look nothing like the way I remember it?'

They found the right key and surprisingly it turned without much trouble. Niall put his shoulder to the door and it swung open, the hinges making a grating noise. 'A few drops of oil should sort that out.'

She turned to him. 'Niall, I feel . . . nervous! I know I'm being an eejit but now that I'm finally about to step inside, my nerves are destroyed entirely!'

He drew her close to him. 'Kitty, this is your dream come true. This is your future home.'

They walked into the hall together and stared around, Niall with something akin to disbelief and Kitty with sorrow.

'Oh, the pity of it! 'Tis a crying shame to let it get like this!' Kitty said softly.

'My God! Kitty, it's . . . desperate! You'll be with the Joyces for months!'

Kitty squared her shoulders determinedly. 'Not at all. Won't I soon get the builders in?' There was a lot to be done, she thought as her gaze went over the damp patches on the walls and ceiling. There were faded squares on the walls where pictures and mirrors had hung. The door to the dining room was sagging and there were holes and gaps in the rotten skirting boards, the result of incursions by vermin, she surmised. The beautiful chandeliers had gone. Everything was covered in a thick layer of dust and there were cobwebs everywhere. Dry, brittle leaves littered the floor, blown in through the broken panes of the fanlight above the door. She turned to him. 'You'll see, this time next year, Niall, no one will recognise the place. Weren't you right? This is my dream. This is my *home*!'

He shook his head but he was smiling. 'You're a very determined woman, Kitty Ellinson, and I admire you enormously.'

She touched his cheek. 'All I ever wanted was your love and then this house and now I have both.'

He took her in his arms. 'Will you marry me, Kitty? I know I have nothing much compared to you but one day I will have the farm and the land and what money is left and you're going to need someone to help you with this place.'

'I wouldn't care if you didn't have a penny to bless yourself with, Niall. I don't want a long, formal engagement, I don't want to wait. I want to marry you as quickly as possible. Hasn't enough time been wasted?'

He buried his face in her hair. 'Oh, Kitty! You'll never regret it, I swear.'

'I'll be a good mother to Aoife, I promise.'

'And I'll be a good father to Edward. A boy needs a father.'

'Will you do something for me, Niall?'

He looked at her quizzically. 'Anything, Kitty.'

'Don't tell your parents that I'm back and that we're going to get married. Invite your mother to meet me here on Sunday afternoon, as Mrs Ellinson.'

'Kitty, what are you up to?'

'I want you to come too, Niall. Isn't it only right that she meets her future daughter-in-law? I want us both to tell her. I want her to realise how wrong she was, how many happy years she's denied us.'

He nodded. He owed it to her. He owed it to them both.

They wandered through the badly neglected rooms and discussed the future, their future. It would take a lot of hard work and money but they would make this into an elegant yet comfortable home filled with love and happiness.

When Niall finally arrived back at his parents' house he could hardly disguise his feelings.

'Don't you look pleased with yourself? Sure, I haven't seen you this animated in years. Where've you been? What have you been up to?' his father asked bluntly.

'I've been up to Harwood Hall, seeing Mrs Ellinson.'

His mother stared at him. He certainly did look delighted with himself. 'Again?'

'Again. She's asked if you will go to see her on Sunday afternoon. Will you go?'

'Sure to God, it's not tea in that place?' His mother was astounded.

'No. 'Tis not fit to house a beast as yet. She's having a bit of the garden at the back cleared. It's an informal occasion. Will you go?' he repeated.

'I will so. Does the invitation include you?' Was there some remote chance this woman had found Niall interesting? She was a widow and a young one at that . . .

He nodded briefly and left the room, unable to hide his happiness.

*

Kitty had confided in the minister's wife, who had listened in silence, shaking her head sadly from time to time.

'I would never have thought Maura Collins would do something like that, but then I once told you I thought she was domineering and manipulative. But if you love him and he loves you, then I wish you every happiness, Kitty, you deserve it,' she had said when Kitty had finished speaking.

Kitty dressed with as much care that Sunday as she had all those years ago when she had first met his mother. The difference this time, she thought, was that everything she wore was her own and not Elizabeth Harwood's cast-offs. The expensive oyster silk dress, shot with palest pink, was fairly new and with its handkerchief hemline, short split cape sleeves and softly draped 'v' neckline was the height of fashion. It had a full-blown shell-pink silk rose attached to one shoulder and the wide-brimmed sugar-spun straw hat that would keep the sun off her face matched it perfectly. The colour suited her, bringing out the pink tones of her complexion. Her silk stockings were white as were the calf leather shoes with the hourglass heel and the strap across the instep. She had a matching leather clutch bag and short white Nottingham lace gloves.

Critically surveying herself in the mirror on the

wardrobe door she thought she looked elegant, stylish and attractive. Was she beautiful, as he had sworn she was last night? Had she grown from that ugly ducking into the swan as her mam had promised she would? No, she could never be called beautiful, but she was satisfied with the way she looked.

She took the trap up to the house; Gloria, with Edward and young Mary Wrafter, had gone for a picnic on the canal bank. Mrs Joyce was having a nap and the Reverend was in his study. She didn't intend to stay long, just as long as it would take to explain everything to Maura Collins.

A corner of the garden had been cleared and a garden table and three chairs had been taken up from the rectory. As she made her way along the overgrown path she plucked a pink rose from the blooms struggling for space with the weeds and tucked it into the flap on the front of her bag.

She felt excited, a little nervous and yet strangely serene. She did not feel angry or even bitter now towards the woman who had caused her so much unnecessary heartache. The past did not matter any more, it was the future that was important. She would not let bitterness or animosity or any desire for revenge spoil that.

She didn't have long to wait before she heard them arriving. She stood up and surreptitiously smoothed down the silk of her skirt. Her heart leaped with joy as she caught sight of him. He looked so handsome in his dark suit and pristine white shirt and he seemed to carry himself with more dignity and presence, as though for the first time he had a real purpose in his life. He had, she reflected. He knew what he wanted; he knew where his future lay. They had made their plans last night, talking long into the deepening dusk of the summer evening.

She looked as though she was dressed for a wedding, he thought proudly as he drew closer. She looked the equal of even Amy Harwood and far more beautiful than Elizabeth had been. He couldn't see her eyes, the brim of her hat shaded them, but he was certain they would be sparkling with joy and love.

Maura Collins fixed her gaze on the elegant figure in pale oyster silk. That outfit must have cost a small fortune; if this was the way she dressed she would be the talk of the county. She couldn't see the woman's face clearly but she was surprised to note that this Mrs Ellinson was much younger than she had anticipated. She only looked to be in her twenties. Hadn't Niall told her the woman was a widow with a young son and Myles had informed her that she had been very successful in business? She didn't seem old enough to have a child and she looked far too refined and ladylike to have done well in what was a man's world. Still, she was very wealthy. Maura arranged her features in a smile that did not quite hide the lines of discontent etched deeply around her mouth.

Kitty came forward to meet them, a smile hovering on her lips. There was no malice in it, no hint of triumph, just curiosity at how Niall's mother would take the news that was about to be broken to her. The woman's blue and white print dress was old-fashioned and much worn although freshly laundered, she noticed. The bag and gloves she carried were good but serviceable and the small plain straw hat did not suit her. Her hair was liberally sprinkled with grey, giving it a salt-and-pepper colour, and she had aged considerably since the last time she had seen her.

Niall stepped forward and took Kitty's hand and she smiled up at him, her grey eyes shining.

'Ma, I want you to meet my future wife. Thanks to you I lost her years ago but now I've found her again and I'll not let her go. You'll never come between us again. I love her and we're to be married next month.'

Maura Collins stared at them both, unable to believe what she had just heard. 'Marry! Mrs . . . Ellinson!' she stammered.

Kitty smiled and reached out for her hand. 'I'm Kitty Ellinson or Doyle as I used to be. Is the blacksmith's daughter good enough for your son now? I've always loved him and I promise I will make him happy

and little Aoife too. She will be as a sister to Edward
my little boy.'

Maura felt dazed as she took Kitty's hand. 'Kitty
Doyle!' she whispered, feeling suddenly ashamed and
overcome with regret.

Niall put his arm around Kitty, not knowing what
his mother would say next.

Maura nodded slowly, tears blurring the image of
her son and the woman he loved, the woman she had
so wronged but who for all her elegance and wealth
had not spoken in anger and who was holding her
hand.

'You're . . . you're more than welcome into this
family, Kitty Doyle, I mean that,' she said softly but
with a catch in her voice.

Kitty squeezed her hand as Niall bent and kissed
her cheek. 'Now I truly feel that I've come home. I'll
never leave again – ever.'

Every Mother's Son

Lyn Andrews

Molly Keegan and Bernie O'Sullivan have been friends forever. As young girls they left Ireland seeking exciting new beginnings in Liverpool. And now, as young women, they are marrying their sweethearts and looking forward to enjoying the lives they've worked so hard to build. But as the Liverpool Blitz begins, it seems as if their dreams are about to be destroyed.

Night after night, horrific bombing tears the city apart. Every day Molly and Bernie struggle to keep their families safe. As wives and mothers, both know that they could face great tragedy. But they also know that their friendship, and their love for their husbands and sons, will give them the strength to find the happiness they deserve . . .

Praise for Lyn Andrews' unforgettable novels

'Gutsy . . . a vivid picture of a hard-up, hard-working community . . . will keep the pages turning' *Daily Express*

'Lyn Andrews presents her readers with more than just another saga of romance and family strife. She has a realism that is almost tangible' *Liverpool Echo*

978 0 7553 0842 2

headline

Friends Forever

Lyn Andrews

In 1928 Bernie O'Sullivan and Molly Keegan catch their first glimpse of the bustling city they're about to call home. Both seventeen, and best friends since childhood, the girls have left Ireland behind to seek work and an exciting new life in Liverpool.

The girls are dismayed to discover that the relatives they are to stay with have barely two pennies to rub together; the promised grand house is a run-down building in one of Liverpool's worst slum areas. Desperate to escape the filthy streets, Bernie secures a position as a domestic servant, while Molly is taken on as a shop assistant. Soon they have settled in new rooms and find themselves in love with local men. For both, though, love holds surprises and the danger of ruin in an unforgiving world.

Bernie and Molly have tough times to face but the bond of their lifelong friendship gives them the strength to rise to every challenge and to hold on to their dreams.

Praise for Lyn Andrews' unforgettable novels

'A compelling read' *Woman's Own*

'Gutsy . . . A vivid picture of a hard-up, hard-working community . . . will keep the pages turning' *Daily Express*

0 7553 0840 9

headline

From This Day Forth

Lyn Andrews

Next-door neighbours Celia and Lizzie are the best of friends. But their families, the Miltons and the Slatterys, are the worst of enemies, divided by religion and by their men's status at the Cammell Laird's shipyard. Lizzie and Celia must keep their friendship a secret – for if Celia's violent father Charlie ever found out about it the consequences would be appalling.

But one day the unthinkable happens. Joe Slattery, Lizzie's brother, does a good turn for the Milton family. From that day forth, Celia Milton just can't get the dark-eyed Joe out of her mind. And, despite himself, Joe Slattery finds that he is increasingly drawn to the girl next door and to a love that seems doomed to heart-break – unless they can find a way around the prejudice of generations and the terrifying bigotry of Charlie Milton.

Praise for Lyn Andrews' unforgettable novels

'A compelling read' *Woman's Own*

'Gutsy . . . A vivid picture of a hard-up, hard-working community . . . will keep the pages turning' *Daily Express*

'The Catherine Cookson of Liverpool' *Northern Echo*

0 7472 5177 0

headline

Now you can buy any of these other bestselling
books by **Lyn Andrews** from your bookshop
or *direct from her publisher*.

FREE P&P AND UK DELIVERY
(Overseas and Ireland £3.50 per book)

Every Mother's Son	£6.99
Friends Forever	£6.99
A Mother's Love	£6.99
Across a Summer Sea	£6.99
When Daylight Comes	£5.99
A Wing and a Prayer	£6.99
Love and a Promise	£6.99
The House on Lonely Street	£6.99
My Sister's Child	£6.99
Take These Broken Wings	£6.99
The Ties That Bind	£6.99
Angels of Mercy	£6.99
When Tomorrow Dawns	£6.99
From This Day Forth	£6.99
Where the Mersey Flows	£6.99
Liverpool Lamplight	£6.99
Liverpool Songbird	£6.99

TO ORDER SIMPLY CALL THIS NUMBER

01235 400 414

or visit our website: www.headline.co.uk

Prices and availability subject to change without notice.